Where Arrows Fall

M.J. Piazza

DEDICATION

To Grammy.
If I didn't use your computer to snoop around on YouTube,
This book would have never been written.

CONTENTS

O Death, I have watched you in silence,
I have watched as you ravage and steal.
But now, foolish Death, I will fight you,
My prayers and sword you will feel.

Leave me, dark angel! Touch not my home!
Take with you the fear in my heart!
Touch not this cradle, touch not my kin,
Or a much greater war you will start.

Death seems to laugh as it circles,
Surrounding my home as for war.
I stand my ground yet undaunted;
With God, I've fought Death off before.

ONE

"Shh—you hear that? It's probably a ghost."

Tarin looked in the direction the rustling noise had come from. "Lukas says ghosts aren't real," he said. He wasn't entirely convinced of the point—the eerie woods around him, damp and grey and dripping with moss and mist, lent themselves entirely to the existence of the paranormal. But if Lukas said something, it had to be true.

Tarin's companion Brett gave a derisive chuckle. "So what? Lukas says you can tell if someone's dying by looking at their pee. He can't be right about everything. Besides, everyone knows that this island is haunted. They say that, forty years ago, the chief's daughter was eaten by a water-*draugr*."

"Sure, and it was fairies that ate the last piece of cheese out of the cupboard last week," Tarin said.

"Go ask Leif—ask anyone you like. It's true. Her name was Ragnhild. She was six years old."

Tarin shivered. Brett was eighteen, an adult in the loosest sense of the term, and certainly old enough for thirteen-year-old Tarin to trust and admire. But Brett also had a habit of teasing his younger classmate, and Tarin was never quite sure when he was serious. Part of him wanted to go home. But there was a party at home—the worst sort of party, where grown-ups talked too much and the smell of food drove you mad because Mum wouldn't let you eat any of it until dinnertime. So he trudged forward into the woods, wiping away a drip of condensed mist that had fallen off a pine bough and onto his freckled face.

"What's a *draugr*, anyway?" Tarin asked. "Some sort of ghost?"

"They happen when people aren't buried properly," said Brett. "Their corpse turns black with rot and reeks of death, but they're still able to run around and attack people. They tear them apart with their teeth and claws, then eat them. This one's a water-*draugr*, so it's a man who drowned in the stream between here and the village."

"I've never seen it," said Tarin.

"You've never seen God, either. Doesn't mean He's not real."

The pair continued on in silence. Tarin kept his eyes open, nervously scanning the forest for anything that looked like a half-rotted corpse. Something touched the back of his neck; it felt like cold phantom fingernails. Tarin jumped and whirled around, only to see Brett laughing, holding a stick. Tarin squared his shoulders and shoved him. His spindly arms were powerless against Brett's bear-like frame, but his intentions were loud and clear.

"You know somethin', Brett? 'Tis a maggot you are. A horse-eatin', addlepated maggot!"

"You're a goat-eyed fool," Brett shot back.

Tarin's eyes gleamed. This time, he knew Brett was teasing. "You're a fat gomey with a chicken's brain!"

"You're nothing but a—"

Brett's voice trailed off, and he stopped walking. One hand shot out and grabbed Tarin's narrow shoulder. There was another rustling in the woods. Tarin froze to listen to it; it sounded like footsteps, and then a thud, as if something had fallen. And then there was silence. No matter how hard Tarin listened, the only thing he could hear was the whispering of the wind in the pine boughs and the eldritch hum of the mists.

"It's the ghost," said Brett. "It's probably a *huldra*. It's a forest spirit that looks like a pretty girl with a cow's tail. If she kisses you, you're her slave for the rest of your life."

"I'll bet 'tis a merrow," said Tarin. "We're fierce close to the ocean."

"Or it might be the same *draugr* that ate the chief's daughter."

Tarin grabbed the stick out of Brett's hand. "Let's go find out," he said.

"You're mad! You'll get eaten!"

Tarin whirled around to face his friend. "Devil mend it, Brett! It was just last week that you prayed Mum would find her tablet weaving shuttle, and you'd hardly said 'amen' before it showed up. Don't you think we can take on a ghost?"

Sighing, Brett made his way towards the source of the noise, and Tarin followed him with a mixture of caution and excitement. Brett's enormous height and broad build were more suited for a wrestling contest than a silent trek through the woods. He had to stop every two paces to duck under a twig or turn sideways to get between two close-growing trees. Tarin's curiosity was overwhelming his patience. When Brett got tangled in the underbrush, Tarin nimbly darted ahead of him, finally reaching the spot the noise had originated from.

There it was.

Tarin froze. Whatever it was, it didn't look human. Its limbs were too long, and they stuck out at odd angles. It moved like a spider, slowly, limb by limb into the underbrush. Tarin took a small step away from it. By the time Brett caught up, brushing twigs out of his beard, the creature had all but disappeared. The only thing Tarin could see was a hand—or at least something that looked like a hand—with fingers that clutched at the dirt as if in pain.

"What is it?" Brett whispered.

"I don't know."

"Did it see you?"

"I think so. 'Tis trying to run away."

"Then it's harmless," said Brett. Grabbing his stick back, he took a few steps further into the woods. "In Jesus' name, come out!"

Tarin flinched. There was a noise—a guttural, instinctual cry, like that of a wounded animal or a dying infant. Brett lashed out with his stick. The creature moved—there was a flash of something sickly white, mottled with dirt and fresh blood and dried scabs. Then Brett gave a cry of his own and came crashing back towards the path.

"It bit me," he said. Blood reddened the torn edges of his sleeve. Tarin's heart skipped a beat.

Brett grabbed Tarin's arm and stared running. Tarin glanced over his shoulder, hoping the creature wasn't following them. It wasn't. Or if it was, Tarin couldn't see it.

From her seat at the hearth of St. Anne's Monastery, Alynn the Dauntless could hear three or four conversations going on in two languages. She wasn't following any of them—she was too tired. Her daughter Elspeth was nursing herself to sleep, and there was nothing Alynn wanted to do more than fall asleep along with her. There was something about having Elspeth snuggled up against her, warm and drowsy, that filled Alynn with the sort of peace and comfort that inevitably brings sleep along with it.

Nevertheless, she stayed awake and tried to listen to everything around her. But she did close her eyes.

The men were closest to her, sitting and standing around her at the hearth. There was the voice of her father Rowan, his Irish lilt rising and falling like waves on a gentle night. Then there was Lukas, the monk who spoke with a scholar's vocabulary and a Highland brogue. Then there was a laugh, and Alynn's husband Drostan said something in Norse. This incited another round of laughter from everyone except for

Rowan, who was stubbornly refusing to learn the language.

Elspeth gave a mighty squirm; Alynn opened her eyes to look at her. Elspeth was half-asleep, but still eating contentedly like the wee piglet she was. Alynn smiled and stroked her daughter's fiery red hair. She'd gotten her hair from her father, but her eyes—a stunning celestial blue, even when they were glazed over with sleepiness—she'd gotten from her mother. Mostly, at least. Alynn's eyes were a greenish-blue, but perhaps Elspeth would grow into hers.

There was another round of laughter. This time, it came from the kitchen, where the women were making the final preparations for that night's feast. Part of Alynn felt bad for not helping. But, she reasoned, her mother Caitriona and Valdis the hired girl could handle everything. They were both better cooks than she was.

And besides, this was Elspeth's party. A celebration of her first tooth, which was hardly visible in her lower jaw. Alynn's Irish mind didn't quite understand the Norse tradition, but any excuse for a party was welcome. Alynn touched her finger to Elspeth's palm and smiled contentedly as her daughter wrapped her tiny fingers around it.

The sweet child—her eyes were half-closed now. Her eyelids drooped until her lashes almost touched her cheek, then fluttered open, then drooped again…was she sleeping? Alynn hoped she was….

A sudden noise turned every head in the monastery. Elspeth started crying.

Sighing, Alynn opened her mouth to yell at whoever had woken her daughter, but her admonitions quickly died on her lips. Her brother Tarin, red-faced and sweating, flew through the front door.

"Da! Lukas! There's somethin' in the woods!" he cried out. "It bit Brett! He's hurt!"

Brett landed on the threshold as if he'd jumped over the two small steps that led into St. Anne's Monastery. Tarin slammed and barred the door behind them. The women were out of the kitchen. The men rose from the hearth. Everyone was talking and Elspeth was screaming.

The boys were quickly led to the hearth. Brett was all but shoved into a seat next to the fire as Lukas slit his bloodstained sleeve from elbow to wrist. Caitriona, meanwhile, was checking Tarin over for injuries.

Words flew like arrows. Cries of "What happened?" and "Who did this?" and "Were you followed?" rang out in both Norse and Gaelic, with the occasional "I'm grand, Mum! Leave me be!" thrown in by Tarin. Finally, Lukas's voice rose above the clamor.

"Excuse us—pardon—Rowan, if ye wouldn't mind stepping—och, *Christe eleision*. Will everyone *please stop yelling* and stand back? We need room to think, thank ye, now someone go fetch us some bloodwort and bandages. Tarin, are ye hurt?"

"I'm grand," said Tarin. He didn't look grand. He was still panting, and his face was as red as his sweat-damp hair. But when Lukas took a ring of keys from his belt, Tarin reached out a trembling hand and took them.

"Good. Thank God," Lukas said. "Bloodwort and bandages, and there ought to be some strong ale on the top shelf. Hurry up."

Tarin scampered down a dim hallway, keys jingling loudly in his hands. In the meanwhile, Lukas took the hem of his frock-like scapular and wiped some of the blood away from Brett's wound.

"This looks like a knife wound," said Lukas, using Brett's native Norse. "Assuming Tarin didn't stab you, what happened?"

"Something bit me." Brett's breath still came quickly. "I didn't see it well. It was cloudy, there's fog—and everything happened so fast—" He paused and wiped his brow. "It might have scratched me. Maybe with its claw or something. I couldn't see all of it."

"Well, it's no bite," said Lukas. "And if it were an animal, it would have left multiple claw marks. This is a single scratch. I still say it's a knife wound."

"Or a sword," said Valdis as she offered Lukas a damp rag to finish cleaning Brett's wound with.

"Then whoever did that is still out there," said Drostan. He was gripping the back of Alynn's chair. "Were you followed?"

Before Brett could answer, Caitriona gave a cry of "Oh, God!" and flew through the kitchen out the monastery's back door. While she was gone, no one spoke. Even Elspeth's wailing turned into a milder fussing. Tarin returned with bandages, ale, and a sack of dried herbs. He too refused to break the silence. He set everything on the stone floor as gingerly as possible, then sat quiet as a mouse next to the fireplace.

Caitriona returned with a two-year-old clutched to her chest. The little girl had no respect for the silence of the hearth; she was crying "No! Mammy! Go pay ow'side!" with the vehemence only a toddler can possess.

Finally, Caitriona said "Hush, Mercy!" in the same tone that had silenced everyone at the hearth. It worked on the toddler, but not as well; Mercy gave a mighty "Hmph!" and settled into a sulk.

"I'll play outside with you tomorrow, my wee heart," said Rowan. He took Caitriona and Mercy into his arms. "'Tis gettin' late. 'Tis almost time for dinner. Are you hungry?"

Mercy nodded and stuck two fingers in her mouth. Rowan smiled and kissed the faint blonde wisps of his daughter's hair.

Caitriona and Mercy had been followed into the kitchen by Drostan's father Leif. His greying auburn hair had been tousled by the wind, but his eyes were sharp, authoritative, and slightly worried. "What's wrong?" he demanded.

"There's somethin' in the woods," said Tarin. "It attacked Brett."

"Something like a person?" Leif asked.

Brett looked at Tarin, who looked back with wide and innocent eyes. "We think it was a *draugr*," said Brett. "It...didn't have a face. It had hands, with long, bony fingers.

And it didn't walk upright. But I didn't see much of it. It's dark in the woods."

"Its legs were black with the rot, and there was dead skin hangin' off its arms," said Tarin. "And there was blood all over it."

"Dried blood," said Brett. "It might have been mud."

"Uncle Leif," said Tarin, looking up with curiosity tempered by respect, "was there really a chief whose daughter got eaten by a *draugr*?"

Leif was silent for a moment, deep in thought. Suddenly, his eyes grew wide. "It was my sister," he said. "Ragnhild. She was six years old. All we found was her frock, there was blood on it—"

Alynn's breath caught in her chest, and she held onto Elspeth a bit tighter. Elspeth let out a squeak of discontentment before latching onto Alynn's breast again and nursing greedily.

Lukas left Brett's arm half-bandaged. Drawing his knife, he quickly looked out the narrow window next to the front door.

"It doesn't seem ye were followed," he said. "We're safe in here. Will someone make sure that the back door is barred, please?"

Leif checked the back door, and Rowan forced a smile. "Well, Lynder, I'm sorry yer party had to end this way," he said.

"Och, don't be," said Alynn. "I mean—I'm just glad Tarin's alright. And you too, Brett. Lukas is the best doctor on the island, you'll be alright."

Brett scoffed. "My sister's a shieldmaiden. She used to practice on me. This is nothing." He finished bandaging his arm. "Lady Cait, can we eat now?"

"Yes. Of course." Caitriona gave her toddler a quick kiss before setting her in Rowan's arms.

"Keep some warm for me," said Leif. "I'm going to look for this thing."

Caitriona eyed him disdainfully as she dished up a plate of well-seasoned fish, fresh-caught that morning. "Leif, you're daft."

"Besides, Father, I'm the one who ought to be looking into things," Drostan objected. He set a hand on the hilt of his sword. Alynn was beginning to wish she'd brought her own sword.

"That would make you daft too, wouldn't it?" Leif asked. He grinned at Drostan and ruffled his flaming red hair. "It's your daughter's party. Stay and enjoy yourself. It's probably just a drunkard."

"Or a madman," said Caitriona.

"Well, good thing we know who to send after those." Leif directed his smile towards Alynn now, and she blushed. Leif nodded a quick goodbye to Lukas, Rowan, and the boys before drawing his sword and heading out the door.

"Bye, U'cle Lay!" called Mercy.

Leif smiled. "Bye, Mercy."

Carefully, so as not to disturb Elspeth, Alynn moved one hand so she could set it over Drostan's. "What do you think it is, love?" she asked.

Drostan shook his head. "I should be going with him," he said. "At least that way, I'd have some semblance of a clue as to what the devil's going on."

"Father's right, though. 'Tis yer daughter's party. And besides, he's got a sword. He'll be alright." Alynn turned her head as far as it could go to look up at Drostan. He smiled at her. Then, softly, he bent down to kiss Alynn's head and stroke Elspeth's soft, downy hair. Elspeth didn't move; she must have been asleep.

"Why don't you lay her down somewhere?" he asked. "It's time to eat."

"I know. I'm afraid she'll wake if I set her down."

"Och, she's a sound sleeper. Just like her mum."

A thousand other worries ran through Alynn's mind. The monastery was huge; what if no one could hear her crying? Elspeth's cradle at home hung from the rafters and was always swinging; what if Mercy's old cradle was too uncomfortable?

Alynn's worries were absurd, she realized. Mercy had been born and raised in St. Anne's Monastery, and she'd turned out fine. A bit spoiled, of course. No child could be born to parents as old as Rowan and Caitriona, and raised with an adoptive grandfather as doting as Lukas, and not be spoiled. But at least she was healthy.

Eventually, though, the smell of the well-seasoned fish won Alynn over. She went to a nearby bedroom and carefully set Elspeth in the wooden cradle kept in the corner, praying she wouldn't wake. She didn't. Alynn didn't leave right away, even though the merry clattering of forks and plates and glasses of small ale was calling her to the dinner table. She stayed to look at her daughter.

She was beautiful.

There were footsteps behind her. Alynn turned to see Lukas with a book tucked under his arm. "Are ye in here, Alynn?" Lukas asked.

"I'm here."

Lukas felt his way through the dark and eventually set a hand on Alynn's shoulder before pressing the book into her hands. "It's mostly Bible stories, wi' a bit of yer mother's poetry thrown in," he said. "It isn't quite finished, though. We thought we'd have a bit more time afore Elspeth got her first tooth. And to be fair, I don't understand why the occasion calls for a gift. I'd have put in more resources, had I known Leif was going to give her that bracelet."

"Don't compare yerself," Alynn said. "Leif's rich. He's probably had that bracelet since his family was still in the slave trading business. And I know you worked hard on this. Elspeth will love it, assumin' she doesn't eat it first." Alynn opened the book. She couldn't see much in the dim light, but lines of text broken up by imaginative illustrations caught her eye.

"Did you draw the pictures?" Alynn asked.

"Yer father did most of them. Brett and Tarin did a few of the more—ah—creative ones."

Alynn brought the book into the hallway, where there was

a bit more light. The picture she thought was a unicorn was actually a soldier riding into battle on a…what the devil—

"Lukas, is that a snail the soldier's riding on?"

"Aye. Brett drew that. Long story."

"And is this soldier wearin' trousers?"

"He'd better be." Lukas took the book, brought it to the hearth to see it in the firelight, and snapped it shut before striding into the kitchen. "Brett Oddson!"

Brett looked up, and his eyes went wide. Knowing him, Alynn figured his mind was going down the list of things he might be in trouble for. Lukas grabbed him by the ear and pulled him out of his chair at the kitchen table. It took some doing, as Brett was a good half foot taller than his teacher.

"Ow—ow—Lukas, I just got stabbed, could you please—"

"I told ye to put trousers on the snail soldier."

"I'll do it—you had me conjugating irregular verbs, I didn't get the chance—"

Lukas thrust the book into Brett's arms. "Ye're not allowed dinner 'til ye're finished. Off wi' ye."

Brett scampered off, rubbing his ear. Lukas looked rather pleased with himself as he sat down to dinner, stealing a piece of bread as he did so. Caitriona set a plate of fish in front of him with something like sympathy in her eyes. "Lukas, the lad was just attacked by a phantom in the woods. You might have been gentler with him."

"I was gentle. I was whipped fer less as a lad." Lukas swallowed his mouthful of bread. "Och, Brother Eamonn—my first Latin teacher, God rest his soul—actually, I take that back. I doubt he's anywhere pleasant right now. Anyway, when I was ten, I was given the opportunity to write an entry in the monastic annals. I chose to include the fact that I'd stepped in a cat's hairball first thing that morning, and Brother Eamonn yelled at me fer the better part of an hour. I'd have preferred a whipping, frankly."

"Do we still have those annals?" Tarin asked.

Lukas looked at Tarin over the top of his mug of small ale.

"Don't ye dare go looking fer them, laddie."

Caitriona was unusually slow in setting the table, but she refused any help—even from Valdis, who stood rather awkwardly and lost-looking near the table. Caitriona kept glancing towards the hallway Brett had disappeared down. It wasn't until he reappeared that dinner was officially served, although Lukas and Tarin had been sneaking bites for quite a while.

The merry meal was halfway through when Leif returned. It had apparently started raining. Leif was dripping wet and shivering even though it was summer. His eyes were unusually grave. Alynn's first worry was that he had been injured. Drostan, from the way he stood from his chair and ran to his father, was thinking the same thing.

"I'm alright," Leif said as soon as the door was bolted behind him. "Just damp, it's raining now."

"Did you see it?" Tarin asked.

"I didn't see anything. No man, beast, or ghost. There's a sign of a struggle in the woods, but the footprints leading away from it stop after a dozen yards. It's as if whatever attacked Brett just vanished into thin air."

Alynn had a sudden desire to hold Elspeth, and Tarin's face turned white.

"Is it safe fer ye to go home, then?" Lukas asked.

"Thor, no. Not with the baby, anyway. If you'd be so kind as to put us up for the night—"

"Ye're more than welcome here. Ye know that, Leif." Lukas stood from the table, disappeared down a hallway, and returned with a blanket. Leif wrapped himself in it gratefully.

Drostan returned to his seat with a sigh of disappointment. "I'll be late to work again," he said.

"You're the chief of the village, love. You can be late to work whenever you need to be," Alynn said quietly.

"I know—technically. I still like to set a good example. And besides, I don't like Father setting up in the mornings. His back's been hurting him."

"Well, lucky for both of ye, ye'll be equally late to work." Alynn heard Elspeth crying and lost no time in fetching her. The babe had soiled herself. Alynn cleaned her up quickly—she was an expert at such things by now, although Elspeth was getting increasingly wiggly—and returned to her meal. Everyone was eating more slowly now, as if they'd collectively lost their appetites.

"I think I saw a whale washed up on the beach," said Leif. "Rowan, if you'll join me and Drostan in the morning, we ought to get a few months' worth of lamp oil."

"Will ye need our help?" Lukas asked, looking at Brett and Tarin.

"It's a small whale. I think we can manage."

"I don't want the lads out there anyway," Caitriona said, wiping fish out of Mercy's hair. "We don't know if that knife-wielder is still out there, and Mercy, my heart, did you get any of yer fish in yer mouth? Or are you just wearin' it?"

"Let's have Elspeth try some fish," said Tarin.

"She's got half a tooth," Alynn said. "She'll choke on it."

"What about a bannock?" Caitriona suggested.

"Alright. Everyone watch. Elspie's first bite of solid food." Alynn sat her daughter up on the table and set the smallest crumb of bannock bread in Elspeth's mouth. Almost immediately, Elspeth's invisible red brows furrowed into a confused frown. She stuck out her tongue and spat out the bread.

Everyone laughed and forgot about the knife-wielder until the next morning, when Leif, Drostan, and Rowan returned early and empty-handed from their trip to the beach. Apparently, Leif had not seen a whale at all. Alynn's heart flew into her throat when Drostan told her that they had found an overturned landing boat.

A landing boat that was smeared with blood, cracked by rocks, and made from wood that did not grow on St. Anne's Cleft.

TWO

No one at St. Anne's Monastery could explain the lifeboat, so, reluctantly, Alynn and her family made the nerve-wracking trip back to the Norse village. Valdis immediately set about washing Elspeth's diapers and Leif went to work at the shipyard, but Drostan went off to ask anyone if they knew anything about the lifeboat. He was gone late that evening and almost didn't make it home in time for dinner—rather, Leif was so hungry that he almost started eating without him. It was all Alynn and Valdis could do to not join in, but fortunately, Elspeth distracted everyone until Drostan came home.

"Nothing," Drostan said as he hung up his rain-damp hood. "I've talked to everyone who might know anything. Drunkards, parents of teenagers, people who have bought boats from other islands. Even Folkvard and Havard down at the shipyard, though God forbid they know more about boats than Father or me. And no one knew anything!"

"So today was a complete waste?" Leif asked with his mouth full of soup.

Drostan bent down to kiss Alynn. As he did, he gave a mild sigh of frustration and disappointment. Smiling, Alynn ran her fingers through his flaming red hair. "Of course today wasn't a waste," she said. "You found out that no one knows anythin', and that means somethin'. We'll just have to figure out where to look next."

"I hope you're right, love," Drostan said, sitting down stiffly on the sleeping bench that doubled as an eating bench during mealtime. He took a deep drink of his small ale. "Sigmund, God bless him, knew more than anyone. Our mystery boat is made from spruce, right? Well, apparently, spruce grows on Darsidia, Hrafney, and Gythia. Someone from any one of those tribes might be hiding in our woods somewhere."

"Spruce trees grow in Norway, too," said Valdis. "I used to climb them with my brother."

"None of that matters too much," said Leif. "The ship might have been stolen during a raid. The English might be sailing it for all we know."

Alynn slammed her drink on the table. "Faith, if there's an Englishman on our island—"

Drostan laughed. "Lynder, even if there was an Englishman daft enough to steal a Norse ship, do you honestly think they'd get away with it?"

"It depends," said Alynn. "Brett's half English, and he could get away with it."

"The smaller half. Besides, he was raised on Hrafney. He doesn't count."

Elspeth squealed in agreement. Drostan gave a tired smile and took her from Alynn.

"How's my wee Elspie doing today, hmm? Were you good for Mammy?" The sound of his voice made Elspeth grin and squirm with delight. "Och, we're squiggly today, are we? Come here, Squiggly." Drostan kissed Elspeth, which made her grin even more, before setting her in his lap and taking a bite of his soup. "Isn't she usually asleep right now?"

"She is, but she's takin' extra naps because she's teething," said Alynn. "I think she's workin' on that second bottom tooth. 'Tis makin' her nose run, you might want to wipe it—"

Drostan drew his sleeve over the bottom half of Elspeth's face. Alynn breathed an exhausted, contented sigh. It was so nice watching Drostan take care of Elspeth. Partially because it meant Alynn wasn't doing it. She was slowly learning how to savor the small moments of freedom.

Valdis spoke up. "Master Drostan, I've been thinking—if you don't mind—"

"Go ahead."

"How do we know that someone was even in the boat? Aye, you said there was blood in it, but that might have come from a thousand places. Wounded wild animals, a dead body—"

"We didn't see any footprints," said Drostan. "You might have a point."

"Aye, but it had been raining," said Leif. "The footprints would have washed away. And if there was a corpse or a wounded animal, it would have been nearby."

Valdis ducked her head. "You're right, Master Leif."

"All the same, that's good thinking, Valdis." Leif smiled warmly before taking another piece of bread. "And good cooking."

This made Valdis smile and Elspeth put both fists in her slobbery mouth. Dinner was finished, the table was stored in the rafters, and everyone started getting ready for bed.

Alynn had the hardest part: getting Elspeth to sleep.

At first, Alynn hoped that nursing her would get her to drift off. And it half-worked. But instead of sleeping, Elspeth started fussing. She would unlatch from her mother's breast to complain, she would kick her little legs and wave her fat little hands. Her fingernails, sharp as daggers, grazed Alynn's chest with the same well-intentioned cruelty as a cat's claws.

Alynn sang, she walked, she bounced, she lay down and set Elspeth on her chest. By the time the baby was finally asleep, everyone else was in bed. Leif was snoring, his trousers and undershift lying crumpled on the ground beside his portion of the sleeping bench. Valdis was curled up like a hibernating stoat, and her blonde hair flew loose like a proud rooster's tailfeathers. Alynn set Elspeth gingerly in her hanging cradle before quietly joining Drostan in the paneled-in bedcloset, reserved for the master of the house.

When Alynn and Drostan had gotten married nearly three years ago, there had been no question about who got the bedcloset. Leif might have been the patriarch, but he was unmarried. Besides, thanks to a legal conundrum, Drostan was chief of St. Anne's Cleft rather than Leif, who ought to have inherited the position (and the bedcloset) from his brother. Fortunately, Leif didn't seem to mind his inferior position. Alynn couldn't blame him. Being chief came with a good deal of pressure and responsibility.

Alynn settled into the bedcloset next to Drostan and gave a tired sigh. She must have fallen asleep, because it seemed that not five minutes had passed before Elspeth started crying.

Groaning, Alynn shoved Drostan awake. "She needs changed," she said.

"Mind your hands, Ulfrik," Drostan mumbled. He was sleep-talking—sleep-working, rather. Sometimes, Alynn would wake up to find him rubbing her arm as if he were sanding a strake. With many silent protests, Alynn sat up, stumbled out of the bedcloset, and picked up Elspeth. Her hands met with something sticky.

"Grand," Alynn mumbled. "Pure grand. You just had to get poo all over the place, didn't you, love? Would you at least stop cryin'?"

Elspeth ignored her mother and kept crying.

Alynn took Elspeth into the adjoining workroom, changed her diaper and her clothes, and nursed her to sleep. Her hands were still covered in something sticky. So, setting Elspeth carefully in the bedcloset (the cradle needed washing, too), Alynn went outside to find water.

It was a short walk to the well. Fog filled the wood-paved streets, as dense as the steam from a witch's cauldron. The full moon was covered by thin, wispy clouds, giving it a vague, spectral glow. The wind was cool. Alynn shivered; she wished she'd grabbed a cloak.

As she approached the well, she heard a voice.

It was something less than a voice. There were no words—perhaps they were gasping breaths. As Alynn drew closer to the well, she realized that what she heard was a child crying. Her mother's instinct welled up within her, and she hurried onward.

"Hello?" she called.

The child must not have heard her. It continued crying, its breath coming in patterns of ragged jerks that Alynn recognized from her own childhood. The child was not crying with grief, but with hunger and cold and exhaustion. This was a cry of empty stomachs and dizziness, a cry of cold fingers and chattering teeth.

"Child, where are you? What's wrong?" Alynn asked.

The child must have heard her, because the crying stopped with a frightened gasp. Alynn kept walking until she saw a mist-blurred figure standing at the well, dark and angular and out of place.

The figure made a single, sudden movement, and then vanished as if into thin air.

Alynn's first thought was that the child had jumped into the well. She ran the last few steps, but the well was empty. At least Alynn thought it was; she never heard a splash, and when she sent the bucket down, it hit the water without striking anything solid first.

"I'll help you!" Alynn called. "You can come home with me. I'll make you some tea—some soup if you'd like—we'll get you warmed up."

The child gave no response. Alynn felt as if she were talking to the mist.

Wondering if she'd imagined the entire thing (she was chronically sleep-deprived, after all), Alynn drew some water and filled her own bucket. But when she stepped away from the well, her bare foot touched something that didn't feel like a stick or a stone or anything else found in nature. Alynn bent down and picked up a piece of leather, worn and cracked and reeking of salt water. It was probably part of a shoe.

Alynn quickly washed Elspeth's poo from her hands, picked up the broken shoe, and hurried home. Drostan was in the bedcloset, holding a still-crying Elspeth. "Where were you?" he demanded as soon as Alynn shut the bedcloset door behind her. Alynn didn't answer right away. Instead, she put her cold feet on Drostan's legs to warm them up. He jerked away from her.

"For Njord's sake, put some socks on."

"There's someone crying outside," Alynn said.

"It's a cat. Feed the baby and go to sleep."

"It was a child." Alynn pressed the piece of leather into Drostan's hand. "A crying child with broken shoes."

Sighing, Drostan set Elspeth in Alynn's arms and wrapped himself more thoroughly in the blankets. "Boy or girl?" Drostan asked.

Alynn started nursing Elspeth, and she settled down almost immediately. "I couldn't tell. They cry alike."

"Where'd you see them?"

"By the well. They disappeared when I offered to help."

"Sounds like an abuse case. I'll look into it tomorrow."

"Thank you, love." And with that, Alynn lay down, made sure that Elspeth was nursing contentedly, and fell back to sleep until morning.

THREE

Elspeth decided that, for the next two days, she would be as difficult as possible.

Alynn tried everything she could think of. She rocked Elspeth, shushed her, sang to her, nursed her, bounced her around, and made funny faces. She played peek-a-boo and patty-cake and everything else she could think of playing with an infant. Elspeth stubbornly refused to find her mother's antics amusing. She spent most of her time either crying or eating or spitting up.

On the second day, a Saturday, Alynn sleepwalked through her laundry. Elspeth lay squalling next to her. Valdis kept taking over the washing so that Alynn could pick her up, try to nurse her, or see if she needed her diaper changed. Nothing worked.

By noon, even Valdis—quiet, longsuffering, kind-hearted Valdis—had had enough. She marched out of the house as soon as the last undershift was on the clothesline and returned with a visitor.

Alynn gave a sigh of relief when she saw the guest. It was Nora McKenzie, a dear family friend with a blessedly level head.

"Help me," said Alynn.

"Och, she's getting her teeth in, isn't she?" Nora asked,

taking Elspeth into her arms. She spoke with a Scottish brogue, which seemed to have a calming effect on Elspeth. She stuck a finger in Elspeth's mouth. "Ye're a bit warm, aren't ye, lassie? And look at yer wee red cheeks!"

Alynn paled, and her tired mind began to race. Was Elspeth feverish? Was she sick? "She gets red when she cries, I just thought—is she alright? Do I need to take her to Lukas? Can he even—"

"Don't fret, Lynder. This hardly counts as a fever. And it's normal wi' teething bairns. How's her poo been?"

"Softer than usual."

"Aye, that's normal. And she's been eating well, I take it?" Nora squeezed Elspeth's fat little arms and her chubby little thighs. "She's round as a wee suckling piglet."

"'Tis the only thing that stops her crying, nursing is," Alynn said.

"Elspeth, yer poor mammy. Ye've got to let her get on wi' her chores, now. Let's find something else fer ye to do wi' yerself. Alynn, do ye have a metal spoon or a bracelet?"

Quickly, Alynn fetched the silver bracelet that Leif had given Elspeth as a tooth-gift. It was heavy even for a grown-up to wear; maybe something smaller would be better. In the end, Alynn wound up with a metal serving spoon.

"Perfect," said Nora. She dipped the spoon in a bottle of ale and stuck it in Elspeth's mouth. She chewed on it contentedly and stopped crying. "The metal's nice and cool once it's wet. Feels good on the gums. She ought to calm down now."

"What about the fever?" Alynn asked. What kind of mother was she, to not realize her infant was sick?

Nora gave a comforting smile and set Elspeth back in her mother's arms. "Whisht, lassie. She'll mend in a day or two. Just keep her comfortable, give her cool things to chew on, and let things run their course."

Still, as soon as Nora left, Alynn sat down with a damp rag and wiped Elspeth's tiny red face with it. Surely that felt good to her. But still—Alynn usually felt cold when she had a fever. Did Elspeth want a blanket? Did she ache? Willow bark tea would help with pain—could you give it to a baby, though?

Someone knocked at the door. Alynn hoped it was Nora coming back with more knowledge. It wasn't. Alynn was met instead by a woman with strong Norse features, blonde-haired and sturdily built and curtly mannered. Alynn knew her. Not well, but since she'd become the chieftainess of St. Anne's Cleft, she'd made it a point to know all of the villagers.

But what was her name?

"Good morning," Alynn said, giving Elspeth one last stroke with the damp rag. Was it Gudrun? Geirhild? No, none of those. But for some reason, those were the only names she could think of. She was probably more tired than she realized.

"I'm here to report a robbery," the woman said.

"You really ought to take this up with Drostan," said Alynn. Elspeth took the metal spoon out of her mouth just long enough to spit up. Alynn wiped away the half-digested milk absentmindedly.

"He's not at the shipyards. I'm missing a pair of dark green winningas. Someone stole both of them off the clothesline this morning."

"And you're certain they didn't blow off? Alynn asked. "It was windy this morning."

"Milady," said the woman, in a tone that turned the word into an insult, "those winningas were six feet long and tied in a knot around the clothesline. They'd have stayed put if a hurricane hit. And besides, I've scoured every last inch of the yard and asked everyone in the family. No one's seen them."

Alynn stifled a frustrated sigh. Winningas were essentially bandages that the Norse wrapped around their feet and legs like impractical socks. No sane person would want to steal them. Nevertheless, Alynn made herself nod politely. "I'll let Drostan know as soon as he gets home. Thank you...Geirhild?"

"Nidbjorg."

"Thank you, Nidbjorg."

The lady nodded her farewell and left, and Alynn completely forgot about the whole matter until that evening during dinner, when Elspeth spit up on her again. This time, Drostan was there to hold Elspeth while Alynn cleaned herself up.

"A lady came by today, said that someone stole a pair of winningas from her." Alynn's dress wasn't coming quite clean, so she dipped her handkerchief in her tea and kept scrubbing. "Insists they couldn't have blown off a clothesline. I can't remember her name."

"What did she look like?" asked Leif.

"I don't know, she was here for all of two minutes. Blonde, around my height, not too pretty." She'd just described half the women on St. Anne's Cleft.

"Was she friendly?" Drostan asked.

"Not terribly. And she didn't even acknowledge Elspeth."

"Probably Nidbjorg the cooper's wife," Leif mused, dipping his bread in his soup. It was starting to get cold and harden, rendering it practically inedible. "Strange, really. Ulfrik came to work late this morning because he couldn't find his comb."

"And Erik wouldn't share his?"

Drostan chuckled, chewing a particularly large bit of meat that had found its way into the stew. "Either that or Ulfrik's particular. There's only one hammer he'll use. If it breaks, we're all doomed."

"Still," said Leif, "if I had a twin, I'd have been more understanding. Erik just seemed enraged by the whole thing."

"You don't think they're connected, do you, Master Leif?" Valdis asked.

"Erik and Ulfrik?" Leif asked.

"The robberies, sir. I mean, it's strange that two people would be missing things so close together."

Leif shrugged, tearing off a bite of bread. "It's a comb," he said with his mouth full. "Ten to one it'll turn up in a corner somewhere. Besides, who the devil steals a comb? Or a pair of winningas?"

"Fairies," Alynn said.

"Fairies don't live in Orkney," Drostan said. Elspeth, still in her father's arms, fussed loudly at the notion. He kissed the top of her head. "Don't cry, sweet. I'll take you to Ireland to see some for yourself. Would you like that?"

Elspeth grabbed a fistful of Drostan's tunic and tried to eat it, and Drostan laughed. "Maybe when she's a bit older," said Alynn taking Elspeth back into her arms and nursing her. She could still eat her soup. She'd never been more grateful that she was both-handed.

As soon as the dishes were washed and put away, Alynn went to bed, but she didn't sleep. She took Elspeth into the bedcloset with her and kept one hand on her chest, making sure it rose and fell with every breath. As tired as Alynn was, Elspeth entranced her. She was so perfect when she was asleep. So precious. Her soft pudgy cheeks, her tiny chin, her sweet little nose.

Alynn loved her.

She once thought she'd loved Tarin the way a mother loved a child. After all, she'd practically raised him for four years. She'd learned how to skip meals so that he could have enough food. She'd sung him to sleep and patched his clothes and made him tea when he was sick. But Elspeth? She'd take an arrow for her. She'd do anything for her.

Alynn was nearly asleep when there was a knock on the door. Drostan answered it, and she heard him talking to a man in low tones.

"I'm sorry to bother you at this hour, sir, but my wife insisted…a silver cloakpin. Your father-in-law made it, it's got a Celtic knot on the pin. My wife took it off the cloak to wash it this morning, but she couldn't find the pin afterwards."

"And she's searched the house, asked your family if they've seen it?" Drostan asked.

"Aye, sir. She insists that someone took it."

Drostan was silent for a moment. "Well, if I see anyone wearing it, I'll let you know. Ten to one it's still in your house, hiding under a blanket."

"That's what I told my wife, but she wouldn't listen to me. I'll try looking for it again, sir. Sorry to bother you."

"Not at all, Sveinn. Thanks for dropping by. Let me know if you find it."

"Of course. Thank you."

When Drostan finally made it to bed, Alynn was still awake and nursing Elspeth. "Cloakpins don't just vanish, you know," she said as Drostan settled into the blankets beside her. "When a woman looks for somethin', the first thing she'd do is shake out all the blankets. Ten to one Sveinn's wife is right, someone took it."

"So?"

"Ulfrik's comb goes missing, no one bats an eye. What's-her-name loses a pair of winningas, we think 'tis a strange coincidence. Now we're missin' a silver cloakpin, which is functional and valuable. Something's up, Drostan."

"You think there's a thief in the village?"

"I think 'tis a possibility. A strong one. And that rude lady was right. 'Tis strange enough that she lost one winninga off a clothesline. What are the odds she'd lose a matchin' set?"

Drostan was silent for a moment. Alynn wondered if he'd fallen asleep; if he had, she was going to smack him for it. Finally, with a tired sigh, he said, "I hope you're wrong, love."

Elspeth was falling asleep, so Alynn handed her to Drostan so he could burp her. Then, finally, Alynn fell asleep.

For an hour and fifteen minutes, anyway, before Elspeth woke her up demanding the next of her midnight snacks.

Somehow, the next day, Alynn made it to church.

She and Elspeth took the wagon. For the past year, ever since a better bridge had been built over the stream that ran through the woods, a system had been in place. Half a dozen families took turns hitching up their wagons or oxcarts for the benefit of mothers with children, the elderly, and anyone else who needed help traversing the not-quite-three miles between the village and St. Anne's Monastery. This time, it was a neighbor's oxcart. The trip was nearly an hour. A toddler screamed the entire time.

But finally, when they came to the stream, things began looking more familiar for Alynn. There was the willow tree that she'd always admired. There was the bramble of bearberries where she'd spent countless merry afternoons. There was the patch of spotted orchid and shepherd's purse.

And there was St. Anne's Monastery itself, its belfry pointing to heaven.

Alynn went inside as soon as the wagon stopped. It was a thrill to listen to the voices of churchgoers as they rang through-out the stone hallways. Children laughed, mothers talked, and occasionally, a baby would let out a wail.

Washing the last of the breakfast dishes was Caitriona, arrayed in a lovely gown of dark teal. Her golden hair was partly hidden by a kerchief, but most of it trailed down her back and nearly to her knees.

Elspeth hiccupped, and Caitriona noticed. Letting the dishes fall to the bottom of the washbasin, she flew to Alynn and embraced her, dishwatery hands and all. Her eyes were alight like a church at Christmas.

"Lynder, how are you?"

"Grand. Exhausted. Elspeth's gettin' her second tooth, and I can't see how I'll get through the next few days."

Caitriona gave a sympathetic smile and took Elspeth into her arms. "Och, my wee heart, you've grown since I've last seen you! You must be eatin' like a wee piglet. Does yer mammy take good care of you? Of course she does. Look at what a grand job she's doing! You're nice and fat and happy, aren't you, Eppie?"

Alynn smiled and took a deep breath. With Elspeth in good

hands, she was free to socialize—something that didn't happen very often nowadays.

Her first instinct was to talk to Lukas, but he was in the middle of praying with someone, and Alynn didn't want to disturb them. So she went instead to the kitchen table, where Brett and Tarin were deep in a board game called *hnefatafl*.

"Morning, lads," she said. The moment he heard her voice, Tarin looked up with a grin and hugged his sister. Alynn gave a contented smile and ruffled Tarin's red hair for good luck. "Who's winning?"

"Hard to say," said Brett, which was what he always said when he was losing. He glanced at Tarin, then at the game board, and moved a piece diagonally.

"Can't do that," said Alynn. Brett quickly moved the piece back. Tarin moved a piece that was different from the others— that was the king. Brett moved one of his pawns, and Tarin moved his king again, this time into a corner space that had a rune carved into it. He grinned in victory.

"Twenty-eight to thirty-two! Brett, you can't even win when you cheat!" Tarin said.

Alynn raised an eyebrow. "Tarin, 'tis better than that we've raised you. What do you say?"

"Sorry. Good game, Brett."

Brett stared at the board dumbfounded for a moment, then glanced up at Tarin. "Rematch," he said.

"Ye'll miss worship," Alynn said. "Why don't ye wait until after Mass?"

"Can I hold Elspeth?" Tarin asked.

"If you can snatch her from Mum."

Tarin bounced off happily just as a shrill squeal rang throughout the monastery. Alynn glanced down to see Mercy, stark naked, streaking across the hearth. Quickly, Alynn scooped her up and set her on her hip.

"Mercy, where are yer clothes?" Alynn demanded.

Mercy laughed. Alynn glanced around the room. She couldn't find a pile of toddler clothes, but she did see Rowan approaching them with an embarrassed smile. There was something vaguely different about him—he looked more handsome than usual. Had he done something different with his hair? Alynn gasped; the long braids of his mustache were gone.

"Da, what happened?" she asked.

Rowan took Mercy from Alynn and wrapped her in his forest-green-and-royal-blue plaid. "She took her clothes off. Nothin' uncommon. You used to do the same thing."

"No—yer mustache—"

Rowan smiled and stroked his beard. He'd only had it for a few weeks, but it was respectably full and red where the rest of his hair was a reddish blonde. "Mercy kept pulling on it. Besides, Mum thinks I look nicer this way."

"You look like a rich man," Alynn said.

"That's the one thing I like about the Norse. Any man can wear a beard." Mercy squirmed, and Rowan tightened his hold on her. "What do you want, my wee heart?"

"Go pay ow'side."

"Outside? We can't play outside. 'Tis Sabbath. Deydey's about to tell everyone about Jesus. We can't miss that, now can we?"

"Ow'side!"

"Tell me where yer clothes are, and then we can play outside after Mass. Alright? Where's yer clothes?"

"I do it." Mercy wriggled out of her father's arms, and Rowan sighed as he followed the naked creature throughout the crowded monastery.

Leif, who had arrived at church earlier, caught eye of Alynn and approached her. "So," he said with a smile in his laugh-lined eyes, "when's the last time you saw your father without that ridiculous mustache?"

"Never," Alynn said. "He's had it my whole life. 'Tis all he was allowed to wear back in Ireland."

"What do you mean, allowed?"

"There's laws for poor people in Ireland. Father was just a

wanderin' craftsman, so he couldn't wear a beard, and he could only put three colors in his plaid."

"Good Lord. And you think we're the backwards ones." Leif chuckled, spotted a friend of his in the crowd of churchgoers, and left Alynn to her own devices. Alynn glanced around and saw her friend Brynhilde, her two sons Matthew and Gunnar playing at her feet with one of Mercy's toys. Before Alynn could approach her, though, she was stopped by a smiling man who smelled like fish.

"Alynn, it's good to see you," he said.

"I can't believe I'm saying this," said Alynn, "but Rothgeir, it's good to see you, too."

Rothgeir's smile deepened, and a newfound light in his eyes shone more brightly than ever. Once the surliest man on St. Anne's Cleft, Rothgeir had surprised the entire island by converting to Christianity shortly after Drostan became chief. He'd become a different person since then, and he had brought his wife and four children to Mass every Sabbath for the past three years.

"Where's your little girl?" Rothgeir asked. "Rumor has it she's needing her tooth-gift already."

"Aye, she's just got her first tooth in. And you're best off finding my mother. I don't know where she's taken Elspeth to." Alynn glanced around the room; perhaps Caitriona had taken her into a bedroom to change her diaper.

"All my children were six months old before they got their first tooth. Perchance Elspeth's stronger than them all. No wonder, considering who her parents are." Alynn felt her ears turn red, but Rothgeir seemed not to notice. "She's a fine lass. The Lord's got big plans for her."

"Thank you," said Alynn. "I've no doubt you're right. Speaking of Elspeth, though, she's probably hungry. I'd best go find her."

Rothgeir nodded his goodbyes. "God bless you, milady."

"God bless you too, Rothgeir."

A familiar wail nearly turned Alynn's heart inside out. She

followed her ears until she found her daughter trying to eat her way through the top of Caitriona's dress. Alynn grabbed Elspeth and helped her start nursing.

"I could have fed her," said Caitriona.

"I've got her, thanks."

When Alynn was finally free to divert her attention from Elspeth—no simple task, as the babe was dragging her kitten-claw fingernails across her mother's chest—she saw that Caitriona was watching them with a bittersweet smile. "My sweet wee girl," she said.

"Which one of us?" Alynn asked.

"You, mostly. I feel like 'twas only yesterday that yer father set you in my arms for the first time. I remember it was freezin' in the house, so Da pulled the straw tick in front of the fireplace, wrapped his plaid around us, and we just lay there, the three of us, snug and warm. 'Tis one of my favorite memories."

Alynn smiled. "It was one of my favorite stories to hear. Da would tell it to us every year on Epiphany."

"The whole story?" Caitriona asked.

"He'd tell us about the snowstorm, and how he sent the neighbor for the midwife so he wouldn't leave you alone."

"The neighbor never came back with the midwife. Da was the one who caught you—did he never tell you that?"

Alynn shook her head. "Go away."

"I can't believe he never told you."

"Who never told her what?" asked Rowan, who had returned with a fully-dressed Mercy on his hip.

Caitriona's eyes were shining with fond memories. "The day she was born, you never told her the whole story! Are you just embarrassed because you panned out afterwards?"

"Of course I panned out! She looked like a frog!"

"A beautiful frog," Caitriona scolded.

"She was purple!"

Alynn hid a laugh. Elspeth hadn't exactly been a picture of beauty the day she was born, either. Coming to himself, Rowan recovered his tact and smiled with paternal fondness in his eyes. "You've turned out nice though, my heart."

"Me too," said Mercy.

"Och, of course, you too!" Rowan kissed the soft yellow wisps Mercy had for hair and tickled her ribs. She laughed, her face lighting up with infectious joy before looking at Elspeth and pointing at her.

"Eppie mick?" she asked.

"Yes," said Caitriona. "Elspeth's drinking milk. She's hungry."

"Eppie want gi'cakes?"

"Say what?" Alynn asked.

"Eppie want—Eppie want gi'cakes."

Rowan smiled. "Elspeth's too little to eat griddle cakes. She doesn't have enough teeth to chew them with."

"Lemme see."

"No, she's eatin'. You can't see her tooth right now."

"Lemme see!"

"No, Mercy."

At that, Mercy's face turned red, and she let out a wail. Rowan sighed and took her upstairs. Alynn turned to Caitriona, who had a look of defeat on her face. "I've got quite a bit to look forward to," said Alynn. "Elspeth's challenging enough right now. I don't know what I'll do when she starts walkin' and talkin' and throwin' fits."

"You just have to love her." Caitriona turned her gaze to the floor and blinked. "And I know 'tis hard when they're little, but 'tis a good thing when yer child's got spirit—it means they'll fight when life gets hard. They're the ones that make it."

Alynn clutched Elspeth a bit tighter to her chest and caught her tiny hand in a firm grasp. Elspeth's fist instinctively coiled around her mother's index finger.

"I didn't mean it that way, Lynder," Caitriona said quickly. "I just—I look at Mercy, I look at you, I look at Tarin, and it makes me think—but that doesn't matter. God's gotten ye both this far, He's no reason to abandon us now."

Alynn was quiet. St. Joseph's Church in Limerick had two little graves that she'd been thinking about quite a bit recently. Louisa would have been sixteen or seventeen now—probably planning her wedding, and Alynn would have helped her with it. Britta would have been ten. Would she be learning Latin along with Tarin, or helping Caitriona with Mercy?

As a child, Alynn had never thought too much of her dead sisters. People died. It was part of life. But now that she had a daughter of her own, Alynn couldn't imagine how her parents had managed to bury two of their children. Rowan especially— he had lost Caitriona to a Viking raid and Britta to a broken heart within mere weeks of each other. It was no wonder that Alynn couldn't remember what his laugh sounded like.

Tarin scampered past Alynn and scurried up the stairs; he was on his way to ring the bell. Alynn forced her memories aside and turned to find her seat in the chapel.

The bell started pealing just as Alynn opened the double doors into the chapel. It was there that her anxieties melted away in the colored light from the stained glass windows. The solemn pews, the delicate railing of the upstairs hallways, the vaulted ceiling—all of it seemed to point her towards heaven.

Alynn wished that Elspeth would look up from her meal to enjoy the ecclesiastic beauty, but Elspeth had no such interests. Wee piglet.

FOUR

Service was over. The chapel was empty and strangely dark. Lukas was quite used to the dark, as well as the layout of the room; his right hand lightly skimmed across a row of benches as he made his way to the lectern. He touched the last bench, took two steps, and tapped the raised speaking platform with his foot before mounting it.

It hadn't been this dark fifteen minutes ago. A storm must have been blowing in. That, and the windows needed washing. Lukas had always been terrified of touching the windows. He had broken one of them as a lad, the year after St. Barnabas the bell had been installed. He had been whipped rather violently for it, then made to go without dinner for three days. A bit harsh for an eight-year-old, in retrospect.

What had he been doing, anyway, to break the window? Playing catch in the cemetery with Eoghan? Aye, it sounded like something the two of them would do. Eoghan had been seven years older than Lukas, but he was still the closest thing Lukas had ever had to a childhood friend. Unless he counted Everhild, but he'd only seen her once a year. Lovely girl, though.

Lukas picked up his Bible and turned to leave, but something caught his attention. He thought he saw movement. Lukas blinked and squinted; there it was again.

"Hello?" he asked.

The motion stopped, and part of Lukas thought he saw a grey figure standing in the middle of the chapel. Between his old eyes and his habit of seeing ghosts, however, he couldn't be sure of anything.

A small voice began speaking in Norse. "Forgive me, father, for I have sinned. It has been three years since my last confession."

Lukas rubbed his eyes and ran his hand across the smooth wood grain of his lectern. Focusing on something real usually helped him come to his senses when he heard or saw something that wasn't there. It didn't work as well when he smelled or tasted blood—or oatmeal with cheese, which had been everyone's last meal before the massacre. Watching it ooze, half-digested, out of abdominal wounds—he couldn't think about it. He could hardly bear to watch the McNeils eat it.

The voice spoke again. It seemed to belong to a young person. "Did you hear me, father?"

"I heard you, but I can't see you." Lukas had spoken to ghosts before; this usually silenced them. "My eyes are old. Come closer."

"I'd rather not."

Well—strange ghost. Lukas began to suspect that the figure was, in fact, real. "Fair enough. Confess what you will, my child."

"It isn't something that I have done, father." The voice quivered a bit. "Although I've done plenty of wrong—it's something I'm about to do."

Lukas clutched his Bible a bit tighter. He stroked the edge of the pages, the plant-based paper of his own invention soft and wilted under his thumb. "What is it you're about to do? And if you know it's wrong, why are you doing it?"

"I don't belong to myself. What I'm about to do—I don't want to do it. Does God—does God see that?"

"God sees everything, my child. And he knows our motives

better than we ourselves do." Lukas turned to the Lord in silent prayer. *What do I say, Lord? What do I do?*

Don't worry, answered a still, small voice.

I'm not worried. I just need to know what to say.

Tell her I still love her, and that she's forgiven. She's in turmoil. She needs a friend. She needs loved.

"God wants to tell you that He loves you, and He forgives you," said Lukas. "And my dear, if you ever need food or a dry bed to sleep in, or simply a bit of company, you're more than welcome here."

There was a moment of silence. Lukas wondered if his hallucination was finally over. But the voice rose again, trembling with tears. "I can't. I'll hurt you. You've got such a nice family here—and such a sweet baby. I can't hurt your baby."

Lukas was wondering how Mercy came into all of this when the grey blur in front of him moved. It disappeared for a moment before reappearing next to the door in the eastern wall that opened out towards the cemetery. It was only used during funerals. Lukas normally kept it locked, and he'd often get remarks from congregants saying they'd never noticed it until they saw it opened to allow a coffin's passage.

The door opened, as if of its own accord, and the grey figure slipped through it easily.

His Bible clutched tightly against his chest, Lukas went to the door and looked outside. He saw no one—not a person, not a ghost, not even footprints in the grass. Even if there were footprints, he knew, his old eyes would be unable to see them.

"Lord," Lukas found himself saying aloud, "I'm seeing things again. Am I going mad? Did I imagine that thing?"

Lukas, you weren't imagining things.

"Please tell me I was, Lord."

You weren't.

Lukas mumbled a single Latin profanity. "Then what the devil was that thing?"

A child in need. No one you need to be afraid of.

"I couldn't see—the way it spoke, it wasn't natural—Jesus, Lord Jesus, what do I do?"

Lukas got the impression that God shrugged. *Fret if you want to, laddie. I won't stop you. Just remember where I am if you change your mind.*

"Right. Thanks." With another deep breath, Lukas locked the door and felt his way through the dark chapel until he reached the double doors that led to the rest of the building. He'd forgotten why he needed his Bible in the first place.

"Are we playing with shield wall?"

Alynn looked up from the *tafl* board at her friend Sigmund. He was holding Elspeth in his lap, letting her chew on the carved thumb of his wooden left hand, but his mind was focused on the game in front of them.

"We won't need it," said Alynn.

There was a smile in Sigmund's eyes. "You're sure about that?"

"Sure, I'm sure. Your move."

"You know," said Sigmund, moving one of his pawns one space away from a corner, "for as good a fighter as you are, I'd think you'd be better at *hnefatafl*."

Alynn moved one of her own pawns. "I'm a berserker, not a strategist."

"Fair point." Sigmund moved another piece, so that he had the corner flanked. "It would be interesting, though—if you were both. You'd be an unstoppable force."

Alynn said nothing as she studied the board. She didn't want to admit that she hadn't held a sword since she'd learned she was pregnant. She didn't even know if her hands would remember what to do with a weapon. She moved a piece and immediately regretted it when Sigmund captured it.

Lukas emerged from the chapel with his Bible clutched to his chest and a bewildered expression on his bloodless face.

"Lukas, are you alright?" Alynn asked.

"*Insanus sum*," Lukas muttered under his breath. There was a silver cat asleep on a chair at the hearth; Lukas picked it up and cuddled it. The cat seemed to enjoy it. Alynn returned her focus to the game of *tafl*, saw where Sigmund had moved, and slid another pawn across the board.

Drostan came up behind Alynn and leaned against the back of her chair, taking a stray strand of Alynn's hair and twirling it around his fingers. "Who's winning?" he asked.

"Too early to tell," said Sigmund, moving again.

Alynn looked at the board, but had wrapped his arms around her chest in a makeshift hug and was resting his cheekbone on the side of her head. "You're distractin' me, love," Alynn said.

"I know. I just wanted to ask if you were in a hurry to get home."

"I'm not. Why?"

"I'm going to go check on the lifeboat."

"Not by yourself, you're not. Not with the person-thing that stabbed Brett out loose in the woods." Alynn twisted around in her chair so she could look at Drostan. He went back to playing with her hair.

"He's got a knife. I've got a sword. I'm fine."

"You could still use an extra hand. Especially if you find him, try to arrest him."

Drostan glanced at Sigmund's narrow frame and wooden arm, then turned to see Lukas sitting at the hearth. "Lukas, are you up for an adventure?" he asked.

Lukas stroked his cat, as if he hadn't heard anything.

"Lukas," Drostan said again. This time, Lukas glanced at the group at the hearth and realized everyone was staring at him. He stared back.

"Hmm?"

"Do you want to go for a walk? Just bring your sword, in case we run into trouble."

"I don't trust myself with a sword right now." Lukas buried

his face in the cat's fur and squeezed it tight. "Och, sweet Theophilus. *Insanus sum creditne?*"

The cat mewed and bumped its head against Lukas's mouth, as if asking for a kiss. Sigmund, who had picked up a smattering of Latin, had a puzzled look in his eyes.

"Lukas, did you just ask the cat if you've gone mad?"

"Nay, I asked him if he *thinks* I've gone mad. Cats tend to lie, ye know."

"Did he answer?" Alynn asked.

"He said that he loves me either way. *Et te amo*, Theophilus."

Sigmund glanced from Lukas to Alynn to Drostan and back again, a slightly worried look on his face. Alynn shook her head. "He'll snap out of it," she said. Then, a bit louder, she said, "Lukas, can I borrow yer sword?"

Drostan cut in. "You're not going—"

"Well, you're not going alone. Your father's already left for home, Brett's hurt, Lukas is askin' the cats questions, and no one else here knows how to use a sword."

"She has a point," said Sigmund, bouncing Elspeth on his knee until she squealed with delight. "Are you trying to laugh, sweetheart?"

Elspeth squealed again, biting Sigmund's wooden thumb with renewed vigor.

"Lukas?" Alynn asked again.

"My sword's under my desk. Take it home wi' ye if ye want."

"Why is it under your desk?" Sigmund asked.

"I reached fer it during a nightmare about a month ago. Rowan nigh lost one of his mustaches. Asides, I don't have much need fer it these days—" Lukas stood up abruptly and, finding that the teakettle still had a bit of water in it left over from breakfast, put it in the embers of the fireplace.

Another awkward glance was exchanged between Alynn, Sigmund, and Drostan. This time, even Alynn didn't dare defend Lukas. Instead, she went upstairs, fetched the sword and the belt that went with it, and returned downstairs armed. Lukas's sword belt was only slightly too big on her. A year ago, it would have fallen right off. Alynn blamed Elspeth.

Before she left, Alynn knelt in front of Elspeth and looked her in the eye. "You be a good girl for Uncle Sigmund, now," she said.

Elspeth stopped chewing on Sigmund's wooden thumb just long enough to smile. Alynn's heart melted, and she kissed her daughter's downy red hair.

"Mammy loves you, and she'll be right back. Alright?"

Elspeth gave a long and meaningless vocalic shriek.

"Alright. I won't be long. I promise."

Then, with the feeling that she was forgetting something, Alynn left with Drostan. The sky was coal-grey with clouds, and thunder rumbled low in the distance. It wasn't raining quite yet, but the air was heavy with the warning that a deluge was coming.

Drostan seemed not to mind the weather, but he kept one hand on his hilt. After half a mile and a particularly loud clash of thunder, Alynn reached out and held his free hand. Drostan squeezed it.

"How do you do this every day?" Alynn asked.

"Do what?"

"Go to work and leave Elspeth behind. It would break my heart."

"Well, we do what we have to. I've got a family to feed. And speaking of food, are we out of butter?"

"Aye, I'll churn more tomorrow."

"Did it go bad? I thought we had half a pound of it."

"Well, Elspeth's growin' so fast and eatin' so much, and 'tis hungry work nursing a baby. Butter's one of the few things I can eat with one hand and not have to cook it first."

Drostan shook his head. "Love, I'll never understand you."

"And I can't believe you've never just eaten a spoonful of butter."

"You're one to talk. You were the only one at my cousin

Idunn's wedding to pass up the *hakarl.*"

"Five-month-old fermented shark meat, I was the only one in my right mind!"

Drostan shook his head with a smile in his eyes. "You missed out," he said.

Alynn was about to give a spirited reply, but they walked out of the forest and onto the beach before she could speak. And what she saw there silenced her.

The woods had been eerie, almost terrifying. The darkness and the distant thunder and the rustling of branches gave the impression that Alynn and Drostan were walking on the branches of the world tree Yggdrasil into another of the Nine Worlds—a cold and evil world, an eternal winter's night. Perhaps there were giants watching them from the shadows; perhaps elfin spirits were following them.

All the same, the woods had a certain comfort to them. The calling of birds and the constant crunch of dirt, and certainly the deep smell of fragrant pine and fresh rain, were familiar and never-changing. But when the dirt turned to sand and the trees gave way to small shrubs and finally to plain emptiness, the familiarity was gone. Alynn felt as if she were standing on the very edge of the world, staring into a void that, if she fell into, she would never return from.

The sky and ocean were similar shades of grey; it was hard to tell where one ended and the other began. Even the sand seemed more grey than usual. The wind whipped Alynn's skirts about her ankles and sent Lukas's sword knocking against the back of her leg. Strands of hair stuck to the corners of her lips no matter how frequently she tried to clear them away.

There were exactly two things that stood out in the void. The first was a small fishing pier. The second was a faering boat, several yards to the right of the pier and dragged halfway up the beach. It looked small and out-of-place, as if it had been placed there by a deity with goals beyond human under-standing.

Alynn looked at everything and shivered.

"Well, the boat's still there," said Drostan. He approached it, and Alynn, unwilling to be left alone at the edge of the forest, went with him. "I thought that our mystery guest would have used it for firewood."

"Isn't it too wet to burn?" Alynn asked.

"This is Orkney, Lynder. Everything's wet, all the time. You learn how to make things work." Drostan reached the boat and looked at the sand around it. Alynn focused more on the boat itself. It was ten feet long, riddled with cracks, and still stained with dried blood.

"He hasn't been back to this area recently," said Drostan. "No footprints. And no signs of a fire. It looks like he left immediately."

Alynn glanced from the wrecked boat to the sea to the forest. She thought of her childhood—all the time she and Rowan and Tarin had spent between houses after Caitriona had been kidnapped by Vikings and Rowan was too heart-broken to stay in one place for very long. She thought of the day she was shipwrecked on St. Anne's Cleft. And she heard herself saying aloud, "None of this makes sense."

"Why not?" Drostan asked.

"You're shipwrecked, you wash ashore, the first thing you notice is how cold you are. If you're not injured, or shiverin' too hard to move, or panned out like I was, the first thing you do is either build a fire or make a shelter. Leif checked the woods the day Tarin and Brett were attacked, he should have found signs of—something."

Drostan was silent for a while. He looked at the boat and turned it right side up; a small crab scuttled away. Other than the crab's claw marks, the sand was smooth. "He didn't turn the boat into a shelter, either," said Drostan.

Alynn glanced at the forest. She could see the path she and Drostan had followed. But if a stranger had arrived on the island—probably on a dark and stormy day—he might not have noticed it. "Our ghost probably started walking along the beach," said Alynn. "If I were him, I'd be looking for a settlement of some sort, and they're usually near the ocean."

"Poor fool," said Drostan. "St. Anne's Cleft has a lot of shoreline. If he turned east—all the farms are inland, do you think he'd try looking for them?"

"He'd probably have a camp near the shore, then venture inland for supplies," Alynn said.

"How well does he know the island by now? I mean, it's been days. He could have walked around the entire coastline. Maybe he's moving from place to place so no one notices the missing supplies."

"Unless he's hurt," Alynn said. She looked again at the bloodstains on the faering—the tiny bit of it that had gotten lodged in a crack between the strakes and somehow survived the rain—and guessed that their mystery guest had been badly injured. "Livin' out in the woods is difficult. If he's too hurt to find food, he's probably starved himself half to death by now. And if he isn't lookin' for the village, he'll be lookin' for a source of fresh water."

"Since when were you such a survival expert?" Drostan asked.

Alynn shrugged. She never liked talking about the times she had spent between houses growing up. Besides, she didn't remember too much about it. Most of her childhood blurred together into a damp, cold, hungry mess.

"My father taught me a lot of things," she said. She looked out over the water and shivered. "Let's go home. Elspeth probably misses me."

Alynn and Drostan turned to leave, but a noise caught their attention. Alynn's gaze darted upwards to see an eider duck tumbling out of the sky with blood flowing from its breast. Curious, Alynn approached the duck. By the time she was within ten yards of the creature, two things were obvious. The duck was dead, and there was an arrow lodged through its heart.

Ignoring the duck, Drostan drew his sword and approached the forest. The bushes were rustling. Suddenly, a figure darted between two trees and then disappeared into the underbrush.

"Ho, there! Stop!" called Drostan. He chased after the figure, and Alynn tried to draw her sword and follow. But Lukas's sword was longer than her own, and far heavier than she anticipated. By the time she was armed, Drostan was nowhere to be seen. Alynn ran into the forest anyway.

Her heart was pounding by the time she caught sight of Drostan—not from fear, but from exertion. She hadn't run this fast since long before Elspeth was born. But her fear certainly increased when she realized that Drostan wasn't moving. He stood frozen, staring at an arrow that was lodged into a tree inches away from his head.

"What happened?" Alynn asked, panting.

Noiselessly, Drostan raised a hand, and Alynn froze. They stood still as statues together, hardly breathing, listening to the faint crashing of footsteps as they retreated into the woods.

Alynn's thoughts were all on Elspeth. Was she safe? Would this stranger find the monastery? If he did, would he spare Elspeth? What if Elspeth grew up without a mother, or father, or both? Who would take her?

Drostan took a cautious step closer to Alynn, placing himself between her and the creature that had shot at him. Alynn inched closer to him so that her chest touched his back. They stared into the woods together, swords clenched in white fists.

A knife-wielding ghost, they could have taken on together. But not an archer. Alynn wondered what might have happened had the stranger been more inclined to fight. He would have shot Drostan first, doubtless. Alynn might have stood frozen for a moment, wondering if she should help her husband or avenge him. And in that split second of indecision, she would have been struck down as well.

After a few more moments of silence had passed in the forest, Drostan stepped forward and grabbed the arrow that had almost killed him. His hand shook. Then, wordlessly, they found the path and walked quickly and cautiously to the monastery. A steady rain set in, and although Alynn detested the wet pieces of hair that clung to her jaw and neck, she ignored them.

"Do you think that was the same man who hurt Brett?" Alynn asked when she was almost certain they were out of danger.

"Probably," said Drostan. "All I know is that I want a wall between us and whatever shot that arrow."

Alynn agreed, and nothing more was said until they were safe inside the monastery, and Elspeth was safe in her mother's arms.

April 25, A.D. 969—

I might be going mad again. I had an entire conversation with—something. I know not what. My spirit says that it was a real person, a young one, who is frightened and alone. But the way it disappeared—it left out the cemetery door—and it spoke unnaturally.

Then again, I have the voice of the Holy Spirit telling me that what I saw was real. But if I cannot trust my own eyes, I cannot trust the voice in my head I deem to be God's. So either I'm entirely correct or entirely wrong. I wish I could talk to an actual person about this, but everyone is on edge over the fact that Alynn and Drostan got shot at by our mystery guest. Brett and Tarin are afraid to go into the woods and enjoy the few short years of youth they have left. Caitriona hardly lets Mercy play outside anymore. I have no doubt that church attendance is going to drop. I'll go about business as usual. Whether it's because I trust Christ to protect me or because I look forward to meeting Him in person is any man's guess.

I suppose, if I am going mad again, I'll find out sooner or later. Easter was last week and I'm wondering if the anniversary of the massacre is affecting me. I'll see if the hallucinations get better or worse, and in the meantime, I'll keep my suffering to myself. What choice do I have? I'll pray about it.

I'm tired of prayer being my only course of action. I always hoped that having a family would include the sharing of problems. But the lads shouldn't be burdened with my pain, and Caitriona is busy with Mercy and the household chores, and Rowan—even if he cared to talk to me, he'd think me dangerous and start distancing his family from me.

I'll hold my tongue. Or perhaps I'll talk to Theophilus. He's currently warming up my bed for me, and holding him as I fall asleep is one of the greatest pleasures in my life.

—L. McCamden

FIVE

By some miracle, Elspeth slept through most of that night, and Alynn had a bit more energy than usual the next day. She managed to get up and dressed at a decent hour, and the breakfast dishes were even put away by noon. Alynn had just laid Elspeth down for a nap and was putting some wool on her carding combs when Drostan came home. Alynn was surprised—he never left work unless something was terribly wrong—until she noticed a man in a faded black captain's coat who had come with him.

Alynn gasped. "Captain McMahon, what are you doin' here?"

The captain grinned, revealing a few missing teeth. "It's good to see ye too, Lynder," he said. Alynn hugged him, ignoring the wetness of his coat from the gentle rain falling outside. "Och, I've missed seeing yer family around. How long's it been? Eight months? How is everyone?"

"We're grand, pure grand—come inside! I'll get you a drink."

"I'll have milk, if it's no trouble."

Curious, Drostan gave him a sideways glance. "We have ale and mead if you'd rather, Captain."

"Many thanks, man, but I've been living off bread,

stockfish, and small ale since autumn. It gets auld fast."

In that case, Captain McMahon should probably have whole milk instead of the mixture of whole milk, skim milk, and buttermilk that Alynn drank daily. Unless the whole milk had gone sour. Had it? Alynn sipped it, guessed it good enough, and poured a glass. When she turned around, she saw Captain McMahon hovering over Elspeth's cradle, which swung suspended from a ceiling beam.

"What's this?" he asked.

"That's Elspeth."

"So! Ye've made Rowan a grandfather, have ye now, Lynder? Och, she's precious. What is she, six months?"

"Four and a half, she's just fat. And if you wake her up, I'll kill you."

Captain McMahon took the threat seriously and stepped away from the cradle. "She's got her da's hair, that's certain. A bit of her mum's spunk, I'll reckon. How's it going wi' her?"

Alynn smiled. "I love her more than I knew I could love anyone. 'Tis wonderful, and exhausting. You can hold her in a bit. Have you been well, Captain?"

"Well enough—just tired, recently. We've come from Iceland, and we would have stopped in the Faroes, but there was a storm and we got blown off course, and blast it, I'm too auld to spend more than a fortnight at sea." Captain McMahon took the milk Alynn handed him and sipped it gratefully as he sat down on a sleeping bench. "Many thanks, lass."

"Not a bother. We're glad you're here safely."

"How's Iceland?" Drostan asked.

"Warmer than usual. So is every place I've been this year— the past few years, in fact. Och, and there's news."

Drostan sat down near Captain McMahon, his ears perked for listening. "Good or bad news?"

"A bit of both, I'd say. Ye've heard of Thrand the Infamous, I assume."

Valdis, who had been spying from the workroom, cracked the door open a bit wider. Even a scolding glance from Alynn couldn't tear her away from the doorway. It seemed that Valdis knew a bit more about Thrand the Infamous than Alynn did—which wasn't much. He was an unsavory character, but Alynn didn't know why she was supposed to dislike him.

"Wasn't he outlawed three years ago?" Drostan asked.

"Two. And he deserved it. Rapist, murderer, Viking marauder of the worst sort—anyway, he and his children disappeared after he was outlawed. I've heard he's been in Kiev since then, but I won't sell that more expensive than I bought it."

In other words, no one knew with any certainty where Thrand the Infamous had been for the past two years.

Captain McMahon took a swig of his milk, then wiped it out of his beard. "The good news is, Thrand's been killed. Bad news, some of his men are still out there."

"Where are they?" Drostan asked.

"God knows at this point. A Darsidian trading vessel found him about a week ago and slaughtered the lot of them. Thrand's in hell where he belongs, and if anyone's seen his mates since then, I've not heard of it."

"Are any of his children alive?" Alynn asked. "'Tis vengeance they'll be after."

"Three of them that we know of. Two of his lads weren't accounted among the dead. Ivar the one, and—maybe Hrut. I forget. And his daughter, Eyja. From what I've heard, she's the one who takes after her da the most. And then a few non-relatives, of course. Sailors, friends, co-conspirators. Hopefully no one close enough willing to start a war over him." Captain McMahon took another drink and wiped his mouth, smearing his sleeve and mustache with red.

"Captain, are you bleeding?" Alynn asked.

"Och, not again. Half a moment—" Pressing a hand to his mouth, Captain McMahon hurried out the back door, bumping Elspeth's cradle in the process. Elspeth started screaming.

"Sorry, I'm so sorry," said Captain McMahon as he shut the door, eyeing Alynn a bit worriedly. A gust of wind blew raindrops inside.

Sighing, Alynn scooped up Elspeth and bounced her around, shushing her and kissing her until her screaming turned into a gentle fussing. When she quieted down enough to be talked over, Alynn asked Drostan quietly, "You don't think he's got consumption, do you?"

"He's not coughing, and it looked like his gums were bleeding. Ten to one he's got scurvy."

"Will he get better?"

Drostan said nothing. He only looked at the back door, and then at Valdis, who was slowly edging her way into the main room. Discovered, Valdis meekly fetched Captain McMahon's mostly-empty mug of milk and wiped the blood off with her apron.

"Don't fret, mistress," said Valdis sweetly. "He's going to the monastery to visit your father, isn't he? Surely Lukas can pray for him, and the Lord's worked greater miracles through him."

"That's right, Valdis," said Drostan. He took Elspeth into his arms, and she finally stopped fussing. Alynn looked on in frustration. She was starting to think that Elspeth liked Drostan better than her.

"Aye, thank you, Valdis. How's the weaving coming along?"

"I'm halfway up the loom, mistress."

Alynn smiled. "Good. Let's see if we can't finish the fabric by the end of the week. I'd like to dye it afore Elspeth's second tooth starts botherin' her too much."

Valdis nodded respectfully and retreated into the workroom. Elspeth, meanwhile, had decided she wasn't going to go back to sleep. She sat upright in her father's arms, blinking at the firelight, and returning her father's warm smile.

A cold gust of wind made Elspeth fuss again, and Alynn hoped that Captain McMahon was coming inside. Instead, she saw a young man at the front door, brushing his dripping blonde hair out of his vaguely familiar face. "Chief Drostan?"

he asked.

Drostan squared his shoulders and handed Elspeth back to Alynn. "Aye?"

"Is Captain McMahon here?"

"He is. He's indisposed at the moment."

"Come inside in the meantime," said Alynn, fetching another mug from the cupboard. "Milk or ale?"

"I'll have a good strong ale, if you've got it, milady. Many thanks."

"I've got it," said Valdis. She poured the ale, then froze when the mug was half in the hands of the stranger. She gave a strange squeal, then clapped a hand over her mouth.

The stranger looked at her curiously before his eyes grew wide. "Valdis?" he asked.

"Oh, Vali!"

Valdis dropped the mead and leapt into the stranger's arms before Alynn could ask herself what the devil was going on. Then it clicked. She realized why the stranger looked familiar—he was essentially the male version of Valdis.

"What are you doing here?" Valdis asked.

"I signed on with Captain McMahon. He was in Trondheim five months ago. My gods, are you alright? Where's your collar?"

Valdis had to think for a moment, two fingers tracing her throat where she used to wear the thrall's collar that marked her as a slave. "They set me free," she said.

"And you stayed?"

"Are you mad that I stayed?"

"No—oh, Valdis, how could I be mad? You're alive! I'm just—surprised. I guess they treat you well?"

"Ever since Master Konar died, everyone's treated me like family. Here—this is Mistress Alynn the Dauntless, you might have heard of her—and Master Drostan. I've known him since he was twelve, he's a good man. And their new daughter, Elspeth." Valdis turned from her male counterpart, and Alynn saw the tears in her eyes. "Mistress Alynn, Master Drostan, this is my brother, Vali."

"A pleasure to meet you," said Drostan, shaking Vali's hand. "Are you twins?"

"For one month a year, we are. Thank you for taking care of my sister, milord—milady." Vali kissed Alynn's hand and let his gaze linger on Elspeth for a while. "Lovely babe you've got."

"Thank you," said Alynn. "Go into the workroom and catch up. We'll let the captain know what's happened."

"Thank you," said Vali again. He kissed Valdis and kept a protective arm around her as they went into the workroom. They were talking to each other in what sounded like a different dialect of Norse, speaking so quickly that Alynn didn't bother trying to make out the words. But Valdis's face had a light in it that Alynn had never seen before. She was radiant.

Alynn felt Valdis's joy in her own heart. Life had taken her own family away from her, slowly pinching one relative in wizened fingers and savoring the despair before selecting and stealing another. But what life had stolen, God had restored, and very few things in life compared to the joy of reunion.

"Are you thinkin' what I am?" Alynn asked.

"Unless you're worried about who's going to cook dinner from now on, probably not."

Alynn shot Drostan a sharp glare. "I can cook."

"And I can nalbind a nightcap, but it still turns out better when Valdis does it." Drostan finally noticed Alynn's angry glare and sheepishly took his hood from its hook beside the door. "I suppose I'd better get back to work."

"Don't you dare. You've company out back."

The hood went back on the hook. Drostan reached out for Elspeth, but Alynn held her tighter. "Fine. I'm sorry," said Drostan. "But you talk bad about your own cooking all the time. You know you aren't the best at it."

"Aye, but you're not supposed to agree with me! I don't go about tellin' you that you can't talk in front of a crowd, now, do I?" Alynn's Irish lilt got stronger, and Elspeth grinned at the singsong meter. Drostan sighed.

"Fair play, love. Can I hold the baby now?"

Alynn was too tired to hold a grudge. "Apologize like you mean it."

"I'm sorry."

Alynn handed Elspeth back to Drostan, and he smiled as he kissed his daughter's fuzzy head. "Now, let's play a game," he said. "I'll call it What Sort of Idiot is Shipwrecked on My Island? Elspie goes first. What do you think, wee darling?"

Elspeth wiggled, squealed, and started gnawing on her tiny fist.

"Good guess. Ten points if you're right. Lynder, your turn."

"'Tisn't a single clue I have."

"Alright, and my guess is that it's someone connected with Thrand the Infamous."

Captain McMahon came back inside, a bit paler and quieter, but with a smile in his eyes. "Sorry about that. I guess my humors needed balanced."

"Not a bother, Captain," said Alynn. "You're alright?"

"Pure grand, as ye Irish say!"

"That's good," said Drostan. He glanced at the workroom as Valdis's and Vali's laughter arose from it. "Your deckhand Vali is going to be indisposed for a while."

Captain McMahon raised an eyebrow. "Is he sick, dead, or in legal trouble?"

"Turns out our hired girl, Valdis, is his sister," said Drostan, disentangling Elspeth's sticky fingers from his beard. "Now, I don't want to take up too much of your time. Where was Thrand killed, exactly?"

"A good day and a half's sailing north of Durness, they told me. Why?"

"There's a Faering on the southern shore," Drostan said. "It isn't one of ours. We were shot at yesterday while trying to investigate it."

Captain McMahon rubbed his eyes. "Christ have mercy,

that's not good." He thought for a moment, pinching the bridge of his nose with work-worn fingers. "From what I know of Thrand's children, all of them are better wi' swords and spears than they are wi' bows. He considered distance weapons cowardly—he'd never fight unless there was a chance he could get hurt. Joke's on him, he was killed wi' a throwing axe. Cleaved his skull in two."

"Not in front of Elspeth," Alynn said.

"She doesn't know her own name yet. It's not like I'm frightening her."

Alynn glared at Captain McMahon, eyes burning like the flaming sword of an angel, and he stammered an apology. Then, quickly, he gave Drostan twopence for a docking fee and asked to borrow a horse. He was off to visit Rowan.

Despite still being a bit mad at him for frightening Elspeth, Alynn was a bit sad to see Captain McMahon leave. Seeing him sick hurt her heart. But now that she thought of it, she'd seen him ill before, and it had never bothered her. Perhaps becoming a mother had softened her heart a bit.

Shoving her emotions aside, Alynn set about making soup for dinner. It wasn't nearly time to eat, but with Valdis busy and Elspeth needing almost-constant attention, Alynn knew she needed to get an early start. Valdis had helped with dinner nearly every night for the past three years. Alynn hoped she remembered how to cook without her.

Drostan surprised her by staying for a while. He fetched water for the soup and got the table down from the loft so Alynn could have more space to chop vegetables. Then, after giving Alynn a kiss on the head, he donned his hood again.

"We've got a small karve just about finished," said Drostan. "It should be seaworthy in a week or two."

"Very nice," said Alynn.

"Can we take it for a float in the harbor?"

"We've got Elspeth to look after," said Alynn.

Drostan smiled. "We can make a nest of blankets for her in the prow. The waves should rock her to sleep. And we can do whatever we want."

"Anything?" Alynn asked.

"Anything," said Drostan.

Alynn smiled as she transferred a handful of chopped carrots into the soup kettle. "I'd like a nap and a shoulder rub."

"Can I at least get a kiss or two?"

"Deal."

Drostan left, and Alynn started chopping vegetables a bit faster. She had gotten almost everything in the soup pot when Elspeth started crying. Should dinner be late, or should the soup be without onions? Alynn could do a lot of things while nursing Elspeth, but chopping onions wasn't one of them. Her first thought was to call for Valdis, but she was still eagerly conversing with Vali in the workroom, blissfully unaware of the passage of time, and disturbing her was not an option.

Dinner could be late. That, or the onions could be undercooked in the soup. A bit of crunch might be satisfying.

"At least you're cute," said Alynn as she got Elspeth situated at her breast. "You're very, very cute. I need yer help, wee heart. If Da and Afi come back before the onions are done cookin', I need you to distract them for me. Do you think you're cute enough to do that?"

Elspeth wriggled.

"Och, what's Mammy sayin'? Of course you're cute enough. Of course you are!"

Elspeth turned red and grunted, and a familiar stench filled the air. Alynn sighed. Aye, dinner would be late.

Luckily for Alynn, Leif and Drostan came home later than usual. Leif's broad shoulders drooped, and his hair was disheveled and in need of a trim. But there was still a smile in his eyes as he took Elspeth into his arms and kissed her head. "How's my wee Valkyrie this evening?" he asked. "Drostan, every day, she looks more like you did at her age."

"There's no way my face was that fat," said Drostan.

"You were fatter than this, lad. You looked like a squirrel hoarding acorns." Leif grinned, and he seemed a bit less tired.

"Och, you were beautiful. And so are you, Elspie. You're such a pretty lassie. Aye, you are! Aye, you are!"

Alynn smiled as she set the table. It would be forever strange to hear baby-talk coming out of a six-foot-three man with a soldier's build. It was beautiful. Alynn had never known her father's parents; she was glad Elspeth had that experience. She set five glasses of small ale on the table, remembering that Vali would be joining them.

Well—they might be too excited to eat. Alynn popped her head into the workroom to find the pair conversing rapidly in the same strange dialect that she could only understand a few words of.

"Dinner's ready," said Alynn as soon as there was a lull in their conversation. "There's soup if you'd like it."

Valdis jumped up. "I'm so sorry, Mistress, I should have been—"

"Valdis. Don't." Alynn made herself smile past the lump in her throat. "Do you want to go home with him?"

"I—I'd love to, but—I can't leave you now. Not with the baby."

"Don't worry about us. I started raising Tarin when I was nine, I ought to be fine." Alynn stepped into the workroom to take Valdis's hands in her own. "I know how important family is. I know what it's like to be apart from the ones you love. And it's high time you went home—not that I want you to leave, of course. We'll all miss you terribly."

Valdis was silent, and her blue eyes glistened. She looked at Alynn, then at Vali, then through the open door at the family she'd come to call her own. Finally, a tearful smile creeping onto her face, she embraced Alynn. "Thank you," she said. "I'll miss you, too. All of you."

"Och, I know. Come eat dinner."

Valdis nodded and helped dish up the soup. Alynn held Elspeth in one arm—it was getting harder every day, the way she wriggled—and took a bowl of soup with her free hand. Leif stopped her as she started to sit at the table.

"You're sure you're alright with Valdis leaving?" he asked in a low voice. "It's hard to find good help. You'll be alone for a while."

"She's a free woman. We can't very well force her to stay," Alynn said. "And besides, I've been keeping house since I still had baby teeth. I'll manage alone."

Leif shook his head sadly. "Well, this is the right thing to do. We'll all miss Valdis. And I'm proud of you."

Dinner was bittersweet and longer than usual; no one seemed to be able to eat. Stories were shared. Vali told most of them. By the end of the evening, Alynn knew twice as much about Valdis as she had before—who could have guessed she'd been a tomboy growing up? Valdis just sat and blushed through most of her brother's stories, only jabbing an elbow in his side whenever his tales crossed a line. She cleared the table once everyone had finished, and when Leif and Drostan left to announce that a village meeting would take place the next day, it was Vali who stowed the table and the three-legged stools in the loft.

Alynn tried to card some wool while Elspeth took her evening nap, but her mind kept wandering. Finally, she felt Valdis's hand on her shoulder.

"I'll watch the baby, Mistress. You can sleep now," she said.

"But the yarn's for a new dress for Elspeth. I need to finish it before she grows any more."

"I'll do it. It's not like I'll sleep much anyway, talking to Vali and all. I might as well keep my hands busy."

Tears threatened to spill from Alynn's eyes as she embraced Valdis tightly. "You're such a dear," she said. "Thank you for everything."

SIX

The village meeting was held in the feasting hall of Samkoma at an ungodly hour the next morning. Elspeth had been up and crying much of the night before. Part of Alynn had contemplated staying home and sleeping instead of attending the meeting. But the rest of her desperately wanted adult company, so she found herself standing half-asleep in a corner, feeding Elspeth her second breakfast.

A drop of water landed on Alynn's shoulder. She glanced up to see a leak in the sod roof. Sighing, she stepped aside. At least it was a warm rain. According to Vali, it was an unusually warm year everywhere. Norway, Iceland, England, Francia— and even farther south, in places like Rome and the Holy Land. Alynn didn't mind so much. Better too warm than too cold.

"Pray for me," said Drostan for the fifth time that morning. He ran his sweat-damp fingers through his flaming ginger hair—a motion he'd been repeating almost constantly for two hours. He'd been pacing, too, in a manner quite unbecoming for the Chief of St. Anne's Cleft. Alynn sighed.

"Come off it, love. If I can tend a baby with three hours of sleep, you can say a few words on stage. You'll do fine."

Drostan chuckled. He kissed Elspeth, then Alynn, then leapt nimbly onto the speaking platform at the far end of the building. Someone blew a horn. The chatter stopped; every eye was fixed on Drostan.

"Thank you all for coming this morning," he said. His voice sounded stronger than it had during the last speech he gave, but it still wavered a bit. "I'll start with the good news," he said. "Thrand the Infamous is dead."

The crowd—mostly men, as the women were still cooking breakfast—cheered. "What killed him?" someone shouted.

"The Darsidians."

"Best thing they've ever done," someone else said.

"I know—strange for the Darsidians to do something for the greater good." Drostan wiped his hands on the hem of his tunic. Alynn scowled. He'd stain the tablet-woven trim she'd worked so hard on. "Unfortunately, this good news does come with bad news. Some of Thrand's crew is still unaccounted for. And we have reason to believe that some of that crew is here, and that they pose a threat to our security."

The crowd started murmuring amongst themselves. Some shouted questions, but they were all lost in the general din. With a lost look in his eyes, Drostan glanced worriedly at the crowd before remembering the man with the horn. Drostan gestured, the horn blew, and the room grew quiet again.

"As far as we know, there is a single fugitive on the island," Drostan continued. His voice shook a bit harder now. "He is an armed and dangerous archer, and he has already attacked two people. Listen to me." His voice grew stern. "I order all of you to use caution. You cannot fight a bow with an axe or a sword. You will be dead before you're in combat range."

"What are we supposed to do, then?" someone cried.

"Use your head!" Drostan snapped before drawing a breath. "Don't leave the village unless you have to. If you do leave the village for any reason—hunting, fishing, going to church—go in groups of at least three. Five or more is better. If you have a distance weapon, carry it with you. Shields, carry one with you at all times. Stay armed. Keep an eye on your little ones. Do not—I repeat, do not—engage this creature alone."

The crowd murmured again. "Is it even human, then?" asked one man. "It can't be that bad," said another. "It's one man. I can take him!" boasted yet another.

Drostan looked lost again. This time, his gaze rested not on the trumpeter but on his father, who was standing near the front of the room. A few exchanges of facial expressions later, Leif mounted the speaking platform and faced the crowd with squared shoulders.

"Gentlemen!" Leif said.

Silence followed.

"I've fought battles, defended my honor in Holmgang, and even gone Viking. I know combat. And the first rule of combat is this: you cannot win against a foe you cannot see. And this shadow we're dealing with managed to shoot a duck in midair from a distance of at least fifty yards, then disappear without a trace. He drew blood from Brett Oddson and escaped unharmed. This man is skilled with his weapon and extraordinarily dangerous. My son speaks wisdom. Listen to him!"

The crowd remained silent, save for a few affirmations. Nodding his thanks to his father, Drostan turned again to the people. "Any questions?"

"Where is this shadow?" someone called out.

"He was last seen Sunday afternoon, on the beach near Treacherous Landing. He could be anywhere on the island by now."

Sigmund raised his good arm. "I suggest we form search parties."

"Good idea. We'll discuss that later in a council meeting. Anyone else?"

"Is it safe to go to church?" someone asked.

"I'll leave that up to everyone's discretion. Personally, though, I'd say that we need Jesus more than ever. I'll be taking my family."

"Are you offering a reward for his capture?"

"Besides the peace of mind from knowing your island's

safe?" Drostan checked himself. "The stranger's belongings will go to the man who captures him. Now, I need a group of volunteers to relay this information to the farms. Hakon—Bjarki—Bjarki the Farrier or Bjarki Fishguts, pick one—Steinmar—Gerimund. Thank you, sirs. How many of you can use a bow? Two of you. Grand, and don't forget your shields. Again, everyone, thank you for being here today. May God bless and protect you. Enjoy your breakfasts. Meeting adjourned."

The crowd dispersed, eager to go home for the morning meal. Soon, Alynn was left alone with Drostan, Leif, and Sigmund. Wait—there was one other man who hung behind. Rothgeir the fisherman.

Rothgeir approached Drostan quietly, as if he was afraid of bothering him. "Do I have leave to go fishing alone, Chief?" he asked.

Drostan seemed surprised. "What about your son—Tormund?"

"Torsten. He doesn't go whole into the forest—was up coughing all last night." Rothgeir tugged on his tunic sleeve. "I'll be out of arrow range, and I don't intend on coming ashore. I figured I'd best get your permission first, though."

"You're a free man, Rothgeir. You don't need my permission to do anything. The only order I gave today was to use good sense, and you've plenty of that. All the rest was advice."

"And good advice it was, sir. Many thanks for it." Rothgeir shook Drostan's hand, then Leif's, then turned to Alynn and smiled. "Here's Elspeth's tooth-gift. Sorry it took so long."

Rothgeir held out his hand and offered up a wooden fish, carved and sanded and perfect for chewing on. Alynn smiled. "Och, she'll love this! She's been needing something to chew on. She's about gnawed her hands off."

"And trust me," said Sigmund, brandishing his wooden arm, "no one wants that."

Rothgeir smiled, and there was a strangely happy light in his eyes that Alynn wanted to ask questions about. He saved her the trouble of asking. "It seems like yesterday I held Torsten for the first time. He's sixteen now. A man full grown. Hold her while you can, milady. Blink, and she'll be taller than you."

With that, he nodded a respectful goodbye to the men and left to start his day. That left the Council—or three-fourths of it, since Lukas wasn't there—alone in each other's company. Alynn yawned.

"Did we miss anything?" Drostan asked.

"Breakfast," said Sigmund. "And my boys. I haven't gotten my good-morning hugs from them yet."

Alynn smiled. "Och, I can't wait until Elspeth's old enough to give hugs."

"I'd bring that up with Brynhilde. Once they're old enough to hug, they're old enough to run places, climb things, jump off things—she hasn't gotten a moment's rest since Gunnar started walking. I should probably go home, make sure they eat their breakfast instead of pouring it down each other's tunics...."

"That's something toddlers do?" Alynn asked a bit worriedly.

"Not all of them," said Leif. "When Drostan was little, he used to—"

"No. No. No more stories." Drostan set a hand on Alynn's shoulder. "Go eat breakfast and hug your boys, Sigmund. Thanks for your help."

"I'll lend a hand any time, chief." Sigmund grinned. "But just the one, it's all I've got. I'll be at the chandlery if you need me."

Everyone bid goodbye at the door, and Drostan made sure that Samkoma was locked and secured before it was left abandoned until the next town meeting. "It's not like you'll need my help finding this shadow," Alynn muttered as they began the short walk back to the longhouse. "But if you do, I'll be at home, as always."

A gust of wind had snatched her words away, and Drostan

turned to her. "Say again?"

Alynn sighed. "Nothin' important."

Valdis had breakfast ready. Leif and Drostan ate quickly and left in a hurry, eager to get in a full day's work. Alynn's day of housekeeping and child-tending was uneventful, if not a bit sad. It hurt to know that Valdis was leaving in only two days' time with Vali and Captain McMahon.

The thought of Captain McMahon tempted Alynn to visit him at the monastery. Logic demanded she stay home. She only had so much time with Valdis. And besides, the shadowy archer and Elspeth's erratic feeding schedule were both powerful forces keeping Alynn firmly at home with the door shut and the latch-string pulled inside.

Alynn and Valdis were just putting the dinner bread to bake in the coals of the fireplace when there was a knock on the door. It was Rothgeir's son Torsten, dark circles under his eyes and angry red scabs around his nose. "Have you heard from my father?" he asked.

"Come out of the rain, lad," Alynn said, shepherding him inside. The rain was more of a misty drizzle than anything, but Alynn knew from experience that any precipitation made being sick even more miserable. "There's no reason I'd have heard anything. Haven't you checked the docks?"

"I have, but Chief Drostan wasn't there—" Torsten coughed into his sleeve— "I thought he'd be here. I thought he'd know something."

"Well, I don't know where Chief Drostan is, and I haven't heard anything about your father." Alynn glanced at Elspeth, who was napping peacefully in her crib. "He's a capable fisherman. You oughtn't worry about him."

"Aye, but he's never out this late. And with this shadow person—"

"I'm sure he's fine," Alynn said. "Go home, drink some tea, get some rest. Ten to one, your father's sprung a leak and had to pull ashore somewhere. If he's not home by sunset, though, let us know. We'll send someone after him, alright?"

Torsten nodded and mumbled a "Thank you, milady" as he left.

Alynn nearly forgot about the incident—people coming to her when Drostan couldn't be found at the shipyard was a fairly common occurrence—but after dinner, there was another visitor. This time, it was Torsten's little brother Bjarki. The poor boy was wet and shivering; Alynn worried he was catching his brother's illness. She had him inside and wrapped in blankets before she let him say anything.

"Torsten was going to come and tell you that our father's not back yet," said the little boy. "But Mother wouldn't let him out of the house, his fever's getting worse."

"He won't be the only feverish one in the house, if you're not careful," Alynn scolded. Elspeth was tearfully fighting sleep; she was given to Valdis for the time being. "Do you want some tea?"

Bjarki shook his head. "I want my father back. He's always home by now. Something's wrong, I can feel it." He set a pleading gaze on Drostan that Alynn couldn't help but copy. "Please, Chief Drostan, sir—can you help me find my father?"

Drostan sighed. His shoulders drooped with a long day's work, and his hands were too tired to even brush the hair out of his face. But he took a cloak, a hood, and his sword. "Alynn, watch the house," he said. "Father, make sure Bjarki gets home safely. Take a shield. I'll go out to look for Rothgeir."

"Take some friends," Alynn cautioned.

Drostan smiled, and a spark managed to come into one of his eyes. He kissed her deeply, then took his shield and left. Leif waited until Bjarki was sufficiently warmed and dried before wrapping him warmly against the rain and leading him home.

Alynn glanced at Valdis, who had nearly gotten Elspeth to sleep. As soon as the babe's eyes were closed and stayed that way for long enough, she was carefully set in her cradle for her first stretch of sleep. "I'll be packing my things," said Valdis softly. "Most of it's in the workroom—I'd ask for your company, Mistress, but…."

Alynn shook her head. The front and back doors, not to mention the door to the stable, all needed guarding. Valdis kept the door open, but they dared not speak to each other—partly from fear, and partly for Elspeth's sake.

When Alynn was sure that all the doors were locked and no one was visible outside the house, she carefully lifted one of the boards that comprised the sleeping bench. The space beneath it stored various things—mostly winter blankets, wool in various stages of processing, and changes of clothing. Nestled carefully in the corner was Alynn's sword.

She took it and drew it from its wonderful birchbark scabbard. The blade was still perfectly sharp.

The sword felt like an old friend. She'd put it away when she learned she was pregnant with Elspeth and hadn't seen it since; she realized she'd missed it. She'd had it for six years now. With this sword she had defended St. Anne's Monastery from Drostan's murderous uncle Konar the Mad. With this sword she had protected her family from Darsidian raiders. She'd even used it to impress others in competitive sparring matches.

Oh, a friend—and yet such a dark and twisted one! One that had taken lives as well as saved them—destroyed families as well as preserved them! Well, it wasn't the sword's fault, Alynn reminded herself. And she hadn't had much of a choice, either. Seeing a sword poised to strike someone she loved elicited an automatic response of berserker's rage in her. She struck before they could, and there was little she could do to stop herself.

That automatic response very nearly overtook Alynn when someone tried to open the door. She leapt to her feet, sword naked and gleaming in the firelight, her heart pounding in her chest. Tunnel vision engulfed her, narrowing her line of sight until she saw nothing but the door—every splinter in its wood, every irregularity in its grain, every tremor as someone pulled harder on it.

Fortunately, it was Leif's voice on the other side. "Lynder, you've locked me out," he said, as if terrified and trying to make a joke all at once.

Alynn let Leif in and, as if trying to keep out a violent snowstorm, shut the door immediately behind him again. This time, she didn't lock it. Drostan was still out there, and Leif was here to help keep things safe.

Leif glanced at Alynn's sword—she held it in a shaking hand now—but said nothing about it as he took off his cloak and boots and put his shield away. "I'll watch the house," he said. "Go to sleep."

"I'd rather sit up for Drostan."

"Suit yourself."

Alynn glanced at Elspeth, peacefully snoring in her cradle, and picked up her comb. It was made of antler, but it still struggled to brush through Alynn's tangled curls. She'd even managed to snap one of the tines off.

It took nearly an hour for Alynn to brush her hair, and Drostan still wasn't home by the time she finished. Elspeth woke up hungry, so Alynn nursed her and put her back in her cradle, and Drostan still wasn't home. Valdis finally emerged from the workroom, put the oats to soak for the next morning's breakfast, and went to bed. Drostan still wasn't home.

Leif stayed in his own little section of the sleeping bench. Shadows hid most of him, but Alynn could see his thighs glowing white where his undershift stopped too soon for comfort, the mug of tea in his hand, and the sword gleaming on the bench beside him. His trousers and tunic were crumpled on the ground. Alynn got up and folded them.

"Go to sleep," Leif said. He spoke quietly, but with an authority that made Alynn murmur a "Yes, sir," and climb into the bedcloset. She started praying but did not sleep.

Or maybe she did sleep, because it seemed that hardly a moment passed before Elspeth was crying again. Groaning, Alynn sat up only to hear Leif's voice in conversation with

Drostan's. Alynn slipped out of the bedcloset and absently took Elspeth from her cradle. Neither of the men noticed. Instead, Drostan kicked up the fire and sat down on the sleeping bench.

Alynn sat next to Drostan and turned her attention to him as soon as Elspeth was settled at her breast. Rainwater dripped from Drostan's hair and beard, and his clothes clung to his skin. His eyes stared past the fire and into some ethereal dimension, one with terrors and nightmares and haunting visions.

"What happened, love?"

Silently, and without moving his eyes from the ethereal dimension, Drostan wrapped his arms tightly around Alynn and Elspeth. His wet clothes dampened both of them. When Alynn tried to brush a comforting thumb over his hand, she noticed blood beneath his fingernails and tinges of red on his sleeves. She gasped.

"Drostan—you're not hurt, are you?"

"We found him." Drostan's voice was low—it was the same tone he used when he talked in his sleep. "It almost looked like wild animals attacked him—he was all torn up, Lynder. Just— swimming in a pool of his own blood…."

Ignoring the wetness that drenched her undershift, Alynn pressed herself against Drostan and held him as best she could. He pressed his lips against the top of her head and started shaking—was he crying? Alynn drew a deep breath and held him closer.

"Drostan—death's part of life. You know that, love."

"I do, I know, it's just—I had to tell his family. I saw Bjarki—just sort of standing there, he didn't know what to do, or think, or feel—and I felt everything different. I couldn't stop thinking about you. I couldn't stop thinking about Elspeth. I just—"

Leif fetched a horn of mead, and Drostan drank it quickly. When the mead was gone, Drostan looked up at his father with red eyes.

"What do I do?" he asked. "I've got a village to keep safe, I've got my family to keep safe—"

"Whisht, son. You're alright. In the morning, we'll call a council meeting, and we'll get something figured out. But first, you're going to give this to God for the moment, you're going to get dried off, and you're going to get some sleep. Alright?"

Drostan nodded. Leif bear-hugged him, then moved the boards of a nearby section of sleeping bench to get a towel and a clean undershift. Alynn helped Drostan take off the vambrace he wore over his right arm, careful not to disturb the burn scars that lay underneath.

Alynn thought that, once Drostan had dried off, he would go to bed. Instead, he sat down naked on the sleeping bench and stared into the fire. "I think the rain made it worse," he said. "Waters down the blood, makes it look like there's more of it. I just—I can't—what if this—this *grima* finds one of us next? If I find either of you, or Lukas, or Mum—the same way I found Rothgeir—I can't. I can't do that. I can't let Elspeth grow up without her da."

Drostan buried his face in his hands. Alynn kissed his still-dripping hair and let him draw her and Elspeth into his arms. "We do the only thing we can do, love. We trust God."

Wordlessly, Drostan clutched Alynn and Elspeth tighter against his bare chest. Leif went back to bed, and the fire began to die down, and still Alynn and Drostan and Elspeth sat on the sleeping bench.

Elspeth had nursed herself to sleep and Alynn had nearly dozed off herself when Drostan asked, "What *is* the Gaelic word for it?"

"Hmm?"

"*Grima*. It means—a mask, or a shadow, or—or something that isn't quite there. Not a ghost, exactly, but—"

"A fairy of sorts?" Alynn asked groggily.

"Not a fairy. A phantom." Drostan stood up and shrugged on a dry undershift. Alynn took the opportunity to crawl into the bedcloset with Elspeth. The room was settled for the night.

The ashes were banked in the fireplace. Valdis had slept through the entire night's events and was curled in the darkest corner of the longhouse. Alynn only knew she was there because one of her braids fell off the sleeping bench and shone in the firelight. Leif was snoring.

And finally, Drostan joined Alynn in the bedcloset and shut the latch. They were safe here, warm and snug in each other's company. And the moment she was tucked under her blankets and satisfied that Elspeth was content and sleeping beside her, Alynn fell asleep.

SEVEN

Two days later, Alynn woke up to the noise of howling winds and the cries of a hungry baby. She took Elspeth into the workroom and touched her itty-bitty forehead. She wasn't feverish, thank God. Checking her temperature had become a compulsion for Alynn.

When Elspeth finished her pre-breakfast snack, Alynn propped her up in a corner and got dressed. Elspeth chewed on her fist and hiccupped until she fell over sideways. Alynn laughed. Elspeth had been hiccupping since before she was born.

"Och, my sweet Elspeth," said Alynn as she propped up her daughter again. "Mammy's sweet little Elspie. Mammy loves you. Aye, she does! Mammy loves you!"

Elspeth grinned, hiccupped again, and toppled over. Alynn grabbed a blanket and wrapped it around Elspeth's back and hips and fat little legs. It seemed to work.

"Och, Elspeth—Mammy's sorry you'll have to do this. You're too young to go to a funeral, but you're too young to stay here, and Mammy has to be there." Alynn glanced at Elspeth, whose eyes shone a celestial blue in the light of the whale-oil lamp. Surely she wasn't old enough to understand what a funeral was. But still—she was so innocent. Alynn didn't want her to change.

"You know what, sweetheart? I want you to take a nap during Rothgeir's funeral. I'll hold you, all nice and snug and warm, and you can sleep and have happy dreams. Does that sound nice, Elspie? Would you like that?"

Elspeth squeaked and started eating her foot.

"Blast it, Elspeth, I don't want to go." Alynn picked up a comb and took her frustrations out on her hair. "Rothgeir was a strange man. I didn't always like him. But he's a good man now—he has been for a couple of years now—and he's got a wonderful family who misses him. 'Tis them I'm saddest about. 'Tis a hard thing to lose yer da—I thought I lost my da once, and it hurt. I cried a lot. Och, Elspeth, I hope you don't lose yer da. He's a good man."

The softest footsteps sounded outside the workroom door, and Valdis appeared. "The porridge is cooking," she said. "Is there anything else you need, Mistress?"

"I'm alright, thanks."

"Are you sure? It's my last day here. I'd feel bad if I didn't do anything."

Elspeth hiccupped again, and Alynn put down her comb. "You could help with my hair, I suppose. I've always been abysmal at crown braids."

Alynn sat down on the workbench, and Valdis stood behind her, brushing out the last of Alynn's tangles. "I think you tend to do a good job," she said.

"You do a better job."

"Thank you, Mistress."

And with that, there was silence. Valdis effortlessly tucked Alynn's hair into a crown braid, her hands moving a bit more slowly than usual. Finally, she blurted out, "It doesn't seem right to leave you now. Not with the baby. Not with this Grima monster lurking about. You need me, Mistress, and I want— well, part of me wants to stay here."

"Valdis—"

"I've been away from Trondheim for so long. I was a

teenager when Konar kidnapped me, I've lived practically half my life in this house. I love Vali, but he feels like a stranger. And sure, I've got cousins and a few more siblings, but our mother's dead now—Trondheim won't be the same without her."

Alynn prayed for the right words. She couldn't lie. She didn't want Valdis to leave. Rowan was always so good at making a bent truth sound beautiful. What would he say?

"Valdis, you've done so much good for this family. And now, 'tis time for you to be yer own person—and you'll learn, you'll learn how to be free again. Get married. Have children. Enjoy time with yer brother, and whoever else is left for you in Trondheim. 'Tis such a beautiful thing, getting to know yer family again, when you've been gone for so long. And don't you dare worry about us. We'll find someone else—she won't be as good as you, but you needn't worry about us being alone."

Valdis smiled, and her fingers caressed Alynn's scalp as if she were a beloved cousin rather than a mistress. "Thank you, miss. Do me a favor, though, and tell your mother I'm naming my oldest daughter after her."

"You'll tell her yerself. She's comin' to send you off, not to mention Rothgeir's funeral. Why Mum makes such a big deal over funerals, I don't know. She hardly knew the man."

"She still thinks she's Lady of the Island." Valdis took a blunt wooden needle and started sewing Alynn's hair in place with a length of leather cord. "Captain McMahon won't sail off in the midst of the funeral, will he?"

"I doubt it. He's lived long enough in Ireland to know to respect the dead."

Valdis put the finishing touches on Alynn's hair, and Alynn tied her coif tightly under her chin so it wouldn't blow away. As she was fiddling with the bow, a loud percussive noise sounded in the front room. Elspeth toppled over with surprise, and Alynn ran to investigate. Fortunately, the noise had been caused by the front door blowing open so violently that it had hit the wall behind it. Vali stood with one foot on the threshold, his flaxen hair whipping in the winds.

"I'm here for Valdis's trunk," he said. "We leave in an hour."

Wiping the single tear that clung to her eyelashes, Valdis picked up the trunk she'd packed the day before. She struggled under its weight and opened it again. On top of her clothes, combs, and domestic tools sat three ells of fabric and a thick silver bracelet.

"Leif and Drostan thought you deserved a parting bonus," Alynn said.

Valdis handed the trunk to Vali and wiped her eyes again. Vali nodded respectfully to Alynn, and then to Drostan, who was getting the table down from the loft. Breakfast was eaten in a sad yet companionable silence, and before the dishes were even washed, they left for the docks.

A crowd was already there. Rothgeir's body was laid out on a pyre; Alynn covered Elspeth's eyes as she approached it. Rothgeir was bloodless pale with a large cut on his neck, but he was finely dressed, and his hair had been lovingly combed. The only thing besides his coloring that seemed odd about him was his hands, which were folded on his chest with a dagger between them. It took Alynn some time to realize that his fingernails had been plucked out.

Alynn moved her eyes from the corpse and glanced briefly at everything else accompanying Rothgeir into the afterlife. No matter how many times Lukas said that no one could take anything with them into heaven, the Norse insisted on honoring their dead with provisions. Rothgeir had been provided with a fishing net, of course. A spear. Some jewelry and ship's tackle. Jars of mead, baskets of food, and a single live chicken in a crate. A blanket, probably made by Rothgeir's wife Melkorka. A doll—a poorly-carved wooden spoon—

Those gifts were from his children. There were four of them, standing dazed and hopeless beside their father's pyre. The youngest, Bjarki, was only nine.

"I'm sorry," Alynn whispered in a voice so softly only Elspeth could hear her. "Och, little ones—I'm so sorry."

Spotting Drostan in the crowd, Alynn quickly hurried to him. Leif and the McNeils were with him. It was obvious that Caitriona was the only one interested in the funeral, while Rowan and Tarin were merely there to bid farewell to Captain McMahon. The captain himself was nowhere to be seen, probably making sure his ship was ready to sail.

"You're alright?" Drostan asked Alynn in a soft voice.

Alynn nodded.

"Mum can be hostess if you'd rather. She knows Melkorka and the children better than you do, anyway."

"This is my job now," said Alynn stiffly. "I'm grand. Don't worry."

A few minutes passed before Lukas took his place beside the pyre. He was dressed in a loose robe of mournful black that billowed in the wind—a traditional priestly garment called a cuculla. He spoke little, for the clouds threatened rain and the wind snatched half his words out of his listeners' ears anyway.

He spoke about finding joy in the midst of grief, joy that Rothgeir was home with the Lord and that all Christians, someday, would follow him there. He spoke about honoring Rothgeir's memory by staying true to the faith. They were all words Alynn had heard a dozen times before—traditional platitudes that meant everything and nothing all at once.

Lukas himself was aware of the effect his words were having. He looked up at the sky and, with a strange tone in his voice, said, "The day I lost my father, there were no words that could heal the wound in my heart. There was no priest in Christendom who could console me. I turned instead to Christ Himself, and I got the sense that He wept with me. Melkorka—children—if you ever feel the need to weep with someone, night or day, come to Christ. And if you're in too much pain to find Him, come to the monastery, and I'll bring Him to you."

Finally, Rothgeir's oldest son Torsten took a stick from a

fire burning nearby. He was still sick. His face was white and his eyes were red and his sleeves were damp with snot and sweat and tears. But, squaring his shoulders, he shoved his father's pyre into the bay and threw the flaming stick into a puddle of oil. Fire engulfed the pyre, and Rothgeir Torstenston drifted into oblivion.

Drostan approached Rothgeir's family to give his condolences, and Alynn followed him closely. Bjarki regarded Drostan with a teary-eyed reverence, but apparently saw Alynn as a bit more approachable. Taking two small steps towards her, he asked, "What's going to happen to us now?"

With an aching heart, Alynn drew Bjarki into an embrace. "You will live," she promised, disentangling his mouse-brown hair from Elspeth's chubby, sticky fingers. "Aye, you'll miss your father. But you'll see him everywhere. You'll catch glimpses of him in your brothers' eyes, your mother's food, your uncle's stories. There's a part of him that still lives in you. Aye, you'll cry for your father. But someday, you'll smile again. I promise."

Bjarki nodded, wiping the tears from his eyes, and went back to his mother. Melkorka pressed him against her ample bosom and gave Alynn a grateful nod. Alynn nodded back.

"Alynn."

The voice belonged to Rowan; Alynn knew what it signaled. She quickly gave her respects to Melkorka and Torsten before leaving to have a second funeral.

This second farewell would probably be longer than the first. Alynn didn't know if it was just her family or the Irish in general who took forever to say goodbye to loved ones. In this case, though, she didn't mind. She had decided to appreciate every moment she had with Valdis.

Captain McMahon took Elspeth from Alynn's arms and tossed her into the air. She squealed with delight, and the captain smiled. A few good meals and a couple of nights in a decent bed had put the color back in his cheeks and the light back in his eyes. He kissed Elspeth, handed her to Rowan, and almost as an afterthought, took something out of the sealskin pouch he always wore around his neck.

"Ye're sure about this, Cait?" he asked.

"Sure, I'm sure," said Caitriona, trying to keep Mercy from squirming out of her arms. "What would I need it for, anyway?"

"Sentiment," said Rowan.

"Mercy will eat it," said Caitriona.

"Elspeth will eat it," said Tarin.

Caitriona sighed. "Tamlane, just do it."

With a smile, Captain McMahon produced a cloakpin from his pouch. It was made of bronze, but it glimmered like gold, and the thick ends had Celtic knots engraved in them. Alynn gasped as she took it. "I remember this!" she said.

"Of course you do," said Caitriona. "Yer nana wore that to Mass every Sabbath. It took the family a while to figure out what to do with it after she passed away, but they sent it here, and I want you to have it."

"Mum—"

Alynn couldn't find any words. She embraced Caitriona and tried to put the pin on her dress. Its point was dulled with use; Alynn could hardly force it through the fabric. Rowan noticed and traded Elspeth for the pin.

"You dulled it, Tamlane," he said.

Captain McMahon had a teasing edge to his scolding voice. "Ye try bringing a cloakpin from Limerick to Reykjavik to Orkney without getting it banged up."

"Lemme see," said Mercy, nearly wriggling out of her mother's arms. When Caitriona's grip proved too strong, Mercy let out a screech. Rowan turned to her and crouched to her eye level.

"Mercy, if you don't settle down, I'll hang you from yer toenails from the fish drying racks. Do you want that?"

Mercy furrowed her eyebrows into a sulk, then shook her head.

"Alright, then. No more screaming."

Alynn smiled. Rowan had used the exact same threat on her—and it had worked then, too. She watched as Rowan put the cloakpin into a pouch he'd skillfully folded into his plaid. For the first time that day, Alynn realized that Rowan was wearing a red and green plaid instead of his usual green and blue one.

"Where'd you get the plaid from?" she asked.

"Tamlane gave it to me," said Rowan, shaking the folded pocket into place. "Even though my old one's pure grand."

"Ye've only had it forty years," said Captain McMahon.

"Liar," Rowan shot back. "It was my mum who made it, and it looks as good as the day she gave it to me. She was magic with fabric like that." A bit of sadness came into Rowan's eyes when he mentioned his mother, but he quickly blinked it away. "Anyway, Lynder, you're up to thirty-one cousins in Limerick, Uncle Oisin's finally married, and Aunt Ruairi's got the consumption."

"She was so sweet," Alynn lamented.

A voice rose from the deck of the Darting Swallow. "Captain, we're ready!"

"Half a moment!" Captain McMahon called back. He kissed everyone goodbye, even Mercy, who was still in a grump. Then he found Leif and Drostan, who had excused themselves from the funeral party with a horn of mead in each hand. Captain McMahon took one horn, and Valdis took the second.

Leif downed his own horn of mead in one gulp and moved his attention to the McNeils. "The saving grace of funerals, there's plenty to drink. Do you want some?"

"Just one," said Caitriona, taking the horn Drostan offered her. She glanced at it, then, so as not to be rude, drank the whole thing. She wiped her mouth and asked Rowan if he wanted any.

"I'm grand," said Rowan.

"Ye're daft," said Captain McMahon, clapping him heartily on the back. "Och, I'll knock some sense into ye the next time I come around. God love ye, Rowan."

"We'll miss you, Tamlane."

"Not as much as I'll miss all of ye." And with that, Captain McMahon boarded the Darting Swallow, and Alynn turned her attention to Valdis. Her flaxen hair was streaming out of its knotted ponytail, and her cheeks were red and chapped. Alynn thought she had never looked more beautiful.

"I'll miss you," said Valdis. "All of you."

Unsurprisingly, Caitriona embraced Valdis and kissed her as if she were her own child. "Och, dear one. We wish you all the best. May the road rise up to meet you, and the rain...."

Her voice trailed off, and she pressed her sleeve to her eyes. Rowan set a hand on her shoulder and continued the blessing. "May the road rise up to meet you; may the wind always be at your back. May the sun shine warm upon your face, and the rains fall soft upon your fields. And until we meet again, may God hold you in the palm of His hand."

Valdis smiled her thanks, wiping away tears of her own. She hugged him and took Tarin and Mercy into her arms. "Och, I wish I could have gotten to know you better."

"Go potty," said Mercy.

"I'll take her," said Tarin. Alynn couldn't blame him. The poor lad had been raveling the fringe of his plaid, as if to keep his mind off the fact that he was surrounded by people who were either crying or looked like they were about to.

Valdis said her goodbyes to Leif and Drostan, then turned to Alynn. They embraced. "Are you sure you don't need me to stay a bit longer?" she asked.

"Of course I'm sure. I've been keeping house since I was nine. I'll manage."

Valdis took Elspeth and held her close for a moment. "I'll miss watching you grow up," she said. "I'll have to come visit you."

Alynn made herself smile. "Aunt Valdis is always welcome. Isn't she, Elspie?"

"I say she is," said Leif. He was smiling, but he didn't mean it. He may as well have been telling a dying loved one that they were going to be alright, that they were going to wake up the next morning and feel better, knowing full well they probably wouldn't wake up at all. "Godspeed on your journey."

Blinking, Valdis set Elspeth back into her mother's arms, waved, and let her brother help her onto the Darting Swallow. A sudden gust of wind nearly knocked her into the ocean, but Vali's strong hand kept her from falling.

"Until we meet again, my friend!" Captain McMahon called as he set the ship free from its moorings.

"You're always welcome here, Tamlane!" Rowan called back.

"And send our love to everyone in Limerick!" Caitriona said.

With a smile, Captain McMahon nodded and took the tiller. The crew rowed until they were clear of the dock, then lowered the single sail that snapped with vigor as the strong wind filled it. The Darting Swallow sailed out of the bay until it came next to Rothgeir's still-burning funeral pyre. It paused for a moment as the wind died down, as if pausing to pay respects. But then the gale picked up again, and the living outpaced the dead and left it smoldering in its wake.

April 29, A.D. 969—

I hate funerals.

It's not the dead that grieve me. It's the living. Rothgeir's son Bjarki can't be more than ten years old, and he doesn't deserve to live a life without a father. I know his pain and he does not deserve it. Torsten is too young to take his father's place in the world, yet he must. Thank God he has uncles to help guide him into manhood.

I keep feeling guilt creep up on me. The memories of the men I've killed—surely they thought that they were just going hunting or woodcutting or some other mundane activity. Did they have sons waiting for them at home? I have had nightmares every night since I heard of Rothgeir's death, and I fear I deserve them. I keep reminding myself that I have confessed my sins to Leif and been acquitted for them. Legally, I have done nothing wrong. Morally, I might never know.

Or perhaps it's another sign that I'm going mad again. I kept mistaking Captain McMahon's voice for Brother Gregory's. One night, the captain sang Mercy to sleep and I had to excuse myself from the hearth. His singing voice was too like my father's. I keep hearing footsteps that weren't there and seeing phantoms in the shadows. My ribs hurt more than normal.

Anyway, I'm glad the captain is gone. It was nice to talk with a fellow Scotsman, but the McNeils dominated most of our conversations and I could hardly talk to the man. Caitriona made tea for everyone, and I was the one who wound up with the cracked mug. I didn't get to hold Mercy once when he was here. I've always known that I'm not full family to the McNeils, but this is ridiculous. Why should Tamlane get treated like a blood relative?

O, Lord—with all that's wrong in the world, who am I to complain about such trivialities? Forgive me, Lord, and help me to see what's really important.

—L. McCamden

EIGHT

For two days after Rothgeir's funeral, a hush came over the village. Eyvind the goatherd was accompanied by his stepfather Bjorn Sturlason, in whose presence the goats dared not bleat. People walked quickly, eyes nervously darting up and down the streets. The shopkeepers kept an axe or a bow at the ready, and their customers finished their transactions with as few words as possible. Women stayed inside despite the lack of rain, and even the children were kept indoors for safety's sake.

Alynn didn't know what to make of the silence. For a while, it was pleasant. The village was normally bustling with activity, so that it was difficult to visit the marketplace without nearly getting hit by an oxcart or tripping over a small child. But the silence and the tension that came with it grew so thick and heavy that it became maddening.

At one point in her life, being alone had been easy for Alynn. There were few things in life she had enjoyed more than a traipse through the woods, an hour to get some cleaning done, or an afternoon in the vegetable garden. But being alone in a longhouse designed to house twenty people, with an infant demanding constant attention—this was a different sort of alone. It was significantly less pleasant. By the second day, Alynn was trying everything to keep the silence away. She sang, she prayed, she talked to Elspeth and even opened the stable doors so the chickens could keep her company. Nothing worked.

"Finish the weaving, replace the rushes, check the ale, and churn the butter," Alynn kept saying out loud to herself. "Finish the weaving, replace the rushes, check the ale, and churn the butter." And so she swept up the rushes that covered the dirt floor before Elspeth started crying. Alynn changed Elspeth and, forgetting the rushes—she'd grown up on bare dirt floors, anyway—started churning the butter.

But then Elspeth started crying again, this time for her afternoon snack. Alynn couldn't very well nurse Elspeth with one arm and operate the heavy dash churn with the other, so she sat wearily on the bench. Drostan was going to come home to a bare floor and a mess of half-churned butter.

She was such an embarrassment. She'd been keeping house since she was nine. She ought to know what she was doing.

There was a creak, and the door flung open.

Alynn jumped to her feet. Her sword was beside her—she'd been keeping it out for the past couple of days—and she drew it. The blade sparkled as Alynn aimed it at a short, curly-haired waif of a young woman. The intruder's eyes went wide for a moment before snapping saucily. "Fer faith's sake. Lynder! Don't do that!"

"Maggie McKenzie, one of these days, I will kill you, and it's not going to be my fault."

Laughing, Maggie shut the door behind her. "Och, I'm sorry, but I couldn't help it. I couldn't stand another second in that house. I thought my brothers were crazy, I was wrong. Ulfrik's got eight cousins under the age of ten. Their mums won't let them outside thanks to this Grima thing, and good God, the screaming I've put up with—"

Maggie spoke with the same Scottish brogue as her mother Nora, but her voice bordered on irritating, mainly because it was high-pitched and she used it too much. Alynn interrupted. "Maggie, if you're going to talk, you can at least make yourself useful. Can you churn butter?"

"What does that mean, can I churn butter?"

"I think the dash is taller than you are."

"If I wanted to be teased, I'd have gone back to Mum's house. Olvir and Slodi—och, they can be cruel, but they're wee angels compared to some of Ulfrik's kin. Einar, the three-year-auld, he's throwing a tantrum right now because I wouldn't let him tear out a chicken's feathers. He's already got a hold of one of the hens. It probably won't lay fer a week. I'm never having children."

Alynn set Elspeth on her shoulder and patted her back. "'Tis easier when they're yers."

"That's what Mum says. She just wants grandbabies. Ulfrik wants to be a da though—ye should see him, holding his wee cousins and such. He's so good wi' them. Just last week he brought a curly wood shaving back home from the shipyard for Einar to play with. Kept him busy fer a half hour."

Maggie kept talking, but Alynn was distracted by a sudden cry from outside. Leaping to her feet, she gave Elspeth to Maggie and grabbed her sword. There was a shield on the wall behind Maggie; Alynn grabbed it. But at the doorway, she paused.

"Please, Lord," she breathed, "if this is Grima, help us catch him. And don't let anyone get hurt."

Alynn crossed the threshold and glanced around. Voices assaulted her. "Thief! Thief! I've been robbed!" cried one voice. "I saw him! He's this way!" called another. Alynn ran towards the voices, but then she paused. Something looked strange.

Beside the wall of a nearby longhouse sat an old washtub, and next to it lay a neglected pile of laundry. And yet the mass of fabric seemed to move—there—the tip of a bow stuck out from the folds of plaid. A hooded head was raised; behind a fabric mask, a pair of dark eyes blinked.

Drostan was right. Grima was the best name for this creature.

Alynn aimed her sword at the figure and took a few more steps closer. But then, for no reason other than sheer terror, she stopped before she was within stabbing range of the figure.

"Drop the bow," she said.

Grima shrunk backwards. Alynn thought she saw the movement of hands—although they were more like claws, small and white and bony. Alynn hid behind her shield and wished someone was with her. Lukas. Drostan. Leif. Anyone who was good with a sword or, better yet, a distance weapon.

"Drop the bow," Alynn said again. She made herself take two more steps towards Grima. "Refuse, and I kill you."

The bow flinched. It gave a whirring noise—a metallic clang. An arrow had hit the metal center of Alynn's shield. Before Alynn could grasp what was happening, Grima had bolted, his cloak trailing behind him.

Alynn ran after him, giving a cry that would have rallied the armies of heaven.

People emerged from their houses like ants from hills. Most of them stared. Some shouted. A few men hurled spears or shot arrows at Grima; all of them missed. There was a noise that was too close for comfort. Alynn turned and raised her shield in the nick of time, stopping an arrow from lodging into her shoulder.

By the time Alynn turned around and started running again, Grima was nowhere to be seen.

The villagers had produced lamps and firebrands to aid the slanting light of the setting sun. Alynn tried to ignore their frenzied cries and focus. Her gaze darted from longhouse to longhouse and finally to the edge of the nearby woods. The bushes seemed to be rustling. She took off running again.

"Show yourself, coward!" Alynn shouted. She strained her senses. There. A crunch of leaves. Alynn ran towards it, but she lost the trail in a matter of seconds. The forest seemed placid and undisturbed in the slanting golden sunlight, as if no evil shadow had ever touched it.

Pressing her back firmly against an oak tree, Alynn held her breath and looked. She closed her eyes and listened. There. Noise. Alynn turned, aiming her sword at whatever was approaching her only to find a small group from the village armed with whatever spears and axes they'd had at their disposal. Every single one of them was angry.

"Where'd he go?"

"How'd you let him get away?"

"Which way was he headed?"

Alynn regarded all of them with a spinning head and shaking legs. She couldn't remember the last time she'd run that fast. "He's slippery," she said, trying to square her shoulders and hide the fact that she was short of breath.

Slippery wasn't the right word. Grima seemed to have disappeared into the shadows by becoming one himself. Alynn quickly steadied her breathing before borrowing someone's oil lamp and helping the villagers scour the forest floor.

There were no footprints. Not a single broken twig or one leaf out of place. Someone found a kitchen rag that had blown off a clothesline. Someone found a half-decayed boot, and someone else found a dead songbird. But no one found a single sign that Grima had ever been in the forest.

"We aren't safe here," said Alynn. "Everyone, go home. If there was a trace of Grima, we would have found it by now."

Alynn made sure she was the last person to leave the forest. A child, glad to be free of his smoky, stifling longhouse, ran shouting through the forest. His father grabbed him by the ear and led him home. Consumed with the nagging fear that something was wrong with Elspeth, Alynn half-ran home on shaking legs. Maggie would never hurt Elspeth—at least, the rational part of Alynn's brain knew that—but still. She couldn't get the worry out of her mind.

Hardly had she opened the door when Maggie flew at her. Her wiry arms wrapped around Alynn's chest like a spider's jaws on a hapless fly.

"What happened? Are ye alright? He didn't shoot ye, did he?"

"If he did shoot me, Maggie, you'd be makin' things worse."

"Right, sorry." Maggie released her kraken's grip. "Was it Grima?"

Ignoring her, Alynn dropped her sword and shield on her way to Elspeth's cradle. Elspeth was half-asleep as Alynn scooped her into her arms. Instinctually, she put her ear to Elspeth's chest. The pitter-patter of her rapid heartbeat and tiny breaths were comforting.

"I can keep a bairn alive fer ten minutes, ye know," said Maggie.

"Have you ever listened for a baby's heartbeat and not found one?" Alynn asked.

"Nay."

"Then leave me be."

"Lynder—my God, whose baby?"

Pressing her eyelids shut to keep the tears behind them, Alynn kissed Elspeth and held her close.

"Alynn?"

"My sister. 'Tis ten years she's been dead. It doesn't matter."

Somehow, this silenced Maggie. She got Alynn a cup of milk, then volunteered to make some bread for dinner while Alynn caught her breath. Alynn let her. She needed to hold her baby. She needed to feel the warmth of Elspeth's head on her chest, smell her milky sweetness, brush her fingers against her downy hair and softest skin. Elspeth started hiccupping as she chewed her fists, and Alynn was nearly in tears with love for her.

Alynn was half asleep with Leif and Drostan came inside, swords drawn and shields at the ready. "What the devil happened out there?" Drostan demanded as soon as the door was shut and locked behind him. "And Maggie, why are you here?"

"My mum got drunk at a funeral."

"Go home."

Maggie pointed to the door. "I'm not going. Not wi' Grima about, ye're mad."

"Just step into the workroom," said Leif. Maggie obliged, taking the bread she was making along with her. As soon as the door was shut, Drostan took Alynn by the arms and stared at her with a strange concoction of rage and fear in his eyes.

"Did he hurt you?"

"He didn't. I'm alright."

Drostan's fear was gone, but the anger remained. "Then what the devil did you think you were doing, running after Grima like that? He could have killed you!"

"Most things in life can kill me, love. You can't expect me to stay clear of all of them."

"You infuriating little—"

Sighing, Drostan checked himself and took Elspeth, who responded with a perfectly pink and almost-toothless grin. "What do you think, Squiggly?" Drostan asked. "Should Mammy be chasing bad guys around the village? Do you think that's a good idea?"

Elspeth gave a long, vocalic squeak.

"She thinks you should listen to me," said Drostan.

"Lad, fetch the table," Leif interrupted. "My back's bothering me."

"We've got more important problems than dinner," said Drostan.

"Aye, and we can't solve any of them on an empty stomach. Fetch the table."

Sighing, Drostan gave Elspeth back to her mother and climbed the ladder into the loft. Leif gave Alynn a tired smile. "You took a shield?" he asked.

"I did."

"Then you did the right thing, and I'm proud of you." Leif glanced up at the loft to make sure Drostan was out of earshot, then lowered his voice. "He's still getting used to being a father, and seeing you as a mother. He'll come around. But och, I'm too old to be bent over a workbench all day." He stretched his back and groaned.

"Do you want some tea?" Alynn asked.

"What I really want is El—well, my Elspeth—Drostan's mum. Between her hands and her voice and a warm damp rag, she could make anything stop hurting." A brief cloud of sadness passed over Leif's face, but he willed it away with a smile. "Tea works well enough, though."

"I'll make it," said Maggie from the workroom doorway.

"You're sure?" Leif asked. "It's getting dark. I'd best see you home."

"If ye don't mind, sir. My mum taught me well, and I'd rather not hurry back to my personal piece of hell. Asides, if ye're going to keep kissing my mum in the hallways after church, ye'd best get used to having me around." Leif relented, and Maggie was quick to set a kettle in the fireplace. Then, she rifled through the cupboard, carefully choosing the right herbs, mosses, and tree barks.

Drostan had finally gotten the table down, and Leif took Elspeth so Alynn could start dishing up dinner. Elspeth squealed again, coaxing a smile into Leif's face. Elspeth looked so tiny in his arms. When she was first born, she would disappear into his sleeves so that only a flailing arm or a wayward foot would be showing. Even now, her head fit perfectly into his massive, work-worn hands. Whenever Leif held Elspeth, the worry-lines on his forehead disappeared while the laugh-lines around his eyes shone all the clearer.

"How's Afi's wee angel this evening? Were you good to your mother? I hope so. Och, I know you were, Elspie. I know you're a good girl." Alynn smiled as she set drinks on the table. "Och, don't yawn, Elspeth. Yawns are contagious—"

Leif proved his point rather loudly, and Elspeth began to cry. Alynn sighed. "Father, you frightened her."

"Not on purpose," said Leif. Alynn took her daughter, who promptly stopped crying and buried her face in Alynn's bosom.

"Och, of course you're hungry. 'Tis been a whole hour and a half since you've eaten last. Look at how fat you are!" Alynn tickled Elspeth's round belly, and her tiny frown turned into a smile. "Why can't you give Mammy a break? I'll run out of milk at this rate."

"She's got teeth, right?" asked Maggie, tending to the tea and the bread all at once. "Mum says that bairns can start eating real food when they get teeth."

"Elspeth doesn't like real food," said Alynn. "She tried one of my mum's bannocks."

"Och, ye don't start wi' bannocks! Ye chew up some beets or something, then spit them out and give them to her."

Come to think of it, Alynn had a vague memory of Caitriona chewing food for Tarin when he was a baby. She'd have to talk to her about it—sometime later. She was exhausted. "Maggie, are you stayin' for dinner?"

"I wish I could, but I've a husband to get home to. Thanks fer the offer."

"I'll walk you home," said Leif. "How's your mother, by the way?"

"Last I saw her, she's alright. Why?"

"I haven't seen her in a few days. Just curious." He took his sword and shield again, then glanced at Alynn. "Don't let my tea get cold."

Alynn nodded and started to pour the small ale. It was hard working with one hand, and Alynn didn't know what she would do when Elspeth got too big and squirmy to hold with one arm. She carried the mugs one at a time to the table.

"How was work?" she asked Drostan.

"Long. Everyone's on edge. Erik almost sawed his finger off, and turns out two of the trees we cut down yesterday are so covered in knotholes they're only good for firewood. Other than that, everything went well. Did Elspeth do anything memorable?"

"She ate about half her body weight in milk."

Drostan ladled some soup into a bowl so that Alynn could carry it to the table. "Are we ready to stop pretending everything's alright?"

"I'm worried too, love. Call a council meeting tomorrow. I want Lukas's thoughts on all this, and I'm too tired to think straight at the moment."

"Liar. You come up with great ideas when you're tired."

"This morning, I forgot which way I was spinnin' my spindle and wound up unravelling five feet of thread. I couldn't come up with a bad idea if I wanted to, let alone a halfway decent one."

Once the table had been set, Drostan took Alynn into his arms and kept her there for a while, so that Alynn nearly fell asleep. But then he kissed her and squeezed her extra tightly, which meant he was going to let go, so Alynn shook herself awake. Elspeth had grabbed a hold of her father's beard, and it somehow took three hands to extricate her fingers.

"Is she this ornery all the time?" Drostan asked.

"Almost."

"Are you managing alright by yourself?"

"Hardly. Too quiet, it is—when Elspeth's not cryin', anyway. And she eats so much that unless I can do it with one hand, it really won't get done. So cardin', spinnin', sewin', tablet weavin', most of the cleanin'—"

"We'll get someone to replace Valdis. I promise." Drostan set a hand on Alynn's shoulder and rubbed the knots out of it ever so gently. "I get the feeling Maggie would volunteer. We'd pay her, of course."

"I get the feeling she'd pay us for the chance to get out of the house."

Alynn reluctantly shrugged out of Drostan's hands so she could put the rest of the food on the table. By the time Leif returned—later than anticipated, likely because he'd stopped to check on Nora—everyone was ready to eat. After the prayer, no one spoke. It wasn't because the food was particularly delicious—Alynn had forgotten to put any seasoning in the soup, and Maggie's bannocks were still doughy in the middle. Everyone was too hungry to care and too tired to talk.

"I'll fetch the dishwater if you put the table up," Leif said to Drostan. It was the first thing that had been said at the dinner table.

Drostan nodded. "Fair deal."

Alynn washed the dishes, changed Elspeth for the tenth time that day, and was in bed asleep before anyone or anything, including her own guilt for being such a terrible housekeeper, could convince her to do anything else.

Humility was frustrated.

Alynn had known her mare for longer than she'd known Drostan. She knew that Humility's favorite thing in the world to do was to gallop as fast as she could down the three-mile trail that led from the village to St. Anne's Monastery. But with Elspeth tied to her mother's chest with a shawl, squirming and fussing, Humility was forced to travel at a slow jog. And she hated it.

"You know I won't drop you," she seemed to say with a toss of her head. "Look. It'll take us an extra half hour."

"If we're late, we're late. You're a mother, Humility. 'Tis a bit more understanding I thought you'd be."

"You could have left the baby with Brynhilde," said Drostan, who was riding not too far in front of them for protection's sake. Humility snorted in agreement and flicked her ebony tail.

"I can't do that."

"Why not? She's her godmother. It's her job."

"I'm her mother. 'Tis my job. Especially with Elspeth gettin' her teeth in, she needs me."

Drostan sighed, and they kept jogging. Elspeth's fussing got louder and louder until they finally reached the monastery, when Alynn hopped off Humility and started nursing her. Elspeth quieted right down, kicking her little feet contentedly.

Alynn left Drostan to tend to the horses and went inside the monastery. Mercy was the first person to notice her. She ran to greet Alynn, her bare toddler feet loud on the stone floor of the kitchen.

"Hi, hi, hi, hi—"

"Good morning, Mercy." Alynn tried to scoop Mercy up with her spare arm, but she was too heavy. Mercy was content to grab hold of two of Alynn's fingers and lead her to the hearth, where Caitriona was letting down the hem on a pair of Tarin's trousers. Caitriona looked up and smiled when she saw her daughters.

"Och, all three of my favorite girls!" she said, scooping Mercy and Alynn and Elspeth into her arms all at once. "What's this council meeting about? Leif wouldn't tell me."

"Our shadow turned up against last night. Robbed someone, shot at me when I tried to chase him, then left. I'm fine, and no one else was hurt. Promise."

Caitriona turned white and held Mercy even closer. "I don't think 'tis safe for you to be in the woods, Lynder. Especially not with the baby."

Alynn had been so focused on not dropping Elspeth that she hadn't even thought about being shot off her horse. The thought filled her with dread for a moment, but it quickly disappeared. "Drostan was with me. Besides, I'd think Grima would be lying low after last night."

"Wha's Geema?" Mercy asked.

"That's what we're calling the scary person who lives in the woods," said Alynn.

Mercy nodded and, perhaps prompted by the sight of Elspeth nursing, tugged on the already-stretched neckline of Caitriona's dress. Sighing, Caitriona asked, "What do you say, Mercy?"

"Mick, pease."

"Milk, please. Good girl." Caitriona resumed her seat at the hearth and let Mercy nurse. "Leif and Sigmund are in the council room, talkin' to Brett and Tarin. Lukas is in the front yard and asked not to be disturbed, God knows what he's doing."

"Thanks, Mum."

Alynn went out the rarely-used front door and had to tug it

shut. She glanced around and was struck by a sudden wave of nostalgia. This was where the Battle of Faith had happened. This was where she and Lukas had stood together against an army and won with nothing but a few weapons, reckless determination, and God's help.

It was a strange feeling. On the one hand, there was a love that had no business being there. Alynn remembered lying in the snow, seconds away from death, and looking Lukas in the eye. Knowing that he was there with her somehow made everything alright, and it had forged a bond between them that, though stretched thin with distance and time apart, had never broken.

And on the other hand, there was pain. Knowing that she had killed people, and that other people would suffer because of her actions. Looking into the eyes of a little boy and recognizing him, because one of the men she'd killed had those same blue eyes. For years, she'd hated herself for it.

But now? There was at least a bit of peace. Alynn could look at Elspeth, feel an overwhelming love for her, and wonder how any man who had looked at his child with a similar love could even think about raising a sword towards a thirteen-year-old girl. Saying they deserved their deaths was a bit harsh. Alynn wondered, though, if they deserved to be fathers.

A strange noise drew Alynn back to reality; it took her a while to recognize it as the thwack of a longbow. She panicked for a moment before spotting Lukas's silhouette several yards away from the monastery. He had a quiver at his waist and a bow in his hands, and he was aiming an arrow at an old building that had once been sleeping quarters for one of his long-deceased fellow monks.

Alynn approached him, but stopped a safe distance away and called out. "Lukas?"

Lukas lowered his bow. "Alynn?"

"And Elspeth."

"Och, my favorite lassies, here to visit!" A bit more enthusiastically than usual, Lukas embraced Alynn and stroked the back of Elspeth's head. It made her smile and spill milk everywhere.

Alynn glanced around. A crossbow and several arrows were set on the ground next to Lukas. Propped up against the cell wall, perhaps ten yards away, was Lukas's spare habit. It had been stuffed with straw to look like a scarecrow and set on a chair. There were four arrows in the scarecrow, a few scattered on the ground around it, and one lodged in the leg of the chair.

"I figured," said Lukas, "that if our mystery figure was going to use a bow and arrow, that we'd best practice our own marksmanship. Turns out I've got some practicing to do."

"You could shoot perfectly during the Battle of Faith," Alynn said.

"Far from perfectly. Asides, my eyes don't work as well as they used to. When's the last time ye shot a crossbow?"

"Two years, maybe."

Lukas motioned to the crossbow and a basket of arrows at the other end of the hallway. "Let's see yer aim."

Alynn glanced down at Elspeth, then stuck a finger into her mouth to ease the leech-like grip on her breast. "Can you burp her for me?"

Lukas took Elspeth into his arms, gingerly maneuvered her onto his shoulder, and tapped her back with the force he might use to level a cup of flour.

"You won't get anythin' out of her that way," said Alynn.

"I don't want to break her."

"She's a quarter Norse and half Irish. She won't break."

Lukas patted Elspeth's back a bit harder, and Alynn loaded the crossbow. She stared at her target, closed one eye, and fired. The arrow landed in the mannequin's shoulder.

"Not bad," said Lukas. "Try again. Use yer other eye this time."

Alynn fired again; her arrow tangled itself in the habit's dangling sleeve. For a moment, she was a little girl again. She was in the monastery's backyard with Lukas, throwing axes into a target painted onto a tree. She was parrying with her sword, working the same motions again and again until her muscles could do them without her brain telling them to.

Another arrow burrowed into the habit's stomach. And then another.

"You know you'll have to patch all these holes, right?" Alynn asked.

Lukas didn't answer. He'd given up on burping Elspeth and was simply holding her, his clean-shaven cheek pressed against her soft, warm head. His eyes were closed, and he was humming. Elspeth's head lay trustingly against his shoulder, peace in her eyes and three fingers in her mouth.

"Lukas?"

His eyes opened. "Hmm?"

Oh, Lukas didn't care about the holes. That habit was probably older than Alynn was. Caitriona was probably making him get rid of it.

"Sorry. Never mind," she said.

"I wish I'd known ye when ye were this little," Lukas said. "I'll bet ye were the sweetest bairn in Ireland. Yer parents are the luckiest people I know."

"They'd disagree." The sight of two small graves in Limerick filled Alynn's memory, and she couldn't brush it away fast enough. "Let me have Elspeth back."

"Shoot once more."

Quickly, Alynn loaded the crossbow again and fired it. This time, the arrow lodged itself into the habit's heart. "Good enough?" she asked.

"Ye hit the mark all five times, which is more than I can say fer myself," said Lukas. He finally gave Elspeth back to her mother. "Now, I know ye didn't come here to shoot targets. Council meeting?"

"Aye. Our mystery guest, we're callin' him Grima, showed himself in the village yesterday."

"What did he do?"

"He stole—somethin'. I'm not sure what. Then he fired a single arrow and disappeared into the woods. But have you ever heard the sound an arrow makes when it hits the metal bit of a shield? Och, 'tis beautiful. Like church bells, or Da hammerin' the flat part of a serving spoon."

With a half-twitch of a smile, Lukas set a hand on Alynn's shoulder as they headed towards the monastery together. "I'm just glad ye're alright. He hasn't taken anything from ye yet, right?"

"I don't think so. Then again, I've been too tired to notice much of anythin' out of the ordinary. Somebody—" Alynn set a condemning glare on Elspeth— "has been keepin' me up all night."

Elspeth smiled and squealed loudly.

"Thank God fer that," said Lukas. "Yer father's missing his new cloak—the one his captain friend gave him. And Caitriona insists that food's gone missing. Between Brett and Tarin, though—and I'll admit, there's days I have a hand in it—'tis nothing I'd blame definitively on our thief."

"Did you just say 'tis?"

"I said nay such thing."

"Aye, you did! I heard it!"

With a sigh and a Latin muttering, Lukas opened the front door, then followed Alynn past the hearth and down a hallway. The second door on the left led to the council room. It was a spacious room—a wall between two of the downstairs cells had been removed to create the space. In it was a table with several lamps and chairs, and against one wall was a slant-topped writing desk. Rolled and stored in a basket were a few maps that had been created by the monks who had founded St. Anne's.

Leif, Drostan, and Sigmund were already in the room and were studying one of the maps, which had been spread out on the table. Alynn quickly recognized the map as one that detailed the entirety of St. Anne's Cleft. Although one of the oldest maps in the collection, it had been recently edited to show the location of the Norse village and several farms.

Alynn looked closer at the map. St. Anne's Cleft was a

lopsided little landmass, pinched to less than five miles in length in the middle and bulging out towards the east. A cross marked St. Anne's Monastery, near the narrowest part of the island. The area of sea that now served as a harbor for Norse ships had been labeled as Foundling Bay. Alynn smiled.

"Lukas said 'tis," she said.

"Hmm?" said Leif.

"That blasted Irish lilt is rubbing off on me," said Lukas. "That's not important. What do we know?"

Drostan pointed to a narrow-mouthed bay on the south side of the island, close to the monastery. Jagged triangles in the water denoted the presence of rocks. "Grima and his companion landed here, in Treacherous Landing. He was seen in the same place a few days later, and yesterday, he was seen here." Drostan pointed to the southwest corner of the village. "He ran off into the woods to the west, where he disappeared. Moreover, Rothgeir's body was found in his boat right around here." He pointed to the ocean, not two miles west of the village.

"Logically, then, he's somewhere in this area," said Leif, using his finger to circle an area that encompassed the tiny western bulge of the island. "Twenty miles square or thereabouts. It's a rather large area to search, but if we draft enough men, maybe make a grid, we should manage."

"Ye won't find him there," said Lukas.

"Why not?" asked Sigmund.

Lukas pointed at Treacherous Landing. "He was hunting here, which means that he was likely camping nearby. When Alynn and Drostan saw him, he moved here." He pointed to where Rothgeir had been found. "Assuming he knows we've found Rothgeir, he'll be moving again. My guess is to the eastern part of the island."

"And he'd be stayin' close to shore," said Alynn. "He's probably waiting for one of Thrand's followers to send out a rescue party."

"If that's the case, we'll probably find a couple of

abandoned campsites somewhere on the western shore," said Sigmund. "There's a few caves on that rock beach. He might have been hiding in one of them."

"Or maybe he's staying near a source of fresh water," said Leif. "We should probably start by looking near the stream."

"If he's near the stream, we might never find him," said Sigmund. "What if the water-*draugr* gets him first?"

"There's nay such thing as a water-*draugr*," said Lukas.

"We've got a list of missing people that says otherwise," said Sigmund.

With a glance towards heaven, Lukas said with reluctance in his voice, "This doesn't need to leave this room, but I'll take responsibility for most of those disappearances."

Drostan raised an eyebrow. "Pardon?"

"I promised my dying father that I'd keep the monastery safe, and the most effective way of doing so, until recently, was to kill everyone who set eyes on it. I'd leave their bodies near the river because that's where the massacre happened. It felt like—revenge, I suppose." Lukas kept his eyes on the floor during this confession, and everyone stared at him. Even Alynn, who knew more about his past than the others present, felt slightly frightened of him.

Leif, somehow, was completely calm. "It's alright," he said. "He told me everything shortly after the Battle of Faith. The only thing I'm curious about now is what happened to my sister, if the water-*draugr* isn't real."

Lukas pressed his eyes shut, as if conjuring a mental image that stubbornly didn't want to appear. "Did she—och, God help me remember. Red hair. She was about waist-tall, she had freckles—she had a front tooth missing—"

Leif tightened his grip on the table. "Did you kill her?"

"Nay, of course not," Lukas said quickly. "She slipped on the rocks in the river. I found her half-drowned and bloodied, brought her back to the monastery. I didn't know what to do wi' her—I was eighteen, I wanted a friend so badly—but she caught pneumonia and died. She's buried in the cemetery, if ye'd like to visit her sometime."

Leif was silent, but he was still gripping the edge of the table. "Why didn't you tell me?" he asked.

"I didn't know she was yer sister. I'm sorry."

There was silence for a while. Alynn set a hand on Leif's shoulder. Sigmund had an embarrassed look on his face, as if he were sorry he'd mentioned the water-*draugr* to begin with.

Finally, Drostan cleared his throat. "Father, are you alright?"

"I will be."

"You can step out if you need to—"

"I'm alright. Let's get on with this meeting."

Drostan glanced at the map again. "Hiding places. Yes. We can send out some search parties. Now we have to figure out what we're up against. Alynn, you saw him up close. What did he look like?"

Alynn thought. "Well—what with the cloak and the hood and all, I couldn't tell much. He looked to be on the smaller side, built sort of like Tarin or my father, but shorter. I think he's got a hump in his back, or else he walks bent over."

"Strange," said Leif. "Most archers I've met have impeccable posture."

"He might have been running half-ducked, especially if he knew we were after him," said Drostan.

"That's a natural response to fear," said Lukas. "Now, what all's been taken?"

Drostan thought for a moment. "Blankets, clothes, food, some mead and ale," he said. "Mostly survival items, I guess. But then Sveinn said that he's missing a cloakpin, and we've got a few missing combs and bracelets."

"And my father's new plaid," said Alynn.

"Have you noticed anything else gone from the monastery?" Leif asked.

"Just food—and that might have been Brett and Tarin's doing," said Lukas. "We haven't checked fer anything else."

Drostan took a few steps away from the rest of the Council,

running a hand through his hair. "Can someone talk Rowan out of working at the smithy until this all blows over? It's not safe for him to travel back and forth."

Alynn laughed. "Aye, he'll listen to you. The man would work on Sabbaths and holidays if the church would let him."

"Caitriona might be able to talk some sense into him," said Lukas. "Asides, I've some work around here he can help with."

"Speaking of work, what about a curfew?" Sigmund suggested. "Anyone not home by dark will be presumed dead."

"Too harsh," said Leif.

"The women will appreciate it," said Alynn. "But 'tis yer decision, love."

Drostan sank into one of the many chairs around the map table, clearing the hair out of his face so he could think better. Alynn could see his mind racing; she set a hand on his shoulder and realized how tight his muscles were. Drostan set a work-roughened hand over hers and stroked the back of her hand with his thumb.

"I suppose this is the first true test of my leadership," he said. "I'm standing on a hole. No clue what I'm doing. I couldn't do any of this without you—all of you. So thank you for being here. I appreciate everything you do, and all of your prayers."

"Any time, lad," said Lukas.

"And if you ever need me and Brynhilde to watch our goddaughter, we'd be honored," said Sigmund.

Alynn glanced at Elspeth, who had fallen asleep while eating. Wee piglet. She couldn't imagine letting her out of her sight, even if it was with Brynhilde. Nevertheless, Elspeth didn't seem to object to the proposition. "We'll keep that in mind," said Alynn as tactfully as possible. "Thank you."

Leif leaned against the wall with a certain smile in his eyes as he looked at Drostan. Alynn had seen this smile before—it usually preceded a story about Drostan's child self or a statement of "You're just like your mother." But this time, Leif said, "You're not alone, son. And even if you don't have any of us, you've got Jesus, and He's the best Council Member of all."

Drostan stopped playing with his hair and looked at Lukas. "Has God told you anything about this?" he asked.

Lukas turned into a shell of himself for a moment, as if retreating inward to revisit every hour he'd spent in prayer over the past few weeks. "God doesn't seem too concerned about the matter," he said. "He's told me a few things, much of it personal. He's said that I've fought harder battles, and that so long as everyone keeps their heads, we should be fine. But other than that…I'll pray, lad. Never doubt that. But seek the Lord fer yerself over the matter. Why don't ye pray fer a bit? The chapel's empty until noon."

"I appreciate that. Thank you." Then, with a smile, Drostan turned and nodded to the rest of the council members. "Thank all of you."

Then he stood, and Alynn followed him into the chapel. They knelt before the altar they had been married at, and Alynn held Elspeth with one arm and Drostan's hand with the other. A sense of peace and contentment swelled in her heart. God and her family, all in the same place. Who could ask for more?

NINE

Alynn was lying on a chapel bench. Lukas's voice was echoing strong and sweet throughout the room, and Elspeth's hiccupping punctuated the message. Alynn groaned and looked up to see Drostan holding the baby.

"What time is it?" Alynn asked.

"Half past chapel. You fell asleep while we were praying, that was almost an hour ago."

Alynn shifted on the hard wooden bench. Part of her wanted to go back to sleep. But a single memory filled her mind—that of a smelly old man yelling at her for falling asleep during Mass. Where had that been? Alynn ran over the long list of Irish towns she'd lived in and found that she'd forgotten several of them. Well, it didn't matter too much. She sat up, stretched her shoulders, and leaned against Drostan.

"Did God tell you anythin'?" she asked.

Drostan kissed the side of Alynn's head. "Nay, but I'm at peace now, and a bit more confident. Now shush. This is a good message."

The midday chapel service typically consisted of a few hymns and Bible verses read aloud, but on occasion, Lukas would practice telling a few stories that he intended on incorporating into his Sunday sermons. This seemed like one of those occasions. He spoke with a clear voice, projecting into the far corners of the room. Or perhaps he just sounded louder in a nearly-empty chapel.

"Some of us might recall the violent thunderstorm we had a few months ago. The one that brought down three sections of paddock fence and blocked the path to the village with fallen trees. Little Mercy was crying with fear."

"Hi," said Mercy upon hearing her name. Lukas smiled at her, but kept speaking as if nothing had happened.

"But then, Rowan took her up into his arms, and I watched as all her fears melted away. Aye, the storm was still raging. In fact, I believe it picked up a bit afterwards. But what did it matter to Mercy? She was safe in her father's arms, finding comfort in his presence.

"So we must be wi' God. We face greater troubles than thunderstorms in life. Everything from spilled ink and stubbed toes to death, disease, and famines. And sometimes, we forget that our Heavenly Father is holding us closely, protecting us from harm, His loving eye watching over us. To paraphrase the Apostle Paul, if God be on our side, what does it matter if people rise against us? Even if we lose a battle, we have faith that God will win the war in the end."

With that, everyone stood to sing the closing hymn—*Rector Potens, Verax Deus*, which was the traditional hymn for closing out the noon service. It was in Latin, but Alynn had been singing it her whole life, so she knew the words and their general meaning. Caitriona's voice rang out as the most beautiful, and Mercy's was the loudest. Drostan only hummed, and Brett stumbled a bit before switching languages. "*Aufer calorem noxium*" turned into "Refer, color them rocks and run." Tarin noticed and giggled.

The service ended, and Caitriona was quick to glide over to Alynn and Drostan. She always glided when she was in a hurry, her long legs taking long steps beneath her long skirts. "You're welcome to stay for dinner," she said.

"I wish we could, Mum," said Drostan. "But I've got work.

Make sure Folkvard and Havard haven't nailed any strakes on backwards or sawed off their fingers."

"Och, don't take my grandbaby away from me." Caitriona took Elspeth into her own arms and smiled at her. "I miss my sweet little Eppie. Look at this. Peek-a-boo!"

Elspeth grinned.

"Where's Elspeth? Peek-a-boo!" Caitriona smothered Elspeth in kisses, and she responded with a series of high shrieks that sounded like the precursor to a laugh. "Och, my sweet girl. Please don't leave just yet, Lynder. I've hardly seen ye."

Alynn smiled sadly. "I wish we could stay, Mum, but I've a heap of chores to do at home. You can hold Elspeth, though. Drostan, love, could you saddle Humility for me?"

"Sure, if you'll be ready to leave in five minutes."

"Ten. I miss my family."

"Fair enough." Drostan kissed Alynn a temporary farewell, and Caitriona directed her attention towards Elspeth again. Elspeth didn't quite know what to make of all the sweet words directed to her, or the finger that kept touching her wee nose. She stared at Caitriona's finger with perfectly round eyes, as if deciding what to do about this invasion of her privacy.

"You'll give her back if she starts cryin', right?" Alynn asked.

"Och, Eppie won't cry. Nana knows how to take care of a baby. Isn't that right, Elspeth? Isn't that right?"

Elspeth smiled. Alynn, content that her daughter was in good hands, turned to see Tarin staring at her. She grinned and pulled him into a hug.

"Are you growin'?" she asked, her voice muffled by Tarin's hair that came up to her nose now.

"I'd better be."

"Och, you can't get taller! You're supposed to stay little and cute forever!"

"That's Mercy's job!"

"Nay, you're going to be taller than me afore long. What is

it I'm supposed to do then?"

Tarin grinned. "I'm supposed to be taller than you."

Alynn planted a kiss on the top of Tarin's head and smiled as he squirmed with embarrassment. "I love you," she said.

"You too. Now quit coddlin' me."

Tarin's face was nearly as red as his hair when he glanced up at Brett, who was hovering nearby and grinning. "I wish my sister liked me," he said. "She's a shieldmaiden. Used me like a training dummy. She stabbed me once."

Alynn winced. She couldn't imagine hurting Tarin. But still, she was curious—she'd never met Brett's sister, but it was nice to know that she wasn't the only woman in Orkney who could fight. "What weapon does she use?" she asked.

"Brenna mostly sticks to axes and halberds. I'll bet she wishes flirting killed people, she'd be the deadliest warrior in all of Orkney."

Tarin snickered, but Alynn felt a strange sense of motivation. She hadn't used her sword in over a year. Part of her wondered if she was still able to wield it. What if she'd forgotten how to parry? Or lost her strength?"

"Lukas?" she asked.

He glanced up from his game of patty-cake with Mercy. "Hmm?"

"Can we practice sword fighting?"

"Are ye sure ye're up fer it?"

"Sure, I'm sure."

Lukas sighed. "Well—it would do us both good. I'll get ye a spare sword from the armory. And let's go out front. Yer mother's expanded the vegetable garden, and she'll not want us stepping on seedlings."

Alynn smiled as she stretched her sword arm. This was going to be fun.

Two minutes later, she and Lukas were standing in the monastery's yard. The breeze was cool, but Alynn lad left her cloak sitting on the kitchen table. She knew that she'd be sweating as soon as the fight started. Lukas had fitted the two swords with wooden covers, so they would be safe from everything except for a few bumps and bruises.

Alynn readied her sword. Then, because he had taught her to never start a fight, Lukas threw the first blow.

The crack of the wooden cases brought all of Alynn's dormant skills back to her fingertips. She knew how to stand. She knew how to move forwards and backwards, side to side. Her shoulder, elbow, and wrist all remembered how to flex and bend with the blows from Lukas's sword. Along with the knowledge came memories of a different sort—a reminder of the early days, when it was just Alynn and Lukas against the world.

She threw a few offensive blows—diagonal slashes, first up, then down. Lukas blocked them, then tried to twist his blade around Alynn's crossguard. She stepped backwards, flicked his blade away, and tried to strike again. Lukas was too quick for her. He aimed a swipe of his own at Alynn's neck, and she had to pull away from her offensive to block him.

A strange wave of dizziness brought Alynn out of her focused state. She realized that her breathing was labored— that her arm was already tired and her shoulder cramping. Lukas was on the offensive, and Alynn's parries were hardly effective. With a single deft motion, Lukas swiped his way past Alynn's defenses and tapped her side with his sword. Panting, Alynn dropped her weapon, and then Lukas dropped his.

"I'm sorry," Alynn said. "I can't fight. I'm sorry."

"Och, whisht. Don't fret. Ye're out of practice, is all, and that's soon mended." Alynn nodded, her pulse pounding in her ears. Her legs were shaking.

Lukas began to say something else, but he checked himself mid-sentence and put a hand on Alynn's arm. There was fear in his grasp. Instinctively, Alynn grew still and listened. She heard a noise—the distinctive thwack of a bow.

"Get down," said Lukas. Alynn dropped to the ground, hands over the back of her neck, heart pounding with a renewed fervor. All her thoughts were on Elspeth. Was she alright? Was she safe? Who would take care of her if anything happened to Alynn or Drostan?

There was another bowshot—Alynn flinched. And then she heard Brett's voice, unafraid, with a certain teasing quality to it. Then Tarin's voice rang out in reply, and Brett spoke again, and there was another shot.

"Target practice. Those lads—"

Lukas's voice was so close to Alynn that his breath tickled her neck. She opened her eyes to see the brown fabric of Lukas's sleeves shivering in a sudden gust of wind. He had been crouched over her, a living shield, his arms circled around her head. With a groan, he rolled onto his back and stared up at the clouded sky. "Ye're alright?"

Alynn reached out to take his hand. "Shaken up. Not hurt. You?"

"About the same. It's my own fault, really—I ought to have put the bows away. I knew that." Lukas sighed and squeezed Alynn's hand. "Ask yer mum to make us some tea. I've got to yell at the lads. They ought to be studying." There was another thwack of the bow, and this time Alynn turned her head to see an arrow lodged into the straw-stuffed habit. She guessed she had been too busy focusing on her sword fighting to notice the boys earlier.

Trembling, Alynn stood, helped Lukas to his feet, and ran inside to grab Elspeth. She forgot to ask for the tea. She was too busy kissing Elspeth's fuzzy head and running her fingers up and down her satin-soft arm while trying to explain to Caitriona what had happened. Caitriona made the tea anyway.

"Lynder, you oughtn't have been out there," Caitriona scolded. "Anythin' could have happened. Even if Grima didn't show up, a wayward arrow—the lads don't know what they're doing. You've got a baby to think about now, dear heart, you can't be gallivanting all over creation fightin' whatever suits yer fancy."

"I don't fight whatever suits my fancy," Alynn snapped. "I fight when I have to. And devil mend it, I'm proud that I'm able to protect my family. If anythin', now with Grima about and all, I ought to be practicin' more."

Caitriona sighed. "Och, this is what I get for lettin' yer father raise you, isn't it?"

"Mum, 'tisn't like you had a choice—"

"'Tis Drostan's job to protect you. 'Tis yer job to keep him fed and clothed, and raise his children. Those aren't small things, love. Especially since you're the chieftess. The quality of the home you keep reflects on the entire island." Caitriona pulled a kitchen chair sideways so she could sit facing Alynn. "You're an adult now, and part of that means accepting your place in the world."

The door had opened during their exchange. Inside trooped Brett and Tarin, heads bowed in submission, one with a bow and the other with a basket of arrows. Lukas, who held the swords he and Alynn had used in their sorry excuse for a skirmish, stopped at the table.

"She's nineteen, Caitriona," he said. "My father insisted that ye shouldn't be considered an adult until ye're twenty-five. Don't be harsh on her."

"She's old enough to know her place."

"Who cares what her place is? Part of being an adult is doing what needs done, regardless of what anyone else says about it." Lukas kissed the top of Alynn's head. "Now, I've a pair of unruly students who need disciplined."

"You're not going to make us go without dinner again, are you?" asked Tarin from the dark hallway that led towards the armory.

"That depends on how long it takes ye to write yer sentence variants."

"All of them?" asked Brett.

"I want every noun declension and every verb conjugation. And if ye complain, ye'll do it in Greek, too. Now march."

Sighing, the boys departed down the hallway, and Mercy watched from the hearth as she played with her rag dolls. "Paky?" she asked.

Lukas smiled, picked Mercy up, and kissed her. "Nay, darling, they're too auld fer spankings. What about ye? Do ye need a tickling?" He tickled Mercy's belly until she squealed with laughter, then kissed her again and set her down.

"Deydey! Pay wi' me!"

"Och, I can't play wi' ye now, Mercy. Later, alright?"

Sadly, Mercy picked up her doll again and resumed playing by herself. Alynn's heart hurt—she remembered being a small child, her only sibling cold in a grave, trying to entertain herself while Caitriona was busy. It was miserable. She was about to offer to play with her, but Drostan poked his head through the back door. "Alynn! Let's go!"

"Already?"

"I've got to get back to work. Come on."

Sighing, Alynn wrapped Elspeth in her shawl and kissed Caitriona goodbye. Elspeth got into a fight with her wrappings and, by the time they were home, she was squalling like a thundercloud. Drostan summarily left for work, and Alynn found herself trapped with Elspeth's cries echoing off the walls of the otherwise-empty house. Why, *why* did Valdis have to leave?

Well, one thing at a time. Alynn had diapers to wash.

The rest of the day passed in a blur of chores and Elspeth's tears, and just as Alynn was starting to prepare the evening bread, there was a knock on the door. Alynn almost started crying when she heard it. The house was covered in drying diapers, there was a large spit-up stain on the front of her dress, and she felt too tired to hold a decent conversation. Besides, Elspeth was wailing so loudly it could probably be heard from three houses down the street. It was probably a neighbor telling her to get Elspeth to shut up.

Fortunately, her guest was Nora McKenzie, who stepped inside with a kind smile and a helping hand. Alynn gladly let her hold Elspeth, whose screaming-red face was dripping with tears and snot and drool. "Och, these are some difficult days," said Nora, letting Elspeth chew on her finger. She quieted down a bit, but still fussed. "Especially since yer help's left."

"I raised Tarin alone," Alynn said, taking her frustrations out on the dough beneath her hands. "You'd think I'd be able to handle it."

"Tarin had all his teeth when ye got him. Asides, he didn't have to eat every three hours."

"'Tis more often than that. And she's wakin' me up every half hour at night, it feels like. Is that normal?"

Nora laughed. "Hen, when they're teething, anything's normal. Don't fret, though, she'll grow out of it. Another week or so, she'll have that second tooth in."

Alynn groaned, drew a deep breath, and put the bread in a spider-legged skillet to bake in the coals of the fireplace. "I tried to practice sword fightin' today. A good idea, I thought it was, what with Grima about and all."

"How'd it go?"

"I couldn't do it."

"No wonder. Ye're young, ye'll get yer strength back soon enough." Nora turned her attention to the soup bubbling over the fireplace. "Would ye mind if I stayed fer dinner, Alynn?"

"Assuming you help make it. I'll be glad for the company."

"Grand." Nora stirred the stew that had been simmering over the fireplace for weeks. Alynn usually liked to wash the soup pot every week, but everyone else in the village thought she was crazy. Some of the older women had soups that had been simmering for longer than Alynn had been alive.

"Am I mad," Alynn asked, "for wantin' to be a shield-maiden and a mum at the same time?"

Nora chuckled. "Lassie, I thought ye were mad when ye took up the job in the first place. Yer mum told me about the nightmares ye were having. I'm surprised ye've kept at it. That said, ye aren't mad fer not wanting to give it up. There's some days I wish I didn't stop midwifing when Maggie was born. Well—I tried to get back into it. It didn't work out."

"Why?"

"See, I'd been apprenticing with my gran since I was a girl

of ten or so. Tried to help her wi' a delivery when Maggie was about three weeks auld. The bairn died, and I bawled fer a month. Just—the way that poor mum looked at me, when there I was, sixteen, unwed, wi' a perfect bairn, and hers dead. I couldn't go back after that."

Alynn's focus immediately turned from the conversation to her own bairn. Nora held Elspeth on her hip and had put a spoon in her mouth to quell her fussing. It half-worked.

As evening drew closer, Nora took off her kerchief and unbraided her hair. Her hair was the loveliest color—the darkest red or the reddest auburn, Alynn couldn't tell—and it fell past her waist in loose curls. Nora brushed through her hair with her fingers, but she stopped with Leif and Drostan arrived home. She glanced at Leif with an expression that mixed surprise with pleasure as she tried to tie her kerchief quickly in place.

Leif ran a hand over his tunic, sending sawdust drifting towards the floor. Some of it floated into a sunbeam cast by the still-open door and sparkled. "You look lovely," he said.

"Thank you," said Nora.

"You know you don't have to wear your kerchief here if you don't want to."

"It would be rather indecent of me—"

Leif took a strand of hair that hadn't made it into the kerchief and twisted it around his fingers. "I won't tell anyone."

Elspeth chose that moment to spit up all over her little frock. Sighing, Alynn wiped her dry with her apron while Nora dished up the soup, Drostan fetched the table, and Leif poured small ale for everyone. It took Alynn a while to notice that Nora had left her kerchief crumpled on the sleeping bench.

"I take it everyone's hungry," said Alynn.

"Starved," said Drostan. He might have been a grown man of twenty, but he still had the appetite of a growing boy, especially after a long day's work. "Do we have any cheese?"

Alynn grabbed half a wheel of cheese from the cupboard and set it on the table, then returned to the cupboard for a knife. She missed the days when she could use both her hands to set the table. Elspeth was worth a spare arm, of course—but still. Alynn glanced at Elspeth, and she grinned as if she knew exactly what she was doing.

"So, Leif," said Nora, smiling at Alynn and Elspeth, "how do ye like being a grandfather?"

"I don't feel old enough for it. Other than that, it's wonderful. Brings back good memories." There was a strange light in Leif's eyes, a variant of the way he'd look at Drostan when he was holding Elspeth, but it was directed at Nora. "How are your lads doing?"

"Och, they're growing up too fast. Olvir wants to start apprenticing wi' his Uncle Hrafnkell, but I don't want him going out to sea fer weeks on end. Suppose he doesn't come back?"

"Hrafnkell rarely leaves Orkney. Out of all the merchants I've met, he's the least likely to run into trouble. Besides, it's a good job, and it was Svan's job. If I were Olvir, I'd want my father's job."

Nora blinked. "Still, though—I was thinking he'd make a good shipwright."

Leif said nothing, but his eyes were still alight as he sat at the table. Alynn, assuring herself that everything they needed was on the table, sat as well, with Elspeth on her lap. Leif prayed for the food, and everyone started eating. The soup was delicious—much better, Alynn admitted, than the soup she normally made. Leif and Drostan complimented Nora before beginning the customary moment of silence, blowing on their soup and shoveling it into their mouths as quickly as possible.

"Nora," said Leif as he took another piece of cheese, "we've been thinking about hiring Maggie to help Alynn with things, now that Valdis is gone."

"She'll like that," said Nora. "Most of Ulfrik's family is still Pagan. It shows in their manners. She'll be grateful fer the break from them."

"I just hope she'll be able to get a few things done here and there, the way she talks," said Drostan.

"Don't ye worry about that. Maggie's a good girl, she knows how to work. I think, though, that she'd only be able to work half the day. She'll be needed to make the evening meal fer her own family."

Alynn nodded, but part of her felt like crying. She'd been looking forward to having Maggie's help with dinner. Making bread and frying fish and tending to Elspeth all at once was overwhelming, and she hated the masked look of disgust on Drostan's face whenever burned fish or half-baked bread was set in front of him.

"We can manage dinner," Alynn said, not entirely meaning it. Elspeth grabbed a fistful of stray hairs and pulled. Alynn winced.

"Och, don't be daft. Ye hardly managed tonight, and I was here to help. My clan can make dinner without me. I'll help ye, hen."

"You're sure?" Alynn asked. "Maggie won't take it as an insult, will she?"

"Of course not. She's needed at her own house, she knows that. More than that, she knows that the fastest way to a man's heart is through his stomach, and she's newly married enough that she's still trying to play temptress with bread and pottage." She coyly glanced at Leif as she spoke, somehow didn't blush, and took a bite of bread as if she'd been discussing the weather.

"She's a wise girl, then," said Leif. "Did you teach her that?"

"Of course."

Leif smiled. "Well, if you're certain you can be spared, you're welcome to come tempt me with bread and pottage any day."

"I'll tempt ye wi' more than that. Roast chicken, fish fried in butter, boiled mutton—"

"Have you tried my mum's ham?" Alynn asked.

"Aye, and it's very good ham. She taught me the recipe."

Alynn wished they were eating ham now. Oh well. She was hungry enough that she didn't particularly care that the only meat in her soup was the occasional bit of fish or wild rabbit. What was it they'd served at the Christmas feast in Ireland, the year Tarin went out wassailing with a group of neighbors and came home drunk and frost-nipped past midnight? It wasn't poultry, Alynn was sure of that—was it venison? Mutton?

Leif's voice interrupted Alynn's daydreams of lamb and venison. "We'd pay you, of course, Nora—"

"Let me stay for dinner, and we'll call it even."

Leif agreed, and Drostan agreed, and Elspeth squealed in agreement. And when Elspeth squealed in agreement, there was nothing more to be said about a matter.

TEN

The next morning, Alynn hurried into church just as the bell was ringing overhead. Elspeth was screaming. It wasn't raining, she'd just been fed, and her diaper was dry. Alynn was patting her violently on the back, hoping she'd burp and settle down.

Drostan stopped on his way to the chapel. "Do you mind if I—"

"Just go. Save me a seat."

Drostan ducked inside the chapel just as the first hymn started, and Alynn sat defeated at the hearth, joining a pair of older ladies who were too busy chatting to join worship. One of them looked up at her disdainfully. "She wouldn't cry if you swaddled her," she said.

"No, that's a hungry cry," the other woman said. "Are you sure you're making enough milk for her?"

Alynn looked up at the women and was frustrated to find tears threatening to quench the angry fire in her eyes. Blinking, she held Elspeth tighter and went to a nearby cell. The room she found herself in used to belong to the abbot, and it had a comfortable feather mattress instead of a lumpy straw tick. It was mostly used as a sickroom now. Alynn tried not to wonder if anyone had died on the lovely feather mattress as she lay down on it, Elspeth on her chest. A few loud and terrible minutes passed before Elspeth started chewing on the neckline of her mother's blouse. Even though she'd eaten a mere half hour ago, she nursed greedily, clawing Alynn's chest with her tiny dagger-fingernails. Slowly, her eyes closed, and Alynn found herself falling asleep along with her.

The next thing she knew, Tarin was sitting next to her, holding Elspeth and talking to her. Alynn sat up and rubbed the sleep out of her eyes. "What time is it?" she asked.

"Lukas is halfway through service. Drostan asked me to look for you." Tarin smiled at Elspeth and tapped her nose. "You know something, Eppie? You're almost as cute as Mercy was when she was little."

"Nonsense. You're ten times cuter," said Alynn. She sat up and took Elspeth into her arms.

"I hope she turns out with freckles. She'll look just like me."

"Except that she's got her mammy's blue eyes. Come here, Tarin."

Since no one was watching, Tarin sat next to Alynn and leaned against her shoulder. Alynn put her arm around him. He might have been thirteen. He might have been growing like a weed and shaving the three hairs on his upper lip and trying to show off in front of the girls, but he was still her little brother. Sweet, quiet, curious Tarin.

"I wish I could come visit you more," said Tarin. "Lukas keeps me busy, and Da's tryin' to get me to work more at the smithy. I don't like it."

"Why not? I thought you liked workin' with Da."

"Well—I did, back when the smithy was warmer than our house and I didn't have to actually do much. Now, I just hurt myself and come home smelling like coal smoke. And I'm not strong enough."

"You'll get stronger."

"Look at me, Lynder! I'm hair and bones!"

"Aye, my wee owl pellet."

"*Stop.*"

Smiling, Alynn ruffled Tarin's hair. "What's service about?"

"Lukas is talking about balancing faith and works. Do you want to hear the rest of it?"

"Only if you'll sit next to me."

"Only if I get to hold Elspeth."

"Sure. Come on."

Elspeth tried to stick her fingers up Tarin's nose as they walked quietly through the hallways to the chapel doors. They entered silently as mice, crept close to the wall of stained-glass windows rather than walking down the center aisle, and sat with the rest of their family in the front row. Drostan put his arm around Alynn as she sat next to him.

"You fell asleep?" he asked.

Alynn nodded, and nothing more was said.

As soon as service ended, Alynn was kept busy talking to people—aye, partly because she wanted to, but also because she was expected to be cordial. She wished she could find a friend, like Maggie or Sigmund or his wife Brynhilde, and talk about something other than the weather or Elspeth's new tooth or if she knew anything new about Grima. Elspeth, meanwhile, was being passed from well-intentioned person to person, and Alynn didn't like it. She wanted to know where her baby was. The moment Elspeth let out a discontented wail, Alynn snatched her back and set her on her hip.

Fortunately, everyone trickled out of the monastery, leaving Alynn and Drostan alone with the McNeils shortly after noon. Even Leif had left, insisting that he was seeing Nora McKenzie safely home. Alynn didn't miss him. Leif was a good man, but a loud one, and it was pleasant to sit at the hearth and visit with her family in relative silence.

Tarin, however, was growing restless. He sat swinging his legs—a difficult task, since they were nearly too long for it— and bounced around from the kitchen to the hearth to the upstairs cells and back again. Finally, he said, "Lynder, I want to show you somethin'."

"What is it?"

"I disguised the root cellar so Grima can't get into it."

Setting Elspeth in Lukas's arms, Alynn left with Tarin. The outdoors met her with clouds and a cool breeze. "Has it worked so far?" she asked as a single shiver went through her.

"Even Brett tried to get in, and he can't." With that, Tarin scampered ahead to the root cellar. It was behind the stable at the edge of the woods, dug into a small hill so that it looked like a fairy's house.

Tarin had covered the wooden door of the root cellar with a piece of sod so that the hill looked like any other hill. Even Alynn nearly overlooked it. She tugged on the grass where the door had been; it didn't come up.

"I sewed it," Tarin said, proudly moving the sod to show a practically invisible seam. "And if you want to get in, you just cut the sod away."

"That's a grand idea you had, and it worked well." Alynn ruffled Tarin's hair. "I'm proud of you."

Grinning, Tarin stood to leave, but he froze with his gaze on the forest. "Is that Da's new plaid?" he asked. Alynn stood and saw something in the woods, something dark red and dark green and looking for all the world like a pile of laundry. She grabbed Tarin's arm. "Don't move," she said.

The plaid moved. It stretched slowly upwards, growing until it resembled a cloaked and hooded figure, and a longbow appeared from within the folds of fabric. There was a quiver at Grima's hip/ Before Alynn could think, he reached into it, placed an arrow on the string, and fired a warning shot at her feet.

Tarin saw the arrow as an invitation, not a threat. He ran after Grima.

"Tarin, get back here!"

"Let's catch him!"

Grima had bolted into the woods, and Tarin was flying after him. His light frame gave him extra speed, and Alynn found herself lagging behind. She wished she could go berserk and use the extra rush of energy it gave her. Instead, she was stuck running on her normal strength, flagging badly, her lungs burning and her legs protesting at every step.

She focused on watching what was going on. Tarin was gaining on Grima. Just a few more feet. He'd catch up to him, probably jump on him, and assuming he didn't die a horrible death like Rothgeir had, the island's troubles would be over.

But none of that happened. Grima stopped—or at least Alynn thought he did, from the way his cloak stopped drifting—and fired another arrow. Alynn screamed as she watched Tarin fall to one knee.

Fear gave her new strength. She was at his side in an instant, holding him, trying to see if he was bleeding.

"What happened? Did he hit you?"

"We've almost got him! Keep going!"

Ignoring him, Alynn felt him over for broken bones. His torso wasn't hit, thank God. Neither were his arms or legs. It was a while before Alynn found the arrow lodged into his foot, pinning him to the ground.

"What are you doing? Get him!"

"We're getting you home." Alynn winced as she pulled the arrow out of the ground, but she knew better than to remove it from Tarin's foot. She stood and tried to toss Tarin over her shoulder. He shoved his way off her.

"I can walk!"

"Devil mend it, Tarin, are you mad? 'Tis an arrow that's stuck in yer foot!"

"I can hop. You're not carryin' me!" And with that, stubborn Irishman he was, Tarin took off hopping on his one good foot, one hand on Alynn's arm for balance. She wished they could go faster. She kept glancing over her shoulder, making sure they weren't being followed. It was a difficult task. The sound of Tarin's hopping, and eventually of his labored breathing, made listening for ethereal footsteps impossible.

The forest had too many hiding places for comfort. Alynn wanted nothing more than a wall between her and Grima, or a friend to fight alongside her, or absolute knowledge that Elspeth and Drostan were alright. She realized halfway back to the monastery that she was shaking.

Finally, after Tarin nearly stumbled and fell, Alynn sighed and glanced once more around the forest. "Get on my back. Now."

Tarin said nothing as Alynn helped him to his feet and onto her back. Thank God he was light, although his hip bones dug rather awkwardly into Alynn's back. She carried him the rest of the way. It wasn't faster, but it was quieter, and Tarin kept a careful lookout for any suspicious movements. They saw nothing.

When the woods finally dropped away to reveal the monastery, Tarin slid down from Alynn's back and insisted on hopping the rest of the way. Alynn let him, especially because Caitriona was in the yard looking for them. She called out, and Caitriona came running.

"What happened?" Caitriona demanded, taking one look at Tarin and running to steady him. "Did you twist yer ankle?"

"Grima shot me in the foot," said Tarin. "Please don't go all mother hen on me, it doesn't hurt much—"

Caitriona gave a smothered cry, inspected Tarin's foot for herself, then scooped him up like an infant and carried him inside. Her face was white with determination. "'Tis alright, dear heart. We'll get you patched up, and Lukas will pray fer you, and you'll be runnin' around in no time. I promise."

"Exactly! Nothin' to worry about, put me down. I can hop. I'm grand, I swear—"

Caitriona ignored him, and Alynn opened the back door for them. Caitriona rallied everyone to help. On her orders, Rowan carried Tarin into the sickroom, and Lukas took Brett to the armory to gather the necessary medical supplies. Drostan put Elspeth in Alynn's arms and set a hand on her shoulder while she pressed her eyes shut and buried her face in Elspeth's hair.

Within moments, the three of them were left alone at the hearth. The only noise was the distant voices of Lukas giving orders and Rowan and Caitriona trying to comfort their son.

"Grima shot him," Alynn said. Tears threatened to slip onto

her cheeks. "Grima shot my little brother."

"He takes after you," said Drostan. He drew her close and planted a kiss on the side of her head. "He's a fighter. He'll be alright."

"He's too much like me." Alynn started trembling again, and Drostan held her tighter. "He wanted me to keep chasing him."

"Which way did Grima go?"

"West, towards the rock beach. We probably chased him a good half mile through the woods. Tarin nigh had him, too—I wasn't fast enough, I couldn't do anything—"

Alynn let herself cry for a moment before a cry of pain from Tarin scraped her ears. Alynn held Elspeth tighter and wished that she'd been shot instead. She'd felt pain before. She could handle it. Not Tarin. He was innocent—he was a child. He didn't deserve to be involved.

When Tarin cried out again, Alynn gave Elspeth to Drostan and ran to the sickroom. She came to the doorway just as Lukas pulled the long and bloody shaft out of Tarin's foot. She wanted to be sick. She glanced around the room—Brett was holding Tarin's legs down, and Caitriona was comforting him as best as she could. Alynn ran to Tarin, and he quickly squirmed out of Caitriona's arms so she could hold him.

"Tweezers," said Lukas. Rowan, who had been staying out of everyone's way, stepped forward to hand Lukas a small wooden instrument. Alynn turned away when Lukas started digging for splinters. Tarin drew a deep breath and tried not to cry, squeezing his sister's arms with white knuckles.

"Whisht, Tarin. You're alright. Deep breaths, now. Can you breathe with me?"

Tarin took a few deep breaths. Alynn stroked his hair, then glanced at Caitriona, who hovered nearby. There were tears in her eyes.

"Surprisingly," said Lukas, "there isn't much bleeding. Can ye wiggle yer toes fer us, laddie?"

Tarin obliged, wincing.

"Good. Very good. We'll pack the wound wi' salt and bloodwort, to stave off infection. A good washing with mead wouldn't do much harm, either…it'll hurt, Tarin. I'm sorry. Just be glad we don't have to cauterize it."

Wide-eyed, Tarin wrapped both arms around Alynn and squeezed tight. Alynn squeezed him back. "I'm right here, Tarin. I've got you, love. Just take some deep breaths. Everything's going to be alright."

Caitriona smiled and stroked Tarin's hair with a cold, white hand. "Och, of course you'll be alright! You're my big strong lad, aren't you?"

"Mum, stop."

"Come, now, let me help you."

"I'm grand! Leave me be." The dictate seemed not to apply to Alynn. Tarin wrapped his arms even tighter around her, and Alynn wasn't about to trade a hug from him for anything in the world.

Blinking, Caitriona contented herself with sitting on the edge of the bed and squeezing Tarin's hand. Rowan returned from the root cellar with a bottle of mead, and Brett was mixing a solution of dried bloodwort leaves and salt. Alynn closed her eyes, as if the medicines were about to sting her own injuries.

Murmuring prayers in a language Alynn couldn't understand, Lukas poured the mead over Tarin's foot. Tarin tensed and shrank in Alynn's arms. He took a deep and shaking breath, and he released it in a high-pitched whimper. He did his best not to cry out; Alynn was proud of him.

"Steady, laddie. There we go. Ye're doing so well." Lukas's voice was unwavering, though Alynn knew he'd break sooner or later. "That was the mead. Ye can drink the rest if ye'd like, to help wi' the pain."

Tarin shook his head. "Just get it over with," he said. Alynn held him tighter, and Lukas poured the mixture of bloodwort and salt into the hole in his foot. This time, the pain proved too much for Tarin. He screamed and tried to thrash about, but with Alynn's arms wrapped around him and Brett clinging to his foot like a fisherman with an unruly catch, he was held immobile. Tarin shouted something in Latin that left Lukas shaking his head.

"Och, forgive me, Lord, fer teaching him those words." Lukas had both his hands around Tarin's foot to stop the bleeding. Alynn had never been more grateful that Lukas had farmer's hands, strong and gentle at the same time. After a few moments of holding pressure, Lukas wrapped Tarin's foot in a strip of linen cloth. "Well, that's all we can do, besides pray."

Drawing a deep breath, Tarin escaped Alynn's embrace and leaned back on his pillow. "When can I walk on it?" he asked.

"We're not sure," said Lukas, wiping his hands on his scapular. "At least a fortnight. Until then, there's a pair of crutches left over from when Alynn got frostbite. They ought to be yer size. Brett, go fetch them."

"You're stayin' in bed the rest of today, though," said Caitriona.

"But Mum—"

"Mind her, Tarin," said Rowan. He was leaning against the wall, shaking. "Jesus, Mary, and Joseph, will you stop puttin' the heart crossways in me?"

A familiar noise caught Alynn's attention; it was Elspeth babbling. Drostan was standing in the doorway with her, making sure everything was alright. As soon as she gave Tarin's hair an extra ruffling for good luck, Alynn took her daughter and melted into Drostan's arms. She realized she was trembling.

"Can you tell us what happened, Tarin?" Drostan asked.

"For faith's sake, lad, he just got an arrow pulled out of his foot. Leave him be." Caitriona had taken Alynn's place at the side of Tarin's bed and was cossetting him with all the tender love a mother could give. Tarin sat up, scooting away from Caitriona as best as he could.

"I saw Grima at the edge of the woods," he said. "He was wearin' Da's new plaid. He shot at us, and then I started chasing him. I almost had, him too! And then he shot me, and Alynn was five feet from him—"

"Good God," said Rowan.

"—I still say you should have gotten him!" Tarin said.

"Did you want your sister to get shot, too?" Drostan asked. "It's a miracle either of you didn't get killed, Tarin. You did the right thing. Both of you."

Tarin grew silent for a while, ignoring his mother as she tucked her arms more tightly around him. "I swear, though, if I see another kid at his da's funeral because I couldn't—"

"Would you rather see a man at his son's funeral?" Rowan snapped. Every eye in the room was on him; his voice shook with angry tears. "I swear, Tarin, if I have to bury another child—"

His voice broke. Hiding his face behind his sleeve, he turned and hurried from the room. Alynn tried to reach out to him, but he ducked past her. For a moment, the room was silent, except for the occasional cry from Rowan as he tried, unsuccessfully, to stop weeping. Caitriona buried her face in Tarin's hair. Tarin let her.

A moment passed before Drostan cleared his throat. "Tarin, you've handled all of this admirably. And even with your wound, you're bearing up like a real man. But your father's right. It's a father's job to die for his children, and not the other way around. And you very easily could have died today, Tarin. I saw Grima shoot an eider duck out of midair. It's a miracle he didn't—"

"Drostan." Caitriona's voice had a surprising edge to it as she drew Tarin's head close to her chest. He was shaking, finally yielding to her embrace. "Not now."

Lukas stirred. He had long since finished wrapping Tarin's foot and had been sitting so quietly he looked to be part of the furniture. "Well—if I may, I've found that the proper way to react to a close call is to thank God and take action. The next time—"

"We're not going to talk about Grima right now," said

Caitriona. "You can change the subject, or you can leave the room. And get Tarin a cup of tea while you're at it."

"I don't want any tea," said Tarin.

Forcing a worried smile onto her face, Caitriona tucked a strand of Tarin's hair behind his ear. "Do you want some mead? It'll help with the pain."

"I don't want anythin'. My stomach hurts."

"You're just frightened, Tarin," said Alynn. "Take some deep breaths."

"Can you help me?"

Alynn sat on the edge of Tarin's bed with Elspeth on her lap, and Tarin disentangled himself from Caitriona's arms. Alynn ran a hand up Tarin's back as he filled his lungs with air, then back down as he exhaled.

It was an old ritual they had developed back in Ireland. Tarin's toddler self had been prone to fits of fear after Caitriona's kidnapping by Viking slave traders. Alynn would hold him until his crying stopped, then "help" him breathe until he was relaxed. Normally, the ritual ended with a tickle-fight, but this time, Alynn gave Tarin a kiss on the head when she sensed he had calmed down. Tarin smiled.

"Thanks, Lynder."

"You're doing better now?"

Tarin nodded. Elspeth squealed her encouragement, then grabbed at the neckline of Alynn's dress. Sighing, Alynn stood, got Elspeth nursing, and went to stand next to Drostan again. He took her by the arm and led her to the hearth. They passed Rowan on their way; he was hurrying back to the sickroom, doubtless to convince himself that Tarin was going to be alright.

Drostan guided Alynn to a chair and sat across from her, scooting it up so that their knees were almost touching. "Are you alright?" he asked.

"So long as Tarin's alright, I am."

"What do you think?"

"Between everyone's prayers and Lukas's medicine—'tis a

chance he's got, a decent chance, but he could still get an infection and I'm still scared."

"What do you think about Grima, I mean? I think Tarin's got a decent chance too, but outside of praying, there's not much we can do for him. Grima's another story."

Alynn was silent for a moment; she stared at Elspeth as she nursed. "I don't know what to think," she said. "He gave us a warning shot before we started chasing him, he gave you a warning shot when we were at the beach together—when I saw him in the village, he shot at my shield like it was a target, like he wasn't aiming for me at all—but then I look at the way he killed Rothgeir, and 'tis almost like there's two people we're dealin' with."

Drostan set a hand on Alynn's knee. "Did Grima have a sword?"

"No."

"You're sure?"

"He's got a quiver at his hip. You can't wear a quiver and a sword."

"Yes, you can. I've seen dozens of men do it."

Alynn sighed. "In that case, I—I don't know. I don't think so, but—"

Drostan sighed. "Leave that aside for now. Did you notice anything else?"

Alynn thought for a moment. "Tarin would have outrun him," she said. "And Tarin's never won a footrace, except against me. Grima's slow."

"Well, we did see blood on that landing boat," said Drostan. "Maybe he's injured."

"He doesn't limp. And his arms seem to work fine." Alynn shifted her hold on Elspeth as she squirmed. "Dear heart, if you don't mind—"

Elspeth stared up at her mother with round, innocent eyes of celestial blue. And then she smiled impishly, milk spilling from the corners of her mouth, as she jabbed Alynn's ribs with a knee and grabbed her breast with sharp fingernails. Alynn held her breath until the pain went away.

She was distracted from her pain by a noise. It sounded as if a drunken caribou were trying to walk down the stairs. Alynn turned her head as far as it would go only to see Mercy stumbling out of the stairwell, tousle-haired and bleary-eyed from her nap.

"Where's Mammy?" Mercy asked.

"She's taking care of Tarin," said Alynn. "He hurt himself, but he's going to be alright. Are you still sleepy?"

"Yes." Mercy climbed into Alynn's lap and leaned her head on her chest, staring off into space. Alynn wished she'd go back to sleep, so she and Drostan could finish their conversation. Perhaps they could carry on regardless.

"Maybe Grima has some sort of heart beneath his cloak," said Alynn. "He might have something against killing women and children."

"I know for certain that Thrand the Infamous never had a problem with it. If Grima was ever truly in league with him, he'd probably share his master's morals. But still, that's a good thought. What does Elspeth say?"

"She's eatin', Da. She can't think while she's eatin'. What do you think, Mercy?"

"I want Mammy."

"Mammy's taking care of Tarin right now," said Alynn. "I'll snuggle you, though."

Mercy settled down. She stared at Elspeth as she nursed, then she stared at Drostan, and then she picked at her tiny fingernails. Finally, she was fully awake, and she climbed off Alynn's lap to pet a silver cat that had deposited itself in front of the fire. "He's name Teo-pus," said Mercy.

"Do you mean Theophilus?" Alynn asked.

"Yeah! He's Teo-pus. I be gentle." To demonstrate, Mercy knelt down and patted the cat's soft head. Theophilus mewed at Mercy, and Mercy mewed back. Alynn watched the two of them until Lukas came out of the sickroom, wiping his hands on his scapular. Tarin's blood had been long since scrubbed away, but Lukas kept wiping them. It was as if his hands were sleepwalking.

"How's Tarin?" Alynn asked.

"Resting. Bandaged up. He'll mend, in Jesus' name. He'll be alright." Theophilus approached Lukas and pawed at his skirts. Lukas stopped rubbing his hands on his scapular and let the cat jump into his arms. "Och, Theophilus. *Timere sum.*"

"Deydey!" said Mercy. "Up!"

Lukas kissed Theophilus, then traded him for Mercy. Theophilus didn't care.

Drostan stroked his beard, looking worriedly down the hallway, then at Alynn and Elspeth. "We need to get home," he said.

"What about Tarin?" Alynn asked.

"What about him?"

"Mum might need help takin' care of him."

"We'd appreciate yer company, my dear," said Lukas. Mercy was trying to flip upside-down in his arms, but he held her tightly, with an unnecessary and desperate determination. "More than anything, though, I want ye to be safe. Ye'll need to get home eventually, and I feel that now is the safest time fer ye to leave. Grima wouldn't dare show himself now. He knows we're angry at him."

"But Tarin—"

"He'll be fine," said Drostan, with that softness in his voice that could make her believe anything he said. "Your parents are some of the most devoted parents I've ever seen. Lukas is the best doctor in Orkney, and he's got Brett to help him. They'll stop at nothing to see him recover. Tarin could not be in better hands."

Drostan was right, of course. Caitriona would tend to Tarin with all the overbearing love her soul possessed, and Rowan would mask his fear with a smile he didn't mean and convince everyone else of a hope he himself didn't believe in. Beyond that, Lukas was undoubtedly the best doctor in Orkney. He drew from experience alongside his Greek medical texts, and he loved Tarin like a third parent. He would take better care of Tarin than he would of himself.

But still, Alynn was worried.

"Go say goodbye to him," said Drostan. "I'll saddle the horses."

"Be careful."

"Och, he won't come back to the monastery so soon. He's not that daft."

"Do ye want a bow?" Lukas asked, setting Mercy on the ground before she could flip out of his arms like a drunken court jester.

"I've my shield."

"Ye're sure?"

Did Alynn imagine it, or did Drostan turn a slight shade of pink? "I can't shoot."

Lukas seemed surprised, but he let Drostan leave for the stables without another word. Alynn hurried to the sickroom. True to Lukas's word, Tarin was resting quietly. Caitriona held his head in her lap and stroked his hair; his foot was propped up on pillows to ensure the bleeding didn't start up again. Alynn sat on the edge of his bed and kissed him. "You'll get better for me, won't you?" she asked.

Tarin opened one eye to glare at her. "You're worse than Mum."

"Promise me."

Tarin smiled, and Alynn embraced him. This moment was heaven, with Tarin and Elspeth both safe in her arms. Alynn kissed them both. Elspeth squiggled in disapproval.

"Do me a favor, Lynder, and catch this eejit." Tarin leaned back into Caitriona's lap again, and Caitriona resumed stroking his hair. "I got lucky. I don't want this to happen to anyone else."

"I promise, Tarin," said Alynn. She ruffled his hair for good luck. "We'll catch this eejit. We'll catch him."

May 2, A.D. 969—

Lord, have mercy. Tarin is wounded. Shot through the foot by the monster that prowls our island.

He handled the extraction surgery well. The bleeding was minimal, and the nerves appear to be undamaged as he can still move his toes and ankle. My main hope is that the skin doesn't heal more quickly than the inside of the foot, to prevent pus from collecting inside the wound. An infection is my greatest fear for Tarin at the moment, and only God can prevent it. If all else fails, I can amputate the foot.

Alynn was there to help Tarin through the surgery, and I know from experience that her touch is a beautiful anodyne. Still, he screamed. O, the screams! For half a moment I thought I was in the forest with my brothers being massacred around me. God bless Brett for bringing me back to reality.

I'm still shaken, though. About an hour after the surgery, I had an attack of madness the likes of which I haven't experienced in decades. All my old injuries hurt. My heart rate increased. I could taste and smell blood. Terror engulfed me to the point that I couldn't breathe properly, and I felt like either fainting or vomiting. Caitriona and Rowan, of course, didn't notice, as they were busy fretting over Tarin. Brett noticed and I yelled at him (Lord, forgive me!) to leave me alone. He knows. He knows I'm going mad again.

I don't know what to do. I don't know if I can take care of Tarin. I don't know if I should allow myself to be around Mercy or continue to conduct church services. I don't trust mys ———

Brett interrupted me and offered to pray for me. I'm feeling much better now. God was the one who healed my madness the first time. He'll take care of me again. I still haven't told Brett about my insanity, past or present. I'll pray. It might not be wise to confide such information to a pupil.

—L. McCamden

ELEVEN

Alynn had a plan. Step One—wait for Leif and Drostan to leave for work—had just been accomplished. Now for the hardest part. Step Two—leave Elspeth with Brynhilde.

The walk to the tailor's house had never seemed longer, and Alynn spent most of it encouraging herself. Brynhilde had two children of her own. She was Elspeth's godmother, for faith's sake. She was probably better with children than Alynn herself was. She could even nurse her if need be. But still, Alynn worried. Brynhilde's oldest son, Matthew, was three and a half. Toddlers could be violent, or clumsy, or they could play too rough. What if he hurt Elspeth?

Oh, precious Elspeth—she was asleep. In all the four and a half months of her life, Alynn had never left her. Sometimes, in the evenings, she would let Drostan hold her while she stepped outside to collect her sanity. Sometimes other people at church would hold her, of course. But that was never for longer than an hour, and Alynn was never more than a cry away.

Elspeth's face twitched in her sleep—perhaps she was dreaming. Alynn smiled. What did Elspeth dream about, she wondered? Eating? Being snuggled in just the right way? Her time in the womb, warm and cozy, with the constant sound of her mother's heartbeat to comfort her?

Alynn found herself at the tailor's door, and she knocked, only to find Brynhilde trying to comfort Matthew and Ragnar as they cried at the same time.

This was a bad day for Alynn's plan. She should reschedule it.

Brynhilde managed to smile. "It's wonderful, actually," she said. "Ragnar got into the stable and had a goat step on his foot, and Matthew's mad that he can't kill the goat and eat it for supper because it hurt his little brother."

"It's a bad goat," Matthew cried. "It's a bad goat!"

"Och, I don't think it's a bad goat." Alynn knelt so she could look him face to face. "Do you ever step on people's feet by accident?"

Matthew nodded.

"Well, I think the goat stepped on Ragnar's foot by accident. Goats aren't very smart, you know. They step on feet by accident all the time. Let's go see if the goat's sorry." Alynn took Matthew to the stable, made sure that the offending goat had apologized, and returned to find that Ragnar was mostly calm as well.

"Thank you," said Brynhilde. "So, what brings you here? Does Elspeth need a new dress already?"

"No, actually—I was hoping you could watch her for a while."

Brynhilde sighed, and Alynn immediately regretted her choice. What was she thinking? She couldn't leave her baby with a stranger. She'd be overlooked. The two boys were such handfuls, there was no way Brynhilde could watch her—

"Well, I need practice with three, anyway," said Brynhilde, setting a hand on her stomach. "This one started kicking yesterday."

"It did? Congratulations!" Alynn could say that with confidence now; she knew the feeling, and it was a beautiful one. "Now, Elspeth should sleep the whole hour, but if she wakes up, she'll be hungry. She's got a strong latch, so brace yourself."

"Alright."

"And if she starts crying, try singing to her. She likes Christmas music."

"Alynn, she'll be perfectly fine with me." Brynhilde took Elspeth from her mother's reluctant arms. "Go take a nap."

Alynn wanted to cry. She wanted to kiss Elspeth goodbye, or else scoop her up and take her home and cuddle her until she woke up. Instead, she squared her shoulders, thanked Brynhilde, and went home.

Her old sword belt was too small for her, so she borrowed Drostan's spare one. She took a shield and saddled Humility, and she was off cantering towards the forest before she could talk herself out of it.

Step Three of her plan was now underway. She would go to where she and Tarin had encountered Grima and try to track him. Fifteen minutes of cantering brought Alynn to the trail she and Tarin had made in their headlong rush. It was too narrow for Humility to comfortably traverse, so she tied her to a tree and continued on foot.

For a while, the trail was obvious. There were Tarin's footprints, and then her own, but where were Grima's? Perhaps they truly were dealing with a ghost.

Alynn kept walking. She came to a place where the grass was flattened in a broad circle—there was a knee-print, a drop of blood on a brown leaf. This was where Tarin had fallen. Alynn paused for a moment, fought back a rush of anger, and forged ahead.

She couldn't see Grima's footprints, but she could guess where he walked by following the path of least resistance. The occasional broken twig let her know that she was on the right path. There was a particular patch of mud that held a strange footprint—it was shaped like a bare foot, but the toes were indistinct. A person wearing socks, perhaps? Alynn kept walking.

She glanced towards the sun to get her bearings. She was

heading west, straight for the rocky beach where Grima, pre-sumably, was trying to convince everyone he was staying.

Just when Alynn considered giving up, she reached the beach. There was no tracking Grima over rocks, and no sign of a campfire or shelter in sight. Here, unencumbered by vegetation, Alynn could think.

But before she could think, she heard a voice. A child's voice.

Silently, Alynn drew her sword and readied her shield. She walked towards the voice. It seemed to be singing, but Alynn couldn't make out the words. Perhaps the child was singing in a language she wasn't familiar with—it sounded like a witch's incantation.

Suddenly, the melody changed, and the lyrics rang out in Norse:

> *It comes with the dark and it hunts in the night,*
> *Its two teeth are shining like knives in moonlight,*
> *Its bleeding eyes smile with evil delight.*
>
> *The monster will vanish, and out you will call*
> *For someone to help you, anyone at all,*
> *But they will not hear you, for you are too small.*
>
> *Let sleep come and bind you with fetters and chains,*
> *To dreams with no meaning may you be a slave,*
> *And when the dream fades, child, the fear will remain.*

Alynn stood frozen. As soon as the singing stopped, nothing—not the cracking of twigs or the rustling of grass or even the sound of breathing—reached Alynn's ears. All she heard was the rush of the ocean as it tumbled over rocks on the shore, and the occasional seabird swoop overhead. Alynn scanned her field of vision and saw nothing.

Wait—movement. There was a piece of fabric rustling in a tree. Alynn ran towards it, her heart hammering in her throat, and tried to poke it with her sword. It was too high up. And besides, it looked like a grey rag that had long outworn its use. A bird had probably picked it up to build a nest with, realized that it didn't want its children around such filth, and discarded it.

But there were no people. No Grima, no child.

Alynn's stomach twisted, and she ran with her sword still drawn. She didn't try to find her old path—it was too unfamiliar, too dangerous. Instead, she made for St. Anne's Monastery and decided to find her way back to Humility from there.

She was panting by the time she reached the clearing where St. Anne's Monastery stood. A small border of grass separated the woods from the fields where Lukas grew oats and barley. Alynn felt safe enough to slow her pace to a walk. She needed to catch her breath, to still the thundering of her heart and pacify the quaking in her legs.

There was another voice. Alynn froze for a moment, then sighed with relief when she realized it was only Lukas, singing hymns as he inspected his freshly-sprouted barley crops.

"Lukas!" she called.

The singing stopped, and Lukas looked up. Alynn ran towards him, making the mistake of walking on the plowed field. Lukas noticed and called out, "Don't step on the—!"

Alynn retraced her steps, careful not to disturb the growing barley, and walked briskly along the edge of the field until she caught up to Lukas. He took her into his arms. "What's wrong? It's not Elspeth, is it?"

"She's grand—I hope she's grand, she's with Brynhilde—but I just saw a ghost."

"Where?"

"Western shore."

Lukas mused for a bit, talking to himself in Latin and holding Alynn at arm's length so he could think. "Well," he said after a while, "the Bible doesn't specifically say that ghosts *don't* exist. Angels and demons, on the other hand—och, ye'd have known if ye were dealing wi' one of them. What did ye see?"

"I didn't see a blasted thing. It was a child's voice—probably a little girl, I couldn't quite tell—it was singing a song about nightmares. I looked for her. Couldn't find a single soul."

Lukas gazed at the sky. It was unusually bright and blue, with clouds like sheep wandering from horizon to horizon. "Did it speak Norse with a strange accent?" he asked.

"It spoke Norse, aye—'tis hard to judge accents when you're singin', though. I couldn't tell. But—I think it was singin' in a different language before it switched to Norse. It sounded like witchcraft."

Lukas laughed. "Och, thank God!"

Alynn raised an eyebrow. "What?"

"I'm not mad! Sabbath afore last—it was the same thing. I heard it, couldn't see it. I thought I imagined the whole thing. I thought I was going mad again. Och, thank God, I'm alright!" He was smiling far more than his usual half-smile, and his eyes held something like joy in them.

Alynn, however, found herself taking a step backwards away from Lukas. "What do you mean, going mad *again*?"

"I—some—when I was—" The smile was gone, the joy was gone, replaced with a drawn mouth and vacant eyes. Lukas took a deep breath. "I used to see things that weren't there. I'd rather not talk about it."

"After the massacre?" Alynn asked, trying to keep her voice soft and compassionate.

Lukas blinked twice in rapid succession, then nodded.

"Lukas, I've known you for years. If you were mad, I'd have noticed. As for the massacre—I'd be surprised if it didn't haunt you. You're not mad. I promise." Alynn, having assured herself she wasn't lying, took Lukas's hand in her own and squeezed it. He squeezed back.

"I said, I'd rather not talk about it. My burdens aren't yers to bear."

Alynn smiled at him. "There's nothing wrong with you."

"I'm glad ye think that."

"Och, I don't think that. I know it. Come, now. Back to this ghost. You're smarter than me. What do you think it is?"

Lukas thought for a moment. "If ye remember a word or two of the language it spoke, I can place it."

"I can't, I'm sorry."

"That's alright. Do ye remember what the Norse part was about?"

"It was a song about—nightmares and a monster with teeth and sleeping in chains." Alynn shivered just remembering it. "But 'tis not a ghost, though, right?"

"I suppose. Ye're shaking. Why don't ye have yer mum make some tea?"

"I'd love to, Lukas, but—I'm not supposed to be here. Drostan doesn't want me out of the house."

"I can't blame him. I'll ride home wi' ye, if it'll make ye feel safer."

Alynn smiled and slipped her hand into Lukas's. "I've got Jesus and a fast horse. You're a saint for offering, though. Do me a favor, and don't tell anyone I was here."

"Ye won't even see Tarin?"

"I wish I could, so badly. Is he alright?"

Lukas half-smiled. "He's angry at being cooped up. He reminds me of a stoat I tried to keep as a pet once. But he's a wee soldier, doesn't complain about the pain."

At least his spirits were up—that was half the battle, Alynn knew from her own experience with war wounds. It had been—how long, five years now?—since she'd been stabbed in the shoulder, and every once in a while, a phantom pain would twist her muscles in knots. Especially if she'd been holding Elspeth in her left arm all day. She was getting too big.

"Elspeth's probably missing me," said Alynn. "I wish I could stay and visit, though."

"Ye shouldn't have to do all the traveling, my dear." Lukas glanced at the forest. "But I've got the lads, and the farm, and sermons to prepare fer, and the woods aren't safe fer anyone right now. Ye're sure ye don't want me to see ye home?"

"I'm alright, I promise—"

Lukas grabbed her arm, his eyes fixed on a nearby strand of trees. "Did ye hear that?"

Alynn held her breath and listened. There it was—a definite rustling in the bushes.

"Is it—"

"Whisht. Get down." Drawing his knife, Lukas pulled Alynn behind him, shielding her from whatever lurked in the dark woods. Alynn started praying.

Oh, God. Help us, God.

The bushes rustled again, and a pair of ravens took flight. After that, all was silent. Lukas breathed a silent sigh of relief and sheathed his knife again. "Blasted birds. Ye didn't make that much noise."

Alynn shivered despite the unusual warmth of the day. "I need to go home," she said. "I need Elspeth."

Lukas drew her into a tight hug. "Godspeed, and be safe."

Alynn went on her way, comforted by Lukas's presence and warned again by his voice not to step on the barley.

She found Humility quickly enough and got home in record time. She tried to hide all evidence of her foray before she picked Elspeth up. Humility was unsaddled and brushed and put in her stall. Alynn put her sword and shield away and brushed the dirt from her boots and hem. Then she hurried to Brynhilde's house, only to hear Elspeth screaming from ten yards down the street.

She didn't bother knocking. She barged into the tailor's house, spotted Elspeth, and took the red and screaming babe into her arms. "What's wrong? What happened?" she demanded. Alynn could usually tell what Elspeth meant when she cried. She had a hungry cry, a lonely cry, and a cry that meant she needed her diaper changed. Alynn had never heard this cry before. Elspeth was furious.

Brynhilde seemed near tears herself. "She woke up ten minutes ago. She won't nurse, and I tried talking and singing to her, like you said—her teeth are probably hurting her, is the only thing I can think of."

Alynn pressed Elspeth to her chest and started swaying. "Whisht, love! Mammy's back, Mammy's got you, dear heart. Don't cry, love, don't cry."

Elspeth lifted her head, looked at her mother with pure grief in her eyes, and stopped crying. Alynn wiped her tears away and kissed her and nestled her close to her heart. Slowly, quietly, she started to sing a lullaby. Elspeth lay quietly, sucking her fingers.

Alynn looked up at Brynhilde. "I'm so sorry," she said as soon as the first verse of the song was over.

"Don't be. She just wanted her mother."

Brynhilde was right. Elspeth had wanted *her*. It was a strange feeling—giddiness, almost—that crept into Alynn's heart. Elspeth really did love her!

"Did you want yer mammy?" Alynn asked the sweet bundle that warmed her chest. "Och, my sweet baby. I love you, Elspeth. I love you more than anything else in the whole, wide world." She kissed Elspeth's soft little head, and the baby smiled.

Brynhilde summoned Ragnar to her arms. He came, leaning his head against his mother's shoulder. "I miss those days," she said. "When the boys were little. It's hard when they need you for everything, but still—it's beautiful."

Alynn took a deep breath. Maggie would be coming over at noon to help with the housework, and Alynn wanted to at least pretend she'd been competent on her own. So she thanked Brynhilde, ruffled Matthew's hair, and went home.

As much as Alynn wanted to get something done, she needed to rest after her adventures. More than that, she needed to process what she'd seen on the western shore. Elspeth was hungry anyway, so Alynn leaned against a pillar and closed her eyes. It hadn't been Grima singing. That much was certain. So who—or what—was it? Lukas said that ghosts weren't real. It was probably just a child from the village—but that didn't explain the strange language, nor the fact that Alynn had been unable to find them.

Maybe Grima wasn't alone. Maybe Grima had a child of his own, or maybe he had washed ashore with a young slave or deckhand. Maybe it was one of Thrand's children. Captain McMahon had mentioned their existence, but not their ages. Thrand sounded like the type of person to bring an eleven-year-old on a raid.

Before Alynn knew it, Elspeth had fallen asleep at her breast. Alynn felt like nodding off herself, but it was Monday, so she had to start brewing the small ale.

She busied herself so she wouldn't have to think about the ghost. So, taking heather, hops, and bloodwort, along with a dash of seaweed, Alynn went to the outbuilding that was used specifically for brewing small ale. While she waited for the water to boil, she swept the rushes off the floor and replaced them with new ones. While she waited for the brew to steep, she mended a pair of Leif's trousers.

Exhaustion plagued her. Her limbs moved slowly; her mind felt waterlogged. Elspeth, who was sleeping outside in her cradle (a Norse custom that Alynn followed, as it gave her the illusion of freedom for a couple of hours every day), decided to wake up from her nap after only forty-five minutes. Sighing, Alynn took her into the house and lay down with her on her chest.

Now, with nothing to occupy her mind, the fear crept in. The child's voice haunted her, permeating every thought and projecting itself through every distraction she threw at it. Finally, she gave into it.

Its two teeth are shining and sharp as a knife….

The teeth that appeared in Alynn's imagination were nowhere near shining. They were dyed an ethereal dark blue, and they were contorted into a hideous, dripping smile.

Its bleeding eyes smile with evil delight…

Bleeding eyes. Those, Alynn saw. Or rather one eye, soulless, blood slipping down onto a helmet like red tears.

Those tears seemed so strange coupled with the dark smile. As if crying with joy, or else smiling with hatred.

Then the eye stopped bleeding, and the teeth shone crooked and rotten yet untouched by the blue dye. Alynn was a child again. She saw the haunting smile and the gleaming eyes. She heard her mother's screams as the monster dragged her away, fighting and crying, a rough fist grabbing her hair. The hand did not belong to any human. It belonged to a formless body that consisted of nothing but hands and eyes and crooked teeth. And then the creature turned, flourishing a dark hooded cloak, with a quiver at its waist.

And then Alynn turned around, and she saw a cradle.

As she approached it, something less than a thought—something deeper, more urgent—kept telling her to stop. She should get someone, anyone, her father, her Aunt Sorcha, the neighbors, the priest from St. Joseph's. There was something wrong. It was too quiet, too still. But Alynn approached the cradle anyway.

At first, she was relieved. Britta was just asleep. But the longer Alynn looked, the more things she noticed that weren't right. Her skin was white. Her fingers weren't wiggling as usual. She was quiet and motionless and she wasn't white at all, she was grey, and when Alynn reached out to touch her tiny hand, it was cold as ice and stiff like the wings of a dead bird.

Alynn awoke with a start. Elspeth was lying on top of her, quiet and motionless. "Och, Jesus," Alynn prayed, shaking Elspeth as vigorously as she dared. "Wake her up, Jesus. Wake up, my heart."

Elspeth started crying, and Alynn cried along with her. She held her close and kissed her and nestled Elspeth's soft, pudgy cheek against her own. Elspeth grabbed a few stray strands of Alynn's hair and tugged on them with uncanny strength. Alynn smiled before disentangling herself.

"I love you, Elspeth."

Elspeth's cries relaxed into disgruntled fussing. She pushed herself away from Alynn's chest so the world could see her angry face. It succeeded in making Alynn smile through her tears and kiss her daughter again.

"I love you more than anything in the whole, wide world. You promise me, now—promise me you're not going anywhere. Promise you'll stay with Mammy. You like me, don't you?"

Elspeth smacked Alynn in the mouth with a tiny hand.

"Does that mean no?"

Elspeth grabbed at Alynn's cheeks. Alynn held her closer to her face; Elspeth tried to eat her nose.

"Is that a kiss, love? Och, I get it. You don't like Mammy, you love Mammy? Is that it? Is that what you're tryin' to tell me, my wee heart?"

Elspeth let go of Alynn's nose and shrieked.

"Thank you, Elspeth. Mammy knows you love her. And I love you too, my wee darling. Mammy loves you, too."

Elspeth opened her mouth as wide as it could possibly go and dove for Alynn's nose again. This time, Alynn laughed, and her smile didn't disappear when the front door opened.

"What are ye—"

"She's got my nose, Maggie!"

"Take it back!"

"She can keep it." Alynn's voice was skewed, and it made Maggie laugh.

"Isn't this supposed to be the other way around?" Maggie found a kettle of tea that Alynn forgot she made and poured two cups of it. "What needs done?"

Alynn carefully moved Elspeth's mouth from her nose to her breast. "I've small ale out back that needs checked on, thanks. Is it noon already?"

"A bit past. Einar wet his trousers, I had to help clean him up. I was mad, but then he gave me a hug and said he loved me, and—well—" Maggie grinned, plopping down next to Alynn and handing her a mug of tea. "I don't know what to think of that wee twit. He breaks into the pantry and eats himself sick, scares the hens out of laying, but then, when he hugs ye like that—I can't help but love him, ye know?"

"I know." Alynn kissed Elspeth's hand. "He's three, right?"

"Aye."

"He'll settle down if you raise him right."

Maggie looked at Alynn a bit more intently and raised an eyebrow. "Are ye alright?"

"Why wouldn't I be?"

"There's circles around yer eyes, and ye're white as a washed sheep."

"I'm Irish. We all look like this. And besides, with Elspeth teething, I only got three hours of sleep last night. I'm knackered."

Maggie reached down and picked a leaf off Alynn's skirt. Alynn bit her lip. *Please, Maggie,* she pleaded internally. *Please don't ask questions, please don't tell Drostan—*

"Dangerous times to be taking a walk," Maggie said.

"I was careful."

Alynn tried to gauge her friend's facial expressions. Was she accusing? Worried? Supportive? She was too tired to tell. But Maggie had a grin in her eyes as she picked up the carding combs, and she began another narrative of how wild her nieces and nephews were. As soon as Elspeth had nursed herself to sleep, Alynn laid her in her cradle, kissed her, and found her spindle. Work always got done faster when Maggie talked.

TWELVE

"Alynn, are you with us?"

Alynn shook herself. Aye, she was awake. Barely.

"She gave the chicken scraps to Humility," said Leif with a chuckle. "Go on to bed, darling. This isn't a full council meeting anyway."

Sigmund yawned, and then Drostan yawned, and then Alynn yawned so hard she nearly dislocated her jaw. But she shook herself and drew a cold breath into her lungs. "I'm grand. What were we—"

"I just asked if ye've noticed anything missing around the house," said Drostan.

Alynn shook her head. "I haven't, but that doesn't mean anything. I'm surprised I haven't misplaced the baby yet. And if I do, I'll be too tired to notice for half an hour."

"Did Humility eat the chicken scraps?" Sigmund asked.

Leif settled back against a pillar. "She picked the carrots out and left the rest."

Drostan checked a piece of birchbark with runes carved into it. "Horik the fishmonger says he's missing five pounds of stockfish. Ulla the merchant's wife says she's missing half a week's worth of small ale. There's other villagers missing cloakpins, bracelets, meat, milk, and some clothes."

"Any chance they blew off the clothesline?" Sigmund asked.

"If it blows off a clothesline, it winds up in a bush somewhere. If you can't find it, 'tis because someone stole it." Alynn was beginning to wish she'd taken Leif's advice and gone to bed.

Drostan rubbed his eyes. "So we come to the conclusion that Grima's taken everything?"

"Most of it makes sense," said Sigmund. "The ale, the food, all that is to keep Grima alive. But what about the bracelets?"

"He's probably stockpiling valuables and planning to leave the island," said Leif.

"How?" Alynn asked. "He won't steal a ship, will he?"

"Not one of our ships," said Drostan. "I've got Folkvard and Havard guarding the harbor."

"Foolproof system you've got there," said Sigmund drily. "Suppose he tries to leave on a trader's ship?"

Drostan snapped his fingers. "Of course. We'll think Grima's with the merchants, and they'll think he's one of us. When's the next merchant ship due in?"

"We should be getting the *Hraustligr* from Hrafney sometime in the next two or three weeks," Leif said. "We'll warn them not to take on any passengers."

"Grima could try to stow away," said Alynn.

"Merchants have better security than that," said Drostan. "I'll tell everyone to keep an eye out anyway. And we need to make sure that everyone keeps reporting the things that go missing. Even if it's just food. Now, let's call it a night. I'm going to bed."

"Thanks for coming by, Sigmund," said Leif. He shook Sigmund's hand, and so did Drostan, but Alynn's arms were full, so she simply nodded as he left. Drostan wasted no time in pulling off his tunic, then his boots, then unwinding his winingas from around his feet and lower legs. Leif followed suit except that he took off his undershift too. Alynn, not wanting to see Leif in all his hairy, tattooed glory, turned to lay a sleeping Elspeth in the bedcloset. Then she took off her spit-up-covered frock and her slobbery dress before crawling gratefully into bed herself.

Drostan crawled into the bed next to her and planted a kiss on her forehead. "Did you brush your hair?" he asked.

"No. I just want sleep."

"Fair enough, love. If I wake up early enough, I'll help you with it in the morning." Alynn hardly heard him. She was already half asleep.

The full moon cast a strange, pale light on the village. Soft wind rustled the sprouts in the vegetable gardens. The fog seemed to glow in the moonlight. A single bird called out; a dog barked at it.

At the edge of the woods crouched a hooded figure, watching the dark world as it settled into coolness and stillness and sleep. When he was sure that everyone in the village was asleep, Grima adjusted his mask and crept forward.

He felt sick. Part of it, he knew, was because he was hungry and thirsty and physically exhausted. His head spun and ached so that he could hardly walk in a straight line. Every so often, he stumbled like a drunken sailor. But there was no use in dwelling on those things. Mistress was waiting, and if he hurried up, he could get a few hours of sleep.

Quietly, Grima walked between the rows of houses. There was the house he'd been to yesterday—that house, the day, before—there. Perfect. A house he had not yet entered. Had the other houses noticed the things he'd already stolen? The food, the cloak pins, the lamps and the whale oil to go with them. Some of it, surely.

What about the monastery? They'd missed the cloak, of course. But the lady probably hadn't noticed the missing food—or was the lady even in charge of the food? What was a lady doing at a monastery, anyway? It probably had something to do with the boy who'd chased him a few days ago. They had the same green eyes.

Grima approached the door and, quiet as a rabbit hiding from a fox, took an arrow from his quiver. He reached the shaft of the arrow through the crack between the door and the doorframe, easily lifting the latch. The door creaked open too loudly for Grima's comfort, but everyone inside was snoring contentedly.

Grima set one foot over the threshold. No one seemed to notice him. He sneaked into the house, then shut the door silently behind him so no one would wake up cold. Now. Which way to the pantry?

Grima took a few stockfish. A few apples. A kitchen knife. He rearranged the winninga he'd wrapped around his face for a mask so that his mouth was free, then ate a few spoonsful of skyr—

Something stirred behind him. Grima froze, then made himself as small as possible, hoping to disappear into the shadows. He listened closely. The disturbance came from a little boy, asleep in bed with his brother and mother. Such dark red curls, the mother had. A lovely sight. Grima waited a moment, then began to stuff some cheese into the pouch folded into his tunic. The boy was only moving in his sleep.

"Mum?"

Grima froze. He'd been mistaken.

The mother replied in Gaelic, a language Grima knew only a few words of. "What is it?"

"I had a—" The boy used a word Grima didn't know.

"About Grima again?"

"Yes."

The mother spoke comfortingly, but Grima was too nervous to attempt deciphering her speech. His only movement was to fix the winninga so that it covered his mouth. It was hard for him to breathe through the woolen fabric, and he wanted to sneeze, but he held his breath and scrunched his eyes shut until everything was quiet again. Then, slowly, Grima crept towards the door, trying to crush the rushes as softly as possible under his bare feet.

"Mum! Something's here!"

The mother rose and struck up the fire. It was too late for Grima to hide; he froze, his last hope that the woman would mistake him for a pile of laundry. Instead, she screamed.

The family was startled awake. A man leapt out of bed, stark naked, and grabbed the axe that hung above his bed. Grima's eyes darted around the room, and he grabbed the first thing he could lay his hand on—a piece of cheese—and threw it at the naked man. Then, knowing the cheese wouldn't hold him for long, he took a burning stick from the fire and threw it, too.

The man dodged the flaming stick, but it landed in the dry rushes that covered the floor. The house filled with smoke. Somewhere, a baby started crying. A cry of "Fire!" was raised, and Grima was forgotten as people of various ages and states of undress leapt out of bed. Grima was the first out the door, and he made it to the edge of the wood before he stopped to catch his breath and grab the stockfish that had fallen out of his pouch.

Instead of going farther into the woods, though, he paused and looked back at the mess he'd made. A little boy was running from longhouse to longhouse, banging on doors and rousing neighbors to come help. The smoke from the house was beginning to compete with the fog for the right to cloud the sky.

Grima took a step towards the village, his conscience telling him to go back and help. But his self-preservation—or selfishness, he couldn't tell—got the better of him. If he showed himself, they'd have his head. So slowly, quietly, Grima disappeared into the forest.

"Lynder, wake up."

"Unless something's wrong with Elspeth, I swear, I will strangle you—"

"Nora McKenzie's house in on fire." Drostan was tugging on his trousers. Leif was already out the door. "Stay here, watch for Grima. He probably set the fire as a diversion." He raced out the door, and foolishly, Alynn grabbed Elspeth and went with them.

Wattle-and-daub construction wasn't known for its fire resistance. One of the walls and the sod roof were engulfed in flames. A bucket brigade had formed, and Drostan took his place at the well. Leif searched the crowd until he found a frantic Nora, screaming her sons' names.

Leif, who was a foot taller than Nora, easily found Olvir, the older son. Nora ran to him and held him, shaking with relief. "Och, Olvir, thank God! Are ye hurt? Turn around—och, ye're alright, where's yer brother?"

"He went back inside," Olvir said. "He wanted to save the cat!"

Nora screamed and held Olvir even closer. Leif glanced at the house, kissed Nora, and ran inside.

Alynn heard herself scream. She ran towards the fire, but Elspeth started coughing, so she forced herself away from the smoke. "Oh, God," she breathed, "bring him out—please, Jesus, bring him back out—"

Leif came out, with a little boy tossed over his shoulder.

"Och, thank God," Alynn said, holding Elspeth closer to her chest.

Nora snatched her son and carried him farther away from the smoke, crying and brushing his hair. Alynn, not knowing what else to do, joined them. Nora was rubbing Slodi's back and chest, Olvir watching on with terror in his eyes. Leif was on his hands and knees, coughing violently. His face was darkened with smoke, his tunic was singed, and his hair was grey with ash. He clutched his shoulder. A hole had been burned in his sleeve.

"Are you alright, Father?" Alynn asked. Leif was coughing too hard to respond, but he nodded. Alynn set Elspeth beside him and stole some water from the bucket brigade into her cupped hands. Leif drank it eagerly.

"Thanks," Leif gasped. He looked up at her with red and smoke-stung eyes before gazing again at Nora and her boys. Slodi was breathing more easily now. Nora had checked him head to toe and found nothing amiss, and now she was pressing his head to her chest and kissing him and thanking God for him. She finally noticed the kitten in his arms.

"Slodi—we can get another cat, love. I can't get another little boy. Don't ye dare do that again, ye hear me?"

"Aye, Mum," said Slodi, his voice rough and raw with smoke.

"Good lad." Nora kissed him again then looked up at Leif. A smile came to her tear-glistening eyes. "Leif, I can't thank ye enough."

Leif coughed again, wiped the smoke out of his eyes, and set both hands on Nora's shoulders. "Nora?" he said.

"Aye?"

"Life's shorter than we think it is. I'm done waiting if you are." He moved a hand to cup her jaw and brush the tendrils of hair that escaped her braid. "Will you marry me?"

Nora's eyes grew wide, and her hand flew to her mouth. Slodi lifted his head and asked, "Do I get a new da?"

Nodding, Nora buried her hand in Leif's hair and all but crawled into his lap, kissing him deeply. They kissed until Leif pulled away to cough again, and Nora held him until he caught his breath. Then she noticed his sleeve.

"Leif, ye're hurt."

"I know. It's not bad."

"Do ye want me to—"

"It's alright. I'll mend." Leif shivered, and Nora nestled closer to him, drawing Slodi closer to her heart. And they stayed there, coughing and dabbing smoke out of moist red eyes and not caring about any of it, because they had each other.

Elspeth coughed, so Alynn took her farther away from the smoke. She watched from a distance as some people tossed water onto the flames and others beat the fire away with wet blankets and tunics. Slowly, the flames disappeared, the smoke thickened, and it was announced that the fire had been put out.

Drostan emerged from the smoke, coughing and shaking his arms. He had been drawing water for the bucket brigade. Alynn ran to him, and he held her and Elspeth and kissed them both. His hands were shaking as he led Alynn away from the smoke.

"You're alright?" he asked.

"We're fine. Your father went in the house to save Slodi, he's breathed in some smoke, but he'll be alright."

"Anyone else hurt? What about Slodi?"

"He's young, he'll mend."

Drostan sighed, looking up at the smoke-clouded sky. "I spoke with Hrafnkell. He says Grima was raiding his pantry. Threw a firebrand and him and started this whole mess."

Alynn clutched Elspeth tighter to her chest. "What do we do?"

"For one, we need to check our house, make sure nothing got stolen. I told you to stay home and watch for Grima, Lynder. Why can't you listen to reason?"

"I do listen to reason. Fires spread, and we're safer outside than inside. Besides, I'm in no state to handle Grima right now. I thought you wanted me safe."

Drostan sighed. "I want this cur's head. Where's my father? I can't clean this mess up alone."

"Och, I should have mentioned. He proposed to Nora."

"Finally." Drostan scanned the crowd until he spotted Leif, Nora, and the boys. He kept an arm around Alynn as he navigated the crowd, but broke into a run and left her behind when he saw Leif. "Father! Your arm!"

"I'm alright. I'm alright." Leif accepted Drostan's hand to help him stand, then clapped him heartily on the shoulder.

"How's Slodi?" Drostan asked.

"I'm good." Slodi's voice was more like itself now, and he stood easily. The kitten was still cradled in his arms. "I think

Mr. Kitty's scared, though."

"Where are we going to sleep tonight?" Olvir asked.

"You'll stay at our house," said Leif. "Drostan, by the way—"

"You're marrying Nora. Alynn told me. Took you long enough to ask her. What about everyone else?"

"Our house is big enough, isn't it?" Leif asked. "Make the announcement. I've smoke in my lungs."

"Everyone! Hrafnkell's kin!" Drostan shouted. The general clamor calmed down, and every eye on was on Drostan. He seemed not to notice. "Hrafnkell's family will be spending the rest of the night with us. Everyone else, thank you for your help, you're free to return to your homes." Drostan cleared his throat, took Elspeth in one arm and set his other around Alynn's waist, and led Nora's family back to the house.

As far as Norse households went, Nora's was of a moderate size. Her late husband Svan had two brothers who shared the house, along with their wives and children and one elderly uncle who spent most of his time drinking and telling stories. All in all, there were fifteen extra people who crowded into Alynn and Drostan's house. Alynn set Elspeth in her cradle and scurried about finding spare pillows and bedclothes and they were out of blankets, could someone use Leif's cloak instead? Finally, everyone was settled, three and four people to a section of bench that counted as a bed.

Alynn was exhausted. Sheer willpower kept her from collapsing like a toy castle of twigs in a hurricane, and just as she was about to crawl into bed, Elspeth started crying. She wanted a midnight snack. Of course.

A soft noise barely caught Alynn's attention as she picked Elspeth up out of her cradle. It was Hrafnkell's wife Gudrun, crossing the room with her one-year-old at her breast. "I'll nurse her for you," she said. "I won't be able to sleep anyway."

"I don't mean to—"

"If you'd rather I not, I understand. It's just—you're so kind to put us up here. It means so much to us. I want to thank you."

Alynn could see Gudrun smile in the soft light, and she kissed Elspeth before setting her in her arms. "Thank you."

"Thank you, Lady Alynn. Sleep well."

Gratefully, Alynn returned to bed. At first, she was worried that Leif, who was sharing the bedcloset with them, would keep her up with his snoring. But he didn't. She was asleep the moment her head hit the pillow, and she didn't awake until full light.

By some miracle, Alynn made herself look presentable before most of the guests were awake. Drostan helped her brush her hair—it took four hands and two combs sometimes, since it was thick and wavy and often spent several days in the same plait—and she swept it into a crown braid and covered it with her embroidered coif. She donned her dress and her frock and was just putting on her belt when she realized she hadn't seen Elspeth all night.

A moment of panic overtook her before Alynn realized that Elspeth was safe in her cradle, her invisible eyebrows knit in concentration. Alynn stroked Elspeth's downy hair. "Good morning, my dear heart," she said. "Did you have a good night's sleep?"

Elspeth grunted.

"Are you making a poo for Mammy to clean up first thing this morning? You know I've got guests to make breakfast for."

Elspeth clearly didn't care.

"Well, Mammy will give you a few minutes to finish up, alright? Oh, look, Elspeth! There's Afi!" Elspeth turned her head so she could watch Leif climb awkwardly out of the bedcloset. "Say good morning, Afi!"

Elspeth squealed.

Leif stretched. "Good morning to you too, Elspeth."

"Father, can you change her?"

"No."

"Please? I've eighteen people to make breakfast for, and

besides, you took up half the bed last night." Alynn looked at the kettle and started doing math in her head. She'd need six times the amount of stirabout she normally made. Fortunately, it looked like she'd have help. Nora was already up and dressed and carrying two buckets of water through the back door.

"My lads and I are at yer disposal, Alynn," she said. "Slodi especially."

"Why Slodi especially?"

Nora sighed. "It breaks my heart—wi' Olvir being apprenticed to his uncle and all, he's staying at the auld house after Leif and I get married. Assuming we get it fixed up again. The roof and the front wall both think the floor looks like a mighty fine place to lie for a bit."

"You'll have neighbors pitch in to help, and I'm sure Leif will, too. It wouldn't surprise me if Drostan took off work and had Folkvard and Havard replace the beams."

Alynn took a sack of oats from the cupboard and dumped what she thought looked like enough into the pot. Nora added a few more handfuls. "I hope ye're right, hen. What did they do wi' our goats? We'll need their milk. I'll ask Hrafnkell."

"We have milk."

"Enough fer everyone?"

"We'll make do. Besides, Leif won't drink any, and I don't need it, either."

"Whisht, ye're a nursing mum, of course ye need milk. Hrafnkell, wake up. Where's the goats?"

Hrafnkell woke up with a start and groaned. "Starboard aft."

"Our goats, you simpleton." Nora spoke Norse better than Hrafnkell spoke Gaelic, so she switched languages. "Are they here or back at the house? We need the milk."

"Our house. The stable didn't burn." He roused himself and slipped his tunic over his head, then nudged the two men he'd shared the bed with. "Sinfiotli. Uncle Ottar. It's morning."

Hrafnkell's brother woke up, but the uncle snored all the louder, and the two men had no reservations about leaving him be. They took Olvir and the two other oldest children, promised to return for breakfast, and left to start reconstructing their house.

From that moment on, everything was a rapid blur. Children were everywhere, getting dressed and brushing their hair, or else letting someone else brush it for them, and Nora and Gudrun and their sister-in-law seemed oddly adept at controlling the chaos. Alynn found herself in charge and barking orders. "Alright, if someone could fetch the table down from the loft—no, lass, you'll hurt yourself, we need someone bigger—Drostan, love, fetch the table. You know what you can do, my heart? There's some stools in the loft that you can get, as soon as Chief Drostan comes back with the table. Aye, your brother can help you. How many stools do we have up there? Four? Five—thank God. I hope that's enough."

She said half of this while changing a crying Elspeth, then nursed her while stirring the stirabout. "Leif, have you changed the bandage on your arm?"

"Not yet."

Alynn sighed. "We need Lukas to take a look at it. Are the woods safe?"

"No one needs to get Lukas," said Leif. "I'm fine."

"Father—"

"Don't you argue with me, Alynn." The tone in Leif's voice made Alynn drop the subject, but Nora was less easily daunted. She handed her spoons to her niece and tried to pull Leif's sleeve up to inspect. He pulled away from her.

"How bad is it?" she asked.

"I've seen worse."

"That doesn't mean anything. Let me look at it."

"Nora—"

Nora didn't let him argue. She took him by the wrist, bade him sit down, and stripped him down to his trousers. Leif gave a strange cry as she unwrapped the bandage; Nora winced. "Deep breaths, love. Where's...Astrid. Go fetch us some water."

Alynn had experienced her fair share of burns from working in the kitchen. She took some butter from the cupboard and was prepared to rub it on Leif's arm, but when she saw how large and red and blister-filled the burn was, she turned around and pretended she'd never thought of such a suggestion.

"Och, this isn't bad at all, Leif."

"It hurts."

"I'm sure it does. But ye'll mend quickly, I'm sure of it." She kept a tender hand on his shoulder while inspecting the wound further. "Ye saved my son's life, and I can't thank ye enough."

"It's what any man would have done."

"Any good man, perhaps. And the world's running out of those." She kissed his cheek, and he smiled.

"Miss Alynn," a small voice interrupted, "do we have any more bowls?"

"I know we're short a few," Alynn said. "How many do we have?"

"Nine. So we need nine more, right?"

"We can all just eat out of the pot," said Leif.

Alynn was tempted to agree, but it would hardly reflect well on her abilities as a hostess. "The children can," she decided. "They'll have fun."

At least she hoped they would. When the time came for breakfast, the children proved her right. Their mothers probably disagreed as they wiped oats from their toddler's faces. But Caitriona had grown up eating straight out of the pot on a regular basis, and she'd used the same practice once or twice on her own children.

Just as Alynn was preparing to wash the many dishes, Lukas appeared out of nowhere. The children flocked to him before Alynn could so much as ask him how he knew to come, and he spent a good ten minutes holding the little ones and listening as they took turns telling him about what had happened last night. A clap of thunder sounded and it started to rain, but not one of the children seemed uneasy.

"And God protected all of you? No one got hurt?" Lukas

asked, letting a five-year-old squirm out of his arms and scooping up her three-year-old cousin who stood with his arms raised.

"We're good!" said the five-year-old.

"Then let's thank Jesus for keeping us safe. Ready?"

"Thank You, Jesus, for keeping us safe," the children said in unison.

"Very good. Now, someone tell me where Mr. Leif is."

"He's feeding the horsies and the chickies and the piggies," said the three-year-old.

"And the sheep," said a six-year-old.

The three-year-old nodded. "Yes. The sheeps too." He pointed to the door that led to the stable. "He's that way."

"Good! Who wants to fetch him for me?"

All the little ones ran into the stable, clamoring for Mr. Leif to come inside. Lukas chuckled and glanced up at Alynn. "Sigmund came and got me. Poor lad, the woods frightened him out of his wits."

Alynn smiled and patted her hands dry on her frock so she could hug him. "How's Tarin doing?"

"Well enough. No infection, praise God. We found the crutches ye used when ye got frostbite, and he's hopping around just fine. He's a good bit shorter than ye were at his age."

"Girls grow faster than boys. That's normal. Have you had breakfast?"

Lukas eyed the few bites of stirabout that the children had left in the pot and took a spoon out of the washbasin, drying it on his scapular. "Aye, but there's nay sense in letting this go to waste. Sigmund said that Grima burned Nora's house down?"

"Well—it didn't burn completely down. Leif burned his arm getting Slodi out of it, and then he asked Nora for her hand in marriage. You're mostly here to look at his arm."

Leif came inside just as Lukas was hurriedly shoveling the last two bites of stirabout into his mouth. He mumbled something with his mouth full that no one could understand, then paused and swallowed and repeated himself. "Alynn says ye're a hero."

Leif grinned. "Just keeping my future stepson safe."

"Och, congratulations." Lukas fished around in his satchel until he found a small wooden jar. "Another Scotswoman. I'm sure Elder Steingrim is turning in his grave."

"Good. He deserves it."

Before Lukas could inspect Leif's burned arm, Drostan came inside with Sigmund and Hrafnkell. They were damp from the sudden rain, and Drostan and Hrafnkell were covered in ash and smelled of smoke. "Thanks for coming," Drostan said, setting a map on the table.

"Of course," said Lukas.

"Have a seat."

"Are we—" Lukas groaned. "Och, not another council meeting—"

"I thought you liked them," Alynn scolded.

"Once or twice a month, aye! This is thrice in one week!"

"I'll let you hold Elspeth," said Alynn. She took Elspeth from where she'd been placed on the sleeping bench to practice rolling over and set her carefully in Lukas's arms. He set a kiss on her soft little head, and she smiled and squealed.

"Good morning, my wee darling," he said.

Elspeth smiled harder, showing the tiny tooth poking through her lower gums. Alynn's heart melted. "She loves the sound of yer voice," she said.

Lukas gave an honored smile. "Do ye like listening to Deydey talk?"

Elspeth babbled.

"Och, ye're a sweet wee thing. Deydey loves ye, Elspeth."

Elspeth rested her head against Lukas's shoulder, and he wrapped her in his arms with all the love a grandfather could give. Drostan smiled. "Well, let's go ahead and get started before Elspeth distracts the rest of us," he said. "Hrafnkell, if you could tell everyone what you saw last night."

"Slodi saw him first," Hrafnkell said as everyone sat down. "It all happened rather quickly. I heard the lad scream, I woke up, and there he was, crouched over by the cupboard."

"Did you see that he'd stolen anything?" Sigmund asked.

"I think there was a pouch folded into his cloak that he'd put things in."

Lukas kissed Elspeth. "Rowan wears a cloak of the same make. It's very versatile. All he'd need is a few cloakpins, and Rowan's missing two from the smithy."

"Several people from the village are missing some, too," said Sigmund.

"Did you notice anything about his physical appearance?" Leif asked.

"He was—short. Scrawny. And he wore a mask. All but his eyes were covered."

Alynn looked from Drostan to Lukas to Leif; they all wore the same nervous expression. "Are you *sure* this isn't a *draugr*?" Sigmund asked.

"They aren't real, lad," Lukas said. "Besides, if it was a ghost, it wouldn't be stealing food."

Sigmund rubbed his forehead with his wooden hand. "Could it be anything supernatural? Because that's what it feels like at this point. This thing is too good at disappearing."

"If there's anything supernatural about Grima, it's demonic possession. But even that's unlikely. Ye'd be able to sense it when ye're near him."

"Sense it how?" Alynn asked.

"It's…ye know how, when ye're in the presence of God, ye feel this peace deep in yer spirit? Sort of a thickness in the air around ye? It's like the opposite of that. Not quite a fear, but—more of a repulsion."

"Has God told you anything about the situation?" Leif asked.

Lukas grew quiet and thought for a moment. "I've been praying. I keep feeling that we're afraid of the wrong thing. And to be completely honest, I don't believe there are demons involved. I feel…timidity in Grima. He wears this mask and hides from us for a reason—"

"So we won't kill him!" said Sigmund.

"That's why he disappears on us so quickly, aye. But we'd kill him mask or no mask. He's hiding something else."

Everyone was silent for a moment—except for Elspeth, who took the opportunity to squeal again. Alynn took her from Lukas and held her tightly. Finally, Drostan spoke up, his voice low.

"How did the fire start?"

"Grima grabbed a stick from the fire and threw it at me. Must have set the rushes on the floor on fire."

"Was he provoked?" Alynn asked.

"I'd just grabbed my axe."

"So that's a yes. Did he have his bow?"

"I think so."

"But he didn't shoot you?"

Elspeth started fussing, and Alynn started bouncing her on her leg. "He was probably just trying to make a distraction so he could leave," she said.

"Killing someone would make a decent distraction," said Sigmund.

"Aye, but it would incite vengeance," said Leif.

"Grima killed Rothgeir without a problem. Shot Tarin. Why he's suddenly non-violent—well, less violent than he could be—none of this makes sense." Drostan sighed, buried his head in his hands, then stood up quickly. "Well, we've got a house to rebuild. Meeting adjourned. Hrafnkell, can you help me with the table?"

Hrafnkell obliged, and Lukas finally got to treating Leif's arm. His advice on how to keep it clean and dry was largely ignored—Leif had spent weeks, if not months, tending to the burn Drostan had gotten as a child, and he refused to think that Lukas's Greek medical texts were better than his own experience.

Leif left to help Drostan and Hrafnkell's family rebuild the house, but Lukas stayed behind. He looked around the house, then glanced at Alynn. "Ye wouldn't be needing any help, would ye?"

"Well, there's only women's work to be done around here, but I'd appreciate the company."

Nora's nieces and nephews had been hiding in the workroom, but they crept out as soon as they realized the meeting was over. "Pastor Lukas! Pastor Lukas!" they clamored. "Can you tell us a story?"

With a half-smile on his face and a gleam in his eyes, Lukas sat down to tell the story of David and Goliath. There were two children in his lap and one at his side and three more clustered around his feet, and his face was alight with as much wonder as those of the listeners.

May 4, A.D. 969—

Grima, that cur, has burned down Nora McKenzie's house. Well, not burned completely down, praise God. And praise God that no one was injured, save for Leif, who has a simple burn to his arm. I'm still angry, though.

At the same time, a few good things have happened of late. I got to see Alynn today. Perhaps my favorite part of my visit was getting to tell stories to Nora's nieces and nephews. Their affection and admiration fill me with a great joy. And coincidentally, I'm feeling much more in my right mind today. I had no nightmares last night.

This newfound sanity is due in part to the fact that Alynn has seen the same ghost I saw in the chapel recently. Alynn is sane, which hopefully means that I am, too. As to what this ghost is—we both doubt it's Grima, as it seems to be quite young. But everything hidden in darkness shall be brought to light, and we'll find out what this ghost is sooner or later.

—L. McCamden

THIRTEEN

I'm cold. I'm wrapped up in blankets and Tarin has his face buried in my shoulder, but I'm still cold. Shivering, I sit up and look around. State of the house. The dishes haven't been washed in days; I think they're growing mold on the kitchen table. The fire is dead. Quickly, I slip out of my bedroll and coax the ashes to life.

Once the fire is going, I crawl back to Tarin. He's sleeping, breathing softly, tearstains on his face and Monika the rag doll in his toddler arms. I don't dare wake him. When he wakes up, he'll start asking about where Mum is. He's asked every morning for two weeks now. And 'tis my job, every morning, to tell him that Mum isn't coming back.

I'm barely nine. It should be Da's job to tell him. But Da has hardly gotten out of bed since the Vikings took Mum. Nana says 'tis because he's been hit in the head by the broad side of a Viking sword. Uncle Oisin says 'tis because he's sad and misses Mum. I just know that 'tis my job to get Da a glass of milk every morning and convince him to drink it, and 'tis Tarin's job to feed him a few bites of stirabout.

Today, I decide to check on Britta first. Da can get his milk later.

In a few minutes, Aunt Sorcha will come and try to nurse Britta. Britta misses Mum more than the rest of us do—she won't even eat. She sits and fusses before nursing for a few minutes, and she spits up what little gets down into her. Britta has gotten smaller over the past two weeks. It hurts to watch.

Softly, I kneel by her cradle and kiss her head. She's cold, and she doesn't wake up.

"Good morning, Britta," I say, stroking her cheek. Her face is cold and her skin is grey and she still hasn't woken up. Her hand is stiff when I try to slip my finger into her grasp. Is she frozen? She's been wrapped in Mum's old plaid. It should have kept her warm enough.

"Da, somethin's wrong with Britta."

I glance up at the big bed to see a lump in the blankets and a mess of hair on the pillow. The pillow is damp. The hem of the blanket is damp. Da hasn't slept, I realize. He's just laid awake and cried.

"Da."

Nothing.

"Da."

Still nothing.

"Father."

"Go back to sleep," Da mumbles. I pick up Britta and snuggle her close to my chest and kiss her head. I take her to the fire, hoping to warm her up. Britta feels stiff, almost like Monika the rag doll. Something cold and empty grows in the pit of my stomach when I realize she isn't moving.

"Britta. Come on, heart. Wake up. Cry for me."

I look at her face again. Cold. Grey. Drawing a breath, I press my ear against her chest. I wait. I move my ear. I wait again.

Her heart wasn't beating.

Screaming, I half-set, half-throw Britta on the ground and leap away from her. Da's out of bed. He's holding my arms, yelling at me. Tarin's screaming. I don't know if I forget what they're saying or if I never hear it to begin with. What I do remember is Da kneeling to pick up Britta, then freezing. He doesn't need to put an ear to her chest. He just knows.

His eyes grow wide at first, then they fill with tears before he presses them shut and screams. I've never heard a grown man scream before. I start crying. Tarin crawls out of his blankets and runs up to me.

"Da!" he cries. "Lynder, make him stop. Make him stop crying, Lynder."

I can't say anything. I fall to my knees and wrap Tarin in my arms and kiss him. Every time I try to say something comforting, a sob tears my voice away.

"Alynn, what's wrong?"

Before I can form a coherent thought, Da's next to us, crushing us in a one-armed embrace. He's still holding onto Britta. I try to hold onto Tarin so that he can't see her, and somehow, it works. Da kisses us and says through tears something about angels and heaven without sounding like he believes it.

When I'm done crying, I walk to the church and tell Father Patrick that my baby sister is dead. It's the hardest thing I've ever done.

"Lynder."

With a gasp, Alynn awoke. "Where's the baby?"

"I've got her right here. What's wrong?"

Alynn didn't answer. She took Elspeth and pressed her ear to her chest and nearly cried grateful tears when she heard a heartbeat. Elspeth squirmed but quickly went back to sleep.

"Talk to me, love." Drostan's voice was exhausted, but still kind. "Was it about Konar again?"

Alynn drew a deep breath and kissed Elspeth's head. "It was about Britta."

Drostan sleepily nestled closer to Alynn and wrapped his arms tight around her. She inhaled deeply. He smelled mostly like smoke, but also like wood and sea and hard work. His arms were warm. Nothing bad could happen here.

"You're alright now," he said.

"I will be."

"No. You *are* alright, right now, love. Talk to me."

"I let the fire go out—on the night—when Britta—" Alynn swallowed hard. "Sometimes I feel like, if I'd have kept her warm, she wouldn't have died—"

"She'd have cried if she was cold. She'd have woken you." Drostan took a loose strand of Alynn's hair and ran it like a golden rivulet between his fingers. "If she's anything like Elspeth, that is."

"She wasn't. She never complained much. Not until Konar took Mum, anyway." Alynn tried to swallow the lump in her throat. "I remember my father's face—when I dropped her—and he picked her up, and—he just—his eyes—"

"Breathe, my love." Drostan rubbed away the tears that had started spilling down her cheeks. "You don't need to remember that anymore. Think about something else. What about your father's face the first time he held Mercy? Och, the grin on his face—it made me more excited than ever to be a father. Think about the day Elspeth was born, how you were the only person that could make her stop crying. Those big blue eyes— she'd just look at you, and your heart melted. Those are the things we remember, love. Don't worry about anything else."

"She's already so big." Alynn wiped her eyes and kissed the top of Elspeth's head again. "What do we do, love? What if somethin' happens to her?"

"We can't think about that."

"I can't help it. I'm sorry."

Drostan sighed. "You remember how frightened I was when Elspeth was born, right? Scared that I was going to lose you?"

Alynn snuggled closer to him. Drostan's mother had died in childbirth, so he'd had every right to be afraid. "I remember."

"What was it you told me?"

Alynn's sleep-deprived brain struggled to remember. "That I wanted you to get married again if anythin' happened to me?"

"Besides that. You told me that we just needed to trust God, Lynder. No one knows what's going to happen tomorrow. No one knows how much time they have left, or how much time anyone else has left, for that matter. And I'm scared, too, love. When I was little, Father would start singing this lullaby sometimes, when he thought no one could hear him. I asked him about it once, and he said it was Teague's song. He said that my mother would be up in the middle of the night singing it, because it got him to stop kicking her awake. I don't know if Father would sing it because he missed Mother or Teague or both of them, but—he missed them. And frankly, I don't want to know what that feels like."

Alynn held onto Elspeth's soft little hand. "Can you pray for her?"

Drostan set a warm hand on Elspeth's chest. "Thank You, Lord, for this precious wee girl You've given us. We love her. And we don't know why You let some children leave before their time—we might never know. But please let us keep Elspeth. Protect her from sickness, famine, and anything else that might come against her. And please, Lord, give us the strength we need to raise her in Your ways. In Jesus' name we pray, amen."

"Amen."

Drostan kissed Alynn's head. Elspeth stirred in her sleep; Alynn smiled at her. "Thank you, love," she said.

Drostan stroked the soft back of Elspeth's neck. "Let's see. She's got Irish stubbornness, Scottish tenacity, and Norse ferocity. If any baby had a chance at life, it's her."

Alynn drew a deep breath. Her head was on Drostan's chest, Elspeth was snuggled in her arms, everyone was warm and safe and snug. "I love ye both," she said.

"I love you too. You're alright now?"

"I am."

"Good. Now go back to sleep."

"She'll be hungry in five minutes. 'Tisn't worth it."

"Suit yourself." Drostan kissed Elspeth and settled back down in his blankets. Then, he chuckled. "I'm glad Father's not sharing the bed with us tonight."

"I'm glad he wore trousers when he did."

Drostan chuckled again, Alynn smiled, and Elspeth jerked in her sleep. Then, until Elspeth woke up hungry again, Alynn lay awake, listening to the sound of Drostan's breathing and Elspeth's gentle snoring.

Alynn slept fitfully the rest of the night, with Elspeth waking frequently and her own anxieties preventing her mind from successfully shutting down. How many hours did she sleep? Three? Four? Four and a half if she was lucky. Well, she'd survive. Her grandmother, the great Maura Quaid, had produced fourteen children and buried four of them, and she'd only passed away last year. Hopefully, stamina and good parenting ran in Alynn's blood.

Still, she was exhausted and on edge from last night's dream. The fact that her house was full of strange people didn't help. Nora asked her if everything was alright, and she could only nod and say she hadn't slept well. She floundered around trying to keep order until noon, when Alynn stepped out of the workroom only to nearly run into Rowan.

"What are you doin' here?" Alynn asked. Her heart skipped a beat. "Is Tarin—"

"Tarin's alright. He's in high spirits and tired of being cooped up. Nay, I had to run up to the smithy to fix a sod-cutter. Figured I'd stop by and see how it is you're getting along."

"I'm grand," said Alynn, not fully meaning it.

Rowan raised an eyebrow. "Don't lie to yer father, now."

"Och, fine, I'm not grand."

"What is it you need help with?"

"Well—" Alynn ran through the list of things she needed, and a trip to the outhouse was one of them. "If you could watch Elspeth for me—"

"Of course. Come here to Granddad!" He picked up Elspeth and spoke to her in a ridiculous high-pitched voice that made her smile. Grateful, Alynn went outside and took care of herself. When she came back in, she found Rowan hiding in the workroom, playing peek-a-boo. Elspeth was laughing—a sound that never failed to spark joy in Alynn's heart.

She sat down next to Rowan and simply stared at Elspeth. Her grin was brighter than the sun glinting off ocean waves. It gave Alynn a warm feeling, like someone had hugged her heart. Surprisingly, though, Rowan seemed choked up.

"Da, are you crying?"

"Och, I don't cry. I just—" Rowan rubbed his sleeve across his eyes and pulled Alynn close to him, kissing the side of her head. "I never thought I'd get this far in life."

There was something in the trembling of his voice and the glistening of his eyes that struck Alynn. She wrapped one arm around Rowan and stuck a finger into Elspeth's grasp.

"God's been good to us," she said.

"He has for a while, anyway. I'm starting to worry that things are going back to the way they used to be."

"What, with Grima?"

"Partly." Rowan rubbed Elspeth's head, making her smile with delight. "Last night, I told Tarin that I'd miss his help at the smithy. He told me to get used to it, that he doesn't like working there, and that he'd rather study for the priesthood with Brett and Lukas."

Alynn smiled. "You say that like 'tis a bad thing."

"He's my only son. Since the day he was born, I've been looking forward to turnin' him into a man. And he's not givin' me the chance. I mean—imagine if someone else taught Elspeth how to card and spin. That's yer job, as her mum. And the feeling you get, Lynder, when you watch yer children grow up, when you know you've finally done somethin' right in life—"

Rowan's voice broke off abruptly. Alynn set a hand on his arm, squeezing gently. "You're still his da," she said. "Tarin still loves you. He just doesn't want to be a blacksmith. He's not turnin' out how you'd like him to. So what?"

"So what?" There was a certain snap in Rowan's voice that startled Alynn. "The McNeils have been smiths and farriers for six generations. I don't want to be the last of us."

"He's still yer son."

"He's not actin' like it." Rowan sighed and looked at the ceiling. "My da wasn't the best of men, but he taught me nearly everything I know. And the time we spent together in the shop, I got to see all the best parts of him. I've already missed out on so much with Tarin. He needs to have this. I won't be around forever."

Alynn looked at Elspeth, who was completely absorbed in eating her foot. Aye, she'd feel terrible if someone else taught her how to card and spin and sew. When Caitriona had been kidnapped, Alynn relied on the skills she'd taught her—not only to keep house, but to keep sane. She could never start a nalbinding project unless she imagined Caitriona's fingers forming the first two loops around her thumb. It kept her from forgetting her.

For once, Alynn had nothing to say to her father.

Finally, Rowan broke the silence. "Maybe—on Sabbath, maybe, you could try talking some sense into him. He seems to listen to you."

"Of course." Alynn's mind whirred for a bit before coming up with an idea. "I could come today, if you'd like."

"No."

"Why not?"

"I'm not about to let Grima shoot you, too."

"You'll be with me, Da. You'll protect me. And besides, I haven't seen Tarin since Sabbath. Please? I've been stuck in here with Nora's brood for two days, I need some fresh air anyway."

Rowan looked at her, sighed, and said, "Take a shield."

Smiling, Alynn took Elspeth and made sure her diaper was dry before marching out into the main room and telling Nora that she was in charge. Rowan helped her saddle Humility, and the two were off in no time.

Part of Alynn was tempted to be afraid during the ride to the monastery. The other part of her was excited. The fresh air was welcome after spending so long inside, surrounded by smoky fires and too many people. Humility shook her mane happily as she kept close to Rowan's gelding, Reliance. Finally, Alynn looked up through the trees to see St. Anne's Monastery towering before her, with a steep roof and a belfry that seemed to point straight to heaven.

She was home.

She had only lived at St. Anne's Monastery for three years, but those three years were precious to her. There were times when she missed waking up in her own bedroom to the sound of Lukas chanting in Latin. She missed sitting in the upstairs hallway watching the sunrise—gazing through the slats of the railing that separated her from the high-ceilinged chapel at the first golden rays of the sun as they illuminated the stained-glass windows. She missed the evenings when Caitriona played her flute and Lukas told stories and she would sit, sometimes in her own chair and sometimes on the floor leaned up against one of them, simply listening.

But she'd been too busy to miss it much recently. Besides, having her own family was thrilling, and she wouldn't trade it for the world.

A noise jarred Alynn—it was Lukas, who was climbing with surprising ease on the half-destroyed stable roof. He was calling out to Rowan, who reigned in Reliance with a sigh of resignation.

"Well, it took ye bloody long enough," Lukas snapped, trying to glare at Rowan over his shoulder while he climbed down the ladder. "Alynn, what are ye doing here?"

"I'm here to see Tarin," Alynn said.

"I thought Drostan didn't want ye out of the house," said Lukas.

"I was with her. She was alright," said Rowan.

Lukas gave him a derisive glance. "Ye fixed the sod knife?"

"Right here." Rowan reached into his satchel and produced the tool, which Lukas took and handed to Brett. He had the youngest back and a heavy build not quite suited for climbing on rooftops, so Alynn guessed that he would be in charge of cutting sod.

"What happened to the stable?" she asked.

"Nothing. The sod just gets auld after a few years, needs replaced. Tarin's in the sickroom. Don't let him trick ye into letting him out." Lukas sighed, re-tucked the skirts of his habit into his belt (thankfully, he was wearing his braies underneath) and scaled the ladder again.

Alynn hurried inside. Caitriona was nowhere to be seen—probably cleaning the chapel, or upstairs tending to Mercy. Alynn turned the corner into the hallway, opened the first door on her left, and smiled when she saw Tarin. He was sitting up with his bandaged foot propped up on pillows, reading a book by candlelight.

"Tarin," said Alynn.

Tarin glanced up, grinned, and slammed his book shut. Alynn went up to him and wrapped him in a hug. He seemed to enjoy it.

"How's my wee heart doing?"

"Stop."

"Och, fine. Here, hold yer niece." Alynn set Elspeth in Tarin's arms, and Elspeth immediately tried to take a bite out of Tarin's hand. Tarin smiled.

"Thanks for comin', Lynder. 'Tis lonely in here. Mum won't let me do anything."

"I know. You should have seen her after the Battle of Faith. She wouldn't let me lift the kettle for a month."

"You were stabbed!"

"Aye, and you've got a hole in yer foot. Same thing."

"Aye, but you—" Tarin realized his sister was right, then sighed and settled back into his pillows. "Still. I hate this."

"Da says he misses you at the smithy."

"Just stop."

"Stop what?"

"Did Da put you up to this?"

Alynn knelt down, plopped her elbows onto the mattress, and stared at Tarin for a while. "I needed an excuse to see you," she said.

Tarin shrugged. "Not really."

"Why not?"

"You're a grown-up now. You can do what you want."

"Well…" Alynn glanced at Elspeth and wondered how to explain that, as an adult, freedom only worked in certain ways.

"Da doesn't want me in the woods. He's had one child shot, and that's one too many, and I can't blame him."

Tarin thumbed through the heavy pages of his book, then saved Alynn the trouble of asking what he'd been reading. "It's Hippocrates. I'm tryin' to figure out how to get my foot to heal faster."

"I could have told you that. 'Tis rest, time, and prayer you need. Does it hurt much?"

"Only when I move."

Tarin took his hands off his book and looked at Alynn. "What does Da want you to say?"

"I don't care what Da wants me to say. I told him I'd talk to you. Well—I'm here. Let's talk."

"About what?"

"You don't want to be a blacksmith?"

"I know that. You know that. Devil mend it, everyone but Da knows that."

Alynn smiled. "Alright. Why do you want to study with Lukas?"

"Because—" Tarin paused for a moment to gather his thoughts. "Because Latin sounds like a dance. Because reading about the Greeks, 'tis been hundreds of years that their medicine's been helping people. I'm connected to all that history. And then—a couple months ago, Lukas laid hands on me and Brett, and he prayed for us to be filled with the Holy Spirit. 'Tis amazing, Lynder. I can talk to Jesus—just like I'm talking to you right now. And I know how I feel, whenever I learn something new about God. I want to help other people learn, and feel that same way."

He gazed up at Alynn with perfectly round, green eyes. Her heart melted. All of Rowan's arguments seemed baseless when compared to this thirst for knowledge, this pure passion for the things of God. Smiling, Alynn squeezed Tarin's hand and said, "Those are a lot of good reasons."

"I know they are. Why can't Da see them?"

Alynn sighed and took a moment to collect her thoughts.

"Well—Da loves you. He wants to spend time with you. In his mind, that's what fathers and sons do, they work together. To him, it feels like you love Lukas more than you love him."

"Oh." Tarin leaned his head back for a moment before perking up again. "Is that why Da and Lukas don't like each other?"

"What do you mean?"

Alynn tried to remember the times she'd seen Rowan and Lukas interacting and realized she couldn't think of many. They tended to avoid one another, like a pair of cats that were both fond of their personal space.

"I overheard Mum and Da talking," said Tarin. "Da said that he wanted to find another place to live. Mum asked him why, and Da said he was tired of being—well, he said 'beholden to Lukas,' whatever that means. Mum yelled at him for it, and thank God, because that means I'd have to stop studying."

Alynn was stunned. Rowan wanted to leave? Why? Beholden to Lukas—everyone earned their keep. Rowan's job at the smithy paid for all the things Lukas's farming couldn't provide. Caitriona was the hardest-working out of all of them, cooking and cleaning and making clothes and watching Mercy and helping the church. Brett and Tarin were Lukas's shadows, doing anything Lukas asked of them—Brett especially, as Tarin spent most of his spare time at the smithy with Rowan.

No, there was definitely something else bothering Rowan. She sincerely hoped that Tarin's vocation wasn't it.

"If Mum and Da start talking about leaving again, you tell me," Alynn said. "Lukas can't be on his own. It was hard enough on him when I got married, he'd be a wreck if ye left."

Tarin shifted in bed again. "You should have seen him after you got married. For two weeks, he'd just stand in the doorway to your bedroom and look sad. Once, I saw him hug yer pillow and tell you goodnight."

"He did?"

"Aye, but he won't admit to it."

Alynn picked up Elspeth (who had somehow managed to get three of Tarin's fingers in her mouth and protested quite loudly when they were removed) and kissed Tarin's head. "Anything you need while I'm here?"

"You're leavin' already?"

"I wasn't supposed to come in the first place, heart. I've fifteen extra people at my house that I'm supposed to be lookin' after."

Sighing, Tarin reached out to give Alynn a hug. "I'm lonely. Please come back."

Alynn nestled him closer, kissed the top of his head, and ruffled his red hair for good luck. "I can't promise anything, Tarin. I wish I could. I wish I could take you home with me, and you could watch Elspeth while I take care of the house. Maybe once you're all better, and we catch this Grima."

"That sounds nice, if Da and Lukas will let me."

"Just tell them I sent for you, and they'll listen."

Tarin smiled, and Alynn smiled back. She left the sickroom and ran upstairs to look for Caitriona, only to find her asleep with Mercy napping on her chest. Doubtless she was exhausted from worrying about Tarin, so Alynn let her sleep and went outside.

She watched the men working for a while, mostly to prove to herself that Lukas knew what he was doing on the roof. Rowan she was less worried about; he was the one who taught her how to climb trees, and even Caitriona's young brothers in Limerick looked up to him. Heights meant nothing to him, and he knew how to fall. But Lukas was sixty this year. He shouldn't be climbing around on roofs.

Brett was the first person to notice her as he approached the ladder with another bundle of sod. "Do you want a bodyguard home?" he asked.

"I'm grand, thanks," said Alynn.

Brett shrugged and went back to cutting sod. Lukas, however, had overheard the exchange and slid down the ladder. Elspeth gave a shriek of delight when he got close enough for her to recognize.

"There's my wee darling!" Lukas said, scooping Elspeth into his arms and giving her an exaggerated kiss on the cheek. Elspeth smiled and kicked her legs happily.

"She likes you," said Alynn.

"Och, I know she does. I like her, too. I think she's gotten fatter since the last time I saw her."

"Wouldn't surprise me, with the way she's been eating recently." Alynn smiled, grabbing her coif as a wayward gust of wind threatened to knock it off her head. She glanced at Rowan, who'd had the good sense to sit down on a finished part of the roof until the gust was over.

"You're alright, Da?" she called.

"I'm grand," said Rowan, whether or not he meant it.

Alynn turned back to Lukas. "Da wanted me to talk to Tarin about his vocation. Do you think he's called to the church?"

"Doubtless," said Lukas, letting Elspeth chew on his thumb. "He's one of the most intelligent people I know. Blacksmithing would be a waste of his intellect."

Alynn glanced up at the sky, disheartened to see that dark clouds were rolling in. "I gathered as much from talkin' to him. I know that you want what God wants, and you probably think Da's just some stubborn Irishman out to ruin everything. But all he wants is for Tarin to look at him, not you, as his father. I don't know if there's any way ye can work that out—"

"Wait," said Lukas. "He thinks I'm—stealing Tarin?"

"In a sense, aye."

Lukas sighed, gave Elspeth back to Alynn, and swore in Latin. "That man—" he switched to Greek for a moment, then back to Gaelic— "He's got everything. A wife. Three beautiful children. A granddaughter. All blood relatives. And he really can't let me have anything, can he?"

"Lukas!"

"Tarin's my student. He's the closest thing I've got to a friend. All I want is to teach him, I've never claimed him as a son, and if yer father won't even let me have that—"

"Would you calm down?" Alynn asked. "I don't see what the fuss is about. You want to teach someone, you've still got Brett."

"Aye, but he's leaving next year. And asides—I'm sixty years auld. I don't know how much time I've left. I don't want to leave St. Anne's Cleft without a pastor. And if Tarin's not it, then who else is there? Sigmund's got his job, his family—"

"You're always telling me to trust God, that He'll work things out," said Alynn. "Can't you try to do that?"

Sighing, Lukas tucked his hands into his sleeves. "I know I ought to. But I know I can't go home to be wi' the Lord unless there's someone here to replace me, and devil mend it—at my age, Alynn, I want to know that I'm free to go home."

A bit of panic touched Alynn's heart. "You're not ill, are you?" she asked.

"What makes ye say that?"

"Why else would you talk about dyin'? And besides, you're the sort who doesn't complain about anything—I was just hoping—"

Lukas half-smiled. "Besides my ribs hurting, there's nothing wrong wi' me. I suppose this sounds—well, foolish—sixty's just such a big number. I don't like it. And realistically, I can't expect to be around much longer."

"Remember Alva? She was eighty when she died. You could have twenty years left."

"Och, I hope not."

"Why not?"

"When ye're sixty, ye'll understand."

Another gust of wind nearly blew Alynn off her feet and set Elspeth to fussing. Lukas looked at the sky, then at the stable roof, and sighed. He kissed Alynn and Elspeth again and said he needed to get back to work before the wind picked up anymore. Alynn put Elspeth in her shawl and kept a careful eye on the forest around her as she set off for home.

FOURTEEN

What Alynn had failed to notice, and what the men were too busy working to see, was the small figure crouched behind the privy. To their credit, the figure didn't look threatening. From a distance, it looked like a discolored shrub. Up close, it looked like a neglected pile of laundry, except for the single humanoid foot sticking out from under it.

When the noise of the workmen died down, Grima began to move. His feet were wrapped in half a winninga each—he only needed half, given how thin his legs were. But the fabric itched, and it didn't cover the tips of his toes, making them sting with cold. But the winningas at least padded the sound of his footsteps as he dashed across a narrow stretch of the yard to a nearby shed. Grima waited for a gust of wind to cover his noise before venturing into the open and shutting himself into the outbuilding.

For a moment, Grima waited, straining his ears, wondering if anyone had noticed him. But the men were intent on their work. They hadn't seen him.

It would have been wiser to make for the woods, Grima realized. Now he was trapped in this shed. Well, it could have been the privy. What was this shed used for, anyway? The whole interior was lined with shelves—and the shelves, thank

God, were filled with ripening cheeses.

Grima broke off a piece and ate it. It was sour and it squeaked in his teeth, but he ate it anyway. It reminded him of a time when he was five years old, and his older brother had dared him to eat some green cheese. Griffith had been such a twit. Grima missed him anyway. He missed all his siblings— Griffith and Gwendolyn were older than he was, and then there were Ellis, Meilyr, and baby Myfanwy. Were they all still alive?

No matter. He'd never see any of them again, anyway.

Grima ate half the green cheese, then sat down and closed his eyes. His whole body ached almost feverishly, but he knew he wasn't ill. He knew it all came from the scratches on his back, and from the stray red lines that crept onto the back of his arms and legs. He suspected that there was even one on the side of his head, right along his ear, but of course he couldn't look at himself to be sure.

It took a while for Grima to get comfortable in the cheese shed, but once he did, he fell asleep. When he awoke, he was thirsty. He felt around in the darkness and found a bucket of milk. It was a bit sour, but he drank it gratefully before deciding to explore his surroundings. To his left was a large dash churn. To his right was a burlap sack, the sort that oats were probably stored in. Grima opened it and felt around, expecting the dusty softness of seed oats. Instead, he felt metal.

Cloakpins of various sizes. Serving spoons, hinges, and best of all, arrowheads. Grima felt around and collected them one by one, as if searching for berries in a bramble. There were six arrowheads in total. Grinning, Grima shoved them into the pouch he'd made by folding and pinning his borrowed cloak in just the right way. He wanted to secure the pouch further, so he borrowed another cloakpin.

Grima put everything he didn't need back into the bag, then found a knothole in the shed and peeked outside. The men were still at work. The monk and the long-haired man with the pitifully short beard were on the stable roof, and the tall, fat, dark-haired boy would poke his head over the ladder every once in a while with a new bundle of sod. Grima hoped that they would hurry up and finish, or go inside for one of the Divine Offices (surely it was time for Nones, right?) or else decide that it was too windy to be working on the roof and go inside for the day.

It was ages before they went inside, and Grima was finally free to sprint into the woods.

Even though it was late and the sky was dim with clouds and the half-set sun, Grima did not go to the cave he called home. Mistress wanted him home, but he didn't care. He'd care later, he knew, but he wanted this sweet moment of freedom. As cautious as a squirrel and nearly as quiet, Grima made his way to the village, and then to the smithy.

Grima was no blacksmith. In fact, his only skills were archery, getting babies to stop crying, and following orders. But part of following orders meant being good at whatever Mistress told him to do, and so Grima had the slightest bit of experience working with metal.

At least his task was easy. The blacksmith had done half his work for him.

In his pack, Grima had ten whittled arrow shafts with fletching sewn on. The shafts were poorly made, and the fletching was awful. He'd been working mainly with chicken feathers. He wished he had eagle feathers, or even goose feathers, but he'd make do. And besides, even if an arrow shattered when it hit its target, it would still do its job. Shafts and fletching were easily made and easily repaired.

Arrowheads were another issue. Grima had no idea how to make those, so he was grateful for the blacksmith. He was grateful he'd found them. He was grateful to have made it out of that shed alive. If it had just been adults in the house, he would have been fine. Adults have routines, and as a general rule, go outside as little as possible. But the little girl was forever running outside and dragging someone with her, either to carry her back inside or to watch her play for a half hour or to lift her onto the seat of the privy. And little girls were curious, attentive. Grima didn't trust her.

She was a cute thing, though. Little Myfanwy had been about her age the last time Grima had seen her—he missed her now, the wee rascal. But now was no time for reminiscing. Grima shook himself and pulled harder on the bellows.

The work, not to mention the heat from the forge, made Grima sweat. He took off his cloak, and finally, reluctantly, he took off his mask. Dark ringlets of hair were freed as he tossed the winninga-turned-facewrap aside before wiping his olive-brown brow and returning to work. The tangs of the arrowheads were too wide to fit into the arrow shafts, so Grima heated them until they glowed red and hammered them until his shoulder knotted with unbearable pain. By the time he'd finished three arrowheads, he was dizzy.

"What are you doing out?" a voice called. Grima froze and looked up. A strange man was looking at him, a torch illuminating strangely concerned eyes. "It's dangerous after dark with that thief about."

"I bent a serving spoon, and my mistress bade me fix it," Grima lied. He hoped the stranger didn't come any closer.

Fortunately, the stranger left.

Grima drew a trembling breath. He couldn't believe that had worked. He was still dizzy, though, so he went to the nearby well and drew some water from it. He'd never had more delicious water.

His break was short, and Grima quickly got back to work and finished the other three arrowheads. Then, after splashing his sweat-sticky face in what was left of his water, he donned his cloak and wrapped the winninga again around his face. The six finished arrows and the four headless shafts went into a quiver at his waist.

As Grima left, he tugged awkwardly at the leather collar around his neck. Sweat had gotten under it, making it itch. Grima's narrow, jagged-nailed fingers tried to dig under it to wipe the sweat away, but the collar was too tight.

This blasted collar. It seemed an eternity since it had first been put on him—he'd been little more than a child, screaming and kicking and trying to bite the man who put it on him. He'd been deftly smacked for his impertinence. But Master, standing in the corner, merely smiled and said that he'd be broken in due time, as if he were nothing more than an unruly colt that needed taming.

Broken, no. Trained, yes. Grima had always been a fast learner. He'd picked up Norse in eight months, for heaven's sake. And in the first eight days, he'd learned that Master was a cruel man, and that Mistress was even crueler. No, they hadn't broken Grima, but they'd taught him two things about life. First, no one cared about slaves. Second, because no one cared about slaves, their lives were expendable, and only the obedient lived.

It was only good sense, then, that kept Grima subservient to his mistress. It was good sense that had kept them together after the shipwreck. After all, Grima couldn't survive alone on a strange island. And Mistress couldn't either, not wounded as she was.

Grima paused, checking the fold in his cloak to make sure the herbs he'd gathered earlier were still there. Then, quietly, he trudged into the woods.

A twenty-minute walk brought Grima to a rock-covered beach. He hid his cloak, mask, and winningas under the roots of a tree. The herbs and the decorated cloakpin he'd stolen, though, along with his bow and arrow, came with him. The wind blew through the rags he wore, sending a shudder through his bones. Grima kept his scrawny arms tucked close to his ribs for warmth. His shirt was as useless as a cobweb, and his trousers weren't much better. He wore what had once been a jacket, but one sleeve had been torn off for use as a bandage and most of the buttons were missing. It flopped uselessly open.

Grima stumbled over the rocky beach, cursing the pain inflicted on his bare feet, and crawled into a small cave. He dared not speak; he hoped that Mistress hadn't seen him. But she had, and her shrill voice made him flinch.

"Just where have you been?"

The voice came from a lady of twenty with haughty eyes and strong cheekbones, clad in layers of colorful fabric. There was a tear in the bodice of her dress. Blood and bare skin showed plainly behind the child's undershift that had been turned into a makeshift bandage.

"I made more arrows," said Grima.

"Did you get food?"

Grima shook his head and handed the herbs to his mistress, who took and inspected them. "Yarrow, I see…I don't know *what* this is…."

Grima was about to tell her that it was willow bark and that a tea made from it would ease the pain of her wound, but the sharp tongue of a whip flashed out and stung his shoulders before he could answer.

"You fool!" The whip cut again through Grima's cobweb of a shirt and left a line of blood on his bony shoulder. "You worthless wretch! You can't follow the simplest of orders!"

"Mistress Eyja, please—"

"You had a single job!" The lady cracked the whip again— twice—thrice—a drop of blood flicked across the cave, flying off the whip's tail and onto the stone wall. With a cry of fear and pain, Grima weaseled his way out of her grasp. He fell onto his wounded back, then lifted himself onto his hands and feet and crawled away from Eyja and her whip. He ducked his head, letting his dark curls obscure his face and transform him into the monster that Tarin had encountered days earlier.

Grima's hand lighted on the cloakpin. Carefully, desperately, he offered it to Eyja. She took it, wincing as she stooped to pick it up, and admired it. She smiled when she saw the way the metal reflected the faint light that flickered up from the small fire heating and illuminating the cave.

"Well, you haven't made a complete waste of today," said Eyja, pinning the brooch to her dress. She felt its weight on her breast and held her head higher. "Go fetch some water," said Eyja. "Tend to my wounds, then find something for us to eat. This is laughable, honestly. I thought my father had taught you better than this. We'd be feasting on pickled puffin and wheat bread if he were here. He'd have the whole town bereft of goods and food by now."

Grima said nothing.

"As soon as I'm mended, and after we're rescued, I'll have to teach you the art of thievery. You ought to know it by now. I suppose you're too dull to learn, even from such a brilliant teacher as my father."

Grima wanted to say that he'd spent the two years with Master following orders, not raiding cities, thank God. And even if he had studied under Eyja's father, Thrand the Infamous relied more on brute strength than on cunning—the exact opposite of what this strange little island necessitated. But all Grima said was, "I'd be glad to learn from you, Mistress."

"And try to find some good mead. I'm sick of this pain."

Grima wanted to say that he'd gotten willow bark for the pain, but all that came out was, "Of course, Mistress."

There was some rainwater in a bucket he'd set out on the beach; he collected it and heated it in a small spider-legged pot nestled in the fire. He mixed herbs in the water and watched them boil, secretly hoping that one of them was poisonous. All the while, Eyja lay on a bearskin, propped up on a smooth rock, an angry-teared gleam in her eyes.

"Of course," she said, "you won't turn out to be the thief you might have been, since my father isn't here to teach you anymore."

"Master Thrand was a good man, Mistress."

"Talk to me about him."

Grima hesitated; it was hard to find good things about Thrand the Infamous, for he had rightly earned his name. "He was strong, Mistress. Bold and daring. He never hesitated to rush into battle."

"He was a soldier," Eyja said. "He deserved a better death. Do you think he's in Valhalla?"

"Of course he is, Mistress."

"Of course. Of course he is. He was fighting for his ship, my brother's lives, my life, the crew's lives. Even yours, worthless as it is."

Grima seethed. Who was Eyja to call him worthless? *She* was worthless, *she* was intolerable, *she* was a compassionless dog with a coward's heart and a drunkard's mind. Drunk not on mead but on power, the power she'd been born with as a child of Thrand the Infamous.

And in that respect? Compared to Eyja, Grima's life probably *was* worthless. Plenty of good things had come out of Wales, but none of them had come from Grima's hometown of Mostyn. Maybe, just maybe, if Grima had been born in Holywell, one town over—maybe Saint Winifred would have been kind to him. Maybe his life would have gone differently, and instead of washing the wounds of his tormentors, he could be earning an honest living. Or maybe he would have joined the church.

Maybe it wasn't too late. Maybe the people at the monastery would take him in; the monk Lukas seemed kind enough.

Or maybe it was too late. Perhaps Grima had committed too many sins to repent of—too many sins for God to want him anymore.

FIFTEEN

"Lynder, we're home."

Alynn heard Drostan's voice but made no move to acknowledge it. She was crumpled on the ground in the workroom, Elspeth nursing fussily, a lump of butter in one hand. She didn't know why she was eating it, especially so close to dinnertime. She didn't care.

"Lynder?"

The workroom door opened, and Alynn looked up at Drostan.

He stared at her for a while.

"Go away," she said.

He left.

Alynn took another bite of her butter and closed her eyes. She was exhausted. Growing up, she'd felt a lot of things that she thought were exhaustion. She'd been wrong. She'd been so, so wrong. She was empty, lifeless, hollow. Elspeth was sucking the dregs of her vitality along with her breastmilk.

She'd been a fool. She'd thought she could handle it. She'd gone to the river that afternoon and scoured the bank for Grima's footprints, hoping that he'd come to gather water. Half a dozen times, she'd been distracted by tracks that turned out to be her own. She'd found nothing, wasted an hour and a half, and exhausted what little energy she had.

She was an idiot. She was such an idiot.

The door opened again, and Drostan scooped her up—Elspeth, butter, and all—and set her at the table. "The soup's not ready," Alynn said. "I only put it on to cook ten minutes ago."

"We can wait," said Leif. "Where's Nora? Why didn't she help?"

"Gudrun's baby is sick. She needed Nora to help watch the other kids while she went to see if Lukas could help."

"That's not good." Leif got himself a glass of ale and groaned as he stretched his back. "I'm wondering if we shouldn't have let them stay an extra day. All the smoke and sawdust, it's not good for the lungs."

Drostan got into the pantry and found some pickled beets to snack on while they waited for the soup to cook. "Are you sick?" he asked.

Alynn raised her head. "Me?"

"No, the cat. Of course I'm talking to you."

"Why?"

"You've normally got the soup ready by now, and—" Drostan took another bite and continued with his mouth full. "I don't know, put on a black dress, I'd think you were the water-*draugr*."

Alynn sighed. "I've had a decent night's sleep once in the past six months. Besides that, I'm Irish, of course I look like death." She took another bite of her butter. Drostan looked mildly horrified.

"How can you—"

"It tastes good!"

"You'll make yourself sick!"

"No, I won't!" And to prove it, she took another bite, just to make Drostan uncomfortable. "Anyway, how did work go?" She asked even though she had no intention of listening to Drostan's response. She was too tired.

"Well, we didn't get much done. We had people coming by

all day, asking if Grima's been caught yet and reporting stolen items. He seems to be striking randomly. He'll rob two or three houses on some nights, none at all on others. We've got villagers missing everything from blankets to cooking pots to jewelry. Did you do anything interesting today?"

Alynn woke up a bit when she heard the last question. "I would have finished Elspeth's new dress, but I folded the hem the wrong way. Had to tear it out and start over."

"Elspeth won't mind."

"Aye, but I will. I'll keep thinkin' 'tis inside-out when it isn't." Alynn was thirsty. Summoning all her energy, she stood up, leaving her butter on the table, and got herself a glass of milk.

"What if Elspeth grows up and starts eating butter?" Drostan asked.

"I won't let her. 'Tis my butter."

Alynn got her drink and lay down with her head in Drostan's lap. He played with her hair until Leif got too hungry to wait for the soup anymore. Alynn was roused, dinner was eaten, and Leif and Drostan took turns holding Elspeth while Alynn cleaned up.

Alynn had never realized how much she loved washing dishes. She was her own person. No one was crying into her shoulder or latched onto her sore breasts or awkwardly bonking their head into her collarbone.

As soon as the dishes were washed, Alynn brushed and braided her hair and went to bed with Drostan. But only for a half hour. Elspeth woke up screaming and refused to nurse.

Sighing, Alynn took her into the workroom so as not to wake Leif or Drostan. She changed her diaper. Elspeth refused to stop screaming. Alynn spoke as softly as she could, and she sang as happily as she could, but nothing worked.

Alynn picked up Elspeth and started pacing the room with her. She talked and shushed and walked around and bounced Elspeth up and down and tried offering her breast again, but nothing worked. Finally, near tears herself, Alynn just sat down and let Elspeth scream.

A strange emotion ran through Alynn. It was anger. "What's the matter with you?" she shouted at Elspeth. "Why can't you just settle down? Why won't you let me sleep?"

The moment passed just as quickly as it arrived, but the guilt that followed wasn't nearly as transient. Blinking past tears, Alynn set Elspeth on the workbench and half-ran out the back door. Two minutes, she told herself. Elspeth would be fine for two minutes.

It wasn't raining. The sky was clear and cloudless; Alynn could see the stars and the full moon and feel the chill of the wind as it flew down the village streets. The wind was alive, really and truly alive. Not in this sleep-deprived state Alynn was mired in. She drew one last breath of delicious fresh air and went back inside. She hadn't realized how smoky and dark the longhouse smelled.

When Alynn came back inside, she heard Elspeth still crying. That vicious anger threatened to rise up again within her, but she forced it down the way she might swallow the urge to vomit. She saddled Humility, wrapped Elspeth in the shawl that kept her close to her chest, and left for St. Anne's Monastery.

Elspeth screamed the entire journey. Alynn felt herself being driven mad. By the time she reached the monastery, she didn't have the sense to put Humility in the stable or try the various doors and windows to get in. Instead, she pounded on the back door and screamed.

Eternal seconds ticked by. Alynn knocked until her knuckles bled, then gave the heavy wooden door a few deft kicks. Alynn's outburst seemed to stun Elspeth; her wailing turned into a less intolerable fussing. But Alynn screamed at the door again.

Finally, Lukas opened the door. Alynn almost didn't see the cold glint of a knife gleaming in the moonlight. "Who are you?" Lukas demanded.

"Me and Elspeth, for the love of God, Lukas, let me in!"

Lukas dropped the knife with a clatter and reached out. "What happened? What's wrong?"

"Elspeth won't stop cryin'."

"Is she ill?"

"I don't know. She won't stop cryin'. I can't take it anymore. I screamed at her, Lukas, I can't do this. I need my mum."

Lukas took Elspeth from Alynn's arms and brought her to the fireplace. Alynn followed. Her hair was stuck to her face; she tried to brush it away. Why was her face wet? It took Alynn a while to realize that she'd been sobbing.

Lukas had stripped Elspeth down to her diaper and was moving her joints, poking her belly, counting her breaths and heartbeats. "She's not feverish. Everything moves that's supposed to. When was her last bowel movement?"

"A few hours ago."

"Is she eating like normal?"

"I tried nursing her earlier and it didn't work."

"Try again. I'll get Caitriona."

Alynn sat down at the hearth and offered Elspeth her breast. Surprisingly, Elspeth latched on quickly and nursed greedily.

Alynn started crying. Lukas paused at the stairwell.

"Is she alright now?" he asked.

"I knew I shouldn't have been a mum," she said. "I get too angry. She hasn't even done anythin' wrong yet, and I already yelled at her—"

"Och, my dear. My wee darling." Lukas moved a chair close to Alynn so that he could hold her as she cried, kissing the top of her head. Then, he started singing. It was no church song— the melody rose and fell like the waves of the sea, as wild and free as the wind over the highlands.

"In the Straits of Od Odrum, where the seals do sleep,
There are no human voices, only sea-waves and geese.
There a stepfather cradles and sings to his babe,
Who falls asleep lulled by the song and the waves.

"The stepfather cradles and sings to his babe,
Who falls asleep lulled by the song and the waves;
The noble seal's calling, the swan near him sings,
The mermaid of heroes in solitude dreams.

"The noble seal's calling, the swan near him sings,
The mermaid of heroes in solitude dreams,
In the Straits of Od Odrum, where the seals do sleep,
There are no human voices, only sea-waves and geese."

In between the verses, Lukas sang freely—sounds without words. They were used in work-songs and dancing-songs and sometimes in crying-songs, at least in Ireland. There was a comfort in knowing that Scotland also sang songs without words.

"My father used to sing me to sleep with that song," said Lukas. "Even after the massacre, I'd sing it to myself sometimes. Is it the song that's comforting, or just my memories of it?"

"The song's good," said Alynn, three-fourths calm and half asleep.

"Good. That's good. Now, my dear, ye need sleep. I'll wake Caitriona, she'll look after Elspeth fer ye. When ye wake in the morning, roll over and go back to sleep, ye hear me?"

"Aye," said Alynn.

"Alright. Come on, now." Lukas helped Alynn to her feet and led her up the stairs, into her old bedroom. It was a comfort to lie on the straw mattress instead of the wooden bed at home, and even more of a comfort to know that she was surrounded by people who loved her. Elspeth was still nursing. Lukas sat on the edge of the bed, his fingers running idly through the strands of hair that escaped Alynn's braid. She could hear Brett snoring from two rooms down.

"I'll wait here until Elspeth's done eating and bring her to Caitriona fer ye," said Lukas.

"Thank you," said Alynn. She snuggled into her blankets

and kissed Elspeth and the next thing she knew she was alone and the room was dark and she rolled over and closed her eyes again. Elspeth was crying in the next room, but Caitriona's voice was shushing her, and Alynn went back to sleep just as Elspeth settled down.

Alynn had no idea how much time passed before she woke again, but her room was completely dark when she opened her eyes. Sometimes, sunlight would come through the stained-glass windows of the chapel and dance along the crack beneath her door. There was no such light today, which meant that it was either nighttime or a cloudy day.

Regardless, Alynn tried to go back to sleep. But she heard something. Voices. They were quiet at first, but they kept getting louder until she could tell that they belonged to Lukas and Rowan. And they grew louder still, until Alynn could hear what was being said.

"He's not ready fer it," said Lukas.

Rowan's voice was thin on patience. "He was ready for it years ago. I should have started apprenticing him full time when he was ten. 'Tis been a mistake, letting him study with you. My mistake. I'm sorry."

"Ye're not taking him away from me!" said Lukas.

"Excuse me?"

"Ye've got everything, Rowan! Ye've got a wife who loves ye. Ye've got three precious children and a darling grand-daughter. I have a cat. I had a family, until the tide dragged ye in. Ye insist on stealing every shard of my hap-piness, and I've put up wi' it until now. But no longer. Ye're not taking Tarin away from me."

"He's not yer son! You've no say in his life. What's best for him is for me and Caitriona to decide, not you. And don't you dare speak to me that way again."

"Ye never thought of asking Tarin what he wants, did ye? And I will speak to ye however I bloody well please. Ye're under my roof, I'd better have some say in how life works around here."

"You *will not* tell me how to—"

Tired of the arguing, Alynn snatched her blanket and wrapped it around her shoulders as she stepped into the hallway. Lukas was the first to notice her. He dropped his shoulders, muttered an apology to Rowan, and turned towards his own cell.

"No. No. Ye woke me up, ye're going to explain what all this is about," said Alynn. "Da, you too. You can go first while Lukas calms down."

"I told him that Tarin wouldn't be studying with him anymore," said Rowan.

"And this is a decision that you and Tarin have agreed on?" asked Alynn.

"No. But I'm his father, and I say 'tis high time he learned a trade."

"I'm teaching him one!" said Lukas.

Rowan threw up his hands in frustration. "The priesthood is not a trade! He can't support himself, let alone a family."

"What the devil do ye think I've been doing fer the past five years?" Lukas demanded. "Who's kept yer family clad and fed, aye?"

"'Tis two different things, farming and leading the church are, and ye can't teach him both."

"I could, if ye'd stop dragging him off to the smithy every time he's got an extra ten minutes to his day!"

There was a clomping noise, and everyone stopped arguing to watch Mercy finish climbing the stairs. She marched up to Lukas and Rowan and said, very angrily, "Deydey!"

"What?" said Lukas.

"Too loud! Eppie seeping."

"Eppie's sleeping? Alright, Mercy. I'm sorry. Can ye forgive Deydey?"

Mercy looked at Lukas, grinned, and said "No!" as she ran back downstairs. Sighing, Lukas retreated into his cell. Rowan glared at him.

"Mercy doesn't determine the end of our conversations," he

said.

"Tarin's yer son. Do what ye think is best. Hopefully, I'll die soon anyway, and none of this will matter." With that, Lukas shut the door behind himself. Rowan muttered something that probably contained a couple of curse words as he paced a few steps down the hallway.

"Tarin's not going to be happy," said Alynn.

"Don't you start," Rowan warned. "You're not his mum. You don't know what's best for him."

"Not his mum, aye? I only raised him for five years. I might not know what's best for him, but I know him, and I know that he's not going to be happy."

Rowan stiffened, and Alynn flinched. She didn't know why. Rowan turned to look at her, and the anger in his eyes slowly disappeared until it turned into a familiar emptiness. He shook his head, then said "Mum's kept some stirabout warm for you" as he went downstairs.

Alynn thought about the stirabout. She thought about Lukas and turned towards his cell. But then she heard Elspeth start crying, and she hurried downstairs. Caitriona, hair amess and eyes exhausted, was bouncing her. But she smiled when she saw Alynn.

"Look, Eppie! There's Mammy!"

"Och, my sweet wee Elspeth," said Alynn, taking Elspeth into her arms and kissing her. "I'm sorry. Mammy's sorry."

"You didn't do anythin' wrong, love," said Caitriona. "I think 'tis just her second tooth comin' in."

"Are you gettin' another toothy in?" Alynn asked.

Elspeth gave one long, final complaint and started trying to eat Alynn's dress. Alynn let her nurse. She seemed to finally settle down.

"Are you alright?" asked Caitriona.

"I'm grand now. I think Lukas was right, I just needed some sleep." All the previous night's fears, worries, and frustrations seemed so pointless now.

Caitriona smiled. "When you were a babe, you got about

four of yer teeth in all right in a row. You wouldn't let me sleep for a month. I thought about dropping you off at the church once or twice. 'Tis alright to need help, and I'm glad you came here."

"Me too." Alynn looked at Elspeth, then at Caitriona. "Thanks, Mum."

"Any time, my heart." Caitriona rubbed her eyes and straightened her hair, composing herself in the process. "Why was Lukas yelling at Da upstairs?"

"I'm not sure, honestly. It was an argument about Tarin it started off as, but then—I don't know. Lukas is mad about somethin'."

"It must be serious. I can't remember the last time he's raised his voice like that."

"I'll talk to him about it." Alynn glanced at the table, where a bowl of stirabout was sitting. "Can I eat first, though?"

"Heavens, yes, dear heart. Do you want tea or milk?"

"Tea?" asked Mercy, who was playing with Monika the rag doll.

"No, darling, you're too little for tea. It's hot. You'll burn yerself."

"Tea for Ma'kah."

"You want to make tea for you and Monika? That's a grand idea. Make some for Mammy too, alright?"

"I make tea," said Mercy, nearly running straight into Alynn on her way to the cupboard. A few old, cracked cups had been put on the bottom shelf just for her, and she pulled them out and carried them to the hearth one by one.

"Shut the cupboard door, now," said Caitriona.

"I do it," said Mercy.

Alynn smiled as she ate quickly, before Elspeth finished nursing and started getting her grubby little hands all over everything. Caitriona got her a glass of milk, and before she finished, Mercy stretched her little hands up as far as they would go to set an empty cup of 'tea' near Alynn's bowl.

"Here," said Mercy.

"Thank you," said Alynn.

Mercy grinned. "Yo'welcome."

Alynn sipped the imaginary tea and finished her stirabout just as Elspeth finished her own breakfast. Alynn burped her, then kissed her, and for the first time in a while, Elspeth smiled.

"There's Mammy's happy girl! Are you feelin' better, my wee heart? Are you finally feelin' better?"

Elspeth babbled.

"Och, thank God. Mammy's so glad you're feelin' better. Come on, now. Let's go find Deydey and see if he's still sulking. Maybe he needs some Elspie-snuggles to make him feel better."

"Go borrow one of my frocks," said Caitriona. "We can't have you walkin' around in yer undershift."

Alynn donned one of Caitriona's frocks and took a few minutes to pin up the hem (Caitriona was a good three inches taller than Alynn was) before visiting Lukas. She was surprised to see that Lukas's door was completely closed. Unless it led to the outside, Lukas never shut a door all the way.

Alynn knocked.

"Go away," said Lukas.

"Lukas, 'tis me. I've got Elspeth. She wants to say hi to her grandfather."

There was a pause, and then the door opened. Lukas had apparently been hiding in the dark. He hadn't so much as lit an oil lamp. He stood still for a moment, not even reaching out to take Elspeth into his arms.

"What's wrong?" Alynn asked.

Lukas shook his head. "We'll be alright."

"Aye, I know you will be. But right now. What's wrong? Are you mad about Tarin not being able to study with you anymore?"

Lukas nodded.

"Is there anythin' else you're mad about?"

"Ye needn't get involved."

Lukas tried to shut the door, but Alynn stuck her foot in the doorway and said, "Lukas, I'm yer best friend, and I'm helping you whether you like it or not."

Lukas sighed. He opened the door and sat at his desk, where the faint light from the chapel windows congregated. "I'm sorry I yelled at yer father," he said.

"Apologize to him, not me. And you can do that later." Alynn came inside Lukas's cell and set a hand on his shoulder. "I know you'll miss Tarin. You like havin' someone to teach, don't you?"

There was a pause before Lukas answered; when he did, his voice was quiet. "More than anything."

"'Tis not like he's leavin' the way I did. He'll still sleep here, take his meals here. You'll get to talk to him in Latin. Keep secrets from Mum and Da. I know you'll like that."

"It's not that simple," said Lukas, shrugging his shoulder out of Alynn's hand. "And I don't feel this is yer place to interfere."

"I'm not interfering. I just know you aren't the best at sorting yer feelings, and I thought you could use some help." Alynn had been half-asleep when she'd heard the argument between Lukas and Rowan, but she tried to remember it as best she could. "You said that you'd had a family until my father came back. What did you mean by that?"

Lukas was silent.

"*Did* you mean it? Or did you just say it because you were angry?"

"I say what I mean," said Lukas. There was a sigh in his voice, as if he were trying to maintain his patience.

"Alright. What makes you feel that way?"

No response.

"I'm not leavin' until you answer me."

Lukas slammed his fist on his desk. "Would ye stop trying to pry into things that don't concern ye? My burdens aren't yers to carry. Just—go away. Please. I'll work this out wi' the Lord, same as I always do."

Alynn sighed. She walked up beside Lukas and wrapped an

arm around him. "I love you," she said. "Do you know what people do when they love each other?"

"They pester each other?"

"They talk to each other. Help solve each other's problems. You've always been there for me, Lukas, I'm just lookin' to return the favor."

Lukas was silent for a moment. He stroked the back of Alynn's hand with a work-rough thumb, took a deep breath, and relaxed into Alynn. "I miss having ye around," he said.

"I miss you, too," said Alynn. "But you've got a whole new family who loves you. They keep you too busy to miss me, right?"

"They don't love me," said Lukas. His voice was quiet.

"What makes you say that?"

"They don't have room fer me in their family, and—I don't blame them. I'm not a blood relative. But still." There was another pause. "I'm having a hard time making peace wi' the fact that I don't belong anymore."

"Lukas!" Alynn set Elspeth in Lukas's lap so she could hold him tighter. "Lukas, you know that isn't true. My family loves you. Why on earth would you think otherwise?"

"Because it's true."

Alynn searched for words. "You've known Mum for longest. What does she do that makes you think she doesn't love you anymore?"

"Well, fer one, she hasn't given me a hug in over a week. She doesn't talk to me except about household questions, or Tarin or Mercy. She's never even thanked me fer taking the arrow out of Tarin's foot! And I stayed up wi' him half the night because he was hurting too bad to sleep, not a word of thanks from her then. Not from either of yer parents."

Alynn was taken aback. She knew her parents' love and worries for Tarin would cloud their rationality, but she hadn't thought they'd overlook something as important as the physician who saved Tarin's life.

She wanted to tell Lukas that they were just frightened about losing another child, that they'd come around, but she couldn't. It felt insensitive. But she couldn't admit that her parents could be so cruelly ungrateful, because they weren't—they were good people. Finally, she found the words to say

"You saved my brother's life," said Alynn. "There aren't words to express how grateful this whole family is to you. I promise you, my parents will thank you themselves eventually. They just got frightened out of their wits. Remember the Battle of Faith? That story you told me, about how Mum had to tell you that I'd panned out? It was Leif who cauterized my shoulder with the fireplace poker, I'll bet the last thing on yer mind was thankin' him."

Lukas was still for a moment, letting Elspeth chew on his hand. "It did take me a while to thank him properly," he said. "I appreciate yer reminding me."

There was another silence while Alynn gathered her thoughts. "You have to learn to be part of a family," she said. "But you're good at everything you set your mind to, Lukas, and you learn so fast, I've no doubt you'll figure it out eventually. I remember when Tarin was born. I was six. I'd had Mum to myself ever since my sister Louisa died, and having to share her attention—I hated it at first. But then I got used to it, I learned how to share, and now I love Tarin more than anything. You'll get used to it too, I promise."

Lukas gave a derisive half-chuckle.

"What?"

"That's hardly a fair comparison. Yer mother loves ye more than life itself. Always has. She's never cared that much fer me."

Alynn stroked Elspeth's head. "A woman can't love everyone the way she loves her children," she said.

"Och, of course not, and I've never expected her to. I just hoped that the rest of yer family would start liking me, to make up for it, I suppose—and Tarin does, but now he's leaving." Lukas grew quiet for a moment. Elspeth kept trying to grab at his fingers, and he wiggled them for her amusement, but he did so absentmindedly. "I'm probably just being ungrateful about the whole thing. I'm sorry fer complaining."

"Everyone complains. 'Tis alright. But how about you find some good things to think about? What about our family are you grateful for?"

"Everyone's healthy, we get along tolerably well, everyone's provided fer." There was a pause. "Caitriona gave me that hug last week."

Alynn waited for the next statement of gratitude, but it never came. "Tarin gives you hugs too, doesn't he?" she asked.

"Tarin's too focused on impressing Brett to be physically affectionate."

Alynn pushed aside the notion that perhaps Lukas's feelings of being left out were justified. Lukas was a grown man. He shouldn't need the same constant affection that a child would. "I know you love hugs, but there's more to life than them. What else can you be thankful for?"

"Let's see…Tarin's foot is mending well, I'm grateful fer that. Mercy directed my attention to some birds the other day, it's sweet how she notices the little things. Brett's been extraordinarily helpful around the farm so far this year. And Rowan—he helped with the stable roof. I can't remember the last time he's done anything around the monastery."

Alynn smiled. "Do you feel better?"

"A wee bit."

"Good.

Lukas glanced at his journal. "I know that God is love, and that He ought to be the only One we truly need in our lives— it's wrong of me, I suppose, to care so much about earthly affection."

"Of course not!" Alynn hugged Lukas tighter. "Maybe things can go back, not completely to the way they used to be, but just a wee bit. Just tell Mum how you feel. She'll probably give you hugs if you'll ask for them, if that's what it'll take to make you feel like part of the family."

"There's nay point in it."

"What does that mean?"

"I'm not a blood relative. I can't expect her to treat me the way she treats everyone else."

"Och, that shouldn't matter! The two of us aren't blood relatives, but I still love you. Faith, sometimes I feel that you love me more than my own father does. Blood doesn't mean anything."

Lukas was quiet for a moment. "Ye really feel that way? About me and yer father?"

"Of course I do. Especially back when it was just the two of us. Da's changed a lot since he's come here. Used to be, he'd work all day, hardly see me and Tarin. Half the time, he'd—I don't even know if he ate breakfast, he'd be gone by the time I woke up. And he'd stay gone until dinnertime, sometimes afterwards, and he'd be too tired to really spend time with us. At some point, he stopped answerin' me when I called him 'Da,' so I started calling him 'Father' instead. It wasn't much of a life we had together. When you took me in—you taught me to read, to fight, you prayed for me, you talked with me. Lukas, you loved me the way God does."

Lukas held her tighter. Alynn kissed the top of his head and briefly set a hand on Elspeth, who didn't quite know what was going on but was enjoying all the snuggles. She squealed.

"Don't you dare tell my da I said that, though," said Alynn.

Lukas gave half of a chuckle. "I won't."

"Thanks." Alynn took a deep breath and gave Lukas a gentle squeeze, so as not to hurt his ribs, before taking his hand to help him from his chair. "Come on. Let's go talk to Mum."

Lukas gave half a syllable of protest, but rose from his chair, holding Elspeth. "I'll talk to her later," he said. "You need to get home. Drostan dropped by earlier, looking fer ye. He was half mad wi' fright. Thought Grima had kidnapped ye."

Alynn hadn't thought about frightening Drostan. She felt a pang of guilt. "Can I just—see Tarin? Please? I'll be quick."

"Of course. He's in the scriptorium."

Alynn took Elspeth and hurried downstairs to find Tarin

and Brett taking turns reading Scriptures in Latin. Smiling, she ruffled Tarin's hair, and he looked up at her with a grin. He didn't squirm much when she hugged him, either.

"I'm so glad you're mending well," said Alynn.

"Everyone's prayin' for me. I don't have a choice."

"Does it still hurt?"

"Only when Lukas puts mead in it. I know it keeps infection away, but it hurts like the devil."

"Lads?"

It was Rowan's voice, and it was worried. Everyone turned to see his grim expression and worried, slightly angry eyes.

"Neither of ye have taken to eating green cheese, have you?" he asked.

"Not me," said Brett.

"You won't let me outside," said Tarin.

Rowan leaned against the doorframe, brushing his hair out of his eyes. "Grima's been back," he said.

Tarin grabbed Alynn's hand. "Can you stay here?" he asked.

"I can't, heart. Drostan's worried about me. I have to get back to him."

"Don't call me that."

"Right. Sorry."

Lukas appeared in the doorway. "I'll take ye home, Alynn," he said.

Alynn was about to protest, but she realized that she'd have Elspeth with her and be practically unable to defend herself if Grima were to show up. "Would you?" she asked.

"Of course," said Lukas.

Alynn smiled and kissed Tarin's head, making him turn red with embarrassment, before saying goodbye to her parents and saddling Humility. Lukas met her in the stable wearing his sword. He saddled Honor, his white stallion, and the two of them set off for the village at a canter.

SIXTEEN

Humility kept close behind Honor, almost begging to go faster. Alynn had to rein her in more than once. She didn't like going so fast with Elspeth. She glanced down at her baby to make sure the shawl was holding, then looked back up just in time to see Honor stumble and come to a hard stop. Lukas fell forwards. Alynn pulled Humility to a stop just as Lukas tumbled to the ground.

"Lukas!" she cried.

Lukas didn't say anything. Alynn ran to him and was relieved when he grabbed her hand. He wasn't breathing, but his face was moving, and his bones didn't crack as Alynn ran her hands over them. Honor tossed his head, prompting Alynn to grab his reins so he wouldn't accidentally spook and step on Lukas.

"What's the matter with you?" she demanded. Honor took one limping step, and Alynn tied his reins to a tree branch and looked at his feet. Sure enough, he'd picked up a stone.

Alynn glanced over at Lukas. He was breathing now, and had moved himself to a more comfortable position, but he was still lying down. "Lukas, are you alright?"

"Can't talk," said Lukas.

Alynn went back to him and rested his head in her lap.

"You'll be alright," she promised. "You just got the wind knocked out of you. You'll mend."

Lukas drew a slow breath. "It hurts," he got out.

"What hurts?"

"My back. My sternum. Saddle horn stabbed me."

Alynn let Lukas squeeze her hand. "You'll be alright," she said again as she glanced around. Humility wasn't tied to anything, but she was too busy sniffing Honor to go anywhere. The woods seemed quiet.

Was that a hood?

Alynn froze. Directly in front of her, half hidden behind a tree, was Grima. Alynn grabbed Lukas's sword from his scabbard and stood up.

"Don't touch him," she ordered.

Grima didn't move. Alynn started trembling. Should she chase after him? But what about Lukas? What about Elspeth? Grima's hands started moving towards his waist.

"Don't you dare!" Alynn cried. "He's a priest! I've got a baby! Please—don't hurt my baby. You wouldn't dare hurt my baby."

Alynn's voice shifted from a terrified plea to an angry demand. Her vision narrowed, and she felt her heart begin to beat faster. It had been a while since she'd gone berserk. She was glad to know that she still could.

Grima stepped out from behind the tree, and Alynn spun the shawl around so that Elspeth was safely behind her. She braced herself to get shot, wondering if it felt like getting stabbed. She could take it. But instead of hearing the whiz of a bowstring and feeling the pain of an arrow entering her heart, she heard footsteps. Grima took a drinking horn from his belt and held it in an outstretched hand.

When Alynn didn't put down her sword, Grima slowly moved one hand to his belt and unbuckled it. His quiver fell to the ground. For the first time, Alynn noticed what he wore beneath the cloak. His clothes were threadbare, patched in some places, but still full of holes. His trousers were dark, and his short tunic was undyed wool.

Alynn knelt beside Lukas and, putting his sword down (but keeping it within arm's reach), she helped him sit up. Grima handed Alynn the drinking horn. Alynn held the horn to Lukas's lips, and he drank gratefully. Alynn never took her gaze off Grima. His face was wrapped in a dark green winninga; even his mouth was covered. But his eyes were visible. They were dark, and the skin between them was sun-browned. A single curl of hair poked out from his hood. Whether it was black or brown or dark auburn, Alynn could not tell.

Lukas finished his drink, and Alynn gave the horn back to Grima. "Thank you," said Lukas. He was breathing easier now, and his face was getting some color back. Without taking his gaze away from Grima, Lukas said "Go home" in Gaelic.

"I won't leave you," said Alynn.

"Take the baby. Go home. I'll be right behind ye."

Alynn's heart started beating faster again as her berserker energy wore off. But Lukas was right. She had Elspeth to worry about. Her eyes still on Grima, she squeezed Lukas's hand, stood up, and mounted Humility. She let Humility run as fast as she wanted to the rest of the way to the village. She didn't stop until she had ridden past her house, through the marketplace, and straight to the shipyard. Drostan was sanding a strake, but immediately stopped and put his tools down when he saw Alynn.

"What the devil were you thinking? I thought you were dead!" Drostan's tone was furious, and his muscles were tense as Alynn jumped down from Humility and wrapped her arms around him. He didn't hug her back. "It's a good thing I had the sense to check the monastery first, I almost got a search party together to look for your corpse! You can't just run off like that!"

"You have to go get Lukas," said Alynn.

"What does he have to do with any of this?" Drostan demanded.

Alynn realized she was trembling. "Lukas was riding home

with me, but Honor picked up a stone and Grima showed up and he gave Lukas a drink but please, please, Drostan, he might be dead—"

"Which is exactly why you shouldn't be going places." Drostan's voice had that hissing noise that he used whenever he felt like yelling, but was doing his best to control his temper. "I don't want you leaving the house until we catch this thing, do you hear me?"

"Drostan." It was Leif's voice, and it was stern. "She's alright. Take her home, I'll go find Lukas. Can I use Humility?"

Alynn nodded. Drostan grabbed her by the arm and walked briskly, saying nothing until they were safely inside their house. Alynn sat down and watched Drostan as he paced the length of the longhouse. She prepared herself to be yelled at, but was taken off guard when Drostan's voice came out in an exasperated yet quiet tone.

"Do you know what it's like, to only have a single memory of your mother?" He stayed at the far end of the room and turned to face her. "One memory. And it's such an old memory that I don't even know if it's a memory at all, or just something I've conjured out of my imagination. I don't know what sort of person my mother was. I don't know what her voice sounded like. She wasn't there when I burned my arm, she wasn't there when Alva poisoned me, she wasn't there when I got married—do you want Elspeth to live that way?"

"I'm sorry," said Alynn.

"What am I supposed to tell her when she grows up? That her mum got herself murdered because she didn't have the common sense to stay home?"

"I needed my mum. Elspeth wouldn't stop crying."

Drostan knelt in front of Alynn and grabbed her arms. "Get Nora. Get literally anyone from the village! But don't go risking your life again. Do you hear me?"

Alynn nodded. She was quietly trying to fish Elspeth out of the shawl, and when she finally succeeded, Elspeth wasted no time in grinning at Drostan and reaching her pudgy little arms out towards him. Drostan smiled with a familiar sadness in his eyes—the same sadness Leif smiled with whenever Drostan's mother was brought up—and held Elspeth close to his chest.

"I missed you, Squiggly."

Elspeth shrieked. Drostan mimicked her, and Elspeth shrieked all the louder. Alynn smiled, Drostan made a funny noise so that Elspeth laughed, and Drostan hugged her again. He smelled the top of her head and kissed her.

"Don't let Mammy take you away from me again, alright?" Drostan asked.

Elspeth squeaked.

Apparently calmer now, Drostan looked at Alynn with a bit less anger in his countenance. "Can you tell me what happened?" he asked.

"Well, Elspeth wouldn't stop cryin' last night—"

"I got all that from Mum. Tell me about what happened on the ride home."

"Honor picked up a stone." Alynn spoke slowly, trying to remember exactly what happened. "Lukas fell. I tied up Honor, then I went to go help Lukas. He was hurting a lot. And then Grima showed up—he's got a suntan, dark eyes, and dark hair—and he gave Lukas a drink of water."

Drostan raised his brows. "What?"

"He had a drinking horn. He gave it to me, and Lukas drank it, and then Lukas told me to go home. And now I'm here."

Drostan ran a hand through his hair and muttered "Lord, what the devil does this mean?" under his breath. He looked up at Alynn and asked, "Are you sure Honor didn't get shot?"

"Of course I'm sure. Saw the stone in his hoof myself."

"And Grima didn't—threaten you? He didn't try to rob you? Did he say anything?"

"He didn't say a word. And he was still wearing that mask. He's short and skinny. And his clothes—he's wearin' rags beneath my da's cloak. And he's barefoot."

Drostan snapped his fingers. "That's it!" he said.

"What's it?"

"We've had clothes go missing, right? Why isn't Grima wearing them?" Drostan didn't let her answer the question. "There's a second person on the island."

Alynn's heart skipped a beat. For some reason, the fact that there was a second, unknown person hiding somewhere on St. Anne's Cleft terrified her more than knowing that Grima was out and about with his quiver and bow. "What do we do?"

"We think. Grima's wearing rags. Did they look like old rags, or just something that might have gotten torn up during a shipwreck?"

"Both. There were patches and new holes."

"Alright. So Grima's poor."

"No. That can't be right. Old clothes are bloody useless. Especially here. The wind blows right through them. You're shipwrecked, you've got unlimited things to steal, the first thing you do is get yourself some new clothes."

"Alright. Why wouldn't Grima get himself new clothes?"

"Besides my da's cloak." Alynn let her mind wander over the years she spent growing up in Ireland and, surprisingly, nothing really stood out at her. She could remember being hungry and cold and tired, and she remembered her feet hurting from walking from town to town, and she remembered fainting in church because she was ill with pneumonia. Not much else.

But then another memory hit Alynn. She remembered walking from one town to another in the dead of winter. Tarin was whimpering and whining beside her, complaining about how cold he was, so Alynn took off her plaid, folded it so Tarin wouldn't trip, and wrapped it around his head and shoulders. She was cold as ice herself—so cold, she felt like she was dying. So she imagined herself a martyr. Surely the cold would cleanse her soul. After all, the priests always talked about our sins being washed white as snow. And so she would walk until she died of cold, and then her soul would go straight to heaven while the people on earth made reliquaries for her bones and maybe she would be made the patron saint of those who died from the cold.

Of course, she'd never died. Sometimes her fingers and toes would turn red for a few days, but she'd never died.

"Maybe 'tis some sort of penance," she said.

"Penance?" asked Drostan.

"Aye, like—well, Lukas doesn't give penance—'tis when you know you're doing somethin' wrong, and you feel bad about it, so you punish yourself. Or else a priest tells you to do it. Once, Da got in trouble for tryin' to steal a chicken, and the priest told him to give three chickens to the man he was tryin' to steal from, except that we didn't have any chickens, so Da just packed us up in the middle of the night, and we moved towns again instead."

Drostan stood up, brushing Elspeth's wandering hands out of his mouth. He paced, deep in thought. "But he killed Rothgeir—unless the second person did—Alynn, was Grima wearing a sword?"

"No. I'm sure of it this time."

"Alright. So Grima didn't kill Rothgeir, he shot at you, he shot at me, and he actually hit Tarin—unless it was an accident—"

"What do you mean?"

"I mean, if you're shooting to kill someone, and you miss, you're more likely to hit their arm or their leg than their foot, right? And that first time you saw him in the village, he could have easily shot you in the leg, or even the head if he'd wanted to."

Another epiphany struck Alynn. "He hit the metal bit of my shield, right in the middle."

"Like he was aiming for it?"

The front door opened, and Alynn ran to Lukas the moment she saw him. "Lukas, what happened?" she asked, wrapping her arms around him.

"Gentle—"

"Sorry. Come, sit, I'll make you some tea. What happened? Are you alright?"

"He was up and riding when I found him," said Leif. "The stone wasn't deep in Honor's foot. He'll limp it off."

"He's always been a bit dramatic," said Lukas, sitting stiffly on the sleeping bench. "I'll take something stronger than tea if ye have it, Alynn."

"Are you hurt?" Alynn asked, getting some mead from the cupboard.

"Nothing's broken, sprained, bleeding, or dislocated, as far as I can tell. I just got the wind knocked out of me. I'll be sore fer a few days, though." Lukas gratefully accepted the horn of mead and, rather than downing the whole thing as was Norse tradition, he sipped it carefully. "Thank ye."

"Lukas," said Drostan, "what did Grima do to you?"

"He didn't hurt me, if that's what ye're asking. We had a conversation."

Drostan handed Elspeth to Alynn so he could listen better. "What did he say?"

Lukas took another sip of his mead. "Enough. I think I know how we can catch him."

Drostan called a town meeting the next day, and surprisingly, everyone listened to what he had to say. Everyone went about their business, chatting unafraid in the streets, lingering to test the merchant's wares. Women were once again gossiping at the well. And then, that night, every house in the village was full of life and noise. People were either singing or talking loudly or letting their children stay up late and get loud with their play.

Every house except for Alynn and Drostan's house.

Alynn and Drostan were in the main room of the house, hiding in the shadows. Alynn was hiding behind her shield the same way she had once hidden behind her mother's skirts in unfamiliar situations. Drostan was closest to the door, also crouched behind a shield. Leif was in the stable.

Elspeth was safe at Nora's house. Alynn missed her.

Drostan was whispering to himself under his breath; Alynn knew he was praying. The occasional half-prayer would run through her own brain, too. *Thank You, God, for always being with us—God, I'm scared—God, please help us not to be wrong about Grima—*

Alynn's breasts were uncomfortably full of milk. Elspeth normally got hungry around this time of night, and Alynn wished for her baby again. Was she safe? Was she frightened? What if Grima didn't behave as predicted? What if he didn't show up tonight at all?

The door rustled. Drostan stopped praying and clutched his sword tighter. Alynn's heart started thumping before she realized it was only a gust of wind.

Time passed, and Alynn's worry was slowly replaced by boredom and exhaustion. She caught herself nodding off and shook herself. But just when she thought that Grima wouldn't show up, the door creaked open.

A shadow slipped through the door, noiseless as a cat, and crept to the pantry. Alynn readied herself for action, but didn't move. She was just backup. Drostan crept from his place in the shadows and put his sword against the back of Grima's neck.

"Game's up," he said.

Grima kicked Drostan in the shin and bolted.

Alynn dashed from her hiding spot and, not knowing what else to do, hit Grima in the head with the edge of her shield. Grima stumbled, but didn't quite fall, and kept trying to get to the door. But Drostan was up, and he grabbed Grima's cloak, then his arm. Grima struggled, but Drostan got his sword against his neck just as Leif burst through the stable door.

"Let me go! Let me go!" shrieked an unusually high-pitched voice. A child's voice.

Drostan stood shocked for a moment, then yanked down Grima's plaid hood and unraveled the dark green winninga that shrouded Grima's face. It came off like a bandage unwinding from a sprained limb, like a spider unweaving its web. And once it was off, Grima hung his head so that his face was obscured by curls of dark hair.

Leif struck up the fire, and everyone stared at the slight figure in front of them. Alynn had always assumed that Grima walked hunched over, as if trying to duck out of everyone's way. But what she'd thought was a hunched back was actually a pack folded into his cloak. Grima was barely five feet tall.

"Show yourself," Leif ordered.

Grima didn't move, so Drostan grabbed his hair and yanked his head upright. Staring back at them was the face of a fourteen-year-old girl.

May 7, A.D. 969—

What a day! I'm hurting a good bit after falling off Honor, so forgive me if this is a bit disjointed. I can't think straight. Besides, I'm bewildered and angry all at once.

The bewilderment first. I believe that the child I thought I hallucinated in the chapel when this whole mess with Grima started was actually Grima herself. She seems to be a young slave girl, maybe Tarin's age, acting on the will of a cruel-hearted mistress. She gave me a drink of water and conversed with me when I fell off Honor, although she didn't let me see her face. She asked after Tarin with genuine concern. I believe she is ashamed of her actions and shows true penitence. I forgive her, and I know that God does; I just pray that the rest of the village can forgive her, too.

Now for the anger. This morning, Rowan said that Tarin won't be studying with me anymore. That man! Forever a thorn in my side and a test of my self-control. He lives at my house, eats my food, wears the wool that my sheep produce, and all I ask in return is the assurance that my ministry does not die with me. I'd think Rowan would be happy that I'm educating his son, giving him a chance at a meaningful life in the service of God. But no! He won't allow it!

I'm losing a friend as well as a student. Tarin is dear to me. I value the time we spend together, and I'm not ready to only see him in the evenings and on Sabbaths. I'm tired of gaining friends only to lose them. Alynn is gone, Caitriona hardly acknowledges me anymore, Brett will be leaving next year—

Perhaps they mean too much to me. Perhaps I'm foolish for thinking that human relationships will fill the emptiness in my heart. That's God's place, and I ought to know that. Perhaps it would be best for me, for them, for everyone, if they were to just leave.

I can't be alone again. The mere thought of it drives me nearly to tears.

No! What a useless, wretched man am I! My tears are mere

proof that human interaction has taken the place of God in my life. I need to distance myself from the McNeils and seek my fulfillment in Christ alone. I'll send them away—or at least ask them to leave, as I dare not add inhospitality to my list of transgressions—and return again to my life of prayer and solitude. It will purge my heart and benefit my soul.

—L. McCamden

SEVENTEEN

Alynn stared. Leif stared. Drostan uttered a single swear word, glancing from the girl to Alynn and Leif and back again. The girl's brown eyes were glistening with tears, and her voice shook as she spoke. "Please don't kill me," she said. She drew a deep breath, but her eyes grew wetter. "I know I deserve it. But please, please don't—I'm scared—"

She stopped talking, as if she knew it would just get her in more trouble. She wiped her eyes and kept her gaze on the floor, shivering as a chill breeze flew through the open front door.

Every ounce of mother's instinct welled up in Alynn's heart. She sheathed her sword, put her shield down, and took the girl's hands. They were freezing cold. "Don't fret, now. We're not in the habit of killing children. It's late. I'll make you some tea, and you'll spend the night here, and we'll decide what to do with you in the morning."

"Tea, Alynn?" Drostan asked.

"She's shiverin'!" said Alynn in Gaelic, which she hoped the girl didn't speak.

"She's a criminal."

"She's a child. And what did Jesus say, that whatever we do for the least of these, we do for Him? I don't think I've met a lesser 'least of these,' and besides, I wouldn't mind a cup of tea myself. Now, someone fetch Elspeth while I get the kettle on."

Leif kept his gaze on the girl. "I trust you can keep our master thief locked up while I fetch the baby," he said to Drostan.

"I'd hope so," said Drostan.

Leif left, and Drostan released his grip on the girl so he could get a better look at her. "What's your name?" he asked.

"Rys."

"Short name."

The girl raised her chin with all the pride such a small creature could hold. "Cerys ferch Owain ap Cadfael ab Eurig ap Dafydd ap Rhys." The list of names came forth like a memorized Bible verse. "But since Cerys was my mum's name, everyone calls me Rys."

"Alright. My name is Drostan. I'm the chief of St. Anne's Cleft. This here is my wife, Lady Alynn the Dauntless."

Rys nodded hello to Alynn.

"How old are you?" Alynn asked.

"I don't know."

"Are you fifteen?" asked Drostan.

Rys furrowed her brows. "What year is it?"

"969."

Rys was quiet for a moment. "I'm thirteen or fourteen. I don't know for sure."

"That's alright," said Drostan. "I'll take your quiver."

Rys took off her belt and handed it to Drostan. Then, she bent down and took a knife that had been tucked into the half-winninga wrapped around her lower leg. "You'll want this, too," she said. "It belonged to the people whose house burned down. They—they all got out alright, didn't they? I—I didn't mean to, but this naked man just started coming at me, swinging an axe, and I just picked up the closest thing to throw at him—"

"By God's grace, no one was seriously hurt." He took a length of tablet-woven garment trim and tied Rys's wrists together, then tethered her to a pillar. "You're not disappearing on us again."

"No, sir."

Those were the last words spoken for quite some time. The teakettle finally started boiling, and no one spoke. Alynn added bilberries and birchbark, and no one spoke. The tea steeped and cooled until it was drinkable, and still no one spoke. Alynn said "Here you are" as she handed Rys a mug of tea, and Rys said "Thank you, milady" as she took the mug carefully in her bound hands, and after that, no one spoke.

Finally, Leif came home. Elspeth was squalling in his arms, and Alynn lost no time in snatching her and shushing her and putting her to her breast. When she finally got Elspeth situated, she realized Rys was staring at her.

"What's its name?" Rys asked.

"The baby's?"

Rys nodded.

"Elspeth."

Rys smiled. "She looks like my baby sister Myfanwy."

"You have a sister?" Alynn asked.

"Two. And three brothers. And there were two other babies that died when they were little, but my mum never talked about them."

"Goodness."

"I know you won't let me hold her, but do you think I could play peek-a-boo with her? When she's done eating, I mean?"

"We'll see." Alynn had no intention of letting Rys interact with Elspeth, but she'd deal with that later. Hopefully, Elspeth would nurse herself to sleep.

Rys retreated into herself again. Alynn sat and gently rocked as Elspeth nursed, keeping an eye on Rys the whole while. Leif and Drostan were having a quiet discussion in Gaelic, trying to figure out what to do with their captive.

Finally, Leif took a stool and sat in front of Rys. "So," he said. "Cerys ferch Owain. That's a Welsh name, isn't it?"

"It is, sir."

"What's a Welsh girl like you doing in the company of

Thrand the Infamous?"

"He stole me in a raid, about three years ago, I think. Gave me to his daughter Eyja. She's a—"

Rys began to describe Eyja in such profane terms that Alynn covered Elspeth's ears. She was surprised until she remembered that Rys had been around sailors for the past several years. What else should she expect?

Leif seemed almost amused by Rys's choice of words. "Is Eyja outlawed like her father?"

"If she isn't, she ought to be."

Drostan, who had been listening to the interrogation, stepped closer to Rys and Leif. "I'll cut you a deal," he said. "Seeing as you're a slave working under orders, and as you're legally still a child, the hand of the law will not deal harshly with you. If," he said, sitting next to Rys and looking her in the eye, "you tell us where Eyja is."

Rys nodded. "I will."

"Good. Very good." Drostan half-smiled and nodded curtly, then stood up, took his stool, and stowed it in the loft where it belonged. Alynn glanced at Rys just in time to see her squirm.

"Your hands stay tied, young lady," she said, trying to sound stern.

Rys looked up with wide eyes. "I'm not trying to get loose, I swear to God."

"Then what are you doing?"

"My back hurts."

"You're too young for your back to hurt," said Leif.

"Not if—" Rys stopped herself, but Leif stepped closer to her and told her to finish her statement. She took a deep breath before doing so. "Not if you mistress whips you."

Leif took off Rys's cloak, then tried to lift up the back of her shirt. Rys flinched and let out another profanity. Leif patted Rys awkwardly on the shoulder and approached Alynn. "Her shirt's covered in blood and stuck to her back. Do you know how to take care of whip wounds?"

"Not a clue. I say we get Lukas."

"In the morning," said Drostan. "It's late. Lynder, go to bed. I'll keep an eye on Rys."

"What's happening?" asked Rys.

"Your back's hurt pretty badly," said Leif. "We'll be fetching the priest in the morning to look at it."

Rys smiled. "I like Father Lukas. Thank you, milord."

Alynn kissed Drostan goodnight and took Elspeth into the bedcloset with her. She stayed awake for a while, listening to the shuffling of Leif and Drostan as they readied for bed. They spoke to each other in low tones, then Leif chuckled softly and bid Drostan goodnight. Drostan climbed into bed with Alynn, and the last thing Alynn heard as she drifted off to sleep was Rys humming the same haunting melody that Alynn had heard on the beach a few long days ago.

The next morning, Rys was let free for ten minutes so she could wash her face and eat some stirabout. Leif volunteered to send Olvir to fetch Lukas, but he never came back. Alynn wasn't surprised. If he wasn't visiting with Nora—the more likely explanation—he was working at the shipyard, or else telling everyone about Grima's capture.

Lukas was a bit stiffer than usual as he came inside, but he still smiled when he saw Elspeth. Elspeth smiled, too, and reached out for him. Lukas took her in his arms, but winced as he did so.

"Are you alright?" Alynn asked.

Lukas made himself smile. "It hurts to breathe, but other than that, I'm alright."

"If you're not well, you ought to have sent Brett."

"I'm well, I'm alright. Where's Grima? Was I right? She's just a child?"

"Aye, you were right." Alynn nodded towards the derelict still tied to the sleeping bench. "Rys ferch Owain. Thirteen or fourteen years old she is, slave to the daughter of Thrand the Infamous, and her back's been torn to shreds with a whip."

"*Mater Dei,*" muttered Lukas under his breath as he approached Rys. He sat down next to her, stared at her for a moment, and cleared his throat. "*Bore da,*" he said.

Rys's eyes lit up. "*Rydych chi'n siarad Cymraeg?*" she asked excitedly.

Lukas stammered around for a bit before sighing. "Not fluently," he said. "Even with Norse, I'll stumble a bit here and there. It's my fifth language. Have mercy on me."

Rys deflated a bit, but she looked up at Lukas with a bit of a smile in her eyes anyway. "Norse is my third language. Don't worry."

"Och, what's the second?"

"English."

"My student Brett is half English. He says he doesn't remember the language, on account of his mother dying when he was young, but who knows? Maybe you can help him remember, and you could have a nice conversation." Lukas untied Rys's wrists. "What hurts?"

"Mostly my back. Mistress whips me. But I tripped and fell in the woods the other day, and I caught myself, and now my wrist hurts, too, but not bad."

Lukas examined Rys's arms and wrists and hands and said that nothing was broken or sprained, but that she ought to keep it wrapped and try not to bend it too much for a few days. Then, he got to her back. Her shirt was still stuck.

"Alynn, I need hot water." While Lukas typically spoke to Alynn in Gaelic, he stuck with Norse this time so Rys knew what was happening. "Dishwater hot, not boiling. We'll also need a clean rag and something with alcohol."

Alynn set about heating water and fetching rags, while Lukas reached out a hand and carefully touched Rys's hair. "My hair used to be about this color," he said. "It wasn't this curly, but my father, when I was young, and we were sitting next to each other during the Divine Offices—he'd—well, he called it 'springing' my curls. Pull them out, watch them bounce back." He demonstrated, and a bit of a sad smile crept into the corners of his eyes. Rys didn't seem to know what to think of the demonstration. "It made me laugh. I got in trouble for it once or twice."

"How's that work? I mean—did you and your dad join the monastery together or something?" She squirmed away from him while asking, and he stopped playing with her hair.

"I was a foundling, actually. The man I called father was just the man who volunteered to take care of me."

"Oh." Rys retreated into herself again, but then smiled faintly. "My little brother Meilyr used to spring my curls. Except that he pulled too hard half the time. He was four the last time I saw him."

"You must miss him."

"I do—all of them, really. Three brothers. Two sisters. You probably don't care about them. Sorry for bringing them up."

"Och, of course I care. Look at me, Rys. I know what it's like to miss a loved one. You can talk to me about your family, or whatever else you like. That's what priests are for. And asides, us brown-haired folk have to stick together, don't we?"

Rys smiled, Lukas smiled, and Alynn decided that the water was hot enough to use. Lukas bade Rys lie on her back and started gently sponging at her shirt. The fabric came off rotten piece by piece, some of it tearing away completely from the rest of the shirt and being tossed in a blood-tinged, salty, languid heap in the rushes on the floor. Finally, the shirt came completely off. Rys's back was striped with whip wounds— some scarred over, some scabbed, others fresh and oozing. Some of them seemed to move.

Lukas froze for a moment. Then he blinked and shook his head—not in disagreement, but more like a horse trying to chase a fly away—as he stood up and hurried out the back door.

Drostan, who was sitting by the door to make sure Rys didn't try to escape, looked up from his whittling. "What's wrong with him?" he asked.

Alynn looked at Rys, who was red with embarrassment, then followed Lukas out the back door. Lukas was pacing, shaking his hand as if he were playing an invisible lyre. His face was ashen and contorted by an expression of either grief or terror, or perhaps a mix of both. It frightened Alynn.

"Lukas?" she asked.

Lukas drew a deep breath. "Go back inside," he said.

"Lukas, what's wrong?"

He paid her no heed and kept pacing. "Och, God help me. In God I trust, I will not be afraid, in God Whose word I praise, what can mortal man do to me—Ye will keep him in perfect peace, whose mind is stayed upon Ye, because he trusts in Ye—God, help me. God, help me." Lukas stopped pacing and banged his fist against his thigh.

Then, just as suddenly, as he'd left, Lukas drew a deep breath, turned around, and grabbed Alynn's wrists with shaking hands.

"I need yer help," said Lukas.

"Of course. What's wrong?"

"I think Rys has maggots."

"Maggots?"

"Listen. Ye've got young eyes and a steady hand. I need ye to remove them."

"Me?" Alynn's voice came out in much more of a squeak than she intended.

"Ye can use those—what's that instrument, ye pull out eyebrow hairs wi' it—"

"Tweezers?"

"Aye. Ye can use those. Just—it needs to be done. And I need ye to do it." And with that, Lukas all but dragged Alynn back inside before kneeling next to Rys and setting a hand over hers. Rys looked up at him with wide eyes.

"Is something wrong with me?" she asked.

"Well—nothing that can't be fixed," said Lukas, his voice nervous. "Alynn's going to help."

"Can't Drostan do it?" Alynn asked.

"Do what?" Drostan asked. He'd laid his whittling aside and was standing in the middle of the room.

"Alynn, grow up and go get the tweezers," said Lukas. Alynn obliged.

"What do you need tweezers for?" Rys asked in a small voice.

Lukas made a fist and started tapping it against his leg. "You've got a couple of maggots hiding back there—"

Rys panicked, trying to stand up. "Get them off, get them off—"

"Lie down!"

Lukas raised his voice and used a tone that made even Drostan flinch a bit. Rys whimpered a bit, lay obediently on her stomach, and wiped tears off her cheeks. Lukas grabbed her hand.

"I'm sorry," he said. "I know you're frightened, and I don't mean to add to it. Just hold my hand. And keep still, now. Alynn's about to start getting them off. Ye'll be alright."

Alynn grabbed a bucket to put the maggots into, knelt over Rys, and started tweezing. Rys was shivering. Her skin was pulled tight against her bones, both with tension and with hunger. The sight of the bones and the injuries roused Alynn's compassion to the point that her own fear of the maggots was gone. She'd do anything to help this poor creature.

Rys gave a fiercer shiver, and Lukas began to stroke her hair. "Talk to me," he said. "Tell me about Wales. What's it like?"

"It's nice," said Rys. "There's lots of sheep. We lived in a place called Mostyn, one town away from Holywell—that's where St. Winifred lived before she moved off to Gwytherin."

"Tell me about St. Winifred," said Lukas.

"You know more about her than I do," said Rys. "Right?"

"I haven't heard the stories in a while." Lukas spoke in a soft and faltering voice, the way a lost child might ask a stranger for help. "Please. Just tell me about St. Winifred."

"Well, there was this man who wanted to marry her, and

when she told him that she was going to become a nun instead of getting married, he got mad and cut off her head. But her uncle, St. Beuno, was there, and he fixed her, and God killed the boyfriend. And a well sprang up there, and if people go there and ask thrice for a miracle, they get it."

"And you lived one town away," said Lukas.

"We did." The muscles of Rys's back were relaxed now, making it a bit harder to get the maggots out. "A bunch of English people would try to visit Holywell and get lost and wind up in Mostyn instead. A couple families ended up staying because Wales is better than England. Our next-door neighbors were English. They had four children, and two of them were close to my age, and so we played together a lot. That's how I learned English, was by playing with them. Their dad was a really nice man. His name was Jehan and his face got red whenever he did anything remotely physical. You should have seen him after he helped unload my dad's ship one day. He looked like an apple."

Alynn tweezed out the fifteenth maggot and carefully looked over Rys's back to make sure she hadn't missed anything, wiping her wounds carefully with a warm, damp rag as she went.

"Could you please stop touching my hair?" Rys asked Lukas. He wordlessly obliged.

"They're all gone," said Alynn. She looked up from Rys's back to see that, while Rys had calmed down considerably, Lukas was pale, and his eyes were staring into nothingness like a blind man's. "Lukas, are you with us?"

No response.

"Lukas," Alynn said, a bit louder. This time, he blinked and looked at Alynn, but he still didn't say anything.

"Father Lukas, are you having a stroke?" Rys asked. "I can feel your heartbeat just by holding your hand. I don't think that's normal."

"I'm sorry," said Lukas, his voice soft and faltering. "My— the last place I saw maggots was on my father's corpse. I have a habit of—letting bad memories get too intense for my own good. Thank you for telling that story, Rys. And letting me hold your hand. That helps."

Rys seemed a bit more sympathetic. "You can pet my hair some more if you need to," she said.

Lukas gave the faintest twitch of a smile. "Nay, I'll just ask Alynn for a hug later on. Thank you, though. Now, Alynn, how's the, ah—"

"They're all gone," Alynn promised, setting the bucket and tweezers down to give Lukas a hug. He was shaking like the air in a belfry during the last reverberations of the noon bell, but he relaxed within seconds. A deep breath steadied him and brought the color back to his face.

Alynn glanced up at Drostan, who had been standing in the middle of the room for the duration of the procedure, and nodded towards the bucket and tweezers. "Can you take care of these, love?"

"What do you want me to do with the tweezers?" Drostan asked.

Alynn shuddered at the thought of using them on anyone's eyebrows again. "Burn them."

Drostan took the bucket and tweezers outside to clean, or perhaps to throw away. Lukas inspected Rys's back for himself and asked for some ale to cleanse her wounds with. Alynn was happy to fetch it. She needed to step away, to breathe and tremble and begin to forget what she had just seen and done. But only for a moment. Rys needed her. When she came back with the ale, she was glad to see Rys talking to Lukas again.

"Dad was just a sailor. He'd be gone months at a time. I hardly knew him, really. My mum must have loved him, though, because she made eight babies for him. There were six of us still alive when Master Thrand took me, God knows what's happened since then."

During the last sentence, Lukas poured the ale over Rys's wounds. Rys tensed up, then cursed to relieve the pain. Lukas then took a salve from his satchel and anointed her wounds.

"Where did you fall among your siblings?" he asked.

"Third born. Second girl." Rys swore in pain again. "Sorry, Father."

"Just call me Lukas, everyone else does. And I also tend to use profanity to relieve pain." Between Alynn's hug and Rys's speech, Lukas was finally looking more like himself—his eyes, at least, weren't staring into a void anymore, even if his face was still a bit drawn. "I'm afraid the lads I'm tutoring have picked up on it, though. Luckily, I do most of my swearing in Latin, so it's not as obvious."

Rys went white. "Please tell me—the little boy, Tarin, I think you call him—is he still doing alright?"

"Aye, by God's grace and Hippocrates' wisdom."

"Who's Hippocrates?"

"A Greek physician. I've studied his works quite extensively. Well, I've done what I can with your back. You can sit up if you want."

"Can I put my shirt back on?" Rys asked.

"Your shirt's not in one piece anymore, unfortunately. But here—try wearing my scapular. Does this do you any good?"

Rys sat up, tugged the scapular as far down her chest as she could, then put Rowan's stolen plaid in her lap to cover the rest of her. It was just in time, too, because Leif came home, and he brought Sigmund with him. Sigmund simply stood in the doorway for a moment and stared at Rys with wide eyes. Her brown hair was disheveled, her hands unbound, and her clothing ridiculous.

"Are you sure we've got the right person?" Sigmund asked.

Rys's eyes flashed sparks. "I'm sorry, you were expecting Saint Sebastian?"

"Uller, maybe," said Leif.

"How did you learn archery?" Sigmund asked. "What are you, twelve?"

"I'm fourteen. I learned the basics when I was eight. Our neighbor Jehan taught me. Then, when Master Thrand took me, he made me practice four, five, six hours a day. There isn't much to do when you're on a ship for weeks at a time. He wanted me to shoot in raids."

"Where is your master?" Leif asked.

"Dead. It's his daughter I'm with now. Mistress Eyja. She's…that way." Rys pointed in the general direction of the rock beach.

"We searched there," said Sigmund.

"I know. We hid in the woods while you did."

"And how the devil have you kept disappearing from us?" Leif asked.

Rys smiled. "You always looked down for us. Never up. I'd climb trees and stay there until everyone had left."

Alynn let Elspeth chew on her thumb. "So that time I went out looking for you—"

"You did what?" snapped Drostan.

Devil mend it, Alynn thought.

"She wasn't in danger," Rys said. "Mistress Eyja had drunk herself to sleep, and I wouldn't have hurt her."

"Then why'd you shoot the boy at the monastery?" Sigmund demanded. "Why did you burn down that house?"

Rys shrunk. "I—Tarin was chasing me. He would have caught me. And I didn't want him to catch me until I got to the beach so he could find Eyja and arrest us both. I just wanted to trip him up with an arrow and slow him down, I swear to God, I never meant to hit him. And the house—I forgot about the rushes on the floor. We just had dirt floors in Wales."

Leif strode over to her and took her chin in one hand, forcing her to look at him. "Are you lying to us?"

"No, sir."

Leif's voice was firm. "Of course you aren't. You're Welsh. The Welsh can be tricky sometimes, but they aren't dishonest. Is that right?"

"Usually, sir."

"If I find you're lying to me, there will be consequences."

"Yes, sir."

"And you'll help us find this mistress of yours, right?"

Rys hesitated. "What'll happen to me if I do?"

"Well, Eyja won't hurt you. We'll make sure of that." Leif studied Rys's face for a moment before continuing. "But what you've done is wrong, and you've earned a certain punishment. We'll have to discuss what that punishment ought to be, but you can rest assured that it won't be too harsh."

"Thank you, sir, but—where will I go, I mean?"

"We'll probably arrange to have you taken back to Wales," said Leif.

"That could take a while," said Lukas. "You're more than welcome to stay at the monastery until then."

For a moment, Rys was silent again. "Do I have to go back to Wales?" she asked.

"Why wouldn't you want to go?" asked Lukas. "Don't you miss your siblings?"

"Of course I miss them. Especially the little ones. But my sister Gwendolyn was always so good at watching them. And besides—Dad's always gone, and my older brother Griffin started drinking after Mum died. No one wanted to hire him because he's a drunk, and we could hardly keep food on the table. And besides, no one's going to want to marry me because of this stupid slave haircut. I—I want what's best for my family, I want what's best for myself—I suppose you could just drop me off at a convent somewhere. At least until my hair grows back."

Lukas was silent for a moment, perhaps praying silently. "Can you earn your keep?" he finally asked.

"Yes, sir. I'm a jack of all trades. I'll do whatever you ask of me."

"Easy, now. When I tell people they can stay at the monastery, I invite them as kin, not servants. You'll be part of the family, which does mean you'll have chores, but you'll be your own person. We do have one condition, though." Lukas's voice and gaze were unusually firm. "You're going to cooperate fully and show us where Eyja is."

Rys blinked and took a moment to decide. "I'll take you to her, but please, don't kill her."

"Why do you care?" Drostan asked. "She's been horrible to you."

Rys's eyes widened, then closed tightly as tears slipped down her cheeks. "I don't know," she said. "I don't know."

Alynn clutched Elspeth a bit tighter. Lukas looked at Alynn, then at Rys, then sat down beside her and set a hand on her shoulder. "Do you want to be free?" he asked.

Rys nodded.

"Then don't give another thought to Eyja. She has no real power over you. Stop acting as if she does."

Rys wiped her eyes and drew a deep breath and swallowed her tears. "I'm sorry," she said.

"You're alright, child," said Lukas, with a kindness in his voice that could make anyone feel loved. "The salve on your back is dry. We'll bandage it, then Alynn, if you could find something decent for her to wear. We'll take care of you, Rys. Don't worry."

Alynn's mind raced. Her own dresses would be too long. One of Drostan's spare tunics might be the best answer, unless one of the neighbors would mind lending a child's dress. No— no one was likely to volunteer, and besides, it would take too long to ask, so one of Drostan's spare tunics it was. Alynn found an old blue one that came past Rys's knees and forever slipped off one shoulder. But a belt and the rolling of sleeves made it a decent and warm outfit. There were no spare boots to be found, so Alynn put some socks on Rys's cold, filthy feet and wrapped them with winningas.

"We'll find you some boots as soon as we can," Alynn promised. "Now, are you ready to show us where Eyja is?"

Rys nodded. "Can you come with, milady?"

"No," said Drostan.

"I don't trust the rest of you. Someone will kill me."

"Do you trust me?" Lukas asked. Rys nodded, and Lukas half-smiled. "Then I'll go with. I trust you're alright with that,

Drostan."

"Of course. But you, on the other hand—" Drostan turned towards Alynn and switched to Gaelic— "you had no business looking for Grima. Suppose we hadn't been dealing with a child slave controlled by an incompetent master? Suppose you'd been killed?"

"Drostan—"

"I know you want to make the world a safer place, but there's a point where you have to look out for your own safety. Do what's best for Elspeth."

"I know—"

"If you knew that, you'd—"

"Children!" Leif snapped. Alynn held her breath, and even Drostan looked a bit worried as he turned to face his father. It didn't matter that Alynn was nineteen and Drostan was nearly twenty-one. Leif was head of the house, and when he used that tone of voice, he could order the hens to roost, and not a single one would disobey.

"Drostan, you won't admit this, not even to yourself, but your biggest fear in life is raising Elspeth the same way I raised you. Without a mother. So Drostan, do you suppose you could work on overcoming that fear?"

Drostan scowled. "Father, this isn't your place—"

"I will make it my place if I blasted well please. Now answer me."

"Aye, sir."

"And Alynn, can you understand his point of view, and can you trust us men to handle the island's security for the time being?"

"Aye, sir."

"Good. In that case, Alynn, sit this one out. I'll gather a small detachment, and we'll let you know if we need anything. Which we won't. We're capturing a single individual, not taking down an army, and we don't need a berserker."

Drostan nodded. "You, me, and Lukas make three. I say we take three more men, just as a show of force."

"Good idea." Leif left to find the three men. Lukas drew his sword and made sure the blade was sharp enough. Rys adjusted her makeshift shoes, Sigmund went home, and Drostan gathered enough shields for everyone. And Alynn, with Elspeth still gnawing her thumb and Leif's voice ringing in her head, decided to make a belt for Rys. The one she'd borrowed from Drostan was far too long for her tiny waist.

EIGHTEEN

One hour passed, then two, and when a gentle rain started falling, Alynn began to worry. Surely Eyja hadn't been able to overpower six men. Surely Rys hadn't switched sides. But just as she was about to don her own sword belt and venture out after the men, a procession came through the streets. Joyful shouts rang out, and Alynn left Elspeth asleep in her cradle to watch. The six men, led by Leif and Drostan, were clustered around a figure slightly shorter than they were. Rys walked in the back with Lukas, a mixture of pride and fear on her face.

A horde of villagers emerged from their homes, feeling safe in doing so for the first time in weeks, and joined the procession. Alynn went with them. They came to the center of town and stopped, the men stepping back so the crowd could see, for the first time, who was behind the upheaval.

Eyja Thrandottir.

She wore her hair loose and uncovered. Her dress and frock had been ripped during the fight on her father's ship, or else during the resulting shipwreck, and she had mended the many holes as best as she could with clothing stolen from the village's clotheslines. Around her waist was tied a child's blood-soaked undershift; she must have been using it as a bandage.

"Eyja Thrandottir," Drostan announced loud enough for

the whole crowd to hear, "you stand accused of conspiring to commit robbery and for the murder of Rothgeir Torstenson. What is your response to these accusations?"

Eyja tossed her head like a proud horse. "I gave orders to a slave, which is well within my rights as her mistress. Lay her crimes to her charge, not mine."

"So you're saying you had no counts in these over twenty counts of robbery?" Drostan asked.

"You wouldn't blame the master for a dog that bites."

"And for the murder of Rothgeir Torstenson, the fisherman? How do you respond to that accusation?"

"I'd hardly call that murder," said Eyja. "He was trespassing. If you're asking if I defended myself from a strange man who intruded on my habitation, then I'm proud to say that I did."

A shout rose from the crowd. It was Torsten, Rothgeir's son, mostly over his illness and ready to avenge his father. "You liar! You outlaw!" he cried. His mother grabbed him and forced a hand over his mouth before he could say anything that got him in legal trouble, for the Norse took insults very seriously.

Eyja's eyes flashed, and she turned to Drostan. "Surely you won't allow him to speak to a lady like that. Or have you no control over your subjects?"

"Torsten's a free man," said Drostan. "You, on the other hand—I'd hardly call you a lady."

"And you're hardly a man if you will stand for this! What, do you fear his retribution? You're a fool and a coward, sir! And my father's worst hunting dog would make a stronger leader than the sow you are!"

Drostan's sword flashed out of its sheath and fixed its point on Eyja's neck. The crowd gasped and whispered amongst itself, and Alynn was furious. No one spoke of her husband that way. No one spoke of a chieftain that way and lived to see another day.

The crowd held its breath, and Torsten cried out again. The

right to kill Eyja belonged to him, but Drostan's honor had been insulted, and he had to regain it first. Drostan knew this, and he thought desperately.

"Holmgang," he said.

Eyja smiled. "Agreed."

"Alynn, what's a Holmgang?"

Tarin's eyes were wide with excitement and curiosity. He was unused to the excited humming of the village when news was in the air. In fact, he wasn't much used to being in the village at all. Brett and Caitriona wanted to watch the Holmgang as soon as Lukas told them about it, and Rowan decided to make a family affair out of it. So they'd hitched Honor and Patience to the hay wagon and carted everyone up to the village in plenty of time for the festivities, which were set to take place as soon as the rain stopped.

Alynn tried to find the words to explain what a Holmgang was, but she failed miserably after stammering for a bit. Leif looked up from sharpening Drostan's sword and said, "It's just a trial by combat."

"Is it to the death?" Tarin asked.

"It used to be," said Brett, who was watching Mercy to make sure she didn't fall off the sleeping bench and into the fireplace. "But then the lawmakers went soft and said that it should only be fought until someone's blood hits the ground. Unless someone gives up first."

"Whee!" shouted Mercy as she jumped off the sleeping bench. Brett caught her and tossed her over his shoulder. Mercy laughed and contented herself with pulling on his hair.

"Alynn." Drostan's voice came from the doorway, and he held Rys by the arm. "Watch her for me."

"What's she doing here?" Alynn asked. Rys and Eyja had been tied to trees and placed under guard—as if the crowd of curious onlookers would let them escape.

Drostan glanced at the ceiling as a low rumble of thunder vibrated in the rafters. But then he smiled. "I brought her in for questioning."

Caitriona set aside the sewing she'd brought with. "That's Grima?" she asked.

"Lemme see," said Mercy.

"Not now, Mercy," said Caitriona, taking her from Brett.

"Lemme see!"

"No."

Mercy screeched and started crying, so Caitriona smacked her on the bottom and told her to hush. Rys glanced at the ground. "I won't hurt her, miss," she said.

"You'll forgive me for thinking otherwise," Caitriona snapped. "You nearly killed my son."

Rys looked up at Tarin for a split second, then back at the ground. "I'm glad he's alright. You can—you can shoot me in the foot, if it makes things better."

"That's a terrible idea," said Drostan. "I'll talk with my Council to decide an appropriate punishment, but Mum, don't shoot her."

Rowan and Lukas came inside from tending to the horses, and Rowan stopped short when he saw Rys. "That's the one?" he asked, his voice sharp, his entire body growing tense. "That's the one who shot my son?"

"Aye," said Drostan. "Her name's Rys."

Rowan strode across the floor and struck Rys across the face. "If you lay a hand on my son, or my daughters, or my wife, ever again, I will kill you myself. Do you hear me?" He spoke through clenched teeth, and his knuckles grew white as he clutched her upper arm. Rys didn't understand Gaelic, so she didn't respond.

"Rowan." Lukas's voice had a sternness to it that Alynn had rarely heard before. It nearly frightened her. "Leave her be."

Rowan twisted Rys's arm as he looked up at Lukas. "She almost killed Tarin!"

"And? What would you have done differently, were ye in

her place? She tried to give a warning shot to a moving target, and things went wrong. She has more self-control than I did as a young adult. I've been in her place, and I've never been content with a warning shot. I doubt ye would have been, either."

"I wouldn't have killed my son!"

"Well, obviously. But what about a stranger? One that posed a threat to yer life?"

"I wouldn't have—"

Rowan's voice trailed off. He looked down at Rys, her face still red from his slap, and loosened his grip on her arm. Rys looked up at Lukas and said, "I don't know what you just said, but thanks for saying it."

Lukas gave half a smile and put a gentle hand on Rys's shoulder. Rowan finally let go of her, but he maintained a steely glare in her direction. Even if he was thin, he was wiry, and his hands were unquestionably strong. Veins and sinews stood out among the scars and callouses. Combined with the rage in his eyes and the bristling of his shoulders, there was an unspoken promise that he wasn't afraid to slap her again—or worse, if need be. And with that promise unspoken, Rowan sat down between Caitriona and Tarin, never taking his eyes off Rys.

Even Drostan seemed a bit unsettled as he sat on a low stool left over from breakfast and motioned for Lukas and Rys to sit on the bench across from him. "So, Rys," said Drostan as soon as they were all settled, "how long ago did Eyja kidnap you?"

Rys shifted uneasily on the bench. "Three years ago, about halfway through Lent."

"Is there a reason they didn't try to sell you?"

"I knew two languages. They figured I could serve as a translator once I learned Norse. Besides, I was…spirited at first, I suppose. I liked to think they never broke me, but—I've been wrong, I guess."

"What do you mean, they broke you?" Lukas asked.

Rys shrugged. "It was just the word they used."

"They meant it like breaking a horse," said Caitriona. Alynn was surprised to hear her speak, but everyone turned their attention to her. "The master crushes your spirit, makes you think there's nothing good in the outside world, that serving him is all you're fit for. Somehow, he earns your loyalty."

Caitriona kept her eyes on the ground as she spoke, and her cheeks flushed ever so slightly. Rowan, despite not knowing what she'd said, set a gentle arm around her and rubbed his thumb over the back of her hand.

"That sounds about right," said Rys. "I guess that's why I didn't want to turn Mistress Eyja in at first. Even if she is a sow who deserves everything she gets." She swung her feet, knocking them against the hollow bench, then stopped when she realized that she was probably being annoying.

"I saw you'd been lashed quite a bit. Were you particularly disobedient?" Drostan asked.

"I don't know."

"What were some of the things you'd get punished for?"

"Falling asleep late at night when I was supposed to be working. Tying knots wrong. Forgetting to do something. Stealing rations, pickpocketing, talking back, being disrespectful. Things like that." Rys glanced up from the bare floor to look at Rowan, whose gaze had softened a bit. Caitriona was translating for him.

"Tell me what happened when you washed ashore," said Drostan.

Rys collected her thoughts for a moment. "Eyja insisted someone would come back for us, and that we had to be visible on the coast somewhere. But she was wounded—it might have been in the fight or after we bailed out and wrecked the lifeboat, I don't know—so she made me do all the hard work. I found us a campsite, built a fire, stole some things to make her comfortable. One day, I came back with a few blankets from the monastery, and Eyja's standing over a dead man. Her blood, his blood, all of it, everywhere—she thought he worked with Master Thrand, so she hailed him ashore, but she killed him when she realized he wasn't—"

Rys's voice was beginning to shake, so Lukas set a hand on her shoulder. "You shouldn't have seen that," he said. "Drostan, have you gotten all the answers you need?"

Before Drostan could answer, the front door opened, and Sigmund stuck his head into the longhouse. "Sorry to interrupt, but the rain's stopped, and we need to get the Holmgang over before it starts again."

A crowd was gathered in the grassy fields where the villagers' livestock grazed. The goats and cattle had been shooed away for the occasion, and a ring was set up—a three-yard square of fabric marking the field of combat and stakes further defining the corners. While Drostan and Eyja stretched, Sigmund stood in the ring and laid out the rules of engagement.

"The fight will be to two bloods," he announced, his voice carrying surprisingly well through the crowd. "Each combatant is allowed three shields. When those are broken, they will defend themselves with their sidearms. Three marks of silver is the customary reward for the winner, and hence the price for the loser. However, as Eyja possesses nothing that has not been stolen from the village, she will be given to Chief Drostan as his slave for six months. After those six months—or after the fight, if she loses—she will be given over to the family of Rothgeir Torstenson. Does each combatant have their weapons of choice, three shields, and an attendant?"

"Aye," said Eyja. Rys stood behind her, tethered like a horse to one of the corner stakes in case she should try to run away. Her job was to give Eyja shields when hers were broken.

"Aye," said Drostan. He glanced at Alynn, who was standing at his shoulder, in charge of his spare shields. He embraced her, and Alynn was surprised to feel living, breathing flesh beneath his tunic instead of the chainmail she expected.

"Where's your chainmail?" she asked.

"It's not fair. Not in Holmgang."

"Love, she could kill you—"

"I know, Lynder. I seem to recall someone telling me that most things in life can kill you, and that one can't be expected to stay clear of all of them." His eyes sparkled as he kissed her. "Besides, God won't let her hurt me."

Drostan stepped into the ring, and Eyja eyed him head to toe. "Wait," she said. "His vambrace. He needs to remove it."

"But he always wears it," said Sigmund. "It covers an old injury."

"Will you break the rules of Holmgang for the mere comfort of habit? Have him remove it. I want a fair fight, and if your chief is not a coward, then he'll want fairness, too."

Sighing, Drostan winced as he tugged the leather vambrace from his right arm. Alynn bit her lip. He was only five when he'd burned his arm, but his scar still hurt without his vambrace. Would it distract him? Weaken him? It wasn't fair, and she nearly said so, but Sigmund stood at the edge of the ring and called out, "Ready?"

"Aye," said Eyja.

"Aye," said Drostan, a bit less enthusiastically.

"As the challenged party, Drostan delivers the first blow! Fight!"

Drostan rushed Eyja and swiped his sword at her leg. She leapt to avoid him. Quickly and fluidly, he twisted his sword so that the pommel destroyed her shield and knocked her to the ground. She was forced to retreat, taking her second shield from Rys.

Sigmund raised his voice again. "Eyja! Fight!"

With an eldritch screech worthy of the armies of hell, Eyja flew at Drostan and thrust the pommel of her sword towards his chest. Drostan easily blocked the move, but his shield splintered. He made sure Eyja had sufficiently backed off before taking his shield from Alynn.

"She's stronger than she looks," he said.

"How's yer arm?" Alynn asked. Drostan didn't answer, returning instead to strike another blow.

"Drostan! Fight!"

This time, Drostan didn't bother trying to crack Eyja's shield. He aimed as if he were going to strike at her legs again, but redirected his blade at the last second and plunged his sword into her arm. The crowd cheered when they saw the brief spark of blood, but their pleasure quickly turned to upheaval. Eyja twisted her body and, with the grace of a dancer and the strength of a warrior, kicked Drostan in the jaw.

Alynn had seen enough barfights to know that a blow to the jaw could incapacitate anyone. She prayed for a split second that Drostan would be an exception, but he stumbled backwards and fell senseless to the fabric of the fighting ring. Something like lightning shot through Alynn's body, something that filled her with rage and energy. She gripped the stake that held the fabric down.

Laughing, Eyja set a foot on Drostan's chest and raised her sword. Alynn's field of vision narrowed. All she could see was the glinting blade of Eyja's sword, cold and treacherous, with a dim spot on the crossguard where Rothgeir's blood still clung to it.

She took Drostan's remaining shield and threw it at Eyja. She hit Eyja in the shoulder, causing her to drive her sword into the ground rather than Drostan's heart.

Alynn leapt into the ring and ran to Drostan, grabbing his sidearm axe and his sword. "I thought you wanted a fair fight!" she said to Eyja, who was struggling to her feet with a hand pressed against her injured abdomen. "Did you change your mind? Your move, coward!"

Eyja lifted her haughty chin again. "It is my move. Step out of my way, so I can kill this man."

"You broke the rules, Eyja, and now we'll play things your way. Your fight is with me now."

"You're a prissy noblewoman, you think you stand a chance—"

Alynn kicked Eyja's shield with such force that it knocked against her abdomen. The child's undershift began to turn a darker shade of red as her wound started bleeding again, but since the blood didn't touch the fabric of the ring, it didn't count as a blow.

"I am Alynn the Dauntless, and I have earned my name! I fight with honor and the strength of my God! And you will live to rue the day you stooped to trickery and dishonor, and in doing so, roused my anger!"

Cursing Alynn, Eyja rose and rushed Alynn with her sword. Alynn locked her crossguard around Eyja's blade, but Eyja pulled her sword backwards and redirected her attack. They struggled together for a moment before pulling back to breathe. Eyja's sword managed to slip through Alynn's skirts and into her shin as she retreated. Alynn's blood stained the fabric, but she felt nothing.

"You wish your father were here, don't you?" Alynn asked. "How ashamed would he be of you, knowing that you insulted an honorable man for no reason?"

"Shut up," said Eyja. She lashed out with her sword, but Alynn blocked her blows easily. Eyja was angry, and no one fought well when they were angry.

"He sits in hell waiting for you! He writhes with shame because of you! My husband was right. You are no lady. You're a disgrace to womankind!"

"I said, shut up!"

Eyja raised her sword above her head. Alynn blocked Eyja's blow with one deft movement of her own sword and, continuing the motion, found an opening. She meant to slash Eyja's chest and leave her with a deep, memorable scar. Instead, her blade went too high and too straight, and she ended up carving a deep slit into Eyja's throat.

Blood gushed onto Eyja's chest, spurting onto Alynn's dress and the fabric of the ring. Eyja dropped her sword. Her fingers closed around her torn neck in a vain attempt to stop the blood that squelched between her fingers. An unnerving gurgling sound accompanied every breath she took.

Alynn turned towards the cheering crowd—not that she heard a word they said—and found a familiar face. "Torsten," she called. "Come. End her misery. Avenge your father."

Torsten stepped into the ring, white and shaking. He had never watched a person die before. Alynn handed him her sword. "Right between the ribs," she told him.

Wordlessly, Torsten thrust the blade into Eyja's heart. The gurgling stopped. The only daughter of Thrand the Infamous was curled bloodstained and limp at Alynn's feet. Slowly, the noise of the crowd grew louder, and Alynn's field of vision widened until she could see her friends and neighbors. There was cheering and shouting. Somewhere, a baby was crying. Torsten, too, was crying, although he tried his best not to.

"It hurts at first," Alynn said. "It hurts like the devil when you lose a parent. I remember thinking, when my mother was kidnapped, that life would always be dark and hopeless without her. I was wrong. It took time, but I was able to smile again, and even laugh again. And I hope you'll find the same."

Torsten swallowed and ducked his face so he would wipe his eyes without the crowd seeing. "Thank you, milady. Are you hurt? Your face is white."

Alynn realized that she was shaking, and that her heart was beating so strongly and rapidly that her dress quaked. She wasn't hurt. But then she remembered Drostan, forgot about Torsten, and frantically turned around. Drostan was lying, white and still, on the fabric of the ring. She heard herself scream.

"Drostan!" Alynn stumbled towards him and fell to her knees. Her head was spinning. "Wake up, love. Come back to me."

"I've got him." The voice belonged to Sigmund, and so did the wooden hand that slapped Drostan's senses back into him. Drostan groaned and tried to sit up, but Sigmund kept him down. "Easy. Easy. Wait until your head clears."

"What happened?" mumbled Drostan.

"Eyja kicked you in the jaw. It would have knocked out anyone."

Grateful to see that Drostan was alright, Alynn lay down next to him with an exhausted sigh. "Och, I'm knackered."

Drostan slowly turned his head to look at her. His eyes went wide, and his hand flew out to press awkwardly on her chest. "Help her," he told Sigmund. Alynn glanced down to see that her frock was red, and it took her a while to remember that she'd put on her blue frock that morning.

"It's not my blood," said Alynn. "I fought Eyja for you. Saved your life. I'm alright, though."

Drostan sighed with relief and moved his hand from Alynn's chest to her hand, squeezing it with a comforting grasp. "Thank God."

Alynn and Drostan lay still for a while, comfortably holding hands. Lukas came with his satchel of medicines. He felt Drostan's jaw and made him open and close his mouth and told him that he'd be fine in a couple of days, he was young, he'd mend. Alynn's head stopped spinning, and she tried to stand up, but Lukas made her sit so he could bandage the scratch on her leg. Then, finally, he helped Alynn and Drostan to their feet and followed them out of the ring.

The crowd welcomed them with cheers and too-hearty claps on the shoulder, some of which nearly knocked Alynn over. She was still trembling. Caitriona pushed through the crowd until she could hug Alynn, then Drostan, then kiss them both and set Elspeth in Alynn's arms. "Ye're alright?" she asked. "Both of ye?"

"Aye, Mum," they said in unison.

"There should be Holmgangs more often," said Tarin. "That was fun."

"Even the part where I almost died?" asked Drostan.

Tarin's grin disappeared before he realized Drostan was only teasing. Sigmund elbowed his way through the crowd, apologizing to everyone whose personal space he invaded, and handed Drostan a leather whip. "Are you ready to deal with the girl?" he asked.

Drostan sighed. "I guess. How many counts of robbery were reported again?"

"Twenty-two."

"Twenty-two. Thanks." Drostan kissed Alynn's cheek and stepped into the ring again, shouting to get the crowd's attention. Alynn stayed close to her mother's side and was glad when Rowan and Brett came to stand next to them as well.

"As you know, while Eyja Thrandottir may have commissioned the twenty-two counts of robbery carried out on St. Anne's Cleft, she was not the one who actually committed these crimes. This was done by Cerys ferch Owan, Eyja's slave." He motioned towards Rys, and the crowd murmured amongst themselves.

"She shot yer brother-in-law, for faith's sake," Rowan muttered. "The least you could do is mention it."

"Given her status as both a slave and a child under the age of fifteen, I sentence her to return whatever items she can. In homes where the stolen goods were consumed as food or medicine, or were ruined beyond repair, I order her to spend one week as a servant. At the home of Hrafnkell Ormundson, which she set fire to, she will spend three weeks. At St. Anne's Monastery, because she wounded Tarin McNeil, she will spend three weeks. In addition, she will receive twenty-two lashes, one for each robbery."

"He wouldn't," Alynn said aloud.

"She deserves it," said Rowan.

"She's hurt enough," said Caitriona.

Rys knelt obediently when Drostan hold her to, and at his bidding, took off both her tunic and her bandages to expose the marks Eyja had already left on her. Drostan looked at the crowd, which was once again murmuring amongst themselves.

"It looks to me like she has already received twenty-two lashes," said Drostan. "Probably more than that, actually. Consequently, I say she's been punished enough for her crimes. All in agreement, please say 'aye.'"

"Aye," echoed scores of voices.

Drostan said something to Rys, and she began to dress again. "All opposed, say 'aye.'"

Perhaps five voices said "Aye," and Rowan gave an angry shout of "Don't you dare!" Lukas, shoulders bristling, grabbed Rowan by the arm and glared at him.

"Listen here, ye pile of horse dung. Who do ye think ye are, to demand that poor girl's torture? Alynn was her age once. I thought ye'd have a father's heart, a bit of sympathy, an ounce of charity! Even common sense. She's staying at the monastery until we can send her back to Wales, and while I doubt she's dangerous, I still wouldn't want to make myself her enemy."

Rowan yanked himself free of Lukas's grasp. "What did you say?"

"After she's done wi' her community service, she's coming to stay at the monastery."

"No. I'm not letting a criminal stay under the same roof as my wife and children. You're mad! Don't you care about them?"

"Well, it's not your roof. If ye don't like it, ye're free to leave. Now whisht. I want to hear what Drostan's saying."

Drostan had spent the duration of Lukas and Rowan's argument unfastening the thrall's collar from Rys's neck. Once the collar was off, he raised his voice again. "Upon the death of your mistress, Eyja Thrandottir, I hereby declare you, Cerys ferch Owain, to be a free woman. Now show us you're a good person, because the hand of the law won't deal so lightly with you in the future. Do you understand?"

"Aye, sir."

"Good. From my understanding, you've done most of your stealing from St. Anne's Monastery. You'll begin your community service there."

Rowan was still in disbelief. "Lukas—how—what happened to not wanting Tarin to leave?"

"I don't want him to leave. But he's yer son. Ye're the head of yer family, and I'm the head of the monastery, and if our responsibilities bring us in different directions, then so be it."

"Lukas!" Caitriona scolded. "For faith's sake, what's gotten into you?"

Lukas was about to answer, but Drostan had led Rys out of the ring and towards her new, temporary masters. Lukas set a gentle hand on her shoulder and presented her to Caitriona. Rys kept her hands clasped in front of her, eyes on the ground.

"What can you do?" Caitriona asked. She shifted Mercy on her hip and surveyed her new charge with a firm gaze.

"Most everything, miss," said Rys.

"Can you card and spin?"

"It's been a few years. It should come back to me, though. I'm good at cleaning, and I can tend the little one."

"That won't be necessary."

Rys looked up at Caitriona as if she wanted to say something, but she held her tongue and returned her gaze to the ground. Caitriona's resolve broke, and she smiled compassionately. She set a hand on Rys's shoulder as she bent slightly to speak to her.

"I was a slave once," said Caitriona. "I didn't cut my hair or wear a collar, but I was a slave nonetheless. To a man who called me his wife. He'd force himself on me, and he'd hit me—he broke me, the same way Eyja broke you. And I did things that I'm not proud of, just as you've done. I'm not excusing your actions, now, and I still don't trust you. But—I understand."

Rys smiled. "Thank you, miss."

Mercy took advantage of the lull in conversation to reach out to Rys and take a fistful of her hair. "Mammy! So-kohs!" she said.

Rys laughed as she fished her hair out of Mercy's grasp. "You're right, little heart. My hair is circles. My little brother used to say the same thing."

NINETEEN

The crowd dispersed, Eyja's corpse was stripped of its stolen clothes and jewelry before being unceremoniously cremated, and Alynn was finally able to return to life as normal. Well—mostly normal. She was giving Rys a refresher course on the carding and spinning of wool.

Brett and Tarin played with Elspeth and Mercy, and Alynn would often look up from her work to smile at them. Brett and Tarin had taken to tossing Mercy around in a modified game of catch, a sport which Elspeth seemed to enjoy watching and Mercy absolutely adored. Her shrieks of laughter almost masked the argument going on in the workroom.

It had started out civilly enough. Rowan and Lukas needed to finish their conversation about Rys's living situation, and Caitriona insisted on taking part as well. But their voices kept getting louder, and when Alynn realized that Lukas had raised his voice even more than Rowan or Caitriona, she told Rys to keep practicing with the carding combs and silently opened the workroom door.

"Of course I'll miss Tarin!" Lukas was saying. "I'll miss him the same way I missed Alynn when she got married. But I've come to realize that living alone is nay worse than living wi' a family that's not mine anymore."

"My family was never—"

"Rowan, shut yer gob." Alynn was surprised to hear so much fire in her mother's voice. "Lukas was a wonderful father to Alynn, he's been grand with Tarin and Mercy. He's given us food and shelter fer the past three years out of the goodness of his heart. Why can't you just be grateful to him?"

"Whose side are you on?" Rowan demanded.

"I'm not takin' sides. I think ye're both actin' like maggots," said Caitriona. "I will say, though, Lukas, I'm surprised at you. I thought you wanted us to stay with you."

"I did," said Lukas.

"Well, you've all but kicked us out over a legitimate safety issue," said Caitriona.

Lukas was firm. "Rys is not a safety issue."

"How can you know that?" Rowan asked.

"Because she's shown remarkable self-restraint. Now that her life's no longer in danger, I'm nearly certain she'll settle down. And if I'm wrong..." Lukas sighed. "I'll take care of her."

"I'm surprised you're even giving her a chance," said Rowan.

"What else are we supposed to do? Her life story is playing out remarkably like my own, and if there's anything I can do to make her existence less miserable than mine's been, I'll do it."

There was a moment of silence before Rowan said, with a bit of defeat in his voice, "Sounds reasonable. But I want Caitriona armed, and I don't want Rys to be alone with either Tarin or Mercy."

"I'm always home," said Lukas.

"Yer mind isn't. You're either out in the fields or off with the fairies. I don't want you lettin' her out of yer sight."

"Will you quit tryin' to pick a fight with him?" Caitriona asked.

"I am not trying to—"

Lukas cut in. "Well, it's obvious that Rowan's not comfortable sharing a house wi' Rys. And if that's the case, again, ye can—stay with Alynn, I guess. I don't know."

"I'd rather have a house of my own," said Rowan. "I don't think we can buy a plot of land outright, but if the smithy keeps being profitable, we can at least rent a place."

"No!" said Catriona. "No, no, no. Lukas, we're family. Family doesn't leave over petty arguments."

"This is an important argument, actually, and we're not family," said Lukas.

"Of course we are!" said Caitriona. "You're not going to get upset again about not having blood relatives, are you?"

Lukas swore. "Blast it, Caitriona! This is the closest thing we've had to a conversation in weeks! Ye've forgotten about me. Rowan's never cared. And ye're taking Tarin away from me—ye never so much as thanked me fer saving his life! I don't know what the devil this is, but it's not a family."

Caitriona gave a bit of a gasp, and her voice was full of compassion. "Lukas—"

"Aye, and now ye'll say nice things to get yer living situation back. It won't work."

Rowan cleared his throat. "I've been thinking about moving for a while now," he said. "I don't like livin' so far away from town, I don't feel at home in a church, and I know that I'm earning enough money now to provide for my family. So when I say that yer turning us out is the least of my worries, I mean it. Now, that said—good God, you did save Tarin's life, and—Cait? Neither of us said anything?"

"Lukas, I'm sorry," said Caitriona. "I am so, so sorry—"

"I—" Lukas seemed a bit sheepish. "I misspoke. Tarin needed a miracle, and God provided it. He's the One Who's saved Tarin's life, and ye've thanked Him fer it, and that's all that matters. I shouldn't have brought it up. It's alright."

Alynn heard her footsteps as Caitriona crossed the room. She was probably giving Lukas a hug; Alynn didn't dare open the door wide enough to see. "You're a good man, Lukas," she said. Her voice began to tremble. "And I'm sorry—I was so worried about him, and I kept thinking—I kept thinking about

Louisa, and how I had to brush her hair one last time before we put her—in that tiny little coffin—and I'm sorry." Caitriona drew a shaking break and continued a bit steadier. "And I thought I'd have to do that for Tarin, but I don't, and 'tis because you took such good care of him. I can't thank you enough for that."

There was a brief silence before Rowan spoke.

"Tarin's my only son," he said. "Out of all the people in my life, he's the only one who hasn't been taken away from me, and I genuinely don't think I could live without him. 'Tis better than any physician I've seen that you treated him. Caitriona's right. We can't thank you enough."

"I love Tarin," said Lukas. "I wanted to save him—well, I'd say as much as ye wanted to, but as much as I try, I'll never love him the way ye do."

"Stop tryin' to be humble and give yerself some credit," said Rowan. "You do love him. And it was a grand job you did with him."

"Thank you," said Lukas.

"Lukas," asked Caitriona, "is this what you meant, when you said I'd forgotten about you?"

Lukas got a few half-words out, then retreated into silence.

"If something's botherin' you, and you don't tell us about it, we won't be able to help you fix it."

Lukas sighed. "Well, wi' Rowan and Tarin back, and Mercy here—everything's different. I just want my family back. I know I ought to be content wi' what I have, and maybe it's just that I don't know what it's like to be part of a family. I know it's wrong of me to complain. I try not to."

"Och, Lukas, you don't have to go about pretending everything's alright," said Caitriona. "'Tis not wrong fer you to feel like this, or to talk about it. If you've done anything wrong, 'tis that you're a wee bit jealous of Rowan takin' his spot back as head of the household, but you've done a grand job handling everything else."

"Jealous?" asked Lukas.

"Jealous of *me*?" asked Rowan. "Good Lord. The kids like you better, you're the one with the house and the land and the livestock—and besides that, you're so bloody perfect we might as well write to Rome and have them canonize you."

"Rowan, I've killed people. All I am and have is because of Christ's mercy. And I've still fallen so low as to be envious. I should have noticed. I'm sorry—I'm sorry."

"Lukas. Whisht, now, we forgive you. 'Tis alright." Caitriona's voice had that sympathetic tone that all mothers have, and she probably hugged him tighter. Alynn was very tempted to open the workroom door and check, but there was a thud behind her, and Mercy started scream-crying. Alynn turned around, forgetting to shut the workroom door, and saw Tarin quickly scoop up Mercy with a rather guilty expression.

"Nothin' happened," he said.

"Did you drop her?" Alynn took Mercy from Tarin and checked her over. There was a red mark on her forehead; she must have smacked it on the sleeping bench. But at least there wasn't any blood.

Caitriona, of course, came flying out of the workroom and snatched Mercy out of Alynn's arms. "What happened?"

"We were playin' catch with Mercy and she hit her head," said Tarin.

"Och, my wee heart. You'll be alright, Mercy! 'Tis alright. 'Tis alright, Mammy's here. Mammy's got you."

Mercy said something repeatedly through her tears and eventually calmed down enough to be intelligible. "Dey *fowed* me!"

Tarin and Brett gave each other a worried glance.

"You *threw* her?" Caitriona demanded.

"It was his idea," said Tarin.

"She loves it," said Brett. "You should have heard her laughing."

"What, you can't hear her screamin'?"

"We're sorry—"

Stern-faced, Caitriona marched to the cupboard and

grabbed a wooden spoon, with Mercy still on her hip. "Bend over," she said.

"But Mum—"

Caitriona grabbed Tarin by the shoulder, turned him around, and gave him a few deft smacks with the spoon. Brett watched in horror, and Mercy stopped crying and even giggled once. Then Brett got his turn with the spoon. Alynn, after rescuing Elspeth from her close proximity to the fray, went to sit with Rys, who had laid her carding aside to watch the debacle.

Elspeth sat in her mother's lap and stuck three fingers in her mouth as she watched Caitriona hauling off on the boys, squealing her encouragement. Alynn shook her head and gently pulled the wool off Rys's carding combs. "You find this amusing, my wee heart?" she asked.

Elspeth kicked her legs and babbled.

"At least she's turning out better than my sister Myfanwy," said Rys. "The first time she laughed—like, really laughed— was when our brother Griffith got drunk and knocked over a chair, then tripped over it and landed—" Rys stopped to stifle a laugh. "He landed on his—"

"Now, sit down!" Caitriona ordered, in a tone that made Elspeth's eyes widen with surprise. Alynn worried for a moment that she would start crying, but fortunately, she just kept eating her fingers and dripping slobber onto her dress. The boys sat, wincing as they did so. "For shame, Tarin. You know better than to play rough with the baby! Suppose she landed on her head! You could have killed her!"

Rys shrunk when she heard the yelling, and Alynn noticed, so she quickly tried distracting her by babbling about how well she did with the carding combs and a few tricks for pulling the yarn off of them. It half-worked. Rowan and Lukas came out of the workroom, and Caitriona told them what happened so that they could start scolding the boys, too.

"We can go in the other room," said Alynn.

Rys shook her head and grabbed the spindle. "I'll block it

out. How do you get this started again?"

Alynn showed her how to use the drop spindle, and just as Rys was about to spin some yarn on her own, Lukas said, "Alright, everyone. Rowan and I have had a discussion, and we have some announcements to make."

"Are we moving again?" Tarin asked.

"We're not," said Rowan. "Lukas is letting us stay."

Tarin grinned, and Caitriona looked relieved.

"That said," said Lukas in Norse so that Rys could understand, "there are going to be a few changes around the monastery. Rys, are you willing to work wherever we need you?"

"Of course," said Rys quickly.

"Good. You're part of the family now, my dear. That said, not everyone trusts you. And you have to earn that trust."

Rys nodded.

"If you hurt anyone else, you'll be shipped off to Wales whether you like it or not. Understood?"

"Aye, sir."

"Alright. Good. Now, Tarin. One of your father's objections towards your studying for the pastorate is the fact that preaching is not a trade. And he's right. You'll need to make a living somehow. Do you think that you could handle pastoring and blacksmithing?"

Tarin thought for a bit, then nodded. "I can."

Lukas glanced at Rowan and nodded. The faintest hint of a smile crept into the corners of Rowan's mouth. "I'll lend you to Lukas for another year, until Brett leaves," he said. "Then, you'll apprentice full-time with me at the smithy. And—would you tell Rys—"

"Rowan needs some help blacksmithing," said Lukas to Rys. "You're going to help him, just temporarily. Then, you can have your choice of either helping Caitriona with the house or helping me with the fields. Or a wee bit of both. We need you both places, frankly."

Rys smiled. "At least I won't get bored."

"And Rowan, something I forgot to mention," said Lukas. "Afore the massacre, we had a fully functioning smithy on the monastery grounds. I don't have the first knowledge of smithing, so I've let it go to ruin. The forge might need a bit of fixing up, and I don't know where all the tools are—but still. I was wondering if ye'd like to bring yer business closer to home. See a bit more of yer family throughout the day."

Rowan's eyes were wide. "You're serious?"

"Of course I'm serious."

Rowan stood in shock for a bit, then grinned. "Thank you. Thank you. Cait—it'll be just like Limerick. You can come out and visit me while I'm working."

"If you'll stop working long enough to visit with me," said Caitriona.

"I've always got time for a kiss," said Rowan, wrapping an arm around Caitriona and pulling her close to him. He kissed her cheek, then took Mercy into his arms and kissed her too. She grinned and touched Rowan's beard with an intensity somewhere between a pat and a slap.

"Tickle!" she said.

"Does my beard tickle you?" Mercy nodded, so Rowan rubbed his chin on her until she squealed with laughter. Then, he kissed her again and said, "Well, now that that's settled, we'd better go home. I want to see this abandoned smithy."

"You'll have plenty of time for that," said Caitriona. "I want to snuggle my grandbaby."

Alynn handed Elspeth to Caitriona and smiled as Elspeth started chewing contentedly on Caitriona's arm. Caitriona talked to her in a silly high-pitched voice that made her laugh. It warmed Alynn's heart.

Leif and Drostan came home a few minutes later. Drostan seemed tired, but kissed Alynn anyway and handed her something made of metal. It was a cloakpin. Alynn looked at it closer and realized it was the one that had belonged to her grandmother in Limerick.

"Where did you find this?" she asked.

"Eyja was wearing it," said Drostan. He was rubbing his neck.

"Are you alright, love?"

"My head hurts. I'll be alright."

"I'll make you some willow tea."

"I'm grand." Drostan helped himself to a horn of mead from the cupboard and went to sit in a dark corner.

Alynn looked the cloakpin over quickly to make sure it was clean and dry. Rowan had instilled in her from an early age that metal and liquids didn't mix, and after the mess that the Holmgang had turned into, Alynn wanted to make sure there wasn't any blood on it.

"We cleaned it for you," said Leif. "It's good as new and ready to wear."

"I don't think I can wear this," said Alynn.

Caitriona smiled sadly. "Nana would want you to," she said. "At least to Mass."

"Can I see it?" Tarin asked. He reached for his crutches, but Alynn went over to him instead and sat next to him. Tarin grabbed the cloakpin and examined it closely.

"Careful, 'tis old," said Alynn.

"I know. And look. Whoever made this didn't bother to weld the fold of the pin. It'll break easily."

Smiling, Alynn kissed the side of Tarin's head. "You'll make a good blacksmith someday."

Mercy wriggled down from Rowan's arms and ran over to Lukas, tugging on the skirts of his habit. "Deydey! Tory!"

"Ye want a story?" Lukas asked, picking up Mercy and setting her on his hip. "Alright, we'll give ye a story. Let's see…" He switched to Norse. "Rys, would you like to hear a story?"

"If Mistress can spare me," said Rys. She glanced at Caitriona, who looked up from Elspeth to nod her approval. Rys set her spindle aside and sat next to Lukas, eager for a story.

"Can ye stay for dinner?" Alynn asked Caitriona. "'Tis

getting late."

"Och, that sounds wonderful. I'll make some bannocks. Rowan, can you bring the table down?"

Rowan complied—a bit hesitantly, as he'd never brought the table down from the loft before. Alynn and Caitriona set to work in the kitchen, but kept an ear open to hear Lukas's story. It was the familiar tale of how Alynn had come to St. Anne's Cleft, but Lukas was a good storyteller, and Alynn never grew tired of hearing Lukas's side of things.

When the story was finished, Drostan came up behind Alynn and set an arm around her waist. "We're just having salt cod for dinner, right?" he asked.

"Aye. Why?"

"Well—does Mum need help with that?"

Alynn looked over at the fire. The fish was already boiling, Caitriona seemed content making the bannocks, Rowan was holding Elspeth, and Mercy was behaving herself. Just as Alynn was about to ask what needed to be done, Rys stood up and said, "Thank you for letting me hear the story, Mistress. I'm ready to help now. What needs doing?"

"You can start by setting the table," Caitriona said. "Drostan, do you need something?"

"I was thinking that some fresh air might help my head stop hurting," said Drostan. "And if you can spare my wife, I'd enjoy her company."

"Och, off with ye," said Caitriona. "Ye've had a long day. Dinner will be ready before ye know it, though, so don't take too long."

"We won't," Drostan promised. He took Alynn by the hand and led her outside, only to find that the streets were much busier than they had been in the past few days. Everyone was talking and celebrating Eyja's death.

Wordlessly, Drostan took Alynn down to the harbor. There was a small boat that was nearly finished—it only needed benches and a few finishing touches on the trim. Drostan helped Alynn aboard, shoved the boat into the bay, and climbed aboard himself.

The sun, peeking out from behind a cloud, was just thinking about setting. It touched everything with a golden hand set the ocean shimmering. Alynn breathed in the fresh, free air and smiled.

"Nice boat," said Alynn. Drostan had already sprawled out on the ship's floor, and Alynn lay down next to him. The rocking of the ship was hypnotic, and Drostan's warmth beside her was comforting. "Who's it for?"

"Someone from Hrafney, actually. He said he'd pick it up on his way home from Althing, but I wanted to finish it ahead of time."

"That's nice," said Alynn. The motion of the boat was rocking her to sleep. It seemed to have the same effect on Drostan, too; he yawned and held her closer.

Alynn closed her eyes, and when she opened them, it was dark yet clear. There were no clouds, and the night fog had not yet set in. Stars glimmered in the heavens and set the ocean sparkling like rippling fabric spun with silver. The moon was not quite full, but it was so bright that the oar propped up against the side of the boat left a shadow.

Drostan was talking. His voice was soft and reverent, and it didn't take Alynn long to realize he was praying. For a moment, she stayed still in his arms, feeling the vibrations of his chest against her cheek.

"I still don't know what I'm doing, Lord," he was saying. "And from the looks of things, I probably never will. My work needs me, my island needs me, my family needs me—give me wisdom, please. Help me know when to focus on what, how to be a good leader and a good father. I'm surprised You saw me fit to put me here in the first place. But thank You for getting me this far."

"Drostan?" Alynn said, her voice sleepy.

"Hmm?"

"You do a good job, love."

Drostan kissed her. "Can we go home now? I'm starved."

"Let me wake up a bit first. How's yer head?"

"Better. All I needed was a nap, I guess." He kissed her again, then settled back into a comfortable embrace. Then, he pointed up to the brightest star. "That's the lode-star. That one there, that's called Aurvandill. And there's the Great Wagon."

Alynn looked up at the constellation. "I think it looks like a frying pan."

"It's too deep to be a frying pan."

"It doesn't have wheels, though! It can't be a wagon without wheels!"

"Fair play to you, love." Drostan acted like he was going to kiss her again, but he just poked her with his nose. Alynn poked him back.

"How long have you been awake?" Alynn asked.

"I don't know. Half hour, maybe." He smiled. "I started thinking about Elspeth. It won't be long before she's raiding the cupboards and beating Sigmund's boys in sword fights. She's something else."

Alynn thought about Elspeth and smiled. "She's just about got that second tooth in. And she'll be sitting up on her own before we know it."

"She's got so much of you in her, Lynder. The way she looks at you when she's happy, the determination she learns new things with. A fighting spirit, she's got."

"She does. And she's got her da's smile."

"I think she's got your angry face."

"Drostan!"

With a grin, and partially to avoid a playful elbow thrown in his direction, Drostan finally stood to draw the ship back ashore—he'd moored it to a post near the ramp. When the boat was safely docked, he helped Alynn out of it and led her back to the house. As they got close to the house, Alynn heard something. It wasn't quite talking, but she was quite certain that Leif wasn't alone. The noise got louder; it sounded like a cry of pain.

Heart hammering, Alynn rushed inside and made a beeline

for Elspeth, who was lying on her stomach on the sleeping bench. "Eppie, what's wrong?" Alynn asked.

She whirled around to see Leif lying half-naked on his stomach with Nora crouched over him. Her sleeves were rolled to her elbows, and she was holding a towel that had been dampened with boiling water.

Leif raised his head and looked at Alynn and Drostan with a measure of disappointment. "Can't an old man get a back rub in peace?" he asked.

Alynn reddened. "Sorry."

Nora laughed. "Don't be, hen. Although I'd appreciate some help. This man's got more knots than a nautical rope." She pressed her hands again into Leif's back, and he relaxed with a contented groan.

Drostan was already checking the cabinet for anything edible. "Did you save any dinner for us?"

"Kept it warm, too," said Nora. "Still in the pot. Just grab ye a plate." She wiped her hands on the warm, damp towel that had been covering Leif's back.

"Don't stop now," Leif pleaded.

"It's dark, love. I have to get home. And ye owe me a shoulder rub tomorrow."

"Anything," said Leif. "My back hasn't felt this good in months. I'd walk you home—"

"Go straight to sleep," said Nora. Leif rolled onto his back, Nora bent down to kiss him, and then she bid a temporary goodbye to Alynn and Drostan. She would be back soon, she promised. She and Leif had a wedding to plan.

Drostan dished up two helpings of salted, boiled fish and handed one to Alynn. They ate quickly. Then, Drostan brushed Alynn's hair while she nursed Elspeth, sneaking in a few kisses while he was at it. Leif started snoring, so Drostan threw a blanket over him before following Alynn into the bedcloset.

By some miracle, Elspeth only woke up once that night.

May 8, A.D., 969—

What a day. A long day, a good day, a hard day—good Lord. I'm exhausted. But I just wanted to mention that Caitriona, Rowan and I were actually able to talk about our problems— well, my problems, at least—and resolve some of them. Apparently, I've been jealous of Rowan (Lord forgive me) for taking his place back as head of his family. Looking back on the past few years, it's hard to see why I didn't notice this earlier. I have some work to do in my own heart, and then hopefully, Rowan and I can start cooperating a bit better.

However, there are some immediate benefits. I get to keep Tarin. Thank God, I get to keep Tarin. Caitriona said I can spend more time with Mercy and reminded me that I'm still in charge of certain things—the farm, mostly, as well as the building itself—that the family could not survive without. I hope that I can take pride in my own work, my own place in this family, without comparing myself to Rowan. (And praise God, Caitriona's agreed to hug me more often.)

The McNeils aren't leaving. I prayed, and the Lord showed me that loving others—having a relationship with them—is one of the most vital elements of the Christian faith. Losing them hurts, arguing with them hurts, but we are still called to love. As for the emptiness in my heart—God told me that He will, on occasion, use the people around us to share His love in a tangible way. That it is not good for man to be alone, and that loneliness can poison the heart just as unforgiveness can. So the McNeils are staying, and I'm relieved.

Rys came home with us, and she seems sweet so far. She is very quiet, but I get the sense that her true nature is much more outgoing and that she has merely been taught silence as part of her slave training. I intend to help her become more like herself, and I shall continue to pray for her. I should also note that I inspected her back before she went to bed, and she seems to be healing nicely. I pray that her spirit has the same resiliency as her flesh.

Her mistress is dead. Alynn killed her in Holmgang. Neither she nor Drostan were seriously wounded—again, reason to praise God. They disappeared before dinner and never came back, and I was quite sad that we had to return home before saying a proper farewell. Oh well; I'll see Alynn soon enough. I also got to hold Elspeth for quite a while. She nearly chewed my fingernail off.

It's late. If I remember more of what happened today I'll write it tomorrow.

—L. McCamden.

TWENTY

Elspeth grew immensely as the summer wore on. By mid-July, she was able to sit up by herself and, between squiggling and rolling over, move a few feet when placed on the floor. She was also babbling incessantly. Alynn didn't mind it at home, although she did wish that Elspeth would quiet down during church.

Lukas didn't mind. As long as Elspeth was making happy noises, he would either ignore her as he preached or give her the occasional smile. However, on this particular Sabbath, Elspeth was dropping her wooden toy fish with reckless abandon, babbling nonstop, and shrieking so loudly her voice reverberated off the chapel walls. Alynn tried nursing her repeatedly and passed her from relative to relative, but nothing worked.

"And so," Lukas was saying, "by keeping our eyes on the Father, rather than on the storms around us, we are freed from fear. Rather than looking to ourselves for the strength to fight, and the wisdom to come up with a battle plan, we look to God. What happens when we look to ourselves for such things? We're not strong enough. We're not wise enough. We fail more often than not."

Elspeth babbled.

"What do Scriptures say about this?" Lukas asked. "In Philippians chapter four, Paul says, 'Do not be anxious about anything, but in everything, by prayer and petition, with thanksgiving, present your requests to God. And the peace of God, which transcends all understanding, will guard your hearts and your minds in Christ Jesus.' It is when we take our problems, our fears, our hardships to God—"

Elspeth screeched again. Alynn sighed with embarrassment. She was very tempted to take Elspeth out to the hearth and sit with her.

"Elspeth, could you please use your inside voice?" Lukas asked.

Elspeth looked up at Lukas and grinned. "Dey-dey!" she said.

Alynn's eyes went wide. She looked at Elspeth, then at Drostan, and then she laughed. "Is that yer first word?" she asked. "Is that Eppie's first word?"

"Is Eppie talking?" Drostan asked. His startled look turned into a grin, and he grabbed Elspeth from Alynn's lap. "Is my little Elspeth talking already?"

Elspeth gave a loud, happy, affirmative vocalization.

Lukas snatched Elspeth out of Drostan's arms, kissed her, and held her close. He was smiling like he actually meant it. "Ye want to be wi' Deydey?" he asked. "Alright. Come on, Eppie. Ye can help me finish the message. Do ye want that?"

Elspeth shrieked in affirmative again. Lukas hopped back up onto the speaking platform with a youthful energy and a smile that never dimmed, and he finished preaching with Elspeth happily perched on his hip. Elspeth loved it. She only interrupted Lukas a couple of times, content instead to wave her pudgy little arms around and smile.

Alynn couldn't pay attention to the rest of the sermon. She was too busy feeling things. Elspeth was growing up! She was happy! But she wasn't going to be a baby for much longer! All those thoughts and the emotions that came with them brought tears to Alynn's eyes, and she nestled next to Drostan for comfort.

"I'm so bloody proud of her," Drostan whispered.

"When do you think she'll say 'mammy'?" Alynn asked.

"Before you know it," said Drostan.

Church was over soon enough, and Alynn was caught up in a whirlwind of people wanting to talk to Elspeth and congratulate her on saying her first word. But eventually, everyone left, and Alynn was able to catch a breath.

Tarin, Slodi, and Olvir played catch at the hearth while Mercy ran between them, trying to catch the felted ball. Every once in a while, someone (usually Tarin) would let Mercy catch the ball, and she would smile and laugh and do a terrible job of throwing it to the next person.

When Olvir threw the ball a bit too hard, Leif caught it. He had just come out of the chapel and had a strange, sad look in his eyes.

"U'cle Lay! Fow da ball!" cried Mercy.

Leif smiled and tossed her the ball. "Boys, we're going home soon," he said.

"Can't we stay five more minutes?" Olvir asked. "We're having fun. Right, Mercy?"

"My ball," said Mercy.

"We're sharing the ball right now," said Tarin.

Mercy grinned. "No! Is my ball!" She ran off, and the boys ran after her. Tarin caught her and started tickling her while Olvir and Slodi tried to retrieve their prize. Leif laughed at them, but sadly.

"Is something wrong?" Alynn asked.

"Oh, no." Leif took Elspeth from Alynn's arms and kissed her. "I was just in the graveyard, talking to my sister Ragnhild. Wondering what she'd think of Nora and the wedding and all."

"I'm sure she'd love Nora," said Alynn.

"I know, but—I wish I could have gotten to know her a bit more." He bounced Elspeth, and she smiled. "No sense in dwelling on the past. I am ready to go home, though. Have you seen Drostan?"

"I haven't. But go on home, we'll follow before long."

Leif smiled, handed Elspeth back to her mother, and left to collect Nora and the boys. Alynn was beginning to wonder exactly where Drostan was—surely he wouldn't leave for home without her—when he came inside with Rys in tow.

"I guess Rys is coming back to the village with us," said Drostan. "She's due at Sturla Gunnarsson's house, and I forgot that his family doesn't come to church."

"I can't ride a horse," said Rys.

"Don't worry. You'll ride with me," said Drostan. He glanced at Alynn with something like a smile in his eyes. "It's warm and sunny outside. I think we should take Elspeth to the beach to celebrate her first word."

"Elspie, do you want to go to the beach?" Alynn asked.

Elspeth grinned and squirmed with agreement.

"Can my family come with?" Alynn asked.

"Of course," said Drostan.

Lukas was coming back from the kitchen with a half-eaten piece of cheese in one hand. "Lukas, do you want to come to the beach with us?" Alynn asked.

Lukas hurriedly swallowed his bite of cheese. "Why?"

"It's hot out. We can go for a swim," said Drostan.

"I can't swim," said Lukas.

"And how old are you?" Rys asked. "That's alright. I'll teach you. Master Drostan, can I come with? I owe Lukas a favor."

Drostan smiled. "Alright. Rys, you can come."

Rys's face lit up. With a smile in her own soul, Alynn gathered her family, and within the hour, they were off to the beach.

Elspeth, having never been to the beach before, had a mixed reaction. She didn't mind getting her legs wet, and she seemed to enjoy kicking about in the water, but she started crying when a wave doused her from the nose down. Alynn had to take her out of the water so she would calm down.

Eventually, Elspeth decided that she liked sitting on the shore and kicking the waves as they came in, and Alynn was finally able to look around and see what the others were doing. Caitriona sat nearby, keeping an eye on Mercy as she ran around chasing seagulls and splashing in tide pools. Brett, Tarin, Rowan, and Drostan were playing rough-and-tumble in the deeper water, and Rys was teaching Lukas how to swim.

She supported him with two outstretched arms and gave him instructions. "Straighten your legs a bit. Keep your head up and your mouth closed—don't straighten your legs *that* much, they'll be as useless as a fart in a jam jar. There, that's better."

"What do I do with my arms?" Lukas asked.

"Cup your hands and start paddling. How did you get so old without learning how to swim?"

His brows set with determination, Lukas started kicking and paddling and made it a few feet before a wave knocked him off balance. He stood up, wiped the water from his eyes, and said, "I did it!"

"Good job," said Rys. "Now, do it again."

Alynn smiled. A particularly large wave came and splashed Elspeth in the chest. Her eyes grew wide and her arms flailed upwards, and she began to cry. Laughing, Alynn scooped her up and held her tight until she calmed down. Then, so Elspeth wouldn't get a sunburn, she went a bit farther up the beach, held Elspeth close to her chest again, and covered her with a towel.

There was a screech from Mercy. Alynn looked up just in time to see her sister jump into an oncoming wave as if giving it a hug. Caitriona kept a careful eye on her, making sure she came up again. "I think she's part Selkie," said Caitriona.

"She gets that from Da," said Alynn. She looked up at her father, who was trying to grab something that looked like a ball out of Brett's hand. Brett threw the ball to Drostan, who was immediately jumped on by Tarin. But something was off about the whole picture, and it took Alynn a while to realize what was wrong.

"What are they playin' with?" she asked.

"Someone's trousers, probably," said Caitriona.

Tarin's trousers, specifically. Alynn shook her head. At least they all seemed to be enjoying themselves. Lukas, having also realized what was going on, paused his swimming lesson with Rys and donated his scapular to the cause so Tarin could get his trousers back. He himself stayed out of the game, but Rys joined and proved a vicious player. She, like Rowan, was much stronger than she looked.

Lukas came to sit next to Alynn and watch the boys play. When Mercy ran to him, he took her on his lap and kissed her head. "Are ye tired?" he asked.

"No," she said, shivering.

"Are ye cold?"

"No."

"Ye aren't cold? Ye're shivering, lassie!" He squeezed her tighter, and she grinned.

"Is wimdy."

"Aye, it is windy out. And the wind makes everything colder. Snuggle up." Mercy burrowed into Lukas's arms until she nearly disappeared, and it was impossible to tell who was more content with the arrangement. "Caitriona, I can't thank ye enough fer letting me borrow yer daughter."

"You're a good granddad, Lukas." Caitriona had piled her hair atop her head so it wouldn't get wet, but now she was taking it down and braiding it. "Mercy, listen to Deydey. Mammy's going out for a swim."

"Stay clear of the wrestling match," Lukas said.

"Och, I'm going to *win* that wrestling match. I know where everyone's ticklish." And with that, tying her braid with a thread loosed from her hem, she swam out to join the keepaway match and was soon laughing and shouting with the rest. Alynn watched as she got a hold of Tarin, who was protecting the coveted cowl with his life, and tickled his sides and stomach. He laughed so hard he let go.

"I'm glad Tarin's alright," Alynn said.

"Aye. We all are," said Lukas. "To be honest, it's a miracle he didn't end up wi' an infection, let alone that he's walking fine now. The day it happened—I started shaking as soon as we'd finished caring for him. I can't remember the last time I was so frightened."

Alynn smiled, scooting closer to Lukas so she could set a hand on his arm. "You still handled everything well."

"Strangely enough, I'm proud of myself, too. Mercy, darling, are ye warming up?"

The little voice was muffled. "A'most."

"Almost? Aye, stay as long as ye need. Ye're warming up Deydey, too."

Mercy giggled and nestled closer to Lukas. Alynn smiled and glanced at Elspeth, who was chewing on her hand under her towel. She noticed her mother looking at her and smiled. Her two bottom teeth were fully in now, and while part of Alynn missed her toothless grins, she couldn't deny that she was still adorable.

"Do you like the beach?" Alynn asked.

Elspeth kicked her legs and squealed.

"I'm glad. I like it, too."

Elspeth babbled. Alynn smiled and babbled back. Lukas chuckled with the beautiful absurdity of it all, but Mercy shut her ears. "Too loud!" she said.

"Are you loud, Eppie?" Alynn asked.

Elspeth shrieked, then grabbed Alynn's thumb and started chewing on it. Alynn desperately hoped that she wasn't getting more teeth in.

The sun disappeared behind a cloud, and Brett, Rys, Tarin, and Drostan swam ashore. Tarin was wearing Lukas's cowl to protect his narrow shoulders from sunburn, and Rys and Brett were having an argument over some aspect of the wrestling match. Rowan and Caitriona were enjoying having the ocean to themselves, swimming out into deeper water together.

Drostan grabbed the towel that was covering Elspeth to dry himself off with. Alynn tried to grab it back, only to find herself caught up in a game of tug-of-war. "You twit!" she said.

Drostan won, of course, pulling Alynn so hard she lost her balance and wound up falling into his arms. She didn't mind that part.

"We should do this more often," said Drostan, kissing Alynn and taking Elspeth. She didn't know what to make of her father's bare chest and twisted her eyebrows into a confused scowl.

A seagull landed nearby, and Mercy leapt from Lukas's lap to chase it. Tarin joined her. It joyed Alynn's heart to see the two of them running around, Tarin hardly limping. Eventually, though, Tarin placed Mercy in Brett's care and stumbled back to where Alynn was sitting. He plopped down next to her and rubbed the scar on his foot.

"Does it hurt?" Alynn asked.

"It's just a cramp. It'll go away."

Alynn smiled at him. His hair was turning into a fluffy, windswept mess as it dried, and the sun illuminated every single freckle on his cheeks and nose. Lukas's cowl was far too large for him and made him look waifish and ministerial all at once. Aye, he'd make a fine pastor someday. His heart was pure enough for it.

Elspeth still hadn't come to terms with her father's wet arms, so she was given to Alynn while Drostan dried himself. Everyone's clothes and a few towels had been set on a fallen tree a few paces behind where Alynn and Lukas were sitting. Tarin watched Drostan with a suspicious gleam in his eyes, and Alynn turned around to see what was so interesting. Drostan was rifling through everyone's clothes, poking behind the log, scanning the beach. "Has anyone seen my tunic?" he asked.

With that, Tarin leapt to his feet and produced Drostan's tunic, which had been cunningly rolled up and half-tucked into the hood of the cowl. "I've got it! Serves you right for stealin' my trousers!"

"You little—"

Tarin flew away like a bird, and Drostan chased after him. Drostan was faster, but Tarin was lighter and more agile. The chase was like that of a cat and mouse. Brett and Rys stopped bickering to watch, and even Rowan and Caitriona came ashore to see what all the screeching and laughter and half-meant insulting was about. Finally, Drostan snatched Tarin like a hawk setting on a field mouse, got him on the ground, sat on him, and started tickling him.

"Is that how brothers act?" Lukas asked.

"That's how Uncle Micheal and Uncle Stiofan treated Uncle Oisin half the time," said Alynn. She'd put Elspeth to her breast to calm her down and was hoping she'd fall asleep. "But you've met Uncle Oisin, and God knows if he's typical at anything."

Lukas's reply was interrupted by a scream far too high-pitched to belong to either Tarin or Drostan. Alynn turned her head to see Mercy running towards Caitriona. Close behind her scuttled a crab, pincers waving, chasing her at an unsettling speed.

Rys darted after Mercy, snatched the crab, and flung it into the ocean. It sailed for a good ten feet before landing with a splash in the bay. Meanwhile, Caitriona scooped up Mercy and kissed her, and Rowan looked at Rys with a strange emotion in his eyes. It wasn't quite affection and it wasn't quite pride, but there was a hint of acceptance and forgiveness in his gaze. Perhaps it was a look that said, "Maybe she isn't so bad after all."

Lukas stood and shook the sand from his braies and undershift. Caitriona had toweled Mercy dry and was trying to put her socks on. Mercy kept squirming, so it was no easy task. Once her socks were finally on, she kicked and complained about sand in them. Caitriona said that she could wash off when they got home.

Rowan and Brett had a gentle tug-of-war over the last towel. Brett argued that he should dry off first because he was already partially sun-dried, while Rowan insisted that he was thinner and there was less of him to dry. Brett won in the end.

Drostan and Tarin reconciled after their scrimmage, and

Drostan got his tunic back. He kissed Alynn and pulled her into a sideways hug so as not to disturb Elspeth, who had fallen half asleep as she nursed. Her eyes fluttered between open and half-closed, and then, suddenly, she looked up at Alynn with a gaze of pure love.

Alynn raised her daughter's tiny hand to her mouth and kissed it. "I love you too, my heart."

Caitriona smiled. Her braid was in ruins. Broken strands of golden hair flew about her face and her cheeks were slightly sunburned, but her eyes held a rare joy. "I've got a new song for her," she said quietly, so as not to rouse her from her half-sleep. "Can I sing it to her?"

"Please."

Caitriona's voice was gentle. It fit perfectly among the waves and wind and the gentle skittering of the sand over the rocks. It put Elspeth to sleep and quieted Mercy; it made Alynn feel like dozing off herself. A beautiful peace settled over the entire group as they journeyed homeward.

> "Little lamb, little lamb, rest your head,
> Your Shepherd's tucked you safe in bed.
>
> Little lamb, little lamb, be at peace,
> All your fears to Him release.
>
> Little lamb, little lamb, you are safe,
> So grow in strength and love and faith.
>
> Little lamb, little, lamb, God loves you,
> When arrows fall, they won't hurt you."

July 18, A.D. 969—

Elspeth said my name today! And as her first word! She loves me, just as her mother does! I held her on my hip as I finished my sermon today and was overcome with love for her. Her smile is one of the most beautiful things in the world, bright as the sunrise over the ocean on a cloudless day. O joy indescribable!

Afterwards, we went to the beach as a family—all of us, even Rys and Alynn and her family—and spent a pleasant afternoon. Rys is teaching me how to swim, and I'm quite proud to announce that I swam a good five feet before foundering before the day was up.

A wonderful day. For the first time since Rowan's return, I felt like part of a family. And not merely because Elspeth called me Deydey. Everyone—they brought me along. They talked to me. They treated me like one of them.

I feel tired now. A good tired, though—the sort that comes after a long but pleasantly eventful day. And today will likely be but the first in a series of long but pleasantly eventful days. Next Wednesday, I will be joining Leif and Nora in holy matrimony. I've agreed to help watch Mercy for a few moments each day so that Caitriona can have a bit of time to herself, and Rys will be coming to live with us permanently before long. I anticipate that training Rys to become a daughter instead of a slave will take a good bit of work, but the results will be more than worth it.

I am struck by her life—the perfect illustration of Christ's redemption. All mankind is born enslaved to sin, and as much as we may despise our chains, we are powerless to remove them. We are compelled to obey. And even once the physical chains are gone, the strongholds remain in our hearts and minds. Praise God for His grace, for freeing us to serve Him! To love Him, to love His children—the essence of lives worth living.

Rowan must be putting Mercy to bed tonight. He always

tickles her before kissing her goodnight, and I can hear her laughing. He's a good father—Lord, I repent for coveting the blessings You've given him. I know that You see the desires of my heart—the yearning to belong, to feel a part of something. I pray that You would help me continue to feel the sense of love and unity that I felt today. Help me to know that this is my family, regardless of blood and the animosities of the past. Help me to know that I belong.

—L. McCamden

AUTHOR'S NOTE

This book is the product of a Nerf war.

I was fifteen years old, about two years deep into editing *Where the Clouds Catch Fire*. My best friend was over, and my sister convinced us to have a Nerf war. I've never been a fan of shooting people, so I could only be convinced to join in if I got to wear a cloak and fight with a toy bow and arrow.

As I was hiding from my sister and friend in the bathroom, I caught a glimpse of myself in the mirror. Lightning hit. I called for the game to be paused, ran into my bedroom, and scribbled a note for myself. That note turned into *Where Arrows Fall*, and the cloak I wore during that fateful game is the same one I'm wearing on the front cover.

This book has been a difficult one to write. I finished the rough draft just as 2020 and all its craziness began. I've had to navigate the insanity of the past few years all while battling my way through my early twenties and assuming the full burden of adulthood. I wrote the rough draft of this book at my parents' house, the second draft in a college dorm, and the final draft in my own apartment.

But in everything—in the transition from teen to adult, from student to teacher, from dependent to independent— God has been with me. Just as Alynn learns how to trust God in her parenting journey, so I've had to learn the same lesson. And God hasn't let me down yet.

I believe that He'll take care of you the exact same way He's taken care of me.

Blessings,

M.J. Piazza

ABOUT THE AUTHOR

Micalah Elise Janelle Piazza grew up surrounded by books in northern Illinois. Her flexible schedule as a homeschooler afforded her plenty of time to read and write, and she began work on her first novel at the age of ten. Her first novel, *Where the Clouds Catch Fire,* took five years to write and was published in 2019. In 2022, she earned a bachelor's degree in English from Southeastern Oklahoma State University. She currently lives in Oklahoma, where she teaches English and home economics. You can contact her at m.j.piazzaauthor@gmail.com, or on her official website, www.mjpiazza.com